Love
Dangerously

by

Alicia Dean

This is a work of fiction. Names, characters, places, and incidents are either the product of the author's imagination or are used fictitiously, and any resemblance to actual persons living or dead, business establishments, events, or locales, is entirely coincidental.

Contact Information: info@thewildrosepress.com
The Wild Rose Press, Inc.
PO Box 708
Adams Basin, NY 14410-0708
Visit us at www.thewildrosepress.com
Publishing History
First Crimson Rose Edition, 2017
Print ISBN 978-1-5092-1311-5
Published in the United States of America

Contents

Thicker Than Water

Tales of the Scrimshaw Doll

by

Alicia Dean

Dedication

To LeAnne and Faye,
the best bosses in the world.

And to my amazing editor and friend,
Lori Graham.

Acknowledgements

I would like to thank my wonderful critique partners,
Christy, Betty, Sheila, Kathy and Kelly,
for your help in whipping this story into shape.

I would also like to thank the other authors of the Scrimshaw
Story project for making this such a fun and rewarding
venture.

A special thanks to Kelly Cox for helping me brainstorm the
twist that made me start liking this story, and a very special
thanks to my beautiful, precious niece, Amanda, for her
research help.

Lastly, I'd like to thank Lacey, my sweet, adorable daughter,
for her help with proofreading the story.

Chapter One

Julia Bennett averted her gaze as she ordered a cup of coffee, hoping the guy behind the counter wouldn't recognize her. Chances were pretty good he wouldn't. After all, she'd left her hometown of Covington, Oklahoma ten years ago and had only been back a few times since.

Her hopes were dashed when he ducked his head to stare into her face. "Hey," he said loudly. "Ain't you that Bennett girl?"

She was indeed *that* 'Bennett girl' and it had been foolish of her to think he might not remember. Lifting her head, she met his gaze and found him staring at her with a combination of curiosity and disgust.

"Yes, that's me."

He nodded, his reddish-brown hair falling across his eyes. "Thought so." He slid the steaming cup to her, then frowned as if trying to decide whether to say more. He settled on, "Have a good day." He turned his back to her, which said more than words would have.

She looked around the Java Hut. Most of the tables were occupied. One held a harried-looking mother balancing an infant on her lap while she struggled to open a juice box for her toddler. At another table, a fifty-something couple sat. The woman stared at Julia with open hostility. The man's gaze shifted from Julia to his wife, then to the floor. Julia glanced away, but the expressions on the faces of the other occupants weren't any more welcoming.

Message received. The town hadn't warmed to her at all. Guess absence did *not* make the heart grow fonder.

Feeling the need to breathe fresh air, she took her coffee and stepped outside. It was strange that, even though she had a successful career, a nice place to live, and several friends at home in Kissimmee, Florida, as soon as she entered the town limits of Covington, she reverted to that same insecure, troubled kid from years ago whose poor choice had led to irrevocable tragedy.

She glanced around as she sipped her cappuccino. Nothing much had changed. Across the street from the coffee shop was Pickering's Burgers, where she and her friends hung out every Friday night, making fun of the jocks who cruised Main Street in the expensive cars their parents bought them. Now there was a cell phone store next to the burger place and a self-serve yogurt shop down the road. Otherwise, everything pretty much looked the same.

From where she stood, she could see the Covington Sheriff's Department. Was Jake—correction, Sheriff Devlin—there now, or was he out patrolling the town, keeping it safe from bad guys? Thieves…rapists…killers like her?

She shook off thoughts of Jake and the killing. Both had been a long time ago. There was nothing she could do about either.

Hoping to see Pam's SUV approaching, she gazed up and down the street. Her friend was at the mortuary, making funeral arrangements for her husband—and

Julia's friend—Corbin.

Corbin…dead. Hard to believe. Even harder to believe he'd killed himself. Fun-loving, kind-hearted Corbin, suicidal? *Impossible.*

"Julia?" The voice came from her right, and even before she turned, she recognized the owner. No way could she mistake the smooth, deep baritone, tinged with that slight Okie drawl. A sound that had always reminded her of honey oozing over a warm biscuit.

Jake Devlin.

Heart threatening to explode from her chest, she inhaled, then exhaled a slow, steady breath, before she turned to face him. Somehow, he seemed taller than she remembered. He wore cowboy boots and a battered Stetson with a chocolate-brown uniform shirt tucked into blue jeans.

A rush of pleasure, quickly followed by nervousness, moved through her body, stealing her breath. She'd caught glimpses of him during her sporadic visits over the years, but not once during that time had she been close enough to make out the flecks of charcoal in his steel gray eyes.

Finally, she found her voice. "Hello, Jake."

"I didn't know you were in town. I guess you're here for the funeral?"

A knot of tears in her throat temporarily prevented speech. She nodded. "Yes. I'll only be here a few days. Leaving Friday."

"I'm sorry about Corbin."

"Thank you." Awkwardness settled between them briefly, then she pointed to his attire. "Jeans aren't exactly regulation, are they?"

He shrugged. "Not particularly, but I play golf with

the mayor. I let him beat me, so he doesn't say much. No one else complains because… Well, you know." He gestured to his hip. "Gun and handcuffs."

She laughed. "I suppose it's always good to have your bluff in."

"Always." He gave her his signature smile that was something to behold. It was mostly in the squint of his eyes with just a hint of amusement playing over his lips. His smile was the first thing that had attracted her to him, and her weak-kneed reaction to it now wasn't much different. She cleared her throat. "I heard about your divorce. I'm sorry."

"That makes one of us. Thanks, though."

She couldn't help but experience a modicum of gratification that he wasn't heartbroken over his divorce. She and Jake had been nothing more than kids when they dated, but hopeful questions still rattled around in her mind, although they remained unvoiced.

Is it because you married the wrong woman, and it should have been me? Is it because you never got over me? Over us?

The hum of a motor caught her attention, and she turned to see Pam's Envoy pulling up to the curb. Her friend parked in front of a No Parking sign.

Julia cast a quick look at Jake. He didn't react. Didn't appear to pay attention to the fact that Pam had broken the law. Maybe he was waiting for the two of them to commit a real crime, like the old days.

Pam climbed out and came toward them. She was adorable with curly auburn hair and a petite body that made Julia feel large and oafish. When Pam reached them, Julia hugged her, then pulled back to study her friend's face. Pam's eyes were red-rimmed, the green irises looking somehow faded. Her skin was even paler than normal.

"Sheriff Devlin." Pam nodded at Jake. Pam and Jake had known each other most of their lives, but maybe the uniform demanded formality.

"Can I have a private word with you?" he asked Pam, managing to infuse sympathy with the authoritative tone.

Her features tightened. "You can talk in front of Julia."

His gaze landed on Julia. He seemed to consider whether or not to speak in front of her, then finally nodded. "Let's sit."

He pointed to a bench and gestured for the women to precede him. They made their way over and sat. Jake remained standing.

Pam looked up at him, shading her eyes from the sun. "Did you learn something more about Corbin's suicide?"

He squatted in front of Pam and reached out to take her hand, engulfing it in his. Holding her gaze, he spoke softly. "That's just the thing, Pammy. I'm not entirely sure it *was* suicide."

****

Jake rose to his feet, concentrating on Pam. He tried to keep his tone level, and his eyes away from Julia. She'd acquired a tan since moving to Florida. Her sun-kissed blonde hair was tousled in the spring breeze, like she'd just crawled out of bed. She'd filled out some, too. She'd been much too thin when she left. Now, she looked healthy…voluptuous. He gritted his teeth to tamp down a groan.

How can she still have this effect on me after all

these years?

He hadn't touched her silky skin…hadn't felt the softness of her lips against his in over a decade, but his flesh tingled at her nearness. His body tightened, and an ache settled deep in his gut. He had to hold himself rigid to keep from touching her.

Damn her.

"Not suicide?" Pam's pixie face crumpled in bewilderment and new pain. "You're not saying he was killed, are you? Murdered?"

Pam had found her husband in his office, a gun lying inches from his hand. A suicide note had been typed out on his computer. The logical conclusion was he'd killed himself. He'd been working late. The building didn't have security tapes. The cleaning crew hadn't seen anyone come in or out. Nothing appeared to be out of the ordinary.

Until the autopsy. Preliminary findings showed busted blood vessels on the back of the victim's neck, indicating he'd been hit with a blunt object. Not many suicide victims clubbed themselves before taking their life.

"That's just a theory." He was officially investigating it as a murder now, but no need to let Pam know just yet. "There's evidence that brings up a whole new set of questions. Do you know of anyone Corbin had problems with? Any enemies? Any threats in the days or weeks before his death?"

Pam slowly shook her head. "No—no one. Who would want to hurt Corbin? But then—" Her voice broke. She fumbled in her purse, producing a tissue. "But then, I can't imagine he'd kill himself, either. We were happy. *He* was happy."

Jake nodded. That's what the families of all suicide victims said. Few of them ever saw it coming, seldom believed it. But then, as it turned out, Pam likely had good reason not to believe it.

"You said your husband had been working late. He was alone when you found him. Do you think someone else could have been there just before you arrived? Did you hear anything at all?"

She swallowed audibly, swiping at tears on her cheeks before speaking. "Nothing."

"Did you touch anything while you were there, other than the phone to call 9-1-1?"

She paused.

He didn't like that pause. It seemed to mean something. But there was no way she had anything to do with Corbin's murder. He'd known her for twenty years. She couldn't kill anyone, especially not her husband.

At least he didn't think she could. No telling what could make a person snap. And Pam might have had motive. The signs Corbin was having an affair were strong. Emails that indicated an intimate relationship were found on his computer from someone with the screen name of 'Ladyinred224.' They were searching the IP address to find out who this person was. She might know something about what happened to Corbin. At first, they hadn't been concerned with the emails, not until the suicide investigation turned into a murder investigation.

"No. Nothing," Pam replied.

"Did your husband wear a wedding ring?"

Again, the pause. "Yes. Why?"

"I noticed a white mark around his ring finger,

where a ring should have been, but we didn't find the ring. You didn't take it, did you?"

"No. Of course not."

Jake nodded. "Our theory is that the killer took it." He let his gaze roam over Julia, then back to Pam. "I'd appreciate it if the two of you would keep the issue of the missing ring to yourselves. Sometimes, a little clue like this can help us find the perpetrator. You didn't tell anyone the ring was missing, did you?"

"No."

"Good. Let's keep it that way. We don't want to show our hand, maybe tip off a potential suspect. As it stands now, the medical examiner, myself, my deputy, and the two of you are the only ones who know about the missing ring." He slid his hat back and used his sleeve to wipe the sweat beaded on his forehead. "Well," he amended, "the five of us, and—if there is one—the killer."

****

Pam's house was spacious and stately. It had been her childhood home, a white colonial that sat on two acres. Her parents had died and left it to her, their only child. None of Julia's foster parents had ever owned a home like this. It was three times the size of her bungalow in Kissimmee.

Julia put her suitcase in the guest bedroom, not bothering to unpack. She didn't intend to stay long. The packed suitcase would reassure her she'd be gone soon. Briefly, she entertained the thought of hanging around a while longer, doing a little digging into Corbin's death herself. As an investigator for a law firm, she was pretty damn good at getting to the truth. But, Jake was on the case. He was smart, capable. He'd solve the mystery without any help from her. She really just needed to get out of this town as soon as possible.

"You get settled in? Is everything okay in your room?" Pam asked when Julia entered the living room.

"Yes, thanks. It's great."

Julia meandered around, looking at Pam's antiques. Each time she visited, she loved discovering Pam's latest acquisitions. The brass lamp hadn't been there the last time. Nor had the oak jewelry box.

She paused at a silver filigree frame that held a photo of the whole group. Tears filled her eyes as Corbin's smiling face stared back at her. He had one arm slung casually over her shoulder, the other over Pam's. He and Pam had been a couple at the time, but it was easy to forget in the dynamic of their friendship. They'd almost always hung out together, the six of them. He and Pam probably hadn't gone on a handful of dates alone. Although Julia and Jake were dating at the time, he was seldom with their group. He didn't approve of their wild lifestyle, didn't want to do anything to jeopardize his dream of becoming a cop.

"We're all supposed to get together after the funeral."

Julia turned at the sound of Pam's solemn voice behind her.

"Yeah? The whole gang?" She immediately regretted her words. Not the *whole* gang. Never again.

Pam nodded. "At the Rusty Nail. Everyone's looking forward to seeing you."

"Great. Can't wait to see them. I haven't spoken to Tanner since I got into town. Is he coming?"

"He is, but I'm sure we'll have to give him a ride."

Tanner was Julia's foster brother. He'd suffered a

brain injury in the accident they'd had years ago, and hadn't been quite right since. He couldn't drive, couldn't work. It seemed all he could do was hang out, still living with his parents, counting on others to take care of him. She felt a little guilty because she hadn't stuck around to help with that. But, the brief visits since she'd moved away had been an experience in misery. She couldn't imagine actually living here ever again.

"So, how do you stand it?" she asked Pam. "The hostile attitude from people in town. Doesn't it drive you crazy, day after day?"

"They don't really treat me that way, not anymore. And, you know, you aren't *from* here. Plus, you haven't been around the last several years. You're an enigma. A new toy to play with."

"Lucky me." Julia snorted. She gestured toward the lamp and the jewelry box before settling on the sofa. "You have some great 'new' old stuff."

"Wait until I show you the latest," Pam said. A light came into her eyes. "Sit tight."

She left the room, returning in a few minutes carrying a hideous looking doll. It must have been over a hundred years old. The porcelain face was yellowed, the hair missing in patches. The faded, tattered black dress was unraveling at the neck and hem.

"What the hell is that?" Julia asked, turning up her nose.

"It's Rosa. I bought her at an antique store a few weeks ago."

"*Why?*"

Pam laughed. "I know she's ugly, but there's something special about her. When the man at the antique store told me her history, I had to have her.

10

Check this out." She pulled the neck of the dress down and pointed at the center of the doll's chest where a small, perfect rose was carved. "Isn't that unique? So pretty. She's a Scrimshaw doll, carved out of whale bone in the late 1600s. Legend has it there's a curse attached to her…*all those who betray you will suffer.*"

"All those who betray the doll?"

Pam shrugged. "Or the owner. The story kind of changes, depending on which account you hear. I Googled it, and there are all kinds of different theories. Thing is, I sort of believe it."

"Do you?" Julia tried to keep the skepticism out of her voice, but failed.

"I didn't. Not really. Not until Corbin died." The last word ended on a whisper.

Julia frowned. "What does that have to do with the curse?"

"Well…" Pam chewed on her bottom lip. "You can't say a word to anyone. Promise me."

"I promise," she said automatically, although a little fissure of dread worked its way through her system. Something was a bit 'off.' Pam wasn't acting normal, and Julia wasn't entirely sure she wanted to hear what her friend had to say.

"When I found Corbin, he wasn't wearing his wedding ring. I don't know how I noticed that. I was hysterical, in shock, but his hand was splayed out to the side, inches from the gun and the pale band on his finger just sort of glared at me, mocking me. I'd been suspicious for a while, but then I knew. He was cheating on me." Her voice broke and she swiped angrily at the tears on her cheeks. "I dug around in his pockets—"

"You *what*?" Julia pictured Pam rooting around in her dead husband's pockets. A wave of revulsion washed over her.

"I knew he had to have the ring on him and…and I didn't want him to be found like that. Didn't want people to know. We were the perfect couple. Everybody said so." Her voice rose defensively. "I couldn't have people looking at me, judging me, laughing at me. I've had enough of being looked down upon by this town. I wasn't going to go through that again."

"So, did you find the ring?"

"No. I don't know what he did with it. Why he didn't have it on. Had he just been with her? Was she maybe still there? Hiding? And, now—" She broke off on a sob. "After what Jake said, did *she* kill him?" Pam looked down at the ugly doll before meeting Julia's eyes. The glint of determination was unmistakable. "I had to hurry. I'd called for an ambulance, and I heard the sirens coming, so I could only look for a few minutes. He might have had it on him, but I just didn't have long enough to find it."

Julia experienced a small measure of relief that she'd at least called 9-1-1 before her morbid treasure hunt.

"Do you know who the other woman was?"

"No idea." She clutched the doll to her midsection. "Now comes the crazy part."

"Oh? *That* wasn't the crazy part?"

"I think she did it."

"You think his lover killed him?"

She shook her head emphatically. "Rosa, the doll. I think he died because of the curse."

Julia's mouth gaped open. She gasped. "You what? Please tell me you're joking."

"All those who betray you will suffer? I mean, come on. I've only had the doll a few weeks. Corbin cheats. He dies. You do the math."

Julia screwed her eyes shut briefly before opening them again. "Please tell me you haven't told anyone else your theory." *It's the grief. It has to be. She's not thinking straight. She can't possibly believe a cursed doll caused her husband's death.*

"You know, murder or suicide. Either way. He betrayed me." Her lips tightened. "And he suffered."

Julia stared at the doll. The doll stared back with creepy, pale blue eyes. A cold shiver prickled Julia's skin.

Friday could *not* come soon enough.

Chapter Two

After the funeral, Pam and Julia drove up to the two-story white frame house where Julia had lived from the age of fourteen to seventeen. The house didn't conjure any fond memories. Not any particularly awful ones, either. The only reaction it elicited was apathy.

"I wonder if I should go in and say hi to Hank and Teresa?" she said to Pam.

"Yeah, you do that. I mean, they kicked you out when you were a seventeen-year-old kid. They deserve a visit from you." Her tone oozed sarcasm.

Pam was right. After the Morrisons kicked her out, Pam's parents had taken her in. Otherwise, no telling what would have become of her. She'd lived with Pam's family for the six months leading up to graduation. Not long after, she left town. The Morrisons likely didn't want to see her any more than she wanted to see them.

"In all fairness," she said. "I caused them a lot of problems."

Pam honked for Tanner and rolled her eyes. "Their son was involved, too, and he's still living with them. Thirty years old, no job, living with his parents. You don't see them kicking him out."

"He's their *actual* son. I was a foster kid they took in."

She'd bounced around from foster home to foster home since her mother died when she was three. She barely remembered her mother, never knew her father. A few of the foster families had been more loving than the Morrisons, but none had ever made her feel wanted...like she truly had a family, a home. A familiar pain tightened her chest.

"The state paid them to take care of you. Wasn't exactly the world's greatest sacrifice." Pam snorted in disgust. "So, why is it that Tanner couldn't make the funeral?"

"He gets panic attacks in crowds."

"But the crowd at the Rusty Nail won't bother him? It's just *funeral* crowds that make him panic?"

Pam's voice was tight with resentment, and Julia glanced at her. The unforgiving sun shone through the windshield, giving her features a ghastly look that reminded Julia of the doll...ancient and worn.

Julia wouldn't continue the debate about her foster brother. Pam had enough to deal with. Besides, she had a point. Tanner wasn't the most caring, or the most industrious, person in the world and, to be honest, Julia could only partially blame that on his condition.

They fell silent, and in a few moments, Tanner lumbered out the front door of the house. His shaggy hair fell over his eyes, and he flung his head back to get it out of his face. He'd done that ever since she could remember. She wasn't sure why he didn't just get his hair cut. Fondness squeezed her heart, and she smiled. She missed having her foster brother in her life. He'd always been good to her, always made her feel welcome, like she actually belonged in his home.

When he reached the car, a huge smile spread

across his face. Julia stepped out and went into his open arms.

He held her tight. "Great to see you, sis."

Sis. She fought back a rush of nostalgic tears and clung tightly. She could barely get her arms halfway around him. He'd always been a chubby kid, but it seemed since adulthood, each time she'd seen him, he'd gained another twenty pounds.

She released him and slid in the backseat this time, letting him have the front during the short drive to the bar.

****

The Rusty Nail was just as Julia remembered—noisy and smoke-filled, with country music blasting from the jukebox.

They made their way to the table where Emily and Dave waited. Neither of them had changed much since the last time she'd seen them. Emily was dark-haired, dark-eyed, and curvy. Dave had grown a goatee that didn't flatter his round face. His longish brown hair was starting to gray. Everyone other than Tanner wore funeral attire. In his baggy jeans and Guns and Roses T-shirt, Tanner was the only one who looked like he actually belonged at the bar.

Emily stood when she saw Julia. Her eyes brimmed with tears, but a smile spread over her face. "Julia, so good to see you." Emily hugged her, then pulled back. "I've missed you. I just wish I was seeing you under happier circumstances."

"Me, too." Julia felt tears in her own eyes and blinked them back.

"Please don't stay away so long next time, okay?"

"Sure, okay." Julia wasn't at all certain she could

keep that promise. "Maybe you can come visit me in Florida. You'd love it there."

Emily nodded. "That sounds great. I'd love to get away for a while. Things here have been…" Her voice trailed off and she sniffed. "Well, you know."

"I know," Julia whispered, reaching out to squeeze her hand.

Julia greeted Dave, then slid into a chair next to him. Empty glasses and a pitcher of beer sat on the table. Dave poured a glass for each of them, then motioned to the waitress to bring another.

"It was a lovely funeral," Emily said, her voice despondent. She looked almost as haggard as Pam.

"I hear the cops think he might have been murdered," Dave said.

Julia looked at him in surprise. *How had word gotten around so quickly?* "That's just a theory."

"Either way," Pam said tearfully. "I can't believe he's gone."

"Me either." Tanner scowled as he lifted his beer. "He was finally going to give me the break I've needed."

"Break?" Julia lifted her brows.

"Yeah. He was going to help me get my wine-making business going. Now, I'll be starting from scratch."

"Corbin was going to help you start a business?" Emily stared inquisitively at Tanner. "Are you sure?"

"I'm sure." Tanner frowned. "Why?"

Emily held his gaze for a few seconds, then shrugged. "Just wondering. I hadn't heard anything about it."

"Why would you?" Tanner asked.

"I worked with Corbin from time to time, helping out in the office, you know."

"Doesn't mean he'd tell you everything."

Emily nodded and took a sip of her beer. "No, it doesn't."

Julia was a bit surprised herself that Corbin would help. Tanner's wine wasn't the best in the world. As a matter of fact, it was barely palatable. Maybe Corbin was hoping he could get better at it, if someone had faith in him, if he had the right opportunity.

"How's everything else going for you?" Julia asked Tanner. "Any job prospects? Anything new and exciting?"

"I have a girlfriend," Tanner said. "Tessa."

"Tessa Sandler?"

"Yeah." He nodded proudly, looking like a schoolboy who'd just scored his first date.

"That's great," Julia said with only partial sincerity. Tessa was a dancer and a bit of an airhead. She came from a decent family; she just never seemed to have much sense or ambition. When Julia was in the ninth grade, Tessa was in her class, but it had been her third time there. Finally, she'd given up and just quit school. Nothing much her parents could do about it, since she was eighteen by then. She seemed like a nice enough person, though. If she made Tanner happy, that was all that mattered.

"Living the high life, are you, bud?" Dave said. He quirked his mouth in derision. "Dating a stripper, jobless, living at home with your parents. Score!"

Tanner glowered, his hand visibly tightening around the beer glass. "Fuck you, man."

"Hey, please, guys. Come on." Julia said, glancing

at Pam. Her mouth was set in tense lines, and tears swam in her eyes. "Today's not the day, okay?"

"Face it, Julia. The guy's a loser and that's all he'll ever be." Dave laughed. "I'm like Emily. I don't believe, for one minute, Corbin would invest in that swill Tanner calls wine."

Tanner shot up from his seat, toppling his chair. "Look, asshole, you got a problem, let's take it outside. I don't have to listen to this bullshit from you."

"Stop it!" Emily's voice rang out over the music coming from the jukebox, drawing attention from a few people at surrounding tables. She lowered her voice. "Is this any way for friends to act? We just buried Corbin. Can we have a little respect?"

Julia was about to chime in when the door to the bar opened, and Jasper Ramsey's widow and son walked in. Her stomach clenched and tears closed her throat. The memories that were never far away came flooding back…the six of them drinking too much. The joy ride along the narrow, dark lake roads. Jasper Ramsey's body flying in the air before landing in the murky water.

Suddenly, booze didn't taste so good. She pushed her glass away, then leaned forward and spoke quietly. "I thought Donny Ray was in prison."

Not long after his father died, Donny Ray got into some trouble. When he was twenty-one, he robbed a liquor store, was convicted, and sent to prison.

"He was released a few months ago." Pam said. "He's been living with his mother. Can't find a job."

"Tell her the rest," Dave said.

Pam shot him a scathing look, then sighed. "Corbin foreclosed on their home."

"What?"

"They couldn't pay the mortgage." Pam's face flushed, and she dropped her gaze away from Julia's.

Wow. They'd caused the death of the woman's husband—the boy's father—and ten years later, one of those responsible had kicked his family out of their home. Julia shook her head. Had Pam really told Jake no one would want to kill Corbin?

****

Three days after Corbin's funeral, Jake stared blankly at photos of the crime scene spread on the desk. He thumbed through the notes, but his mind was on Julia. She'd be leaving today. He probably wouldn't see her before she left. He tried to convince himself that was what he wanted.

He shook his head and attempted to focus. They'd confirmed the email address of 'Ladyinred224.' It belonged to Emily Green, although they hadn't let that detail slip out to the public. *Poor Pam.* It was bad enough to know her husband had cheated, but when she learned it had been with one of her closest friends, she'd be devastated.

"Sonny wants his iPad; can you believe it?" Jake's deputy, Kurt Schuman, came in from the holding area, shaking his head. He and Jake had gone to school together, graduated the same year, but with his scrawny frame, curly red hair, and clean-shaven, freckled face, Kurt looked like he should still be in high school. "The dumbass is in jail and he thinks we're gonna let him play with his toy?"

Jake took a sip from his coffee cup. "He's been in jail often enough, you'd think he'd have the rules memorized by now."

"You'd think." Kurt cocked his head toward the papers spread out on the desk. "Come up with anything?"

"Nothing helpful."

"Is it because you're thinkin' about Julia instead?"

Jake snorted. "You a mind reader now, or what?"

"Nah. I just recognize that lovesick look. You been wearing it for nearly fifteen years."

"Bullshit." Jake scowled.

"Don't know why you keep holding onto her. You know, she left you without explanation, and she's barely paid you any mind since."

Massaging his neck to ease the tension settling there, Jake said, "I'm not holding onto anything. Don't know where you get that."

"Good thing. If you're of a mind to, just remember, she's the one who left. Didn't give a damn about your feelings."

Jake didn't respond. There was nothing he could say to such a blunt truth.

He forced his mind back to the photos and notes from Corbin's case. "Murder or suicide?" he asked rhetorically.

"My money's on murder. Otherwise, how'd he get that blow to the neck?"

"Yeah. And a note typed on the computer is kind of obvious. A killer wouldn't want to try to copy the victim's handwriting."

"Nope."

Jake picked up the printout of the suicide note left on Corbin's computer.

I'm sorry. I can't keep living like this. Their is just no other way. I love you. Corbin.

"He spelled 'there' wrong."

"What's that?" Kurt asked.

"There. Should be t-h-e-r-e. He spelled it t-h-e-i-r. Corbin was an educated man. Funny he'd get a simple word like that wrong."

Kurt picked up the note and studied it. "Yeah, but most guys ain't that great at spelling. 'Specially them 'there' words. I mean, you got three or four different spellin's for a word that sounds the same but means somethin' different. Confusin' as all get out." He tossed the note back on the desk.

Jake pondered the list of suspects, musing aloud, "Who do we have that might have wanted him dead?"

"We got his wife—cause of the affair. The other woman, Emily Green—if he was breakin' it off. Then, the widow of the man whose death he was partly responsible for. Or the man's son, who just got out of prison."

"That's quite a list for a person formerly thought to be a suicide victim."

The phone rang and Kurt picked it up. "Sheriff's Office."

"Shit," he said into the receiver. "Thanks. We'll be right there." He hung up the phone and looked at Jake with the face of someone about to deliver unwelcome news.

"What've you got?"

"Another body."

****

"I can't believe you're leaving." Pam stood in Julia's bedroom doorway, watching her pack the few items she'd used during her stay. The television was on a local newscast, the volume low. Half of Julia's attention was on the news, but not much happened in Covington. A few petty crimes, nothing serious enough to be interesting. She didn't know of one killing—accidental or otherwise—between Jasper Ramsey and Corbin.

"I know. I wish I could stay longer."

That was only partially true. She did wish she could spend more time with Pam. She was worried about her. Her mind didn't seem quite right, and she was still shaken over Corbin's death. Julia should at least be with her until she was a little stronger—at least until she found out whether her husband killed himself, or was murdered.

But, she needed to get back to work. Besides, this town brought back too much pain, the pain of running into Jake, and the horrible memories of Jasper Ramsey's death. Not that Julia had put it out of her mind. Not a day went by that she didn't think about it. But, when she was in Covington, not a *second* went by without her thinking about it. And seeing the man's family made it all too real, too horribly sad and unbearable.

"Your flight doesn't leave until this evening. Are you going to see Jake before you go?"

Julia halted in her packing to give Pam a disbelieving look. "Why would I?"

"Because, you still care about him, and the two of you have unfinished business."

"Right. We dated more than ten years ago. He married someone else, and we've barely spoken or seen one another in all that time. Yep. Definitely need some closure."

Pam came over to help Julia fold her clothes. "You

never explained why you left. You owe him that."

"He knows why I left. After the accident, the Morrisons kicked me out, Jake was in Iraq, and the town treated me like I had the plague. Why are you bringing this up after all these years?"

Pam released a shaky breath. "After losing Corbin…it just seems so wrong not to let someone know how you feel, not to clear the air. People shouldn't leave things unsaid between them. They might never get the chance to make it right."

Julia was trying to formulate a response that would satisfy Pam when a few words on the newscast caught her attention. She grabbed the remote from the nightstand and punched up the volume. A male reporter stood outside the police department. The bottom of the screen flashed the words *Breaking News: Woman found dead. Bizarre note typed on computer at scene.*

The camera cut back to the news anchor. "Police are conducting an investigation to determine who could have killed the woman and to discover the meaning of the chilling note found at the scene. We'll bring you more details as they become available."

"That's right here in Covington." Julia's insides tightened. *Another death so soon?*

"Jesus. Wonder who it was?"

The doorbell rang, and Pam went over to Julia's window and looked down. She turned, wearing a smile. "Here's your chance to say what needs to be said. It's Jake."

Julia's heart sped up. "Jake's here?"

"Come on, let's see what he wants."

Julia followed Pam downstairs. Breathless anticipation gripped her chest as Pam went to the door.

No matter why Jake was here, Julia couldn't stop the little thrill that ran through her at seeing him once more before she left.

Pam opened the door, and Jake stepped inside the foyer, filling the small space with his presence, bringing with him a light scent of manly cedar soap and the spicy aftershave he wore. He held his Stetson in his hands. His eyes landed on Julia, and he gave a curt nod. His expression revealed nothing, but a trickle of unease wound through her body.

"What is it?" Julia peered up at him. "Is this about the woman who was killed?"

"Damn reporters," he muttered. "Had the story on the news almost before we got to the scene."

"Does this have something to do with Corbin's death?"

Jake twisted his hat brim as he studied her. "We don't know yet. But, I thought you should hear from me who the victim was."

"Who?" Pam's voice shook, the question coming out like she didn't really want to know.

"It's Emily Green."

Julia's knees went weak. She opened her mouth, but couldn't form words.

Pam spoke for her. "What? We just saw her two nights ago. Dear God. How?"

Jake let his gaze rest on Pam for a moment, then switched it back to Julia. "You didn't hear it on the news?"

"We only caught the tail end of the story. Something about a note."

"No question this time about suicide or murder," he said in his soft drawl. "She was stabbed to death. The note at the scene wasn't a suicide note this time."

"What did it say?" Julia asked, dreading his answer.

A muscle twitched in his jaw, and he let out a reluctant sigh. "It said, 'You'll all pay.'"

Chapter Three

Maribel opened Jake's office door and shuffled across the floor. Coffee sloshed out of the cup she carried as she set it gingerly on his desk. She was seventy-two and had been with the sheriff's office for over half a century. Her years of being an asset were well past—and the county had already retired her—but Maribel wasn't really aware of that. She showed up, got paid, and had deluded herself into thinking it was still her job—not acknowledging that she drew a retirement check rather than a paycheck. Jake couldn't bring himself to disillusion her by letting her go.

She wiped her hands on her flowered blouse that was tucked half-in, half-out of the blue stretch pants she wore. "Those folks are here to see you," she said. "Should I send them in?"

Send six people I've brought in for questioning into my tiny office all at once? He held back a sigh of frustration and smiled. "No, thank you, Maribel. Just have them wait outside. Deputy Schuman and I will talk to them one at a time in the interrogation rooms."

She bobbed her head in a nod, making her glasses slip down her nose. "I'll tell them to wait. I gave them all coffee."

Jake barely held back a chuckle. If any of them were guilty of murder, that in itself was punishment enough. "Thank you. That's all for now."

She eventually made her way out of his office. He waited until she was gone, then slid the window up and emptied her coffee into the bush outside. Heading to the closet, he opened the door where he kept a Keurig coffee machine. In moments, he had a delicious, fresh brewed cup of coffee instead of something that tasted like dirty water poured out of a boot.

He carried the cup with him into the lobby. His heart kick-started as soon as he saw Julia. Her face had lost some of its color. Her blue eyes were red-rimmed, her mouth tight with grief. She wore faded jeans and a dark green blouse. The top few buttons were undone, and he found himself wishing the next few were also. He shoved the thought away and scowled as he stalked over to the group. Time to switch into formal Sheriff mode.

"Thanks for coming." He let his gaze roam over the entire group, deliberately forcing it from Julia.

He'd brought in the four remaining friends, along with Jasper Ramsey's widow, Debra, and her son, Donny Ray. He'd asked Maribel to have them arrive two at a time, staggered two hours apart, but like most things, she'd gotten it wrong.

Tension zipped through the air like lightning in a thunderstorm. No surprise since the Ramseys were sitting in the same room with four of the six people who'd caused Jasper's death. The thought of forcing Maribel to stay away from the office flitted once more through his mind. He'd have to worry about that later. For now, he had interviews to conduct.

"What the hell are we doing here?" Dave Owens demanded. "We just lost two of our best friends and you make us come into the goddamned sheriff's department?"

Jake kept his tone level, professional. "I'm aware you just lost two friends. And I'm trying to figure out what happened to them." There was no guarantee the deaths were even linked, but murder seldom happened in Covington. Since both scenes had notes typed on computers, and there was a link between the victims, they were focusing on the theory that the same person had committed both.

"Are all of us suspects?" Tanner tipped back in the plastic chair. Jake briefly hoped the flimsy legs would give and he'd fall on his ass. He'd never liked the guy. Too smug, lazy, and bad-tempered for his taste.

Before Jake could respond to Tanner, Kurt came into the room. Good. Now it was two against six. He liked those odds better.

"Not suspects," Kurt said. "We're just gathering information to help us with the case. We have to do all we can to make sure no one else gets hurt, or killed."

Pam lifted her head, her eyes wide. "Do you think we're all in danger?" She cut her eyes to where the Ramseys sat. No doubt where her suspicions lay.

"Deputy Schuman didn't say that." Jake walked over to the desk and retrieved pads of paper and pens. "This is about solving a case, that's all. The sooner we get started, the sooner you can all go home. Before we begin, I need you to do me a favor." He passed a pad and pen out to each of them. "Write a note stating, in these exact words, '*I wasn't there when the murders took place*.'"

Julia stood and lifted her gaze to his. "I beg your pardon? This doesn't sound like standard police practice."

He moved closer to her. Not a wise decision. Standing near her, inhaling her scent, experiencing that torturous, yet pleasurable sensation that only she could elicit, was a huge mistake. Yet he didn't move away.

Staring down at her, he hoped she read integrity in his expression. "Please. It's not anything anyone *has* to do, but I'd appreciate your cooperation."

She narrowed her eyes, then gave a quick nod. "Of course."

His heart soared at that small concession.

After they'd all passed the notes back, he looked at the Ramseys. "Could you come with me, please?"

There was a snack bar at the back of the office. Debra and Donny Ray could wait there. He wanted the two groups separated while he and Kurt interviewed each person individually.

As he led them back, he quickly skimmed the notes, grimacing in frustration. Not much help. Pam and Julia were the only ones who'd spelled 'there' correctly.

Once the Ramseys were settled, he called Pam into one of the rooms that doubled as an interrogation/conference area while Kurt started with Tanner in another. He and Kurt had decided beforehand how to divide the interviews. Jake made it clear up front that he wouldn't be questioning Julia. A murder investigation required professionalism and detachment. He had neither when it came to her.

Pam sat across the table from him, her face stretched into a grimace.

"Do you have any idea who might have wanted Corbin and Emily dead?"

She shook her head, then sighed. "Well…maybe. Corbin's mortgage company foreclosed on the Ramseys' house. Emily worked part-time for Corbin. And, well, you know what happened years ago. So…"

They'd discovered the foreclosure during the investigation. Definitely a motive. Especially coupled with the fact that Corbin had been partly responsible for Jasper's death. "Did the Ramseys ever make any threats that you know of?"

"No. Not that I know of." She raised her eyes to his. "Do you think Emily was the one Corbin was cheating with?"

The question caught him off guard. How had she come to that conclusion? "Why? Do you?"

She shrugged. "It crossed my mind. I was going through Corbin's office. There was a note Emily had written to him. She dotted the 'I' with a heart. She was awfully broken up about his death. And now—she's dead."

Jake blew out a breath. It would all come out eventually. Emily was dead, so it wasn't like he was ruining a friendship. Pam had a right to have her suspicions confirmed. He reached out and took her hand in both of his. "It's true. Emily is the one he was sleeping with. I'm sorry, Pammy."

She gasped. "Oh, God. How could she do that to me? How could he?" She lowered her head, sobbing softly. Jake handed her a tissue and gave her a moment to compose herself.

When she seemed to be somewhat in control of her emotions, he continued, "You said 'and now, she's dead.' Do you think their affair had something to do with her murder?"

"I don't know, but...I have this doll—" Pam stopped abruptly and picked up the bottle of water from the table, taking a long pull from it before she set it down. "Never mind."

"A doll?" Jake raised his brows.

"I said never mind. It's dumb. Is that all you need from me?"

He rubbed his fingers across his forehead. A headache was forming, and he was barely into the first interview. "Just a few more questions. Where were you just before Corbin was killed? You said you got to the office at eight p.m.?"

Her red-rimmed eyes stared into his. "Am I a suspect?"

He considered a moment before answering. "The spouse is always the first person we look at in a murder case. You found him. He was having an affair. Things don't look great for you."

She shot to her feet. "Jake! How can you say that? My God, you've known me most of my life. I can't believe you'd say something so awful after all I've been through."

He stood. "Calm down, Pam. I don't think you killed them. I have to ask these questions."

Her already wan face paled further. "Do I need a lawyer?"

"You have the right to retain one."

She put a hand over her mouth, shaking her head. "I can't believe this."

Jake reached out and squeezed her arm gently. "Don't worry. I don't believe you did it, okay? We'll find this person and all this will be over."

She nodded jerkily. "For you, maybe. But it will

never be over for me."

He pursed his lips, nodding back. "I know that. And I'm sorry. That's all for now. Thanks, Pam."

He followed her out and called for Donny Ray Ramsey.

Donny Ray wouldn't meet Jake's eyes as he settled in the chair across from him—one that had been purposely positioned so the table was next to the interviewee, and not in front of them. It was an old trick used to keep barriers out of the equation, allowing law enforcement to read body language, get a better feel of whether or not people were hiding something.

Donny Ray drummed his fingers on the tabletop and tapped his feet to the same rhythm.

Jake poised a pen over his notepad. "Where were you on Thursday night?"

"I was shooting pool at the Hog Wash in Seminole."

He spoke as he scribbled notes. "Can anyone corroborate your story?"

"Whole bar full of people saw me. Only one who would remember was Cleve Delaney. Beat him out of two hundred bucks."

"You know how I can reach him?"

"We didn't exchange phone numbers, or promise to call. Wasn't no date."

Jake gritted his teeth and ignored the attitude.

He picked up the phone and pushed Maribel's extension. When she answered, he said, "Maribel, can you get me the number for a Cleve Delaney, in or around Seminole. If you can't find a listing, get me the number to the Hog Wash. It's a bar."

"Well, that's a bunch of hog wash." She chortled at

her own joke…for a very long time.

"Thanks, Maribel." He hung up the phone with her still chuckling, then looked back at Donny Ray. "What about a week ago Friday?"

Donny Ray frowned. "Can't remember right off hand."

"It's very important that you do."

He sat up straighter and glared. "Am I the number one suspect, or something?'"

"No, Donny Ray." Jake quirked a brow. "You're *not* number one." He wasn't sure why he felt the need to throw out the double entendre, but from the mutinous scowl on Donny Ray's face, he got the implication.

The phone rang with an internal call. Maribel had the number for the bar, but didn't find a listing for Delaney. While Donny Ray looked on, Jake dialed the bar.

A woman with a raspy smoker's voice answered. When Jake asked her about Cleve Delaney, she said he wasn't there and wouldn't be for a while. He was on a fishing trip.

Jake hung up the phone. "Can't check your alibi. Delaney's on a fishing trip."

"So, what now? You think I did it?"

"I don't know what to think. Just gathering facts, for now. How did you feel about Emily Green and Corbin McCauley?"

Donny Ray stroked the thin mustache that lined his upper lip, avoiding Jake's gaze. "Didn't care for 'em."

"You hate 'em?"

"They killed my old man."

"They were young. It was an accident."

Donny Ray shifted forward and leaned his elbows

on his knees, now meeting Jake's eyes. "That don't make my daddy any less dead now, does it?"

Jake held eye contact with him for a moment, trying to get a read. He saw bitterness. Self-pity. Anger. No guilt. But guilt was a tough thing to read. Even if he'd committed the murders, didn't mean he felt guilty about it.

"There was a note at the second scene. It said, 'You'll all pay.' Got any idea what that might mean?"

Donny Ray leaned back and tapped his finger on his chin for a few seconds, as if considering. "Could be someone did it for revenge. I can understand how you'd look to me and my family." He smiled without humor. "Or I reckon it coulda been somebody from the IRS."

"I'm guessing revenge is more likely."

He shrugged. "You're the lawman. You should know."

Jake asked the rest of his questions but got nowhere. He advised Donny Ray—strongly—to remember where he was on Friday night, then told him he was free to leave.

Jake talked with Dave while Kurt finished up his interviews with Debra Ramsey and Julia. By the time they all left, Jake's brain felt as though someone had poured oatmeal in his head, and his muscles ached with tension. He was no further in the investigation than he'd been when they started.

Heading to his Keurig closet, he said to Kurt, "You want a cup of coffee, and we'll compare notes before we call it a day?"

"Coffee, or Maribel's piss water?"

"The real stuff."

"That I'll take."

Once they were seated with fresh cups of coffee, they thumbed through their notes.

Jake sipped from his cup, hoping Maribel didn't come into the office and bust him. "What about Tanner? He have anything interesting to say? Any red flags?"

"Nah. Not really. Why? You like him for it?"

"I don't know. Dave mentioned he had a bad temper—the kind that'll get him in trouble some day."

"You mean more trouble than he's already been in?"

Jake rolled his shoulders, trying to release some of the stress. "Passing bad checks and being drunk and disorderly are a long way from murder."

"True. And it looks like things were finally turning around for him. McCauley was investing in Morrison's wine business. They were on the verge of a deal when he died."

Jake scowled as he processed the information. "I can't see a smart business man like Corbin taking a chance on someone so poor at business and finances as Tanner."

"No. But maybe he's really good at making wine."

"What is his alibi?"

"He was with his girlfriend. At home all evening."

Jake took a drink of coffee before responding. "Both nights?"

"Just for Emily. The night Corbin was killed, he was at home with his parents."

"So his alibis are family members and a girlfriend." Jake thrummed his fingers on top of the desk. "Handy, but not exactly airtight."

"Nope. Mighty hard to prove or disprove, if the

other folks back you up."

"Then you got the note. Why would he want Corbin and Emily to pay? Unless it was because they were sleeping together, in which case, Pam would be the prime suspect. But, the note said, you'll *all* pay."

Kurt slowly nodded. "Kind of strange how there was no note with the first one. Almost as though it was an afterthought to point the finger somewhere specific."

"Like at the son or the widow."

"Exactly." Kurt leaned back in the chair and slurped loudly from his cup.

"Helps that Donny Ray just got out of prison. If I was going to frame somebody, he'd be my first pick."

Kurt's brows rose. "Frame? You really think so?"

Jake didn't think so, not necessarily, but it was a workable theory. "Why a threatening note this time and not the first? Why would the killer bother with a suicide note with Corbin?"

Another slurp. Jake considered reminding his deputy how irritating the noise was, but didn't. He'd told him plenty of times before, and it hadn't done any good.

"If it is Donny Ray, could be he planned to make 'em all look like accidents. Then, when the first one started to look like murder, he figured he'd go with that. Let everyone know he was avenging his dad."

"Could be. But it wouldn't be the smartest thing to do. Point the finger right at yourself."

Kurt shrugged. "Donny Ray ain't exactly no Einstein."

The killer wasn't necessarily an Einstein, either. He, or she, had already made a few mistakes. The trick was capitalizing on them and catching a murderer before someone else died.

Jake hated to think Tanner could be involved. Julia cared about the guy and finding out he was a killer would devastate her. He couldn't imagine what possible motive he'd have, but instinct was gnawing at him like a beaver on a log. Problem was, instinct and a shaky alibi didn't mean diddly-shit in a murder investigation.

****

On the day of Emily's funeral, a light mist fell as the mourners made their way across the grass toward the canopy that sheltered her casket. A dozen or so chairs held family members. Julia's heart ached with sadness when she saw the young man in dress blues—Emily's younger brother, home on leave from Afghanistan for his sister's funeral.

What a way to thank him for serving our country. He sat ramrod straight, his military bearing only slightly broken by the quaking of his shoulders.

Julia and Pam had umbrellas, but the rain wasn't coming down hard enough to need them. Julia's heels sunk into in the soft ground as she walked. She wore the same black dress she'd worn to Corbin's funeral. She'd only packed for one. Who would have thought she'd need funeral attire for two?

When she'd called the law firm and told them she had to extend her time off, they weren't happy, but then, neither was she. Two of her lifelong friends died tragic deaths. And there was a killer roaming free who might never be caught. She shuddered. A killer was on the loose who possibly had a vendetta against their entire group. The thought made her want to leave town as soon as the funeral ended, but she'd promised Pam she'd stay on a few extra days. Besides, she'd feel like the biggest coward in history if she fled and abandoned her friends.

Pam had been walking silently beside her, but now said in a stage whisper, "You'll all pay. You know what that means, right?"

"No. I don't." Julia frowned at her.

"It's the doll. *All those who betray you will suffer*."

In spite of the absurdity of the doll-as-a-psychokiller theory, Julia answered as if the topic was logical. "Right. Corbin's affair, but Emily—"

"Was the one he was sleeping with."

"What?" Julia looked at Pam in amazement. "You're not serious."

"Yes," she said bitterly. "I am. Emily was screwing Corbin. They both betrayed me."

"How do you know? Why didn't you tell me before now?"

"I found out at the police station when we went in for our interviews. I had suspicions before, but Jake confirmed it. I didn't tell you, because I was humiliated." She shrugged. "But you're my best friend. I had to tell someone."

Julia's stomach clenched. *How could Emily have done this to Pam?* But knowing what she'd done didn't lessen Julia's grief. In spite of the affair, neither of them deserved to be murdered.

"So, you think the doll killed them because they cheated and betrayed you?"

"No, that's not what I meant. The note threatens more people, right?"

"It sounded that way. What are you getting at?"

"Corbin and Emily are dead. You, Tanner, and Dave might be in danger, too."

Julia had been leaning toward Donny Ray as a suspect, which would mean Pam was also in danger. *Why hadn't she included herself?*

They were almost upon the canopy, but Julia slowed her pace in order to finish their conversation, to try to make sense of what Pam was saying.

"We could be in danger from the doll? But the legend is about those who betray the owner. What have we ever done to you?"

Pam halted, and after a few steps, Julia did, too. She turned to look at her friend. The mist had grown into a heavy drizzle, and they opened their umbrellas. Pam's features were distorted by the curtain of rain falling between them, her mouth drawn into a frown.

"Back then, the night Jasper Ramsey died..." She shifted the umbrella to cover part of her face. "The rest of you squealed. You told the police I was the one driving."

A chill raced over Julia's neck and trickled down her spine. "Jesus, Pam. That was ten years ago. Karma's just now coming around?"

Pam lifted her free hand, palm up. "I didn't own the doll ten years ago."

Julia stared at her incredulously. "You can't possibly think that we deserve to be punished?"

Pam met her gaze. "*I* don't think you do, but maybe the doll does." Her tone was matter-of-fact. Chillingly, matter-of-fact. "Of course, you did try to cover for me. Told the police at first you were driving. The doll might take that into consideration. Then that fucking Tanner had to open his mouth."

"Tanner just told the truth, Pam. He wanted to protect me."

Julia had tried to claim she was driving. She'd had much less to lose than Pam. Pam had a loving family who trusted her, bright plans for her future. For Julia, being treated like an outcast with leprosy, whether she did anything wrong or not, felt normal. She was used to it.

"Yeah, then you *all* told the truth. I'm not saying it's right, what the doll's doing. I'm just saying that could be the reason. You all betrayed me."

Julia gaped at her in stunned silence. *What is wrong with her? What the hell is going on in this town?*

The service was about to start, but Julia couldn't leave this alone. She reached out and caught hold of Pam's hand, moving closer. Pam's flesh was cold, her hand small and trembling in Julia's. "I'm worried about you. This doll thing isn't normal…you know that, right? Thinking some ancient curse is killing people? We need to get you some help. You should talk to someone."

Pam's mouth tightened, and she jerked her hand away. "You think I'm crazy?"

"I think you've dealt with an awful lot and really should see someone. You know it's not logical to think a doll could be killing people."

"Prove it." Her voice took on a pleading note. "Please, would you prove it?"

"What?"

"Prove that I'm wrong. Prove the doll has nothing to do with the murders, and I'll go see someone. You're an investigator. Get to the truth, and we'll know I need help."

"Jake is on the case, he—"

"The cops may, or may not, solve it. They don't

care as much as we do. If you find out something they haven't, it will put my mind at ease. Please."

Pam's eyes implored her, the desperation in them making her look like a drowning victim. Was she really worried about her sanity, about getting to the truth, or did she just not want Julia to leave?

Either way, it worked. Julia couldn't go when Pam needed her. And maybe she could poke around and find something the police hadn't discovered. Not likely, but if it would put Pam's mind at ease, she'd give it a shot.

"Okay. I'll stay for a bit. See what I can find out."

"Thank you," Pam whispered, then turned, and headed toward the canopy.

Julia started to follow, but her eyes fell on a gravestone. The one she and her friends had hung out at when they came here as kids. They'd drink and tell ghost stories, trying to scare one another. This particular grave was that of a man who'd died in the late 1800s. His name was Bertram Scoffield, and the guys had tried to convince the girls they'd seen Bertram's ghost floating through the cemetery. Emily had been half-convinced. Her large brown eyes would brim with moisture as she begged the guys to stop, which only made them taunt that much more.

The cemetery had been their second favorite hangout, next to the lake, and now, two of them were resting here…forever.

"Are you okay?"

She whirled at the low rumble of Jake's voice behind her.

He stood a few feet away, studying her with that intense expression of his, as if he could ferret out her every secret, pull every thought and emotion from her soul.

She took a deep breath. "Just dreading…you know…" She looked back to Emily's casket. Tears knotted her throat, and her stomach clutched in grief. She swayed as the strength left her legs. "I don't think I can go over there."

As if staying outside the circle would make it not true. Would make Emily still be alive.

Jake moved closer, and his touch fell on her forearm, his grip warm and gentle. "Yes, you can. I'll help you."

She peered up at him. Rain dripped from the brim of his hat as he squinted at her, his mouth turned down in sympathy. She wanted to fall into him, to feel his arms close around her, to rest in his comforting embrace. She sucked in a breath, willing the power to resist.

He tugged gently, and she walked along beside him, staying close, feeling his calming presence…his warm strength. During the entire service—through Emily's mother laying a rose on her casket, sobbing, held upright by Emily's brother—Jake's touch never left her.

****

The next night, Julia stood on tiptoe in the darkened alley alongside The Rusty Nail, peering through the window. She'd followed Donny Ray from his house and ended up here. So far, Donny Ray sat alone at the bar, sipping a mug of beer, not speaking to anyone. She wasn't sure what she thought she'd learn, but she wanted to get a read on his habits, his friends. Although, maybe, after spending the better part of ten years in prison, the guy didn't really have any friends.

An unwilling twinge of sympathy seeped through her. After all, he'd lost his father, couldn't find a job, and had no home. *Shit*. Even half of that was enough to drive a person crazy.

Camera in hand, she was ready. If anything noteworthy happened, she'd capture it. If it was really good, she'd take it straight to the police.

Donny Ray eased off the barstool, leaving his empty mug and heading to the back. Probably going to the restroom. She'd wait a little while longer. If he did nothing except drink alone at the bar, she'd call it a night and work a new angle. Check out some of the other suspects on her list, although Donny Ray was definitely at the top.

Her feet cramped from standing on her tiptoes, and her back was starting to ache. *What is taking him so long?* Maybe he had to do more than urinate. She curled up her nose.

Another five minutes passed.

Geez, is there a line for the bathroom? Don't guys usually just whip it out and go whether there was a receptacle or not?

Julia shifted her feet and leaned her butt against the wall to get more comfortable, debating whether to give it up for the night. She opened the camera bag and slipped the Canon inside. The sound of the zipper closing almost masked the crunch of footsteps behind her. She whirled, nearly dropping the expensive camera. She yelped as Donny Ray yanked her close, his face only a few inches from hers. His fingers dug painfully into her shoulders.

"What the fuck do you think you're doing?" he snarled.

Chapter Four

Julia's breath left her body in a single rush. She opened her mouth to reply, but her vocal cords seized. Donny Ray was so close she could see her reflection in his angry blue eyes, could smell the beer on his breath.

"I said…what are you doing? Spying on me?"

"I-I-just…" She shook her head, unable to come up with a plausible explanation.

"I seen you behind me after I left my house but didn't think nothing of it. Then I come out here to take a piss and see you sneaking around with a goddamn camera?"

He shook her, snapping her head back.

"Let me go!" She tried to jerk away, but he tightened his hold.

"It ain't enough you and your friends ruined my family. Now you gotta spy on me? You think I killed your friends, don't you? What the fuck? You think you're some kind of Nancy Drew or something?"

He shoved her against the wall. She grunted with pain, looking up into his livid face, into his crazed eyes. This man had been in prison. True fear took hold, and her heart dropped to her stomach. In a dark alley, the bastard could do whatever he wanted. No one would know. She drew in a breath to scream, but he clamped a calloused hand over her mouth.

"You ain't callin' for help, and you ain't goin' nowhere 'til I get some answers."

Against the pressure of his hand, her demands to be released were muffled. She shoved on his chest, but he didn't budge. She couldn't very well give him answers while he was impairing her ability to speak.

"Turn her loose." The low, controlled voice came from her left. She almost wept with relief.

Jake.

Donny Ray cut his eyes to the side, then back to Julia. "Ain't none of your concern, Sheriff. Me and her was just having a little chat."

He loosened his hold enough that Julia could turn her head. The rough brick wall ground against her skull. Jake stood a few feet away. The streetlight behind him illuminated his silhouette like an angel of mercy. He stood with a hand on one hip—the hip where his gun rested.

He tipped his hat back off his forehead. "She doesn't look like she wants to chat, so I'm thinking you should probably turn her loose."

"And if I don't, what you gonna do about it?"

Jake's shoulders lifted in a laconic shrug. "Don't think you want to find out."

The world stilled. She waited for Donny Ray to react. After the longest seconds of her life, his grip on her shoulders relaxed, and his hands dropped away.

"Yeah, sure." Donny Ray puffed out his chest. "You're real tough with that badge and gun, Sheriff. Wonder what would happen if it was just man to man."

Jake unclipped the badge from his waist and slipped his gun belt off his hip. Squatting, he placed them on the ground, then straightened, and held out his hands, palms up. "Okay. Now it's man to man."

Donny Ray's chin rose, and he took a couple of steps toward Jake, then halted. He stood uncertainly for a few moments, then shook his head. "Hell with it. She ain't worth it." He looked back at Julia and pointed his finger at her face. "You just stay the fuck away from me, got it? Don't be following me. Lawman won't always be around to save your ass."

He stalked away, pushing past Jake and disappearing out of the alley.

"You're not going to arrest him?" Julia demanded. She threw her hands up in the air, then dropped them to her sides, letting anger cover the fear. "You know he's probably the killer. And he tried to attack me."

"Not enough evidence on the murders. No evidence, really. And I stopped him before he did anything to you." He reached down and retrieved his gun and badge, calmly settling them back in place. "What's this about you following him? Maybe I should take *you* in."

"Are you kidding me?" She strode over and glared into his shadowed face. "The guy most likely killed two people. No telling what he would have done if you hadn't shown up." She wanted him to care, to show some emotion, some relief she was okay…a sign he gave a damn.

"Let's get you home. If you're too shaken up, I can run you to Pam's, and you can get your car tomorrow."

She shook her head. "Nothing ever gets to you, does it? Cool and calm, no matter what."

He scrutinized her briefly, then turned away. "Got to me when I saw his hands on you. Would've got to me if he'd hurt you."

His usual honeyed tone held a harsh edge. Her heart sped up at the brief flash of emotion. But she wasn't sure how to interpret it. Did he mean as an officer of the law, or as an old friend? Or someone who still had feelings for her? She couldn't ask him. She might not like his answer.

"Well, that's something then," she finally said.

"Come on, I'll drive you home." He headed out of the alley. She followed.

"I'm fine. I can drive."

"I'd feel better if you didn't. You're still shaken up."

"You just want to make sure I don't follow Donny Ray again."

He glanced back at her, but kept walking. "What was that all about, anyway?"

"I wanted to check him out, see if I could get any evidence that might prove he killed Corbin and Emily."

They'd arrived at Jake's car, and he paused as he reached for the door handle, turning to squint down at her. "You don't think I can do my job?"

"It's not that. I promised Pam I'd check out a few things. I'm an investigator for a law firm, so she thought I might find something to take to the police."

"Your friend wanna get you killed? If Ramsey is the killer, how smart is it for you to be snooping around, spying on him?"

The door of the bar opened and a blast of music carried to them, along with a shaft of light. Julia waited until the door closed, and they were once more in the quiet, semi-darkness before speaking. She pulled the camera strap high on her shoulder and shrugged. "I was being careful."

He gave a disbelieving snort as he opened the passenger door and motioned for her to get inside. She didn't know at what point she'd decided to take him up on his offer of a ride, but she slid in the seat. Truth was, she liked being around him and would take it for a few more minutes, even if it was just a ride home.

He went to his side and opened the door, then got behind the wheel. "Careful, huh?" He shook his head as he started the car and cruised onto the street. "Didn't look like it when I walked up."

She played with the strap on her camera bag, feeling foolish and incompetent. "I guess maybe it didn't."

He fell silent and flipped on the radio. "Suspicious Minds" by Elvis was playing. She glanced at Jake from the corner of her eye. Did he remember how much she liked Elvis? How he'd teased her unmercifully about it? Nothing showed on his face, but he must remember. Had he shoved every memory of their time together out of his mind?

They pulled up to Pam's house to find all the lights off and the house shrouded in darkness. Jake got out of the car and opened her door. His hand rested on the small of her back, singeing her flesh through the thin black fabric of her blouse as he guided her to the porch. A fluttering sensation moved through her chest. His touch always had that effect on her, only now her reactions were that of a woman instead of a shy, awkward teen.

On the porch, he stared down at her, an inscrutable expression on his face. "I'm glad you're okay."

"Thanks to you." She tried not to think of what might have happened had he not shown up. "So, what were you doing at the Rusty Nail?"

"Stopped for a beer. Heard commotion in the alley and went to check it out."

"You didn't get your beer."

"No."

She hesitated a moment. "Pam has beer." She tried to make the offer sound casual, as if she didn't care whether he accepted or not.

His gaze searched her face, then he stared over her shoulder at the house, as if debating the wisdom of entering. "I'm kind of out of the mood for beer. Better just get on home."

She pushed back disappointment and gave a quick nod. "Okay. Sure. Thanks for the ride. And the rescue."

"No problem." He headed down the steps, then turned back to face her. "Let me ask you something. You lived with Tanner for several years. Did you notice any anger issues? Have you seen any in him as an adult?"

"Anger issues?"

"Yeah. Does he have a short fuse? Ever show any violent tendencies?"

She thought about the incident in the bar with Dave, but didn't mention it. "He's a troubled kid. I'm sure he has some anger."

Jake's mouth quirked. "He's not a kid. He's a grown man."

"In his mind, he's not grown."

"Making excuses for him?"

She peered closely at him. "Accusing him of something?"

"Just trying to get a read on all the players."

"Players? As in suspects?" She moved to the edge

of the porch. He stood on the bottom step, eye level with her. "Tanner is a suspect, isn't he? I'd probably be a suspect if I'd been in town when Corbin died."

"Didn't say that."

"No, but you thought it. As far as you're concerned, we're all the same. Nothing but trouble. You think once someone's bad, they're always bad."

"You're putting words in my mouth. I never said anything like that."

"Tanner has his faults, but he's not a killer. You're holding his past against him." She almost said, 'just like you did with me,' but that wouldn't be fair. She'd left him, not the other way around. "You only see black and white, no room for error in your world. You're perfect, and you expect everyone else to be. You've never done anything wrong in your life."

His jaw tightened. "Never did anything wrong, huh? Is that what you think?"

"I can't imagine what it would be. Star athlete in high school, brave soldier risking his life for our country, and now, a sheriff, keeping the town safe from evil. Sounds pretty perfect to me." Bitterness colored her tone.

He moved up a couple of steps. Her breath stalled in her throat, his scent filling her nostrils. A slow, warm thrill uncoiled in the center of her belly. But the look in his eye was far from romantic. Anger had turned the gray to steel, but there was pain there, too.

"You think I never did anything wrong? That I was some hero fighting for our country? What would you say if I told you I was a deserter?"

The words hit her in the gut, rendering her speechless.

He continued, his voice soft, pain-filled. "I went AWOL, abandoned my platoon in Iraq."

No. Impossible. Jake Devlin would never do that. "What? Why?"

"Because, I was terrified. I wish I could say it was something noble, like I didn't want to kill another human being, but the truth was, I was scared shitless of dying. Or worse, of having a limb torn off by a bomb, living that way the rest of my life. Cowardly, right?"

"But you would have gotten in trouble. You're a decorated soldier. Shouldn't you have gotten a dishonorable discharge, or something? Had charges filed against you?"

"I should have, but no one ever found out. I only disappeared for a few hours. My sergeant found me in the desert, out of water, dehydrated, sobbing like a baby."

She waited as emotions chased across his face. She saw pain and shame. It made her want to reach out and touch him, comfort him, but she didn't think he needed that right now. He was working through this himself. He needed her to let him.

"He told me it was my choice, whether I came back or not. Said it'd be our secret, whatever choice I made. He had a son who was killed in the war the year before." His voice choked, and he cleared his throat. "He was the most devoted military man I'd ever met, but he said if he had a choice, he would rather his son had deserted and survived." He let out a long breath. "I chose to go back."

"Then it turned out okay."

He shook his head. "Doesn't change what I did. I live with that every day. So don't tell me I'm perfect, that I don't know what it's like to make mistakes."

She placed a hand on his arm and looked up into bleak eyes. The misery she saw squeezed her heart "It's okay," she whispered. "You weren't much more than a child."

His eyes locked on hers and cleared, finally looking at her, rather than at something a world away. He lifted a hand, running his thumb along her jaw line. Goose bumps pimpled her skin. "Your eyes look like sapphires in the moonlight," he whispered.

She closed her eyes and swallowed against a tide of desire. His warm touch on her flesh made her shiver. "I—thank you," she ended lamely. Her eyes opened to the brilliant silver of his gaze. She couldn't look away, couldn't control the hitch in her breath. The air around them sizzled with electricity.

He peered intently at her for a few heart-stopping moments, then muttered, "God help me," just before his head lowered, and his lips claimed hers.

His mouth was firm, demanding, coaxing her lips open so he could slip his tongue inside. As a boy, his kisses had been sweet, inexperienced, yet thrilling nonetheless. Now, he kissed like a man who knew what he was doing. A man who wanted more than just to slide a hand under her sweater and get to second base.

God, if she didn't want it too. She pressed against him, returning the kiss, ignoring warning bells that clanged loudly in her head. After ten years of yearning, all she could think about was the glorious wonder of being in Jake's arms. She lifted her hands and clenched his hair in her fingers, dragging his head closer, tighter to her. Vaguely, she was aware of his hat landing on the ground, but neither of them stopped.

He lifted his mouth long enough to run his tongue along the sensitive flesh of her neck. A small moan rumbled in her throat before he once more found her lips.

Her mind went back ten years, after Jake graduated and she was still in high school…to the excitement of knowing Jake Devlin liked *her*…wanted *her*. She could almost feel the cool spring breeze against the exposed skin of her back where Jake had lifted her blouse to fumble with the clasp on her bra, could almost hear the sounds of the crowd at the football game while they huddled in the darkness behind the bleachers. An idyllic sense of peace…the rightness of this moment filled her soul, and the awful years between then and now melted away.

The memories shattered when Jake pulled back, breaking the kiss. She bit her lip to keep from crying out in disappointment. His hands moved, gripping her upper arms as he drew in ragged breaths. He screwed his eyes shut briefly, grimacing as if in pain.

"What?" she whispered. "What is it?"

He opened his eyes, looking down at her, his mouth crooking in a self-deprecating grin. "Now, I've made two mistakes."

The words hit her like a blow to her chest. She couldn't control the flinch of pain as she jerked loose from his hold. "Gee, thanks. Just what a woman wants to hear."

"God, Julia. I didn't mean it that way." He scraped a hand through his hair and bent to snatch his hat from the ground.

"Oh? Then how did you mean it?" She crossed her arms over her chest, fighting the anger rising in her heart.

"I just meant…we've got all this history. You'll be leaving in a few days. The last thing we need is to muddle things up by having sex." The corner of his mouth turned up in a mocking grin. "Unless you're looking for a quick fling before you head out?"

She held back tears that threatened. "I had no intentions of having a fling with you." She tried to sound determined, but the raw pain in her voice lessened the effect. "We had a moment. Lost control for a few seconds, but as far as mistakes go, I don't believe you can rank it up there with being a deserter."

Now it was his turn to flinch. With a quick nod, he settled the Stetson back on his head. "Good point. Night, Julia. Call me tomorrow if you need a ride to your car."

Right. She'd walk the three miles before she'd ask him for a ride, but she didn't say it. Nor did she voice the apology she owed him. She stayed silent as she watched him walk away. When he climbed into his car and drove off, she brought trembling fingers to her mouth where his lips had rested only moments before.

****

The next morning, after a sleepless night of waffling between anger and disappointment, Julia was sitting at the kitchen table drinking coffee when there was a knock on the door.

Her heart thumped.

Jake? Here to apologize? Not likely. Besides, Julia was the one who owed the apology. Or, maybe they owed one another apologies—for everything that had gone on between them over the years.

It was probably someone for Pam, who was still

asleep. She'd been sleeping a lot lately. Her doctor had prescribed sleeping pills after Corbin's death, but Julia wasn't sure it was a good idea for her to take them, especially considering the path her mind had been going down lately.

The knock came again. She considered not answering, but instinctual good manners won out. With a reluctant sigh, she rose and went to the door.

The elderly lady who worked for Jake stood on the porch. Wisps of gray hair escaped her bright yellow headband, which clashed with her shapeless blue and green flowered blouse. Her glasses sat askew on her nose.

"Hello, can I help you?" Julia didn't think Pam knew the woman very well. *Is she lost?* She seemed to suffer from a slight case of dementia, so it was possible.

"I need to talk to you, if you have a minute. Can I come in?"

"Certainly." Julia stepped back. "Please come in, Miss, uhm…"

"Maribel. I work for Sheriff Devlin."

"Yes, of course. Maribel." Julia led her into the living room. "Would you like something to drink?"

"I wouldn't say no to a nice cup of tea."

"Have a seat. I'll be right back."

Julia microwaved a cup of tea and brought it, along with creamer and sugar, into the living room. Maribel was perched on the edge of the couch, peering at the Scrimshaw doll resting on the mantel.

"What in God's creation is that?" she asked, turning up her nose.

"It's a doll…a really old doll. Pam bought her from an antique store."

Maribel cackled. "Why would she do a fool thing like that? It's got to be about the homeliest thing I've ever seen."

Julia suppressed a grin. "Pam likes it."

"Hmmmph." Maribel poured a generous amount of sugar into her tea, stirring and shaking her head. "To each her own, I suppose."

Wanting to steer her to the reason for her visit, and just a little irrationally concerned the doll would take offense, Julia said, "What did you need to speak with me about?"

"Oh, that. Yes. Sheriff Devlin told me to call the airline and find out when you rescheduled your flight for, but I thought to myself, why go to the market for eggs when you can go straight to the chicken? So, here I am. When did you reschedule your flight for?"

Julia didn't think this was what Jake had in mind when he gave Maribel the assignment. However, her visit made one thing painfully obvious. He was anxious for her to leave.

"I left my flight open. I want to stick around, see if I can help Jake with the case. Help him find out who killed my friends."

"Sheriff Devlin won't want your help, I can guarantee. Him and Kurt is plenty smart enough to solve the case. Just give 'em a little time."

"Oh, I didn't mean that at all. It's just…I know the victims so well, I thought maybe I could uncover something they didn't."

It occurred to her that, with a little probing, Maribel could provide some useful information. Julia might burn in hell for taking advantage of a feeble-minded old lady, but if it helped catch a killer, well…surely she'd be forgiven.

"You dern right you know the victims well. You was part of that awful thing with Jasper Ramsey. You know, my Herbert worked with Jasper down to the lake."

"No, I didn't know that."

"He sure did." She took a sip of the tea, then lowered her voice to a conspiratorial whisper. "I know you shouldn't speak ill of the dead, but if it eases your mind any about what happened to Jasper, just know he wasn't exactly the best man you'd ever want to meet."

"No?"

Maribel shook her head and more of the precariously contained gray hair escaped. "There was a rumor going around that Jasper had a baby with a woman besides his wife. Some woman from another town. He refused to acknowledge the child, or help the woman. Don't know if it's true and don't know what happened to neither of 'em, but if it was true, you ask me, he wasn't worth the powder and lead it would take to blow him away."

Julia's mind turned over the revelation. *Could it be true?* Could Jasper Ramsey have another child out there somewhere? Could that child possibly have something to do with the murders?

She grimaced. That was a stretch. A huge stretch. First of all, she didn't know if it was even true. Like Maribel said, it was a rumor. Secondly, if it was true, the kid might not know who his, or her, father was, or what had happened to him long ago. On the other hand, anything was possible.

She smiled at Maribel and politely listened to her prattle, but her mind was gnawing on the juicy little tidbit she'd just been handed.

****

The last place Julia wanted to be was the Ramsey house, but that seemed to be her most logical start. If Jasper had fathered another child, his widow might know. She might not be willing to share the information, but it never hurt to ask.

As she stepped onto the porch, she hesitated, reluctant to open old wounds. An image of Corbin and Emily surfaced. They were gone forever. She would never see her friends again, never hear their laughter, never have another conversation with them. The reminder cemented her resolve as she knocked on the door.

Debra Ramsey swung the door open. Fireworks shot from her eyes when she saw Julia standing on the porch. Though the woman couldn't have been much more than fifty or so, streaks of gray lined her red hair. Heavy bags under her eyes and the pinched look around her mouth aged her another ten years. "What the hell do you want?"

"I'd like to ask you a few questions, if you don't mind."

"I mind like hell. Get off my property."

"Please. It will only take a few minutes."

She stared hard at Julia for a few seconds, then stepped back, pushing the door to close it. Just before it shut, Julia shot out a hand. "Mrs. Ramsey, please, this is extremely important, or I wouldn't be here." The door kept closing. Desperate to get her attention, Julia shouted, "Did your husband father a child with another woman?"

The pressure on the door eased. Debra pulled it

back and glared at Julia. "I don't want to talk about the past. It's none of your damned business. I know you think my boy had something to do with the killings. I ain't gonna help you with none of that nonsense."

"I think he might have something to do with the murders…or at least I did. But, if the rumor is true, if your husband had a child with another woman, that opens up a whole new set of possibilities. Please just answer my question, Mrs. Ramsey."

A shimmer of tears glistened in her eyes. "My son could get hurt by all this."

If the rumor was true, Donny Ray must not know. "Whatever I learn here today stays between you and me, unless I have to use it to stop a killer."

Debra pressed her lips together, her face clenching with pain and anger. Julia could see in her expression when she relented. "Let's hope you don't. Donny Ray has been hurt enough for ten lifetimes." Stepping back, she opened the door.

****

Jake was alone at the sheriff's office when he heard the front door open. He went into the lobby, and his heart stilled when Julia walked in. Her eyes met his, and the kiss he kept pushing away exploded in his memory. That dangerous, spine-tingling, soul-rocking kiss. The one that could never, ever happen again. Not if he wanted to survive with his heart intact.

"Can I help you?" He kept his tone level and pushed thoughts of her soft lips pressed against his to the recesses of his mind.

She offered a tentative smile. He considered apologizing for the hurtful words they'd exchanged, but wasn't sure how to begin. So, he left it alone.

"I found out some information that might help your case. I tried to run it down on my own, but got nowhere. You have access to records that I don't."

He bit back his irritation. *So much for warning her to stay out of the investigation.* He heaved a deep breath. "What kind of information?"

She glanced around the empty office. "Can we go somewhere private?"

"Maribel is off today, and Kurt's out handling a vandalism call. Can't get much more private than this." And, in his office—a confined space—Julia would be much too close, much too tempting.

Twisting the strap of her purse, she nodded. "I found out something about Jasper Ramsey. I'm not sure if it will help, but it's possible. Did you know that, nearly thirty years ago, he fathered a child other than Donny Ray? With another woman?" Her face lit with excitement, her eyes shining like sunlight on the ocean.

He knew how she felt. Nothing could compare to the adrenalin rush of putting clues together, finding one piece of the puzzle that fit it all into place. But he didn't think this was it. From what Jake remembered about Jasper Ramsey, he wasn't exactly a ladies' man. "What other woman? What happened to the child?"

She shrugged. "Debra didn't know what happened to either of them. Or who the—"

"Wait. You talked to Debra Ramsey?" His chest constricted. "What were you thinking? Those people don't like you, Julia. You could get hurt."

She brushed off his comment with a wave of her hand. "She wouldn't hurt me. So, anyway, I'm thinking this kid could have something to do with the murders. He, or she, would be about our age, from what Debra said."

"And you think now, nearly thirty years later, Ramsey's bastard child is seeking revenge for his, or her, father's death?"

She sighed. "Well, when you put it that way…"

"Any way you put it, it sounds ridiculous. Does the kid even know about Jasper? Is the kid still around? Still alive?"

The defeated look on her face almost made him wish she was right, that this far-fetched theory were true and she'd solved the murders. Anything to put that glow back on her face.

"No, I don't know any of that. It's just an idea, something to check out. You have resources to do that, where I don't."

"It sounds like a waste of time."

She nodded, her voice quivering when she spoke. "Okay. I understand. You don't have time. Sorry I've taken up so much of it already." She headed to the door, but he couldn't stand to let her leave looking beaten down.

"Hey, I tell you what. I'll check into it. If anything comes of it, I'll let you know. How's that?"

She turned to face him, and the glow was back. "That would be great. Thank you."

The smile that touched her lips made him want to find this unknown person, and if they were innocent, frame them for the murders.

****

Later that night, after Pam went to bed, Julia read over her notes. In case nothing came of Jake checking out the lead she'd given him—which, the more she thought about it, sounded outlandish—she would dig under every rock, search every nook and cranny. Not only did Corbin and Emily deserve to have their murderer brought to justice—and not only were the rest of them in possible danger—but the sooner the killer was caught, the sooner Pam would get the therapy she obviously needed. And, the sooner Julia could get back home and leave Covington far behind…in her past, where it should have stayed.

She rubbed the heels of her hands against her closed eyes. Staring at the computer for hours was going to make her go blind.

Standing, she stretched, leaning back to work the kinks out of her lower back. Time for a break, at least a short one. She went into the kitchen and was headed to the fridge to get a bottle of water when a loud crash sounded through the open window, followed by a masculine grunt. She rushed to the window and pulled the curtain aside, searching the darkness. Her heart thumped a frightened rhythm. Was Donny Ray here to shut her up for good? Or—she swallowed—was it the killer? Was it her turn to pay?

In the faint glow of the moon, she saw a figure lying prone in the backyard. She squinted, trying to make out the features, something identifiable…something that would tell her if it was an innocent person in need of assistance, or a ploy by someone intending to do her harm.

She gasped when recognition dawned. The skin on her neck tingled, and her knees went weak as she muttered a prayer. "Please, God, *please* let him be okay."

Chapter Five

"Tanner!" Julia screamed his name as she tore out the back door. Someone was running through the gate into the backyard. *The killer?* Her pulse raced. She'd been foolish not to bring a weapon. She squinted in the darkness. A wave of relief came over her when she recognized Tessa. But it didn't mean they were safe. Whoever had done this to Tanner could still be out here.

"What happened?" Tessa wobbled on her high heels like a newborn colt. "What's the matter with Tanner?"

"Call 9-1-1," Julia shouted. Tessa nodded and fumbled a phone out of her over-sized purse.

Julia reached Tanner and dropped to her knees beside him. He moaned, and his eyes fluttered open.

"Lay still," she choked. "Help is on the way. Where are you hurt?"

"Head," he mumbled.

She lifted her gaze. Moonlight filtering through the trees provided minimal light, but it was enough. Her mouth went dry when she saw blood streaming from his forehead. She jerked her shirt off, folded it, and pressed it against the wound. Stripped down to nothing more than her black silk camisole, she felt self-conscious, but Tanner's well-being was more important than her modesty.

"They're on the way," Tessa said. The smell of cheap perfume reached Julia before Tessa did. "Are you all right, baby?" The girl bent over at the waist, her boobs spilling out of her tight pink blouse.

"I don't…know—" Tanner gasped. "Hit me with something—"

Julia frowned. "Who did? What happened?"

Tessa answered for him. "We was driving by and Tanner said he saw someone go in the backyard." Her sentence ended on a wail. She sniffled, then continued. "He made me stop. I told him we should call the cops, but he bailed outta the car and hightailed it back here. Chased the dude right out of the backyard."

Julia's blood froze. The killer had been lurking outside. *Am I the target? Pam?* Whichever of them it was, Tanner had risked his life to save them. Gratitude and love filled her heart. In the distance, sirens sounded. She reached for her brother's hand. "Hang in there, sweetie. Just a few more seconds, and they'll take care of you. Everything's going to be all right."

Lights flashed over the top of the house. Two paramedics rushed through the gate into the backyard. Julia rose and stepped back. Tessa remained where she was until Julia tugged her away. Julia shivered, folding her arms over her breasts as she anxiously watched.

One of the paramedics knelt beside Tanner and asked a series of questions. *Where are you hurt? Is anything broken? Can you move?*

He checked Tanner's head, bandaging it before sitting back on his haunches. "You seem to be fine. Just a superficial wound. We're taking you to the hospital to have it checked out, though."

Tanner slowly nodded. "If you think so."

The EMTs lifted him onto the gurney one of them had retrieved from the ambulance. Something white caught Julia's eye. She moved to where Tanner had been lying and saw a folded sheet of paper fluttering in the breeze. Dread filled her gut. She started to pick it up, but this was a crime scene. She was sure the cops were on the way. She needed to go inside and grab another shirt—but couldn't let a potentially vital piece of evidence blow away. Sticking her foot out, she anchored the paper with the toe of her shoe.

"Julia?"

She turned to find Tessa at her elbow.

The girl's lips trembled as she spoke. "I know you're family and all, but would it be all right if I rode to the hospital with Tanner?"

"Yeah. I'll wait here for the police."

Tessa nodded, her big brown eyes swimming with tears. "My Tanner's a hero, you know."

Julia smiled. "I know."

Tessa twisted around awkwardly on her six-inch heels and headed toward the gate.

Moments later, Jake strode into the yard and rushed to Julia's side. "Julia, are you okay? I got a call that there was an intruder?"

She nodded. "I'm fine, but Tanner was hurt."

"I spoke with the EMTs; he's going to be fine."

She let out a shuddering sigh. "Yeah. That's what they said."

His gaze dropped to her chest, his entire body going still. "What…?" He halted, swallowing audibly.

"I used my shirt for Tanner's head wound," she mumbled, trying to cover as much of herself as she could with crossed arms.

He nodded, slowly bringing his gaze back up to her face. He continued, his voice raspy, "I'll need you to tell me what went on here."

"First, grab that." She pointed at the sheet of paper.

Jake took a pair of gloves from his front jeans pocket and slipped them on as he squatted down. She removed her foot, and he picked up the note. He unfolded it, scowling as he read, then looked up at her. "How did this get here?"

"I assume the attacker left it. It was lying underneath Tanner. I saw it when the EMTs moved him. What does it say?"

His scowl deepened as his gaze scanned the yard. He stood and walked over to a spot about five feet from where she had found Tanner. He squatted again, studying something on the ground. She wanted to see, but wouldn't chance messing up important evidence. It took every ounce of effort to remain where she stood.

Commotion at the gate made her turn. A young man came into the yard, carrying a small duffle bag.

"Over here," Jake said to him.

Julia tiptoed, leaning forward, trying to make out the object they were looking at in the dim light. She couldn't see a thing. Jake bagged the note and slid it into his pocket, backing off so the crime scene tech could do his job.

Jake came over to Julia, staring down at her. His gaze roamed her features as if to reassure himself she wasn't hurt. "Now, tell me what happened," he said gently.

She recounted the story while Jake jotted in a notebook. When she finished, he slid the notebook in his shirt pocket. "Did you see the person?"

She shook her head and hugged her waist. "No. He'd already run off by the time I got outside."

"So, Tanner and Tessa were driving by, Tanner sees someone suspicious and has Tessa stop, then takes off after him? Without calling the police?"

"Well, yes. He was acting on instinct. Worried about me."

Jake slowly nodded. "Why were they here? On Pam's street? Were they coming to see you?"

She hadn't asked, but she didn't think so. *Why would he come over this late, without me knowing he was coming?* But that wasn't the real question. She stared up at Jake. "Why are you making him out to be a suspect when he almost died trying to protect me?"

Jake harrumphed. "Almost died? He got a nick on his forehead."

"A nick? It was gushing blood!"

He lifted his brows. She was being melodramatic, but she was pissed at Jake's continued attempts to paint her brother in a bad light. Sure, he had his share of faults, but when it came down to it, he treated her like family. He'd risked himself to protect her. She couldn't remember the last time someone had done that. In a brief bout of self-pity, she acknowledged that she couldn't remember, because no one had *ever* done that.

"Head wounds have a tendency to bleed a lot," Jake said. "Even minor ones."

"What did the note say?" she demanded.

He narrowed his eyes, peering around the yard. "I'd rather keep that to myself for now."

"You don't trust me."

"The more details we can keep quiet, the easier it is

to catch the bad guys." He looked back at her, his lips quirking in a grin. "Surely, as an investigator, you know that."

Ignoring the fact he was mocking her, she gave a short nod. She *did* know that, but she wanted to be in on the investigation *with* him, like a team. She wanted the killer caught, but part of her also wanted to see respect and admiration reflected in Jake's eyes if she helped make it happen.

A flash of light spilled over the yard. Julia turned to see Pam coming out the back door. She wore a robe belted over pajamas. She blinked sleepily, running a hand through her tousled copper hair. She looked to Jake, then to Julia. "What in God's name is going on?"

****

Jake arrived at the station before dawn. He had gone to the hospital to see Tanner the night before, leaving Julia to explain the events to Pam. Jake had to admit, Tanner had been forthright in answering all of his questions. Although cooperative, he'd seemed slightly ill at ease. Jake wasn't sure if Tanner's nervousness was a result of the attack, or something else. The whole situation just felt wrong, but he couldn't figure out why.

When eight a.m. finally came, he tried calling his friend at vital records. Connie could get a name, date of birth, place of residence, and social security number quicker than a prostitute could get an STD. He'd been trying to reach her the past few days, but she'd been out of the office. This time, she answered.

He gave her all the facts he had, then sat on hold, listening to a soft rock radio station. "My Heart Will Go On" by Celine Dion played. Michael Bolton's version of "When a Man Loves a Woman" had just started when Connie came back on the line.

"Got it," she said triumphantly.

Jake grinned. Barely into the second song, and she already had the info he needed. *What a gal.*

"Great. I'm ready." He held a pen over a notepad as he waited, doubting the information would be useful, but determined to make good on his promise to Julia.

"We have records from a hospital in Tulsa that show Jasper Ramsey listed as the biological father. But, when the birth certificate was issued, the father was listed as unknown. Not sure what happened to change the mother's mind. It appears she moved away from Covington while she was pregnant. Died when the child was small. Child went from home to home, ending up with a foster family, right there in Covington."

Ice formed in Jake's chest as he listened to Connie drone on. His hand shook when he placed the receiver in its cradle.

Shit.

Julia would be disappointed that her theory was a bust, and the mystery child had nothing to do with the murders. But she'd be absolutely devastated when she learned that the man whose death she'd been a part of ten years ago was her father.

****

Julia sat across the table from Dave at the Java Hut. He was the only living member of the group she could talk to, could hope to get serious answers from about what had been going on in her absence. Tanner wasn't the most intellectual conversationalist, and Pam was teetering on the edge of the deep end.

"Did you know Emily and Corbin were having an

affair?" she asked Dave.

He took a sip from his coffee cup and frowned, his brows nearly meeting over his dark eyes. "The thought crossed my mind. They worked pretty closely together, and I knew he was seeing someone. Now that they're both dead...the way Emily acted after Corbin's death...yeah, I can see that. I can believe they were having an affair."

"Do you think it had something to do with their deaths?"

"Well...not unless *Pam* killed them. Emily didn't have anyone in her life—or at least not anyone I knew of—who would be upset enough to do something like that."

Her heart raced at the mention of Pam. She refused to believe it. In spite of her friend's worrisome fascination and belief in an ancient cursed doll, Julia could *not* imagine her as a killer. Pam was at the bottom of her suspect list. Although, admittedly, it was probably because the two of them were close friends, and Julia loved her. It didn't mean she was innocent.

"Do you know of anyone Corbin had business dealings with who might have wanted to hurt him? Since Emily worked with him, that's a possibility. It could be the link."

Dave shook his head. "I didn't know much about his business. He never mentioned having trouble with anyone." He set his cup down and snorted a disbelieving laugh. "What about that shit with the doll? Pam really believes the doll has something to do with the killings? That's totally jacked up, if you ask me."

"She doesn't *really* believe that. It's been difficult for her, with everything she's dealing with. She's not thinking straight and just needs some time to get through the grieving process." Julia didn't let her true level of concern show. She wasn't convinced the explanation was that simple, or the solution would be that easy.

Dave sighed heavily. "I don't know. The doll's creepy enough, but the way Pam's been acting over it since Corbin died—that's downright spooky."

A shiver raced down Julia's spine. Dave was right. Pam was being a little freaky over the doll. It didn't, however, mean she was a killer. Steering the conversation away from Pam, she said, "Did you ever hear anything about Jasper Ramsey fathering a child with someone other than Debra?"

Dave's expression tensed. None of them liked to talk about Jasper, but she had to get some answers.

"No, I didn't. Did he?"

She shrugged. "I heard a rumor."

"Are you thinking that has something to do with what's happening now?"

Leaning closer, she lowered her voice. "What if it does? What if this child is coming after us for what we did to Jasper?"

"Why now, after all these years?"

She sat back. "I don't know. Maybe the kid just found out who his, or her, father was. Maybe the mom confessed on her deathbed that the kid was Jasper's."

"Do you know who the mother is?"

"Unfortunately not." She blew out a breath in frustration. "I know almost nothing about the child. I'm not a hundred percent sure the rumor's even true."

"It's a good theory if it is true. I mean, it sounds like someone has a vendetta against our group. That is, if the killings are linked. Since there hasn't been a murder in Covington for years, and now there have been two, odds are they're related. Donny Ray is definitely a good suspect, but if there's another one of Jasper's spawn out there, could be something to it. Stranger things have happened."

****

The Red Sox were playing the Yankees in the first of a three-game series. It was the top of the eighth, and the Red Sox were ahead by three runs. Normally, watching the Sox take the Yankees down would have Jake riveted to the television, but he could barely concentrate. All he could think about was Julia.

How could he even be around her with the burden of the secret he carried?

Knowing the truth would crush her. Not telling her would damn him to an eternity of torment. He owed her the truth. The truth would kill her.

Back and forth, his thoughts circled and collided with one another. He needed to solve this damned case, so she'd get the hell out of town. That way, he wouldn't be forced to hold back any secrets. He could carry it all on his own.

She was in danger here. That much was obvious. According to the note, she'd been the intended victim tonight. The message had been perfectly clear. *Your turn, bitch. You should have never come back.*

His gut tightened at the thought of what might have occurred if Tanner hadn't happened along.

But, had he really? Just happened along? When Jake questioned him at the hospital, he said he was heading home and decided to cruise by to check on Julia. He *happened* to see an intruder, *happened* to catch him before he broke into the house, but was overpowered. The intruder hit him over the head and *happened* to drop the note, leaving it behind. Just like he'd left behind the weapon—a steel pipe Jake found near the spot where Tanner was attacked. What kind of dumbass would do that?

The only suspect on Jake's list, who seemed stupid enough to do that, was Tanner himself. Last night's victim, not the attacker. None of it added up. Tanner knew Jake didn't believe his story. Jake had seen it in his eyes. Tanner was defensive, almost panicky, unable or unwilling to meet Jake's gaze.

If he was the killer, was he there to hurt Julia, or had it been a set up to mislead the investigation, to make himself look innocent?

Pam was a valid suspect, too. Had she only pretended to be sleeping? Had she been the one to attack Tanner? But why outside? If she wanted to harm Julia, she was right there in the house with her, and it would have been simple to do. However, it would have been harder to hide her part in it.

Tanner? Pam? Donny Ray?

The theories roiled around in his head, pounding at him like a defensive line on a quarterback with nowhere to throw the ball. On paper, Pam and Donny Ray were his best suspects. What possible motive could Tanner have? The guy didn't seem the type to physically harm himself, even to provide a cover. He was way too narcissistic, way too self-centered.

Either way, Jake didn't like games. And he didn't like Julia being in the middle of such a dangerous one. Keeping a disastrous secret from her and trying to protect her from a killer was more than he had time to deal with. The best thing would be for her to go home. The sooner, the better.

If not, he might pour his heart out, might tell her how he couldn't watch a football game without thinking about high school, about coming off the field to find her waiting for him—that he could still taste the berry lip gloss from her kiss. He might tell her that, every time she'd come to town over the years, he avoided her, because watching her leave would make him feel the same way he felt when he came home from Iraq to find her gone.

He pushed back the memories, pushed back the ache that surfaced in his chest. Yes, leaving town was definitely the best thing for Julia. But for him, it meant trying to forget her all over again.

****

Julia headed back to Pam's after going to see Tanner. He was recovering nicely. The hospital kept him overnight for observation, and Tessa insisted on nursing him back to health. Julia grinned. He seemed to be milking his injury just a tad, but after risking his life to save her, she figured he'd earned it.

She parked in the driveway and was almost to the front door when a police cruiser pulled up to the curb. Jake climbed out of the car. Julia tried to get her pulse under control as she watched him come toward her.

"Julia," he murmured in his slow, sexy drawl.

How can the sound of my name on his lips make me go weak in the knees?

"Jake. Is there something I can do for you?"

"Can we go inside? I need to have a quick word with you."

"Sure." Nerves had her fumbling with the key until

she was finally able to unlock the door. Pam had gone to visit Corbin's parents, which left her and Jake dangerously alone. The last time they'd been alone in an intimate setting, they'd shared a kiss that was imprinted on her mind for eternity, in spite of the fact it was a huge mistake.

Would she be able to stay cool and collected this time, or would one touch from him ignite that same fire? She probably wouldn't have to worry about that. After the self-disgust he'd exhibited last time, he was unlikely to touch her again.

She led him into the living room, then turned to face him. As always, the sight of him took her breath away. For a brief second, she allowed herself the luxury of drinking him in—his clean-shaven jaw, the slate gray eyes, the curve of his full lips. A tremor of yearning shivered along her skin.

She swallowed hard and cleared her throat. "Have a seat. Would you like something to drink?"

"No, thanks. I won't take up much of your time."

"Did you find out something about Jasper's illegitimate child?"

Jake shook his head. "You can forget that. It turned into a dead end."

"So, there is no child, or you confirmed the child had nothing to do with the murders?"

He studied her silently. "Like I said…a dead end. I wasn't able to find out anything."

"Damn." She bit her lip, fighting back frustration. "What do we do next? Any other leads?"

"There's no 'we.' You're not part of the investigation, Julia. I didn't come here to discuss the case. I think you should leave town. It's not safe for you here."

She smiled bitterly. "I'm sure, along with almost everyone else in town, you'd love that. You'll be glad when I'm gone."

He shifted his eyes from her, then brought them back, shrugging. "It's not like that. I don't *want* you gone. I just think, if you're gonna go, it might as well be now."

"Is it because of what happened between us years ago? You know, I never really explained why I left."

"You don't need to. It's all in the past."

"It doesn't bother you? Leaving things unsaid between us?" She was surprised to hear Pam's words coming out of her mouth.

"We were kids. We didn't know what we were doing, what we were feeling."

"Right. No explanation needed, then. I just figured you might want to know how hard it was for me. You were my first love. You were the first person to ever make me feel like I could be somebody—that I wasn't some loser no one wanted."

Frown lines creased his forehead. "How could you ever think you were a loser?" Before she could answer, he went on, "You never came back to see me. Even when I was on leave from Iraq."

"I tried, but your father wasn't exactly welcoming."

"You tried to see me? When?"

"Not long after you arrived home. You were hanging out with friends, and I went to your house. Spoke with your father."

His brows rose. "Why didn't you stick around until I got home? What did he say to you?"

She swung her gaze to the windows, away from his piercing eyes that saw too much. "Nothing, really. He showed me one of your letters. The one where you said it was better the way things turned out. That you were better off without me." The old ache came back, but it wasn't as severe as it had been at the time. Back then, her heart nearly shredded to pieces. This was more like a sadness…a 'what might have been' longing.

"That was taken out of context."

Turning back to face him, she said, "I read the entire letter." She'd been so desperate for any part of him, just to feel his presence, she'd soaked up every painful word.

"My father had written to me about the way things turned out between us. About how you left me without so much as a goodbye. I was simply accepting…agreeing. Moving on."

She forced herself to nod. "That was best for both of us. I know I should have said goodbye, but I was young, scared. I couldn't stay here after…after what happened. Everyone in town despised me. You were gone. I'd walk down the streets and feel their stares, their hatred. Everything in this town reminded me of that night. What we did." She sucked in a trembling breath. "Sometimes, when I close my eyes, I still see his body flying over the edge of the cliff. Hear the sound it made when he hit the water." She shuddered. "It took almost ten years of therapy before I stopped waking with night terrors."

His voice gentled. "I'm sorry about that. About what you went through…alone. But Ramsey's death was an accident. A complete accident. Remember that, okay? It wasn't your fault." His mouth compressed. "As far as us, though. I guess it was best, the way it all turned out. You're happy in Florida doing what you're doing. I'm happy here. And now, you're in danger. There's nothing left for you here. You really should go."

"I promised Pam I'd stay." Determination filled her soul. She wasn't leaving.

"You promised her you'd try to find out who killed her husband. You and I both know the chances of you doing that are almost non-existent."

She snorted. "Right. I mean, not like the great job you guys are doing, huh?"

A flash of pain shadowed his face, making her regret the words.

Before she could offer an apology, he said, "We've got a few leads. We're getting closer."

"Is Tanner one of those leads? Even after he was injured, you still think he could be the killer, don't you?"

His shoulders lifted in a shrug. "We're checking out everything."

"He told me how you questioned him at the hospital. As though he were a suspect instead of a victim." She moved closer to him. "What's this harassment all about, Sheriff? Vengeance for old pains? For past crimes?"

"Don't be ridiculous."

"Then why aren't you suspicious of Donny Ray? He has more motive than Tanner, who has none. And since you never found the truth about the child Jasper might have had, you don't know if the kid—assuming there is a kid—could be a viable suspect."

"As I said, we're checking out all leads. You'll just

have to trust me."

"Trust you? When you're trying to railroad my brother for a crime he didn't commit? When you look at me like I'm some kind of criminal?"

His mouth twitched, and he narrowed his eyes. The devastating smile took her by surprise. Her body reacted instantly. Desire heated her blood. Her voice trembled as she spoke. "What are you smiling about?"

He leaned slightly forward and said in his low, molasses drawl, "Sweetheart, if you think that's how I'm looking at you, your detecting skills ain't worth a damn."

She couldn't react. Couldn't breathe. She wanted another one of those kisses. One of those he'd warned her about. The kind that shouldn't happen again. She swallowed, needing to wet lips that had suddenly gone dry. But she didn't want it to appear to be an obvious ploy. Didn't want him to know how much she wanted him to kiss her. Her eyes dropped to his lips, and she knew that was a dead giveaway.

With a husky groan of denial, he pulled her to him and fused his mouth to hers.

****

Jake thought his heart would fly from his chest. She felt so good…tasted so sweet

He was completely insane. He'd come over to get her to leave, and now he was all over her like a horny high school kid. More so than the high school boy he'd been when they dated. That dumb kid had no idea what he'd lost.

Julia had been a fun, attractive girl. Womanhood had made her a knockout. But it was more than just her beauty. She called to him, a wounded soul who brought out his protective instincts. But it was her resilience and strength, her emotional fortitude that made him respect the hell out of her.

Right now, though, his respect for her was being edged out by blind crazy lust. His common sense was getting its ass kicked by his desire for her. His soul was getting snared in her scent, her feel, the wonder of holding her in his arms.

She moaned and lifted her hands, linking them behind his neck. Her softness settled into him. His hands cupped her bottom and brought her closer, tighter, until he could feel every curve, every sweet secret place, through her clothing.

He almost cried out when she pulled away. She looked up at him, beautiful blue eyes dazed with passion. "Aren't you going to get that?"

"Huh?" The jangle of his phone hadn't registered. *Shit.* He'd been totally lost in her. Heat crept up his neck.

He stepped back and yanked the cell off his belt, half grateful to whoever it was, half wanting to strangle them with his bare hands. The caller ID said Kurt was the one to whom he owed whichever emotion won the battle.

"Yeah," Jake barked.

"You gotta get over here."

"Where's here?" he bit out.

"The Ramsey place."

Jake stepped away from Julia and moved to the other end of the room, lowering his voice. "Another victim?"

If it was Donny Ray instead of Debra, then that meant the suspect vying for number one with Tanner had been taken out of the equation. That left Julia's foster brother in the hot seat.

"Not another victim. We got an anonymous tip, and I thought I'd check it out on my own in case it turned out to be nothing. Some guy called and said Ramsey was at the bar showing off the ring."

"Corbin McCauley's ring?"

"Yeah. I came here and waited on him to get home. Asked if I could search him. Didn't want to go through the hassle of getting a warrant in case he said yes."

Jake's irritation grew. Not only had Kurt's interruption possibly kept him from making love to Julia—even though it was the last thing he should have done—he was taking a freakin' eternity to get to the point. "You wanna skip all the build-up and give me the bottom line?"

"Bottom line is…we found it. Ramsey had the goddamned ring in his pocket."

Surprise rendered Jake speechless for a moment. "You mean he had the ring, but he let you search him?"

"You ever seen anyone dumber?"

Jake thought about that. "Guess not. I thought I had, but it appears he's not as dumb as I thought."

"What are you talking about?"

"Nothing. Never mind. I'll be right there." He disconnected and walked over to Julia. Taking her hands in his, he looked down at her, trying not to think about what it had felt like to kiss her, about what might have occurred between them if Kurt hadn't called. "I've gotta go. We're making an arrest so you can leave town without feeling obligated."

He pretended that, instead of pain, her eyes held relief that they'd found the murderer.

She nodded. "You got the killer? Who was it?"

"Nothing's for sure yet. You'll know as soon as I can tell anyone. But you might as well go ahead and make your reservation. No telling how long it'll take you to get a flight."

"You're really anxious for me to leave, aren't you?" Her lips trembled, but she clamped them together. "I can take a hint. You don't have to hurt me any more than you already have."

He clenched his teeth so hard his jaw ached. He couldn't tell her the truth, couldn't tell her that the reason he wanted her to leave was to *keep* from hurting her more than he already had.

Chapter Six

Jake glanced up as Kurt stepped out of the hallway, leaving Donny Ray in a cell—their lone prisoner of the night. Tossing the keys up and catching them in his hand, Kurt said, "Finding that ring on him sure was a stroke of luck."

Jake slowly nodded. "Stroke of pure genius, you might say."

His brows rose. "You don't think it was him? What do you think? Somebody framed him?"

"I think a lot of things." Jake expelled a breath. "They ain't always right."

Kurt grinned, dropping the keys on top of the counter. "Not always, but mostly."

"Yeah. Mostly."

"Julia finally leavin'?"

Jake's chest tightened, and it was a few seconds before he could speak in a level tone. "Yeah, finally."

"It's for the best, you know."

"I know."

Donny Ray shouted from the cell, "Hey, Sheriff, come back here. I need to talk to you."

"Want me to go?" Kurt offered.

Jake shook his head. "I got it."

He rose and swung open the door leading into the holding area. Donny Ray leaned with his forearms hanging through the bars.

"This is bullshit," he said. "You got the wrong guy. I didn't do nothing."

"You'll have a chance to prove that in court. You want to call a lawyer?"

Donny Ray scowled. "Don't want no damn lawyer. I want the fuck out of here. Haven't you reached Cleve Delaney yet?"

"He's on a fishing trip."

"Try again. He can't fish forever."

"We found the ring on you, Ramsey."

"Sheriff, you ain't stupid. Neither am I. If I killed somebody and stole their damn ring, would I carry it around in my pocket?"

Jake took a deep breath and let it out. Probably not. Very few people were that stupid. Without responding, he went into his office and dialed the number to the Hog Wash. The same raspy-voiced woman answered.

"Is Cleve Delaney there?" Jake asked.

"Cleve!" she screamed, nearly bursting Jake's eardrum.

A short time later, a man's voice came on the line. "Yeah, this is Cleve."

"This is Sheriff Jake Devlin with the Covington County Sheriff's department. I need to know if you recall shooting pool with Donny Ray Ramsey on May ninth. Would have been a Thursday night."

There was a slight pause, then, "Yeah, I recall shooting pool with the asshole. Beat me out of two hundred bucks. Don't remember what night…wait. Yeah, it was May ninth. Night before I left for Horseshoe Lake in Arkansas to go fishing. Lost part of my trip money to the son of a bitch."

"Thanks." Jake hung up the phone, his mind clicking over the news. Donny Ray never provided an alibi for the night of Corbin's murder, but the one for the night of Emily's had just become solid.

Standing, he slid on his Stetson and headed to the door. Seemed like a good time for another chat with Tanner Morrison.

****

Julia's heart ached as she closed her suitcase. She hadn't booked a new flight—she was tired of canceling and rescheduling. She would just head to the airport and take the next flight out.

Pam stood in the doorway. "I'm going to miss you."

"I'll miss you, too. You'll go see someone, like you promised, right? Now that we know who committed the murders?"

Pam nodded. "I promise. I've already made the appointment, and I'll go."

"Thanks. That makes me feel better. I've been worried."

"I know. I've been kind of worried, too." She gave a small grin. "Dave and Tanner talked about going camping one more time before you leave. Are you sure you can't stay long enough to do that?"

Julia sighed, looking into her friend's sad eyes. Pam didn't want to let go. Didn't want to be alone. Julia chewed on her bottom lip. She'd been gone this long, what difference would a few more days make? It was a weekend, after all, and it wasn't like she had the chance to hang out with her friends every day. Besides, after what they'd been through, a little R and R and fresh air would do them all good.

"Sure. Let's do it. Call the guys while I finish packing. I'll have everything ready, then when we get back, I can just toss it in the rental car and head to the airport."

Pam's face lit with pleasure, making it all worthwhile. "Yes! I'll throw a few more things in the SUV and give them a call. This is going to be great."

In less than an hour, they were all ready to go. On the way down to the lake, Julia changed the greeting on her voicemail to let callers know she might be unavailable. Cell service was spotty—almost non-existent—where they were going. She'd left a message with her boss that she'd be back in a few days, but in case someone from the office tried to get in touch with her, she didn't want them to think she was ignoring them.

The guys were already there when they arrived at their usual camping spot. It was their favorite. Leafy, green trees canopied the area, which offered a lovely view of the lake. Sun danced off the surface of the water like a million jewels. Not many people chose this space, because it didn't have direct access to swimming, or to a boat dock. But, their group never boated and seldom swam. They mostly drank and hung out. *The good ole' days*, Julia inwardly saluted.

Julia breathed in cool spring air, feeling her spirits lift a little. Although Corbin and Emily's absence cast a pall of sadness over the gathering, the hurt of leaving Jake behind was not quite as sharp.

Julia reached into the SUV to unload one of the boxes Pam had brought, gasping when two beady eyes stared out from beneath the open flaps. *Son of a bitch.* The doll.

She turned to Pam, who'd come up behind her to help. "For god sake, why did you bring that hideous doll?"

Pam shrugged. "Didn't want to leave her behind. If she's pissed at those who betray me, do you really think I want to betray *her*?"

Julia frowned at her friend. "Pam, the doll didn't murder Corbin and Emily. It was Donny Ray, and he's locked up."

"Right. But it doesn't mean she didn't have something to do with it. Maybe she led him to do it."

Julia peered into Pam's face, trying to figure out if she was pulling her chain. Hadn't they just talked about how the doll thing was lunacy and Pam needed freakin' therapy?

Blowing a breath out between pursed lips, she decided to ignore it for the moment. Maybe she should try to get rid of the doll during their weekend. Maybe Miss Rosa could meet with an untimely accident in the woods. Julia looked into those faded blue eyes and a shiver passed through her. Crazy, but she felt almost threatened as soon as the thought occurred. Maybe she should just leave the doll the hell alone.

Once they were all set up, Julia said, "How about I gather some firewood and we can get a campfire going, then break out the booze?"

"Cool." Tanner brushed off his hands and stood. "I'll go with you."

Julia smiled. Coming here had been a good idea. Tanner was acting more like his old self. The four remaining friends would be able to say their goodbyes to one another—and in a way, their goodbyes to Corbin and Emily. They all needed this. Now that the killer was behind bars, they were safe. Mystery solved. End of story. End of her and Jake, too. She pushed back the gloom the thought brought. After all, there hadn't really been much of a beginning.

She grabbed some twine and headed into the woods with Tanner. The air was cool with the trees blocking the sun. It felt sort of cozy, nice...relaxing. Julia impulsively reached out and squeezed Tanner's hand.

He smiled, squeezing back. "Glad you came, sis. I'm going to miss you."

"I'll miss you, too. But at least we have these next few days to hang out."

And then, blessedly, she'd be back home in Florida. All the ghosts from her past left behind.

****

Tessa stood in the doorway, one hand on a cocked hip, her bathrobe gaping, breasts nearly exposed. Her coarse blonde hair stuck up wildly all over her head. Apparently, Jake had awakened her at the indecent hour of four p.m.

Her lips puckered in an unattractive pout. "Asshole took off with his friends. Left me a damn note. Didn't even have the decency to invite me along. Guess I'm not good enough for his *friends*."

"Care if I take a look at the note?"

"Don't even know if I still got it."

"Can you check, please?" he said through clenched teeth.

She sighed in a put-out manner, as if he'd asked for a free lap dance, then disappeared. In a few seconds, she was back, thrusting a wrinkled piece of paper toward him.

Suspicious stains marred the paper, and he guessed she'd retrieved it from the trash. He wasn't sure why he even wanted to see it, but instinct told him he did.

He straightened the note and read, *"Sorry, babe. Gonna take off for a few days, going camping with the gang. Won't have cell service when we get their, so I'll call when I get back. Love ya."*

T-h-e-i-r not *t-h-e-r-e.* Beads of sweat gathered at his neck. Jake already had Tanner write a note at the station. He'd misspelled the word then, but so had others. Jake needed more.

"Where did they go camping?" He slipped the note in his back pocket.

"Lake Covington, but I got no idea exactly where. If you find the asshole, tell him I'm mighty pissed."

Deciding to take a gamble, he forced a casual smile. "Listen, while I'm here, Tanner said I could take a look at that ring he found a little while back. We had someone call in to say they'd lost one, and I promised I'd be on the lookout."

"Ring?"

His hopes sank. The gamble hadn't paid off.

The pout returned. "You mean the ring he was supposed to sell to get us some cash? The ring that disappeared before he could? Claims he lost it. Who the hell loses a ring worth that much money?"

Jake's brows rose. "Worth a lot of money? What did it look like? I'm wondering if it's the same ring these folks were looking for."

"Hell, I don't know nothin' about jewelry. All I know was it was a man's wedding ring with some diamonds on it."

His heart raced like that of a hunter closing in on a

kill. "When did Tanner lose it?"

She scrunched her face. "Few days ago…let's see." The frown wrinkles vanished and clarity appeared in her vacant stare. "It was Thursday 'cause I was gonna let him have it that night—it's my night off. I was gonna give him what for and tell him either he was gonna sell it, or I was. Then the stupid mother fucker says he lost it."

Thursday. The day before the anonymous tip that Donny Ray was flashing a stolen ring.

Shit. Tanner was definitely their guy.

A sensation—part euphoria, part dread—surfaced in his chest. He'd nailed the bastard, but he didn't have him in his clutches.

"You don't know the spot where he usually goes camping?" he asked Tessa again.

"Don't know. Probably the same place him and his friends went when they was kids."

That didn't help. Although he and Julia dated, Jake hadn't gone camping with them. He'd preferred spending time alone with her instead of with her wild group of friends.

Jake tipped his hat to Tessa. "Thanks, ma'am. You've been mighty helpful."

As he headed back to the cruiser, her shrill voice followed him, "You tell that cock sucker when he gets home, he might find me gone."

Jake didn't tell her that losing a girlfriend was about to be the least of Tanner Morrison's worries.

He slid into the cruiser and pulled onto the street. Tessa said they'd gone to the same spot they had when they were kids. Julia would know where that was. If he could catch her before she boarded the plane, maybe she could tell him. If nothing else, he'd hear her voice one more time.

He cursed himself for being a damn fool. Entertaining ridiculous notions about Julia was not only detrimental to his sanity, it was dangerous for her. She needed to be far away from Covington and everyone associated with the town. With Jasper's death still haunting her, no telling how she'd react to the news he was her father.

He dialed her cell, disappointment settling in his gut when her voicemail answered.

The disappointment turned to abject fear as he listened to her message. "Hi, you've reached Julia's cell. Please leave a message. I'll be out of range for a few days, camping with friends, but will return your call as soon as I get back."

Son of a bitch. Julia was in the wilderness with a murderer.

He had to find her. Had to get there before something happened. Fear expanded in his chest, as he fought to think clearly. He had no idea how to find them.

A thought suddenly occurred to him, bringing a wave of relief. He might not know where to find them, but he did, however, know someone who would.

****

When Julia and Tanner had gathered as much firewood as they could carry, and secured the loads with twine, they headed back to the campsite.

"Do you think Pam's gonna be okay?" Tanner asked.

"I think so. I know she's grieving, but now that they've found Corbin's killer, I'm hoping she'll start to recover, that she'll get stronger."

"Me, too. But it's gotta be tough. I mean, losing your husband is bad enough, but knowing he was cheating with one of your best friends." He let out a disbelieving laugh. "Jesus. Especially finding him without his wedding ring on. That's gotta be the worst."

His words stopped Julia in her tracks. She slowly turned to look at him, brows drawn into a frown. "How did you know..."

Then it hit her. There was only one way he could know. Jake had told her and Pam the cops were keeping the detail about the ring under wraps. That the two of them were the only ones who knew...other than the killer.

His eyes narrowed. He watched her closely, his expression expectant. In that moment, she knew the truth.

"Ah, hell." He dropped the armload of firewood. "Almost home free, and I had to fuck up." He slammed a palm against his forehead over and over. "You dumb...stupid...idiot. What the hell were you thinking?"

Her stomach roiled with shock. *No way. No way could Tanner be the killer.* But he was. It was written all over his face. She swallowed hard. "It's okay, Tanner. We can work this out."

"No. We really can't, and you know it." He shook his head, blinking back tears. "You're the one person in this world who understands me, the only one I truly care about. And now, I have to kill you."

Chapter Seven

Jake raced to the sheriff's office, rushing past Kurt to Donny Ray's cell, ignoring his deputy's stunned expression, and his shouted, "Hey, what the fuck?"

Donny Ray flew from the bunk to the bars as soon as he saw Jake. "You here to set me free? You know I didn't do it. Why the hell won't you let me out?"

"I need some information. You used to hang out at the lake with your old man. Where did Julia and her group camp? I know you know."

Donny Ray shrugged. "So what if I do? Doesn't mean I'm telling you."

"I don't have time for your bullshit. Tanner Morrison is the killer, and he's out there with them—with Julia—right now. You have to tell me where I can find them."

Donny Ray threw his head back and howled with laughter. "Well, if this ain't rich. Whatcha call it? Poetic justice? Assholes killed my old man, now they can kill each other for all I care."

Kurt came into the hallway. "Everything all right, Sheriff?"

Jake's jaw tightened. "Won't be for this asshole if I don't get some answers."

"Need any help?"

"Nah. For your sake, you might want to just go

back up front. I got this."

Kurt looked from Jake to Donny Ray, then nodded. "Okay, then. You got it, boss."

After Kurt left, Jake unlocked the cell door and flung it open. Donny Ray backed up as Jake stormed inside. He grabbed Donny Ray by the shirt front and slammed him against the cell wall. "You'll either tell me where I can find them, or I'll beat it out of you."

"Police brutality," he squeaked, the pressure on his throat making it difficult to speak. "Why should I tell you a damn thing that's gonna help any of them?"

"Because you don't want them finding little pieces of you all over the cell."

In spite of his vulnerable position, Donny Ray managed a smirk. "You ain't gonna hurt me. You'd be in a world of deep shit, and you know it."

It was obvious Jake couldn't appeal to the man's sense of right, or his sense of self-preservation. "Then how about this, asshole. You need to tell me where the fuck they are, because Julia is your *sister*."

Donny Ray's eyes rounded. "Not possible."

"It's possible. And true." Jake released him. "Your old man had a thing with a woman nearly thirty years ago. Knocked her up. Turns out, it was Julia's mother."

"Jesus." His face paled.

"So, tell me. It could already be too late. I have to get to her."

Donny Ray's eyes glazed. He looked as though he'd stepped in the center of a mine field. He slowly nodded. "I'll take you there."

"Just tell me. You're not going with me."

Donny Ray lifted his chin, a stubborn glint in his eye. "You wanna waste time arguing? Knock me around some more? Or you wanna go save my sister?"

****

Tanner reached into his jacket pocket and pulled out a small pistol, pointing it at Julia's chest.

"Tanner?" Tears and fear choked her voice. "How could you?" Her heart crumbled. The man she'd loved as a brother was a killer?

Tanner grimaced. "Didn't mean for any of this to happen. Once the thing with Corbin went down, it all just snowballed."

"What thing with Corbin? Exactly what happened?" She had to keep him talking. It was her only hope.

He pursed his lips and sighed. "I don't have time to explain. If I don't get back to the others soon, they'll come looking for us. But I gotta think of how to do this, so it looks like an accident. Give me a minute to think."

Yeah, right. Take all the time you need to work out a plan on how to kill me without implicating yourself. No problem.

"Please, Tanner. If I'm going to die anyway, I want to know. What made you this way? How did it come to this?"

He let out another sigh. "It all started with Corbin. I thought he was going to invest in my wine business, but he backed out. We got into an argument about it, and he laughed at me. Said there was no way he'd sink any money into a failure like me. He turned his back on me, dismissing me like I was nothin'. I grabbed a statue off his bookshelf and hit him over the head. I knew he kept a gun in his desk drawer, so I made it look like a suicide."

"The ring? Did you take it?"

He nodded. "I was gonna pawn it once some time had passed. Then, I had to plant it on Donny Ray, so I never got the money for it. Sucks. That ring was worth a shitload of money."

"Yeah, that's what sucks about all this. You not getting the ring money."

"Sarcasm, little sister?" He grinned, his eyes flashing with amusement, and something not quite sane.

"What about Emily? Why did you kill her?"

He went silent for a moment, then shrugged. "You're my sister. I guess the least I can do is explain what happened." His eyes took on a distant look, as if he were reliving the memory. His mouth drew down in a frown.

"Tanner?" Julia ventured. "I think you feel guilty about what happened to Emily. I know you don't want my death on your conscience, too."

"You're right. I don't. But just like with Emily, it's the only way. You remember that night we all met at the Rusty Nail?" Julia nodded. "When Emily starts saying that crap about how she didn't believe Corbin would invest in my business, I started to wonder. I knew he was having an affair, and I was afraid whoever it was might know too much. I might have to shut them up. After Emily acting all broken up, then sayin' that stuff about the wine business, I guessed it might be her. I went to see her, to confront her about it, and she went off on me. I killed her. Planted the note, cause at this point, I'm thinking the Ramsey guy would be a good suspect."

A lump formed in her throat, and she swallowed it back. "The attack in Pam's backyard...Jake was suspicious about that. No wonder. It was you, right?

Only you?"

He laughed. "Yeah. Whacked myself pretty good. Almost too good. For a minute, I was afraid I'd black out before I had a chance to drop the note." His expression darkened. "Jake's an asshole. Thinks he's so damn smart."

Nausea churned her stomach. *How could someone I love be so diabolical? So evil?*

"He is smart," she said, choking on the words. He was also sexy and kind—and the only man she'd ever loved. Now, she'd never get a chance to tell him.

"If he was so smart, I'd be in jail, instead of out here in the woods with you, wouldn't I?" He glanced around quickly, then brought his gaze back to her. "I just have to figure out how to make this look like an accident."

"You don't have to do this. I won't say anything. In fact, I have an idea…a way you can get your hands on some cash so you and Tessa can disappear. No one will ever know you killed Corbin and Emily."

He narrowed his eyes. "What are you talking about?"

It was a total bluff, but he wasn't exactly a Mensa candidate so it just might work. "Pam's doll. That antique doll she thinks is cursed? It's hundreds of years old. Worth a fortune. Pam's getting rid of it, because she's afraid she's going crazy. I can get it for you. You're my brother. I know you didn't mean to hurt anyone. I know you don't want to hurt me."

"I don't *want* to. But I really don't have a choice. I can't trust you to keep your word. But, thanks for the tip on the doll. I'll just steal if from Pam once I've got you out of the picture. You're right. I need to blow this town." He waved the gun. "Now, come on. That cliff where Ramsey went over…that's a good spot for you to have your 'accident'."

She stared at him in disbelief, her heart pounding so loud, she was sure he could hear it. "You can't mean that. You can't really plan on killing me."

"Drop the firewood, then walk," he snarled. "Or I'll shoot you where you stand."

She drew in a sharp breath. This was it. No way out. Good God. She was going to die. The wood fell from her arms. Her idea of holding onto it, of maybe using it as a weapon, was a bust. *What now?*

She took a step, her legs feeling as though they were filled with hot lead. Tanner backed up, training the gun on her, walking behind. She tensed, expecting a bullet to pierce her flesh any second. Tears clogged her throat. She didn't want to die. Not this way. Not at all, but especially not before she had a chance to tell Jake how she felt. She dropped her head, her steps slow and reluctant as she made her way to the place where Jasper Ramsey had died.

****

Donny Ray barked directions while Jake drove. Jake couldn't think, couldn't breathe, couldn't keep his speed under ninety. Even if he never had Julia for his own, the thought of her being hurt…or dead…was unimaginable. Debilitating.

When he got a hold of Morrison, he was going to make him wish he'd never been born. Whether he'd hurt Julia or not, just the fact he'd put her in danger was enough to make Jake want to tear him apart with his bare hands.

"Can't believe she's my sister," Donny Ray

muttered for the hundredth time. "Can't believe you didn't tell me. Tell *her*."

Jake gritted his teeth. "She's gone through hell over what happened to your dad. She was in therapy for years and still carries a ton of guilt. How much worse do you think that would be if she knew he was her father?"

Donny Ray muttered something Jake didn't hear, but he didn't bother to have him repeat it. They approached a turn-in, and Donny Ray pointed. "There. Right there is the campsite. You see the tent through those trees?"

Jake whipped the car onto the turn-in and pulled as close to the site as he could before vaulting from the cruiser. Pam was sitting on a rock while Dave lounged on the ground next to her. They both turned shocked faces up to Jake and Donny Ray.

"What the…?" Dave jumped to his feet and pointed to Donny Ray. "What's he doing here?"

"Where's Julia? Tanner?" Jake barked.

"They're out gathering firewood." Pam frowned. "Why?"

"Shit," Jake bit out. "Which way did they go?"

"I—I don't know…" Pam trailed off uncertainly. "Jake, what's the matter? Is Julia okay?"

"God, I hope so."

He turned, peering into the thick woods. Which way to go? How could he possibly find her with all this ground to cover? And, what if it was already too late? His heart suddenly felt too large for his chest. He opened his mouth and sucked in air. *Think, man, think.*

"Call 9-1-1," Jake ordered. "Tell them we need the police and an ambulance." He wasn't sure about the ambulance, but he had to cover all bases. "The rest of you stay here. I'll be back." *I hope*, he added silently.

He picked a direction and headed that way, having no idea if he was even close. Donny Ray followed. He almost told him to stay put, but why did it matter? He had to find Julia. Now. Anything else was inconsequential.

He'd only gone a short distance when he realized his destination. Something was leading him to the place where the accident happened, the accident that killed Julia's father. Donny Ray realized it too. His expression was tight…determined.

Jake prayed their instincts were correct. And that they wouldn't arrive too late.

****

"Stop right there."

Julia halted. She couldn't have gone much further, anyway, since she was only four or five feet from the edge of the cliff. She hazarded a glance at the lake. Here, where the trees blocked the sun, the water looked thick and murky, just like it had that night. Memories of that horrific evening flashed in her mind. They hadn't seen Jasper Ramsey. Hadn't even known he was there until they felt the thump of his body against the grill. She shuddered.

"You're remembering, aren't you? That night. That was pretty fucked up."

"Yes," Julia whispered.

"But you all made out just fine. You went on with your lives, your successful careers, your happiness, while I suffered. Couldn't get a job. Couldn't find a decent girlfriend."

Disgusted and beyond enraged, she shouted, "No

more!"

Tanner's eyes flew to hers, rounded in surprise.

"I'm sick and tired of your self-pity bullshit. I mean, aside from the fact you're a killer, you're also a lazy, spoiled, self-centered baby. Grow the fuck up, for once. For God's sake. I mean, you've murdered two people—I'd say it's time you finally just grow the fuck up."

Tanner raised the gun. "You sure got a lot of balls for someone at the wrong end of a gun."

"What does it even matter? Whether I tell you what I think, or beg for my life, you're still going to kill me, right? Anything to save your sorry ass. I might as well get it off my chest while I can."

He laughed, sounding a little on the edge of insanity. "I guess so. Famous final words and all that. I am sorry, though. I really don't wanna do this."

"Are you going to shoot me, or make me jump? I don't want to go into that murky water alive. Please, just shoot me."

He shook his head. "Can't do that. The sound of the gunshot will draw attention. Besides, what kind of suicide, or accident, will it look like if you have a bullet wound?"

"No one will believe I killed myself, and you don't have a computer to type a note on, or paper to write on, for that matter."

"Yeah. Accident is better. I'll tell 'em you were overcome with memories of that night and you came over to look at where it happened. You got too close to the edge…I tried to save you…blah, blah, blah. End of story. Tanner the hero fails this time, but he's broken up, grief stricken."

She tightened her lips, but didn't respond. Glancing behind her at the lake thirty feet below, she realized it was possible she could survive the fall. Didn't Tanner know that? His plan might backfire. Wouldn't that just show him a thing or two if she lived? She giggled, a bubble of hysteria rising to her throat.

"What are you laughing about?" Tanner growled. "What's so damned funny?"

"Nothing. Not a damned thing." A movement from the corner of her eye caught her attention, but she willed her gaze on Tanner. Had help arrived? Or was it just a wild animal? Maybe it was a wild animal that would tear Tanner a new one after he killed her. The incongruous thought gave her a measure of satisfaction.

"It's time. Jump." Tanner waved the gun.

"You know, I'd be an idiot to jump instead of making you shoot me. What do I have to gain by following your orders?"

His mouth pulled down in the frowning pout she'd grown accustomed to over the years. It meant Tanner wasn't getting his way.

"Well, I guess you don't have anything to gain. But, if you don't jump, I'll start shooting off little pieces of your body. It would fuck up my *accident* story, but I'll deal with that later. We're probably far enough from the campsite that they wouldn't hear the shots, or wouldn't know what it was if they did. I would imagine, after a while, you'll be glad to end it in the water, won't you?"

A chill swept through her. He was truly fucking, bat-shit insane. *How could I not have seen it?*

Ashamed to feel tears in her eyes, she swiped them away angrily. "You'll have to shoot me. Even if it's a little at a time. I won't make this easy for you."

Her earlier thoughts of surviving a fall were ludicrous. She would die whether she jumped, or he shot her. At least if he shot her, they'd likely catch him, and he'd finally pay for his crimes.

He stood uncertainly for a moment, then tossed the gun aside. "Shit," he growled. Before she knew what was happening, he rushed toward her.

Everything inside her froze. Desperately, she grabbed hold of the branch of a willow tree just as he reached her.

He wrapped his arms around her middle and pulled, but she held tight with both hands.

"Let go!" he huffed. "You know you won't win. You're no match for me."

She was no match for his strength, but as out of shape as he was, she had him beat on stamina. If she could just hold on until he tired out…until help arrived…until a miracle occurred.

Her hands were slipping, the branch digging into the tender skin on her palms. Crying out in frustration, she tried to latch on tighter. She screwed her eyes shut, concentrating with all her power, using all her strength to *just hold on…*

It took her a moment to realize the pressure around her stomach had eased. Tanner had let go. Had he suffered a moment of guilt, a change of heart?

Her eyes flew open. He was right there, his face a few inches from hers. Sweat beaded his forehead, and saliva dotted his parted lips. He gulped for air. She yelped when his hands wrapped around her throat. He squeezed.

She gasped, releasing one hand to claw at his

fingers, her windpipe feeling like a steel vice gripped it. Staring into his eyes, she only half registered the dampness in them.

"This is harder than I thought it would be," he moaned. "Why did you have to make me do this? Why?" With the last word, he jerked his hands forward, nearly snapping her neck. Black spots danced before her eyes. This was it. She was going to die, right here, at the hands of someone she loved.

Just when she thought her chest would explode, when she thought she couldn't hold on a moment longer, a shape launched from her peripheral vision, landing on Tanner with a *whoompf.*

Chapter Eight

Tanner let go, hurtling backward. Julia released the branch and staggered to her knees. Clutching her neck, she drew in deep breaths, watching in confusion while Donny Ray wrestled Tanner to the ground.

Donny Ray? She must be hallucinating. *What is he doing here? He is in jail. Why is he helping me?*

The thoughts were immediately followed by a rush of horror as Tanner's hand scrabbled across the ground. He was looking for the gun. The momentum of Donny Ray's tackle had driven them no more than a foot from where Tanner dropped it. She stood, but before she could get to him, Tanner's hand closed around the butt of the pistol. A shot rang out.

"Oh, God," she croaked.

She glanced around wildly, looking for something to use as a weapon, a way to help Donny Ray. If he was still alive.

Tanner pushed him off and lumbered to his feet. Fear gripped her. Donny Ray was dead. She was next. She opened her mouth to scream, interrupted by the sound of someone crashing through the bushes. She nearly wept with joy when Jake strode toward them, gun in hand, pointed straight at Tanner.

"Aw fuck," Tanner bit out softly.

"Drop the weapon," Jake commanded.

Tanner halted uncertainly, his gaze resting on Jake. His expression set, as though he was considering rebellion.

Julia's heart stalled in her chest when Jake charged forward. She cringed, expecting Tanner's pistol to fire, expecting to watch Jake die.

He reached Tanner in the space of a heartbeat and cracked him in the face with his elbow. Tanner emitted a high pitched squeal and dropped the gun, his hands flying to his face.

"You broke my nose," he cried out.

"I oughta break every bone in your body." Fury emanated from his voice, his stance. Roughly, he cuffed Tanner's hands behind his back, cutting his eyes to Julia. "Are you okay?"

She nodded, the knot in her throat rendering her incapable of speech. Finally, she found her voice. "But...I don't think Donny Ray is." She hurried over, dropping down next to him, scanning his body for the bullet wound, afraid to touch him. She looked over her shoulder at Jake. "What's going on? How did you find me? What's Donny Ray doing here?"

The sound of sirens wailed in the distance.

"I'll explain later." Jake shoved Tanner roughly to his knees. Tanner wept openly, shaking his head and gulping in deep gasps of air. Jake came over and knelt next to Julia, but spoke to Donny Ray. "Hold on. Help's coming. You did good, but I should kick your ass for taking off without me."

"You were...off...course. Knew...where I'd...find 'em."

Julia shook her head, her mind trying to wrap around what happened—how Tanner had almost killed her, and how Jake and Donny Ray had ended up a team.

A squad car with Covington Lake Patrol on the side screeched to a stop on the dirt road next to them. An officer stepped out, and Jake rose. Walking over to the cop, he spoke to him in low tones. The guy hauled Tanner to his feet, pushed him toward the car, opened the back door, and shoved him into the cruiser.

Julia turned away, unable to watch the only brother she'd ever known being hauled away in handcuffs. Even though he deserved it—and much more—it still hurt.

An ambulance arrived immediately. Two EMTs climbed out, rushing to the rear of the vehicle and grabbing a stretcher. She and Jake stood back while the technicians knelt beside Donny Ray, checking his vitals and injecting him with what she assumed was a pain killer. As they were lifting him onto the gurney, Julia hurried to his side.

"Why did you do that for me?" she asked. "You risked your life to save me."

"Because…" He smiled, his eyes drooping sleepily. "That's what family does."

"Family?"

"Sheriff will explain. I think I'm gonna pass out."

She looked at Jake. "What the hell's going on?"

A muscle twitched in his jaw, and a shadow crossed his face, but he didn't answer.

Donny Ray reached out and took her hand. "Two things to keep in mind," he murmured, the drugs slurring his words. "You have family now. A real family. Second thing, he kept it from you cause he loves you. Wanted to…protect…" His eyes drifted shut. "Loved you enough to keep it from you. To keep from hurting you. Then, loved you enough to tell, to save your life. Don't know about you, but I never had no one love me that much."

Confusion warred with concern over Donny Ray. She'd get her answers later. Right now, she had to make sure he was okay.

"I'm going to the hospital with him," Julia told the EMTs.

"No," Donny Ray gasped. "You stay and talk to the sheriff. Mom will be there. You can come see me later."

After a slight hesitation, she nodded. "Hurry, please," she said to the EMTs. "Get him to the hospital."

"You'll come see me…later?" Donny Ray asked.

"I will."

"Promise?"

"Promise."

His eyes closed. He went silent as they wheeled him through the ambulance doors. She watched until they drove away.

Jake came over and took hold of her arm. "You and I need to talk."

She stared up at him, trying to stem the tears. "So, talk. What did Donny Ray mean by family?"

Jake's jaw clenched. "You know the child Jasper Ramsey fathered?" She slowly nodded, but before he spoke, she knew what he would say. He took a deep breath, then let it out slowly. "You were that child, Julia."

Even though she expected it, actually hearing the words stole the air from her chest. Her head spun, and she thought she might pass out. She stared at him, wondering if she looked as green as she felt. "I killed my father?"

"You didn't kill him. It was an accident."

"Oh God," she moaned, her legs nearly giving out. The only thing keeping her upright was Jake's grip on her. "I killed my own father?" Deep sobs shook her body. Jake tried to pull her into his arms, but she jerked loose from his hold, suddenly finding the strength to stand on her own. "You knew Jasper Ramsey was my father, and you didn't tell me? How long have you known?"

"A few days."

"But you were going to let me leave without telling me."

He nodded. "I thought it was best. I saw how you suffered over what happened. I didn't want you to carry that burden."

"That wasn't your decision to make." Her voice trembled with pain and rage. "I had a right to know."

"You did. I just figured you'd had enough hurt in your lifetime."

His image wavered through the tears in her eyes. "How could you?" she whispered brokenly.

"I wanted to protect you."

Pressing her lips together, she drew in a deep breath to stop the sobs wrenching her chest. She couldn't bring herself to speak, all she could manage was a nod.

Jake seemed about to say more when Pam's voice carried to Julia.

"Dear God. What happened?" Pam rushed to her, took her into her arms, hugged her tightly, then pulled back. "Are you okay? Tanner was the killer?"

"Yes," Julia gasped.

"You poor thing. And we let you go off with him. No wonder you're so upset. Come on, let's get you home. Unless you want to go with Jake?"

"No!" Julia shot a glance at Jake. He held her gaze, his eyes filled with torment. She hardened herself against it. "I'd rather ride with you," she said to Pam.

"Sure, sweetie. Okay. Come on."

Subdued, they loaded up. Dave hadn't been all that surprised at the news. He'd never trusted Tanner, anyway.

Julia looked from Pam to Dave, a disturbing realization just now sinking in. Their group had gone from six to three in a couple of weeks. Unbelievable. Not to mention, she'd just discovered the identity of the father she'd never known—a father whose death she'd been partially responsible for. Bile rose to her throat. How could she live with something like that? Thing was, she didn't really have a choice. Like everything else in her life, she'd deal with it and move on.

Alone.

She waited until they were heading back to drop the bombshell on Pam.

Pam's head swiveled to Julia, eyes wide, mouth gaping. She turned her attention back to the road. "Jasper Ramsey was your father? Donny Ray is your half-brother? Dear God. What a day you've had. I mean, like it wasn't bad enough finding out your foster brother is a killer, nearly getting killed yourself…then this? I think you're the one who's going to need therapy."

"Yeah. It's not every day you learn you killed your father."

"Don't think like that." Pam reached across the console and took hold of Julia's hand. "You didn't kill him. You can't blame yourself. That's not fair. You've been through enough."

"I have to blame myself. It's my fault."

Pam let out an incredulous snort. "Look at me." Her voice was firm, authoritative. Julia lacked the strength to disobey. "Do you hate me?"

"What? Of course not."

"You don't hate me for killing your father? You don't blame me?"

Julia shook her head adamantly. "No way. Not at all."

"I was driving, for heaven's sake. If you can't blame me, you can't blame yourself."

Julia took a deep breath. Pam had tricked her. And, she had to admit, her friend had a point. She wouldn't have the luxury of wallowing in blame, guilt, and self-pity. Not unless she wanted her best friend to join her.

Pam smiled. "Nothing to say? Not even, *Gee, Pam, you're right, as always. Thanks for putting things into perspective.*"

Julia gave a half-hearted chuckle, feeling marginally better. "How about just, good point, and let's drop it?"

"Works for me." Pam released her hand. "You're going to be fine, sweetie. I promise. Are you still leaving today?"

"No. I've changed my mind. I need to stick around, talk to Donny Ray. Just a few more days. I have to make sure he's okay before I go."

"That, my dear, sounds like a plan."

****

The next day, Julia called Donny Ray to say goodbye. She'd gone to the hospital and stayed with him for hours last night. He'd told her about Jasper, the kind of dad he was, the fact that, while he was decent to Donny Ray, he hadn't exactly been the most loving father in the world. And, knowing Jasper cheated on his mother, then abandoned Julia and *her* mother, Donny Ray's love and respect for his father diminished considerably. Debra hadn't been happy to hear the news about Donny Ray's newfound sibling, but she'd grudgingly accepted it.

"You sure you want to leave?" Donny Ray asked over the phone. "I said I was sorry about the alley thing."

She choked out a laugh. "That's not it. I have a job to get back to."

"Yeah, I know. But I was hoping we could spend some time together. I might be kind of an ass, but I'm not all bad. I always wanted a kid sister."

His words warmed her heart. She might have lost one brother, but she'd gained another. And this one was blood. "I'll call and email often. We'll visit one another as much as possible." She thought about running into Jake again. "But, next time, you come out to see me in Florida."

"Sounds good. I'll have to find a job first, save some money."

"Pam and Dave both offered to help you on the job search. You'll find something."

"I know. Thanks. See you around."

Julia hung up and turned to find Pam standing behind her.

"So, you're really going?"

"I'd say it's about time. Donny Ray's on the mend. I've been here for over two weeks. My boss said if I didn't get my ass back, I might not have a job waiting for me."

"You okay? About Tanner and all. Can you believe it? I mean, I know he's an asshole, but who would have thought he'd be a killer?"

"Not me. That's for sure." She forced a smile. "And yes, I'm fine. How about you? You sure you're over the doll thing?"

She nodded. "The spell is broken."

"I beg your pardon?"

"I don't need therapy now. The curse of the Scrimshaw doll is broken."

"How do you figure?"

"True love."

"You've fallen in love?"

Pam rolled her eyes. "Not me, dummy. You. And Jake."

Julia lifted a brow. "Uhm…since you're the owner, don't you have to be the one to fall in love?"

"Not sure. Maybe the curse will stay with me, but is it really that bad to have people who betray you suffer?" She grinned impishly. "All that really matters is you and Jake love each other."

"Don't be ridiculous."

"You mean, more ridiculous than believing an ancient doll was causing people to die? Now, I know how crazy that sounds, but I think I went a little nuts after I lost Corbin, then found out he cheated. It's especially hard, knowing he cheated with Emily. It's not fair. I can't even grieve for them like I should after what they did."

Julia squeezed her hand. "I know it's rough. But you'll be fine."

"Yeah. I'll just have to work that out. It's not me I'm worried about now, though. It's you and Jake. I can't believe you're leaving him. That's crazy."

Julia rolled her eyes. "Is that right?"

"Yeah. And if anyone knows crazy, I do." Pam grinned, and Julia forced herself to grin back. "You can't leave him. He loves you so much."

"I don't know where you get that idea."

"He's always loved you."

"He's been trying to get me out of town since I got here." Julia huffed out a breath. "Doesn't sound like someone in love to me."

"Because it was dangerous for you here."

Julia tried to tamp down her impatience. Pam meant well, but she needed to just let it go. "He never said he loves me. And, even if he did, you know I could never make him happy. He needs a different kind of woman. One who belongs in this town. One who would make a good cop's wife. It's best that I leave."

"Are you out of your mind? Are you saying you're not good enough for him?"

"You know it's true. Can you imagine…me…a sheriff's wife? They'd laugh us out of town."

"You're a fool, Julia. I always thought you were so smart, but you're about as dumb as they come."

"Let's drop it, okay?" Julia slipped the strap of her overnight bag on her shoulder.

"You have friends, a brother, a man who loves you. You're leaving all that?"

"I also have a lot of heartbreak here. I'm sorry."

Pam crossed her arms over her chest mutinously.

"Apology not accepted."

Julia shrugged. "Then, I don't know what else to say. I'll see you soon, all right? Love you."

"Love you." Pam said, her voice petulant. She hung on tightly when she hugged Julia, then stood in the doorway and watched as she left.

Julia climbed into her car and drove away, barely able see the road through the tears in her eyes. She'd left this town half a dozen times. *Why does it hurt so much more now?*

Was it because of what had happened with Tanner? Or, because she'd fallen in love with Jake all over again? During her previous trips back to Covington, she'd barely seen him. This time, she'd touched him, felt his lips on hers…been betrayed by him.

He did it for your own good and you know it.

Yes, she knew it, but what she'd said to Pam was true. She could never make him happy.

A sound in the distance snapped her to the present. *Is that a siren?* She looked in her rearview mirror.

"Shit," she hissed through gritted teeth when she saw the flashing lights. She was barely out of Covington, and she was being pulled over?

She eased onto the shoulder and slowed to a stop, squinting through the sun's reflection in her side view mirror.

A Covington squad car? If so, that meant Kurt, or Jake, was giving her a ticket. *Assholes.* Couldn't they just let her leave, so she'd be out of their lives for good?

She waited breathlessly to see who would climb from the squad car. *Please let it be Kurt.* Her heart couldn't take another goodbye.

When she saw the tall figure move toward her with that familiar, lazy stride, her pulse rate hiked. She slid down her window.

"Get out of the car," Jake barked, reaching for the door handle.

She shaded her eyes with her hand and stared up at him. "What?"

His jaw was set, his eyes flashing molten silver fire. "Step out of the car."

She frowned, but obeyed when he swung the door open. "I don't understand, what was I—"

Slamming the door shut, he snarled, "What the hell do you mean you aren't good enough for me?"

Damn. Pam had a big mouth. And she was fast.

He leaned toward her. She tried to pull back from him, but she was against the closed door. He slammed his hands on the car, one on either side of her. She was trapped.

"I can take it if you say you don't love me. If you say you can't forgive me for holding back the truth. But don't you dare say you're not good enough for me. You're smart, kind, and beautiful. I've never met a woman like you in all my life." He paused to take in a deep breath. His voice lowered. "As a girl, you stole my heart. As a woman, you haven't let it go. So, you can tell your friend you don't love me, that you're not good enough for me, you can tell your brother, or whoever. But look me in the eye and tell me you don't love me. That you're not good enough for me."

She opened her mouth, but she was lost in the fire of his gaze, in the nearness of him, in the heat from his body. Nothing came out.

"That's what I thought. You know it's a damn lie."

He took hold of her upper arms. "Admit it. We've had all these lies between us all these years. We kept our feelings inside, but too much has happened. I can't go on like this. I'm exhausted…drained, and I hurt like hell. So, tell me. For once, let's have the goddamned truth between us."

She stared up at him rebelliously. The words hung up in her throat, fear keeping them from surfacing.

He waited a few beats, scrutinizing her features before releasing her with a shrug. "Okay. Fine. If that's the way you want to leave it, then fine." His eyes crinkled, but there was bitterness in the curve of his lips. "Take this with you, though. I love you. More than I've ever loved anyone. I never meant to cause you pain, and I'll never hurt you again. I'll let you be on your way." The absence of his touch chilled her like an Arctic wind. He headed back to the cruiser.

Her heart ached, and her head swam with confusion. Jake had just confessed his love for her, and she was letting him walk out of her life. Suddenly, all the fight, the anger, the resentment, the hurt fled.

"Then don't leave me," she choked out. Jake didn't pause. He hadn't heard her. He'd reached the squad car, and her words had come out in barely a whisper. She raised her voice. "Jake, please. Don't leave me."

He halted, lifting his head to stare at her. "What was that?"

She started toward him, and he stood, waiting. His eyebrows drew together. She reached him and lifted a hand to touch his face. "I said…then don't leave me. If you love me, don't leave me. Because, I love you too. Always have. Always will."

Tension melted from his features. The sexy grin

came back, this time filled with happiness. He took her face in his hands and stared into her eyes. "I promise. I won't. Not ever."

"We've wasted so many years," she whispered, not believing this moment was actually here, that Jake loved her. That she'd admitted loving him.

"Don't think about it. Maybe we had to go through it all to get where we are now. All that matters is I love you, and you love me. I'll never let you go again. I'm sorry I didn't tell you about Jasper—"

"Shhh." She placed her finger over his lips. "I know you did it out of love."

He brushed a finger tenderly along her hairline, his gaze roaming over her features, as if drinking them in. "I did. You've been hurt so much. I only wanted to protect you."

She nodded. She knew that. Knew he would never intentionally hurt her. "I'll have to find a job around here. Not much call for legal investigators in Covington."

"Oklahoma City is forty miles away. You could commute. Or we could move. Or whatever it takes. I'm not letting you go again."

"Promise me?"

He gave her that squint-eyed smile she loved so much, then lowered his head and claimed her lips. His kiss was all the promise she needed.

End of Lonely Street

by

Alicia Dean

Dedication

To all the Elvis Presley fans out there
(especially to my wonderful sisters,
with whom I grew up listening to Elvis,
and to my kids, who also love Elvis: my daughters Lana
and Lacey, and my son Presley.

~

There will never be another entertainer like Elvis,
whether people like his music or not,
there's no denying he had something magical
and left a legacy that will never be matched.

Acknowledgments

I would like to thank my fabulous editor, Nicole D'Arienzo, for liking my story enough to contract it, and for being talented enough to help make it shine. I would also like to thank the entire team at The Wild Rose Press, from the owners, to the talented cover artists, to the marketing guru, and all the editors and authors. You guys are the best! A special thanks to my beta reader and friend, Monique DeVere, who was the first to read my story and tell me what worked...and what didn't.

Chapter One

Mapleton, Tennessee, November, 1957

Toby Lawson closed her eyes and shut out all sounds of the diner, except for Elvis Presley's voice. He was crooning about how she was the only one for him…no matter where he went or what he did… he'd spend his whole life loving her…

Rough hands landed on her waist and shattered the fantasy. She caught a whiff of hair tonic and too much cologne and snapped her eyes open. Wes Markham's hateful face replaced the image of Elvis' beautiful, crooked smile and smoldering blue eyes.

"Let me go." She gritted her teeth, keeping her voice low. If her boss, Mr. Winstead, knew there was trouble on account of her, he'd explode. He'd barely let her have the job in the first place. Everyone in Mapleton knew the Lawson women were trouble.

"Come on, honey. If you like that hip swivel, Presley ain't the only one who's got it. I got it too." He released her with his left hand so he could run it over his slicked down hair and gave her a big-toothed, wolfish smile. "Only we'd be naked." He shot a cocky grin over to his two companions—Chuck Stenson and Billy Garfield—who were leaning against the jukebox making kissing and whooping sounds.

Toby gripped his right wrist with one hand, tightening her hold on the utensils she held in the other. "I said let me go. Now!"

"Aw, be a sport, Green-Eyes."

The bulge of his pelvis pressed into her abdomen, and she gasped in shock. Nausea tightened in her esophagus. "Wes Markham, I'm warning you…"

She shoved against him, but he didn't budge.

He pulled her tighter. "Your momma's a whole lot friendlier than you are. They say the apple don't fall far from the tree, so how's about you cut the pretense and we go someplace quiet? Winstead won't miss you for a few minutes."

Her cheeks heated. She didn't dare look around. No doubt the customers were watching, listening. Elvis had stopped singing, and everyone in the place could hear what he'd said about her mother. It wasn't like they didn't all know, though. Constance Lawson hadn't exactly kept her escapades a secret.

Toby clenched her teeth and brandished the utensils. She spoke loud enough for everyone to hear. "Release me this instant, or I swear, you'll be pulling this steak knife out of your eyeball."

He held her gaze for a split second, then gave a laugh that was somewhere between nervous and furious. "Sure, sure. Okay." He released her and stepped back. "I was just foolin' around anyway. I got better things to do with my time than waste it on a used up chick like you."

Muffled laughter rose around her. Oh God, she could crawl into a hole.

"How about you apologize to the lady, then beat it?"

Toby whirled at the male voice. Noah Rivers stood

behind her, looking handsome and sharp in his police uniform—even with his dark hair in the military buzz cut. Her knees weakened, and tingles swept over her skin. She swallowed against the sudden dryness in her throat. She'd heard he was back but hadn't seen him until now. And what a time to have a reunion.

Wes licked his lips and darted a glance around the diner. He stuck his hands in his pants pockets and shrugged. "I didn't mean no harm. Like I said, just funnin'."

Noah narrowed his eyes. "Like *I* said, tell that to the lady."

Wes frowned, then turned a glare on Toby. "Sorry. Didn't mean nothin' by it."

She nodded, suppressing a shudder. His words might have sounded amiable, but his eyes made a threat she couldn't ignore.

"Now get out of here." Noah gestured with his head.

Wes tugged on the edges of his letterman jacket—three years out of high school and still couldn't let go of the jock mentality—then stalked to the door, his two buddies following behind.

"Thank you." Toby brushed her hands over her paper apron—self-conscious of the soda stains on her pink uniform blouse and her hair coming loose from its ponytail—when Noah looked like, well...*that*. "I was doing fine on my own though."

"Yeah, sure you were. But he ticked me off, so that was just for me." He crossed his arms and studied her with hypnotic, golden brown eyes. "How have you been, Toby?"

"Good." She tried to take a deep breath, but it got

stuck somewhere between her chest and her throat. "You? I heard you were back. A police officer. I never would have pictured that for you."

"Why not?" He grinned. "Because I was hell on wheels?"

She smiled back, keeping her voice low so as not to continue attracting attention from the diners. "Something like that."

"A couple of years in the Marines will take the rebel right out of a guy."

She nodded, and an uncomfortable silence settled between them. Toby searched for something to say, but failed. What more could she say?

I've missed you...

No other guy can make me feel the way you do...

Wish I hadn't caught you kissing my mother...

In all fairness, her mother had kissed *him*, but since Toby could never erase that image from her mind, the blame didn't matter.

"Well, I'd better get back to work." She placed the utensils in the dish bin.

"Yeah, me too." He glanced around the diner. She followed his gaze. The counter was lined with customers. A jukebox sat in the corner. Patsy Cline's "Walkin' After Midnight" now belted from its speakers. He brought his eyes back to her. "What happened to college? I thought you were getting your teaching degree."

She shrugged and took the dish cloth from her apron pocket. "That was the plan." She wouldn't go into how she'd had to put off her schooling to come home and see after her mother. Surely he'd heard the story about Constance falling asleep with a lit cigarette and almost burning down the house—with her inside it—from the town gossip mill. "I finished my three years at University. Now I have to complete my Post-Graduate Certificate of Education. I had to put that on hold for a while, so in the meantime, I'm doing this."

"Great. That means I'll see you often. Maybe we can get together for a movie or something? *Jailhouse Rock* is showing at the Bijou."

Elvis and Noah at the same time? Her heart wouldn't take it.

Before the break-up, she'd gone to the drive-in with him to see *Rebel Without a Cause*. James Dean had died less than a month earlier, and she cried throughout the entire movie. Noah had held her, comforted her. Let her cry on his shoulder. That was their last movie together. The night remained a sad memory for more than one reason.

"Thanks, but I don't think so. I'm awfully busy with work and the high school committee."

His mouth turned down in a frown, but he gave a quick nod. "Fine, then. I guess I'll just see you when I see you. Take care."

She nodded. "You too."

He left, and it took all her willpower to refrain from calling him back, telling him she'd changed her mind. But the pain from their break-up had just started to heal. And there was no way on Earth she ever wanted to experience that again.

****

Toby hurried home after her shift. She had just enough time to get ready before she had to head to her meeting with the alumni group. They were almost finished with plans for the benefit for their former

129

principal. Miss Murdock had been so kind to her the entire time she'd been at Mapleton High. She'd retired last year due to illness, and her health was deteriorating while her medical bills continued to grow. Toby had been appointed head of the entertainment committee, and, after Miss Murdock's endorsement, had managed to get approval from the school board to play rock and roll at the dance. Tickets were selling like crazy.

She let herself into the white frame house she'd grown up in. Her father passed away when she was five, but his business partner paid her mom a salary in order to keep her from selling her half of the auto business he'd owned with Toby's dad. Thanks to that same auto business, she'd gotten her two-tone blue and white '55 Bel Air for a steal.

Agitation coursed through her when she stepped into the living room and saw the mess. She did her best to keep the place clean, but her mother was a slob, so it was an uphill battle.

The odor of booze mingled with the scent of lemon furniture polish. Two empty vodka bottles were strewn on the carpet next to a pile of her mother's clothing. Magazines and her mother's coat and shoes littered the turquoise sectional sofa. Where had she been? Toby had taken her keys away after the last drunk-driving incident when she'd plowed into a mailbox. If her mom had gone out, someone else must have driven. She couldn't imagine who it would have been. Constance had no real friends.

"Mother? Where are you?" Toby yelled up the stairs. She didn't have time to fool with her mom, but she had to check on her. The last thing she needed was another *incident*. She couldn't trust her mother. She'd kill herself before it was all over.

And then I'd be free...

Toby shook the horrible words away. What kind of person thought such awful things about their own mother?

"'Mm-in'ere, baby girl. Need...help."

So what's new?

Toby huffed out a sigh and climbed the stairs. She entered through her mother's open bedroom door. Constance lay on the floor, her head cradled in her arms.

Fear raced through Toby as she rushed to her mother's side. "Mother, are you okay?" She knelt, checking her mom's slight frame for possible injury.

"Can't...make it...bed." She puffed out the slurred words on a breath filled with alcohol fumes. She lifted her head, but her eyes remained shut.

Satisfied her mom wasn't injured beyond stupefied drunkenness, Toby grimaced. Anger warred with sympathy, but the anger definitely had the lead.

She bent over and tucked her hands beneath Constance's arms. The smell of vodka and stale perfume wafted to her. She wrinkled her nose. How long had it been since her mother last showered? Sober, she was immaculate and well-groomed. Drunk was a whole different story.

"Come on, let's get you to bed." Toby tugged, but she was dead weight. "Please, Mom, you have to help a little."

Constance pointed her finger, aiming somewhere over Toby's left shoulder. "Don'you sass me. I'm sti-still yer mother."

"Right. So why am *I* taking care of *you*?" She let out a sigh and tugged again. "Help me out. I can't lift you." Although she should have been able to. Constance had wasted down to skin and bones. She'd never been fat, but she'd had curves. Toby had always thought she looked just like Tuesday Weld, but her good looks were fading, and she appeared older than her thirty-nine years. She hardly ever ate, did nothing but drink. She'd gotten so much worse in the six months since Toby had returned home. Even if Toby prevented her from going up in flames, she was slowly killing herself with booze.

"Okay, okay, okay, okay," her mother mumbled. She pressed her feet against the floor, and Toby lifted at the same time. With a few more tugs and stumbles, she managed to get her mother into bed.

"Here you go." Toby pulled the covers up to her chin. "You just get some rest." The doorbell rang. "That's probably Daisy here to pick me up for the meeting. I have to go. Will you be okay?"

She nodded. "Fine. Just bring me a drink."

Toby headed to the door. "I'll get you some water."

"No water! Bring me my bottle."

Toby opened her mouth to argue, but clamped it shut. It wouldn't do any good. She'd get the booze, and hopefully, her mom would pass out before she drank it.

Downstairs, Toby opened the door to Daisy Abersol, her best friend since the third grade. She wore a pink cashmere sweater with a white scarf knotted to the side and a slim white skirt. Her dark hair hung loose around her shoulders. Toby pushed back a twinge of envy. She could never make her own blond hair lay in soft curls like Daisy's, so she usually kept it in a ponytail.

"Ready?" Her friend stepped inside.

"Not quite yet. I just put my mother to bed. She

wants me to take her vodka to her."

"You aren't, are you? That's the last thing she needs."

Toby snorted a humorless laugh. "Yeah, but if I don't, she'll try to get it on her own, and she'll probably fall down the stairs and kill herself."

She grabbed the bottle of vodka and took it up to her mom. She found her snoring, so she set the liquor on the nightstand and headed out.

They climbed into Daisy's red rag top and cruised out onto the road. Daisy tapped her long pink fingernails on the steering wheel and slid a look at Toby. "So, are you going to spend the rest of your life taking care of your mom?"

Toby shrugged. "What choice do I have? I'm just hoping I can find a way to finish school in the meantime."

"Well, even if that doesn't happen, you'll be fine. You're smart and pretty. If you aren't able to finish your education, you can easily find a husband."

"I don't want to find a husband. I want to be a teacher."

Her friend's perfectly arched brows scrunched in a frown. "And die an old maid like Miss Murdock?"

"Hey, that's a lousy thing to say."

"I know." Daisy blew a breath up, ruffling her dark bangs. "Sorry. I just, I want what's best for you. Noah's back, and you can tell he's still nuts over you. Don't let him go a second time."

Toby grimaced. "I won't let him go, because I don't have him."

Her friend tightened her mouth and shook her head, but didn't respond.

When they arrived at the Mapleton Public Library, the other committee members—Johnny, Suzette, and Blanche—were waiting for them in the meeting room. Johnny was in charge of the ticket sales and venue, Daisy the refreshments, and Blanche and Suzette the decorations. They had all graduated together in '54, and were part of the honor roll, so they'd been chosen to sit on the alumni committee.

Once Daisy and Toby were seated, Johnny consulted a spiral notebook. "Mr. James agreed to let us use his concert hall for free. He doesn't have anyone scheduled on the twentieth, and he wants to help with Miss Murdock's bills. Thanks to Toby getting permission for us to play rock and roll at the dance, we've sold three-hundred thirty-two tickets at a buck apiece so far. Kids from schools in nearby towns are planning to come. This could be gigantic."

"Good going, Toby." Blanche, a plump, pretty brunette, twisted her red scarf in her hands and leaned her elbows on the table. "Guess what? I heard Miss Murdock was a women's rights activist. She was a member of the National Woman's Party."

Toby laughed. "You're putting me on. Sweet, proper Miss Murdock?" She couldn't imagine the matronly woman being an activist.

"What's the National Woman's Party?" Johnny sneered. "Sounds like a drag."

"Shows what you know." Toby scowled at him. "They were instrumental in getting the nineteenth amendment passed, giving women the right to vote. That's quite impressive."

The brunette's mouth turned down. "Yeah, she's the coolest. So sad she's dying."

The words pierced Toby's heart. "We don't know that. Soon, she could be strong enough for the surgery and be fine." She wasn't as sure as she pretended, but she had to keep saying it. Maybe that would make it true. Miss Murdock had been more like a mother to her than her own mother. She'd taught at Mapleton High, then became principal in Toby's senior year. Sometimes, she didn't know how she'd have made it through school without the woman's kindness.

Blanche didn't reply, but the sympathy in her eyes spoke for her.

Suzette thumbed through her notes. "Now for refreshments. I thought we could charge for cookies and provide punch for free."

"Swell." Johnny grinned. "And with free punch, it will be easier to sneak a little booze into it."

"No!" Toby spoke more adamantly than she intended and all heads turned to her. "No alcohol."

"Hey, look. Just because you're a square doesn't mean we all have to be."

"She's not a square." As usual, Daisy jumped to her defense. "It's just that we could get into a lot of trouble. We're adults, responsible for the kids. We can't sneak them alcohol."

Johnny snorted. "Yeah, sure. We all know the score. It's 'cause Toby's mom is a drunk."

Sadness squeezed her chest, and she fought back tears, but she didn't argue. She'd spent most of her life defending her mom. But all the horrible things people said about her were true. Her mom was a drunk, and she was a square. But she'd rather be a square any day than be like Constance Lawson.

Chapter Two

Friday was Toby's only day off, and she had tons of things to do. First on the list was visiting Miss Murdock at the hospital. The poor thing was out of it most of the time, but it made Toby feel better to visit her, whether or not she was aware.

She brought in the bottle of milk from the porch and poured a bowl of cornflakes. She ate them quickly, then checked on her mom, who was still sleeping. She was about to head out when the phone rang. She answered, surprised to find Mr. Rivers, the school principal and Noah's father, on the other end.

"What can I do for you, Mr. Rivers?"

"I need to see you in my office, right away."

She chewed on her thumbnail, dread settling in her stomach. He wasn't the friendliest person under the best circumstances, and judging by the tone of his voice, these were not the best circumstances. She'd better swing by before visiting the hospital. The last thing she wanted was to incur his wrath by putting him off.

"Yes, sir. I'll be there shortly."

She glanced down at her pedal pushers. Not the sort of outfit one wore for a professional meeting, especially with an application pending at the school. She had practically been guaranteed a position once she finished her year of teacher education. It was the last step before obtaining her Post-Graduate Certificate of Education. She wasn't going to do anything to mess up her chances of obtaining a teaching position at Mapleton High. She dashed upstairs and changed into a powder blue cardigan set and cream-colored pleated skirt.

At the school, Mr. Rivers' secretary, Georgia, showed Toby into his office. He scowled at her from behind the desk, not bothering to stand.

Like his son, Daniel Rivers was handsome. The black hair was peppered with gray, and his eyes were a darker brown than Noah's, but the similarities were striking. Physically, that is. Unlike Noah, Mr. Rivers was a hard, cold man.

Toby cleared her throat nervously. "You wanted to see me, Mr. Rivers?"

He pointed with his cigar to a chair across from his desk. "Have a seat."

She perched on the edge of the chair and waited silently.

He frowned and clamped the cigar between his teeth, picking up a sheet of paper off the top of his desk. He held it up for her inspection. She recognized one of the flyers for the dance. "What's this all about?" he demanded.

She shifted and wiped damp palms on her skirt. "It—it's the flyer. For the dance we're holding. A benefit for Miss Murdock. She—she's ill, and needs help with medical bills." She gave an uneasy chuckle. "Did you know she once marched for Women's Suffrage? Who could picture Miss Murdock doing that? I know I couldn't—" She halted abruptly. Nerves were making her chatty. And she was babbling like a fool.

"I'll have none of this nonsense at a school

function. Rock and roll? Are you out of your mind?"

No rock and roll? No Everly Brothers or Little Richard or Buddy Holly? No....Elvis?

"But, sir. The kids are really looking forward to it. We've sold more than three-hundred tickets so far, and we just know we'll sell more. That's over three-hundred dollars for Miss Murdock's expenses. Many of the kids will want their money back if we don't have rock and roll music at the dance. Besides, Miss Murdock already gave her approval, before she had to retire."

Mr. Rivers crossed his hands on the top of his desk. "It doesn't matter how many tickets you've sold. I'm in charge now, and I'm not going to coddle students like Miss Murdock did. I won't have my kids exposed to that devil music, especially that vulgar, immoral Elvis the Pelvis."

"Vulgar? Devil music?" Toby clenched her fists. It made her so angry when older people spoke that way about rock and roll, especially about Elvis. He was a nice boy, respectful and polite. Kind to his fans, to his mother. And he was the dreamiest. "Rock and roll is not devil music. It's just a way for kids to have fun, to have their own—"

"That will be enough, Miss Lawson. I should expect this kind of attitude from someone with your...upbringing—your lack of morals." He smirked. "The only reason you're even on the committee is because you made straight A's. It certainly wasn't my idea to allow you to serve, and I assure you, I will do all in my power to have you removed if you cause me any more trouble."

His words were like a fist to her gut. She couldn't believe this stuffy, hateful man was Noah's father. Noah was kind, fun, with a sense of humor. This man was a total boor.

"You don't understand. This is extremely important. Miss Murdock needs—"

"The discussion is over. I've made my decision, and I'll hear no more about it. No rock and roll, and that's final. And you listen to me, young lady. I'm involved in the decision-making as to whether you get hired here. If you buck me on this, I'll ensure that you'll never get a job here, or anywhere in this school district. Understand?"

Toby gave a quick nod. "I understand." She rose and walked to the door, feeling as though she were walking to the electric chair. How could she tell the others on the committee that they would have to change their whole plan? That they would have to refund money when the kids learned they wouldn't play rock and roll after all. What teenager wanted to go to a dance where they played nothing but Frank Sinatra and Glenn Miller?

She could fight, dig her heels in and refuse, but would that really get her anywhere? He would have her removed from the committee, maybe even shut down the dance altogether. And what about her future? She could help the kids more by becoming a teacher and following in Miss Murdock's footsteps. The woman had done more than educate, she'd connected with her students and changed lives. Toby wanted to be that kind of person, too.

But Miss Murdock also marched for equality. She didn't back down when things got rocky…

She pushed the thought aside.

Her hands were tied. She would have to make the best of it and hope to find another way to help the woman who meant the world to her.

****

The hospital sat at the edge of town, just past Mapleton Park. Orange and gold leaves drifted from the trees that lined the street. On the drive over, Toby kept telling herself this wasn't a big deal. There were a lot of ways to raise funds. The dance would be smaller, but they would still bring in money. Any would help.

She went into Miss Murdock's room to find her niece, Shelley, sitting by her bed. Shelley's mother had passed when she was young, and Miss Murdock had taken her in. The woman was in her thirties, pretty, tall and thin with an easy smile and auburn hair the shade her aunt's used to be before she'd gone gray.

Shelley looked up and smiled. "Hi. She's awake. You picked a good time to come." She stood. "I'll let you two visit while I go down and get a cup of coffee. Need anything?"

"No, thank you." Toby moved over to the bed. Miss Murdock looked even older and frailer than she had last time she had seen her, just a few days ago. Her skin was sallow and looked…crumpled. Her breathing was labored, a sign that her heart ailment was worsening. The doctors were waiting for her to gain the strength to withstand the surgery she needed. In the meantime, her bills were piling up. If they didn't come up with money soon, the hospital would release her.

"Toby, is that you?" Miss Murdock lifted a hand. Toby took it gently. The older woman's skin was thin, papery and cool. "Thank you for visiting me, dear."

"My pleasure." Her heart ached to see her so weak and helpless. "How are you feeling?"

She gave a raspy chuckle. "I've been better, but I

can't complain."

Toby glanced over at her bedside table to where a bouquet of bright pink and yellow carnations rested in a crystal vase. "Those are beautiful. Who sent them to you?"

"They're from Noah Rivers. But I hear he didn't send them, he brought them. I hate that I slept through his visit." Her face softened when she turned to look at the flowers. "He's such a nice boy." She brought her gaze back to Toby. "You two made such a lovely couple. I hope you work things out."

"You shouldn't worry about us. You need to focus on getting well."

"Nonsense. It does my heart good to have hope for you and Noah. He's mad about you, you know."

"He's a great guy." That much was true. He just wasn't the guy for her. Not anymore. "I heard something interesting about you," she said, anxious to change the subject.

"Oh, what was that?"

"You were a tiger in your day. You were a member of the National Woman's Party? You marched for women's right to vote?"

Miss Murdock chuckled. "That I did. I even got arrested once."

Toby's mouth dropped open in shock. "No! Not you."

"It was in 'eighteen. We were in Washington D.C. What a night. Six of us were taken to jail." Her eyes twinkled. "It was scary, but I've never felt more alive."

"You're something else. All your years as a teacher and principal, helping kids. And now I learn you were a rebel rouser."

"You know, you remind me of myself when I was your age."

"How so?"

"You've got that same passion, that fire. There's nothing you can't do if you set your mind to it."

"I'm not sure that's true. If so, I'd find a way to take care of everything you need, to help get you better."

Miss Murdock pressed her palm to Toby's cheek. "Don't worry about me. I'm an old lady. I've had a full, wonderful life, and I have no regrets. Now is your time. Your time to have fun, to make your dreams come true."

"Nonsense. You have a lot of good years left."

She shook her head. "No, I don't believe I do. I'm not…strong enough for the surgery I need. I've accepted that the end is near."

Toby dropped her gaze and blinked back moisture. She didn't know what to say, so she simply laid her hand on top of Miss Murdock's. After a few moments, the older lady's eyes drifted shut, and she fell asleep.

Toby sat by her bedside and waited for Shelley. In a few moments, she returned, carrying a plastic cup with steam rising from it. She came over and looked down at her aunt.

Her voice low in the quiet room, she said, "We're fighting two battles." She took a sip of coffee and shook her head. "Her being strong enough for the surgery, and getting money for the bill so they'll keep her here. She couldn't get the care she needs at home."

Toby rested a hand on Shelley's forearm. "We're working hard to raise money. Don't give up hope."

She nodded. "I know. You've been so good to her. She admires you a great deal. She said she saw a lot of herself in you in your determination and strength. Also a little stubbornness."

Toby laughed. "Maybe the stubbornness. I'm not so sure about the strength." She sighed. "You're very lucky to have someone like her in your family."

Shelley smiled and patted Toby's hand. "I would say we both are."

****

After work that night, Toby wasn't ready to go home, so she sat in her car in the parking lot of Winstead's, listening to the radio. "Love Me" by Elvis came on, and she cranked the volume.

Nothing else calmed her and lightened her heart like listening to him. She could escape into his music and all the bad just…faded away. When Elvis sang, there was no drunken mother, no failed dreams, no dying Miss Murdock. Toby didn't only listen to his music, she *felt* it. It seemed to vibrate through her blood.

Although she was embarrassed to admit it, sometimes listening to him, watching him on television, made her all squirmy and hot—just like Noah made her feel. Especially that one night, when they had almost gone all the way.

Toby had been a senior in high school, and he'd graduated the year before. He picked her up and they drove out to the bluff, known as Make Out Row, overlooking downtown Mapleton.

The town was shrouded in darkness, but scattered lights shone, as though a starry sky were laid out below them. There were other cars around, but closed up in their cocoon, it was as though they were the only two people on Earth. Noah had kissed her, deep and long, whispering love words, telling her she was special, beautiful. She'd fallen in love with him at that very moment—wanted to be with him forever. He'd been the one to halt their make out session. She would have willingly gone all the way that night. She was helplessly under his spell...the feel of his lips on hers, his hand covering her breast through her thin blouse...

A tapping sound on the window made her jump. She looked through the glass to find Noah standing outside the car. Was he real, or just part of the fantasy world she'd drifted to? When another tap came, she blinked away the memories. He was definitely real.

She rolled down the window. "Is something wrong?"

"That's what I was going to ask you. Are you okay?"

"I'm fine."

"Then what are you doing sitting out in the parking lot after closing time? All alone? It's not safe for you out here."

She laughed. "Come on, this is Mapleton. What's going to happen around here?"

He grinned, his eyes glinting like gold in the dim light. "Now if it was all that safe, I wouldn't be needed, would I?"

"Are you? Needed, I mean? What's the worst crime you've had to handle? A stolen bicycle?"

He chuckled. "That and a couple of three-oh-sevens."

"Three-oh-sevens?"

"Drunk and disorderlies."

She laughed again, and he leaned down and rested his arms on her door. It brought his face too near, his lips too close to hers. She swallowed a lump in her throat. He was so handsome, so...Noah. No matter what she told Miss Murdock and Daisy, and even herself, she wasn't over him.

He didn't speak for several moments. He stared into her eyes, then let his gaze roam over her hair and to her lips. Finally, he said, "Can we talk, Toby? We never really spoke much about what happened. You never let me tell my side."

She dragged her gaze away and stared through the windshield across the street at the brightly painted awning over Sweet and Tasty Bakery. She couldn't keep looking at him, doing so made her weak. "You told your side. You told me what happened, and I believed you."

"Then why did you break up with me? Why aren't we together?" When she didn't answer, he took her chin in his hand and gently turned her to face him. "I thought about you the entire time I was away. Every day. I slept with your picture at night and prayed that God would bring you back to me."

She pulled from his touch and pressed her fingers to his lips. "Don't. Please, don't." Hearing him say the words tore her apart, even though they were the words she wanted to hear. "It doesn't matter anymore. I can't be with you." Regret ripped through her heart "Not ever."

He gripped her fingers and placed a soft kiss on the tips. She shuddered and tried to draw in a breath.

"Don't say that." His words were a tormented whisper. "Please don't say that. I can't lose you forever. I won't."

She squeezed her eyes shut. "I can't, don't you see? Every time I think of you…with her. I get sick to my stomach. And every time I see you, I think of that night." She opened her eyes and stared directly into his.

"Looking at you makes me sick."

He flinched. "You can't mean that."

"I do. Don't you understand? My mother has tainted you…tainted us. She taints everything she touches, and I'll never be free of her."

He compressed his lips, his voice harsh when he spoke. "That's your choice. You can't define yourself by your mother's actions. We're responsible for our own lives, our own destiny."

She snorted a laugh. "That sounds awful nice, but I haven't ever had control of my destiny, my life. I'm tethered to my mother as long as she's alive."

She turned away from his scrutiny—afraid he could see her darkest thoughts. See that sometimes, she wished for her mother's death. Would he still think she was the girl of his dreams if he knew that?

Chapter Three

The next night, Toby sat on her front porch, eating a dinner of macaroni cooked in tomato juice and watching dusk settle over the quiet neighborhood. Behind the walls, families were sitting down to dinner…mothers, fathers, and children gathered around the table sharing the events of their day. Inside the house, her mother was staring drunkenly at the TV screen, apparently unaware she was watching American Bandstand, a show she despised. Dick Clark's voice filtered out, then a song she didn't recognize played.

Her solitude out on the porch was peaceful yet…lonely. As if all the world had faded away, and there was only Toby, her mother, the crickets, and Dick Clark spinning records for just the two of them. A train whistle sounded in the distance, accentuating her isolation.

She tipped a bottle of orange Crush to her lips and once more focused on the pages of *The End of The Affair*. She was halfway into the book and was enthralled by Bendix's obsession with Sarah. What would it be like to have someone love/hate you that much?

The phone shrilled from inside the house, and she jumped. The sound was somehow ominous, although she had no idea why. Her mother likely wouldn't answer it, so Toby set her bowl on the porch swing, rushed inside, and snatched up the receiver.

She'd barely gotten the 'hello' out of her mouth when a sob came over the line. "Please come quickly."

Shelley's tear-filled voice set Toby's warning meter to high. "What is it? Has something happened to your aunt?"

"She's taken a turn for the worse. You must hurry if you want to say goodbye. There isn't much time."

Chills washed over Toby's skin, and she dropped the phone into the cradle. *No, she couldn't be dying.* They needed more time to help her get better.

Fighting back tears, she grabbed her keys and hurried to her car. She hardly remembered the drive to the hospital. There seemed to be a haze settling over her brain. Nothing registered until she reached the door to Miss Murdock's room.

Shelley sat by the bed, holding her aunt's hand. Her profile was to Toby, and her shoulders shook with silent sobs.

She turned when Toby entered, then looked down at the bed. "Aunt Florence, Toby is here to see you."

Shelley stood and stepped back. Toby walked to the bed, her heart sinking into her stomach. Miss Murdock's eyes were closed, and her face had gone from pale to gray.

Toby suppressed the urge to weep and took hold of her hand. "Hi," she managed to choke out.

"Toby...so nice of you to...come to..." a weary breath sighed from her. "...say goodbye."

Toby brought her hand to her lips and kissed it. Grief welled in her chest, and tears streamed down her face. "No, no, this isn't goodbye. You're going to be fine."

A small smile touched Miss Murdock's lips, and her eyes opened. "You're...such a...good girl. So strong. Don't let...anyone take that away."

"I won't, I promise."

"But...don't be so...so strong you..." She drew a labored breath. "...are afraid to...love."

Toby bit back a cry. "Save your strength. You just need to rest and get better."

"I'll be...better...soon." She looked up, and a joyous smile touched her mouth, reflected in her blue eyes. "I'm...going home."

****

That night, Toby slept fitfully. She would doze off and when she awoke, for a split second, would forget Miss Murdock had died. Then the realization would come flooding back, and she'd cry all over again.

She had stayed at the hospital until they took Miss Murdock away. Her entire body felt numb, yet she hurt so much she could barely draw a full breath. She was gone. Toby would never hear her infectious laugh, never be held in her comforting hugs again.

At seven a.m., she dragged herself out of bed, sleep-deprived and grief-stricken, but determined.

Miss Murdock had said Toby was like her, that she was strong. But what had she done? She'd let Rivers push her around. Let him make her back off instead of helping Miss Murdock. Now she was gone. She most likely had life insurance, and that would cover the medical bills and funeral costs, but she deserved more. She deserved to be memorialized, and Toby needed to know the woman she idolized wouldn't be disappointed in her.

She dressed in a black pencil skirt and white blouse

with a ruffled collar and drove to the school. Georgia rang Mr. Rivers, then said Toby could go in.

His signature frown firmly in place, he stood behind his desk, arms crossed. "What can I help you with? I thought we settled all the business about the dance."

She lifted her chin and channeled Miss Murdock's spirit of fortitude. "I've changed my mind. We will play rock and roll after all. The kids are expecting it, the tickets are sold, and I plan to go through with my promise."

He pressed his hands atop his desk and glowered. "I thought I made myself clear. There will be no rock and roll." A cold smile touched his mouth. "Aren't you forgetting about your potential career here? I can end it before it even starts."

"Maybe so. But that's a chance I'll have to take. I won't be bullied."

He picked up the phone. "I'm calling the board now and suggesting you be replaced." He dialed as he spoke. "And if you get any ideas about one of your cronies taking up your cause, I'll have them replaced, too. You will *not* win against me. If you keep pushing, I'll make sure you never work in this school district."

His words sent chills of dread racing over her skin, but she made an effort to keep her expression impassive. "You do what you have to do, and so will I."

Without waiting for a response, she turned and strode from his office. Once she was on the other side of the door, an attack of nerves combined with elation washed over her.

She'd done it. She'd stood up to him and held her ground. Now she just needed to figure out what to do next. What would Miss Murdock have done?

An idea occurred that increased her nervousness. Mr. Rivers might get rid of her, but she wouldn't go quietly.

****

Toby spent two hours gathering materials at the Five and Dime and making signs. She thought about asking the other committee members to join her but didn't want them to risk their positions. So, it would just be her. And four protest signs.

She drove to the Rivers' house—the home Noah grew up in, although she'd heard he had his own apartment now. Two-story houses lined either side of the street. When she and Noah had gone steady, she hadn't come here. His father didn't approve of their relationship, and although Noah insisted she should feel comfortable at his home, she couldn't bring herself to venture into unwelcome territory, to face the condemnation, the looks that said she wasn't good enough for their son.

Shaking off the memories, she climbed from her car. The neighborhood was quiet, the only sound the distant barking of dogs.

She opened the back door and retrieved a sign that read, 'Principal Rivers is a square.' Holding the sign up high, she walked back and forth in front of his house. A car cruised by, slowed, then moved on. Other than that, there was no activity, no one stirred.

She'd been marching for fifteen minutes— beginning to wonder why she was bothering, what if they never discovered she was protesting?—when the front door opened, and Mr. Rivers stormed down the porch stairs. Her stomach dipped, but she took a deep breath and squared her shoulders.

"What's the meaning of this?" Even in the semi-darkness, she could see the purple veins sticking out on his forehead. "You'd better get out of here, now! Before I call the police."

"I'm not doing anything wrong." She tried to prevent her voice from warbling. "I'm not even on your property."

He lifted his fist in the air. "I swear you'll be kicked off the alumni committee. I'll do everything in my power to make sure you pay for this, whatever way I can."

Without a word, she set the sign on the ground and picked up another that read, 'Rivers hates teenagers' and once more began marching along the sidewalk, ignoring Mr. Rivers. Although it wasn't easy to do, she blocked out his yelling and threats, and after a few moments, his front door slammed. Good. He'd gotten the message. She wasn't backing down.

Ten minutes later, a police cruiser pulled up and stopped by the curb. She chewed on the thumbnail of her free hand, waiting. She wasn't sure whether to feel relief or dread when Noah stepped out of the vehicle.

"What's going on, Toby?" He slowly walked toward her, arms crossed, his handsome face drawn into a scowl.

"Your father is a stubborn bully, and I'm protesting. I would think it's pretty obvious."

"Yes, I know what you're doing, what I want to know is why?"

"Why? Because, he's got no good reason to forbid us from playing rock and roll. Not only do the kids deserve to have fun at the dance, Miss Murdock—" Her throat clogged and she swallowed back tears. "—

deserves a memorial. Your father doesn't even care. Apparently, neither do you."

Noah blew a breath out and rested his hands on his belt. "I do care, but this isn't the way to go about it."

"No? Then maybe you can tell me what is."

He shook his head. "I don't know exactly, but you're causing a disturbance, and I have to stop you."

"Stop me?" She halted and crossed her arms, the sign dangling from one hand. "Are you going to arrest me, Noah Rivers?"

He looked away, then at the ground and back up at her. "I don't think it will come to that. Just be a good girl and head on home."

"I'm not going anywhere. You'll have to arrest me." She met his gaze in challenge.

His golden brown eyes flickered with uncertainty, then with resolve that should have warned her. He took the sign from her hand and looped his arm around her waist, lifting her off the ground. She was pressed against his warm, strong body, and lost her breath. Tingly sensations moved through her lower belly.

"Noah! You put me down this instant. What do you think you're doing?"

He ignored her and carried her to his car. He opened the back door with the hand that held the sign and plopped her down on the back seat.

"You can't do this to me." She scrambled to get out, but he blocked her way. "I didn't break a law."

"We'll come get your car tomorrow when you've had a chance to come to your senses. I'm not taking you to jail, I'm taking you home."

"Then I'll call Daisy to pick me up, and we'll come back here and protest again."

He closed his eyes and leaned his head back, shaking his head. "Damn, stubborn…"

"That's right. I'm not giving up, so you can either arrest me, or leave me be. You're just like your father, thinking you can bully—"

With a growl of frustration, he took hold of her shoulders and hauled her from the car. His lips landed on hers, cutting off her gasp. He cupped a hand behind her head and pulled her to him. She went willingly, swept away in a fog of yearning.

Noah's tongue slid past her lips, and she clutched his shoulders, wanting to push away, but not having the strength. He slipped his hands beneath her blouse and caressed her lower back. With his warm hands against her skin, his hard body pressed to hers…all thoughts of protest fled, there was only this moment, this man she'd never stopped wanting.

With a groan, he pulled away. She bit back a cry of disappointment.

His voice husky, eyes heavy-lidded, he said, "I'm sorry. I shouldn't have done that."

She nodded and wiped her mouth. "It's okay. I guess it was the only way to shut me up."

His mouth curved in a wry grin. "Yeah, that's all it was. It had nothing to do with those kissable lips of yours, that soft as velvet skin. Or the hole that opened up in my heart the day you ended things." A dark look came over his face. "Go home, Toby." He heaved a sigh. "Or don't. Stay out here all night and drive my old man crazy for all I care. I'm done."

He set her on the street and shoved the sign in her hand, then climbed into his car and peeled away.

She stared after him, a cold, hard knot of sadness

settling in her chest. Noah was done with her. That was what she wanted, wasn't it? Then why did it feel like her heart was splintered into a million pieces?

Chapter Four

The following day at work, Toby was exhausted. Even though she'd shut down the protest and gone home after Noah left, she'd barely slept.

Her spirits lifted a little when Daisy came in and settled at a booth. Toby stood next to the table while her friend scrutinized her. "Geez. You look like hell."

"Yeah, I *feel* like hell." She rubbed the back of her hand across her forehead where a headache was pushing at her skull. "The usual?" Daisy always ordered a burger, fries, and an RC cola. She only ate half so she could keep her figure, but she wouldn't give up the food she loved.

"Yes, please."

Toby placed her order on the cook's wheel and poured a cola. When she returned to the table, Daisy grinned. "I heard what happened last night."

At first, she thought she meant the kiss, then realized that would be ridiculous. Noah definitely wouldn't tell anyone, and neither had she. Not even Daisy. "You mean the protest that went sour?"

"Yeah, that was a pretty brave thing to do."

Toby rolled her eyes. "Pretty stupid. And useless. We still can't play rock and roll. We've already had almost a hundred people request a refund."

"That stinks." Daisy slurped from the straw. "No other ideas?"

"Nothing. You have any?"

"Well…" She swirled her straw in the soda and shot Toby a look from beneath her lashes. "You could use your charm on Noah. Then maybe he can convince his dad to change his mind."

Charm Noah? Sure, the way he looked at her last night, she'd have more luck charming a snake. "I don't think that would work. Noah probably has no influence with his dad, and I certainly have no influence with him."

"Since when?"

Toby shrugged. "Listen, I need to get back to work. My shift's almost over, and I have to finish my side duties. We'll talk later, okay?"

"Sure. Later."

After work, Toby headed across the nearly deserted parking lot to her car. A breeze chilled her, and she closed her sweater more snugly, wishing she'd worn a coat. The night was still, thick with fog. She squinted, trying to peer through the darkness that was only slightly diminished by the street lights. She heard a sound like footsteps but didn't see the man until he was directly in front of her. A small yelp of fear escaped her, then she halted and brought a hand up to her chest. "Good grief, Wes, you scared the daylights out of me."

Wes shoved his hands in his jacket pockets and leaned against her car. "Oh yeah? Made your heart pound, did I?"

She was in no mood for his smarmy Casanova shtick. "Get out of my way."

"How about you make me?" He pushed off the Bel Air and stepped closer to her. "No steak knife this time, huh? No big bad ex-boyfriend cop either. Looks like you're kind of in a spot."

Her heart thudded in her ears. She glanced around the darkened parking lot. All alone. And Wes didn't look like he was messing around. His eyes held a feral gleam that was part satisfaction, part revenge. She'd known him for years, and never thought he would hurt anyone, even though he was a creep. But the look he gave her now told her he was capable of anything.

"Get lost, Wes. I mean it. I just want to go home."

"Oh, sure, you can go home, but not 'til I've had a little taste of what you've been sharing with Rivers. Your momma ain't nearly as stingy as you are. You just ask my old man."

Oh God. Her mother had screwed Wes's father? Nausea crawled to her throat. How many men in town *hadn't* she slept with?

She clenched her jaw and made her voice firm. "I don't give a damn who my mother fooled around with. I am *not* her, and if you don't get out of my way this instant, you'll regret it."

The smirky smile dropped off his face, and anger replaced it. "Who you think you're talking to, girlie?" He grabbed her forearms and jerked her to him. "I think it's time you learned a lesson you won't soon forget."

He smashed his lips on hers, then his tongue probed at her clenched mouth. She fought back bile. His kisses were nothing like Noah's. Wes's wet mouth disgusted her, where Noah's touch made her swoon. She pressed her palms against his shoulders and pushed, but he didn't back off. His breath sped up, and he panted into her mouth, his breath reeking of beer and onions. He grabbed a handful of her hair and jerked her head back, straining the tendons in her neck.

"No!" Her muffled scream against his mouth only seemed to incite him.

He gripped the front of her blouse and tugged. Buttons scattered, bouncing on the ground with tiny pings. Cool air hit her skin, and panic skittered through her blood. He was going to rape her...Noah wouldn't be her first. This jerk, this disgusting pig was going to take her virginity.

With an enraged cry, she shoved against him as hard as she could. He stumbled away, tripped, and slammed backward into the concrete. A sickening thud resounded in the darkness. Wes lay still.

"Oh God," she whimpered. "Wes?" She knelt beside him. "Wes, wake up!" She was afraid to touch him, in case he was... No, he couldn't be dead. But a stream of blood leaked out from beneath his head.

She shot to her feet and staggered back. "Help!" Her scream reverberated off the silent buildings. "Help! Help! Please, somebody help me!"

Holding the edges of her sweater over her torn blouse, she ran back to the diner, pounding on the locked door. "Mr. Winstead, it's me, Toby. Please. Open up."

The door opened and Winstead appeared, bushy gray eyebrows drawn together in a frown. He wiped his hands on his greasy apron. "What in Sam Hill's going on?"

"Call an ambulance. Wes is hurt."

"What happened?"

"He fell." No need to go into the entire story right now. "Just please, please, call for help."

"Sure, sure." He disappeared inside.

Toby's entire body trembled. She wrapped her

sweater tighter around her, but it didn't help. She was cold on the inside, deeply, thoroughly frozen.

Sirens sounded, and a police cruiser pulled up behind an ambulance. A part of her prayed that Noah would climb from the car, but the other part prayed he wouldn't. What would he think of her now? Now that she might have killed a man?

Relief swept through her when Officer Fullerman stepped out of the cruiser. Paramedics were tending to Wes, but Officer Fullerman strode over to her. "Toby? What happened?"

Tears chilled on her cheeks, and her words came out in a hiccupping sob. "He...he attacked me and I..." She drew in a shaky breath. "I only tried to get away from him, but when I pushed him, he...fell. Hard. His head hit the ground and...it sounded like..." She pressed her lips together and shook her head. "Like a watermelon bursting, and..." The trembles increased, and Officer Fullerman put his arm around her. "Oh, God. I think I killed him."

He glanced over to the ambulance, then led her to his car. "Let's get you somewhere warm. I'll take you down to the station so you can give your statement."

Toby nodded. Her teeth chattered so hard she could barely hear his words. She climbed into the car and prayed with all she was worth that Wes would be okay.

****

Noah wasn't at the station when she arrived. They gave her coffee and questioned her for hours. The officers were polite, but suspicion hovered in their eyes. And why not? She was a Lawson. No telling what she might be capable of.

Every five minutes, she asked for news of Wes's

condition. She finally learned that he was okay. His head required stitches, but there would be no lasting injuries. Her entire body sagged with relief. Regardless of what a creep Wes was, she couldn't live with herself if she'd killed him.

Officer Fullerman finally took her back to her car, advising her that pending an investigation, charges could possibly be filed. She was so bone weary, so emotionally drained, she couldn't bring herself to ask what he meant.

When she got home, she took one of her mother's sleeping pills, stripped her clothes off, and dropped into bed. Blissful sleep soon claimed her, but she was jerked out of it by a ringing phone. She blinked sleepily at the clock on her night stand. Nine a.m. Wow. She'd really been out of it.

She brushed hair back from her face and answered the phone.

"Miss Lawson, Principal Rivers here." Before she could form a response, he went on. "Your…escapades of last night have come to my attention."

Escapades? She'd nearly been raped, nearly put a man in the hospital. He made it sound like she'd been caught doing the Twist naked in the town square.

"I have contacted the board, and we are in agreement. You are off the committee. They left the final decision up to me. After this incident, you have no defense."

She sat up in bed, too numb to even decide how she felt about it. Still, she made a half-hearted attempt to state her case. "Last night wasn't my fault. Wes…attacked me and I—"

His gruff laugh cut her off in mid-sentence. "Please,

Miss. Lawson. We both know the kind of girl you are. Tramps are always found out in the end. Now the whole town knows, including my son. We've always known he was too good for you. Now he realizes it, too."

Her heart ached with hopelessness. He was right. Maybe this was best. She would never be free of her mother. She and Noah could never be together anyway. Who was she kidding? She was nothing like Miss Murdock. The woman deserved to be honored, but Toby wasn't the person to do it.

Chapter Five

Toby slept most of the day. When she finally dragged herself out of bed, she found her mother stretched out on the sofa, wearing a dingy pink bathrobe, a half empty vodka bottle dangling from her fingers.

"Hey, sugah." Constance often imagined herself as Scarlett O'Hara and an incongruous southern accent appeared. She attempted to rise, tottered, then finally struggled to a sitting position. "I thou-thought you were goin-ta sleep your life away."

Toby rubbed her hands over her face. "I wish I could."

"Ah, come now, surely it'sssnot all that bad."

"No? It's worse."

"Tell Momma all about it." She patted the cushion next to her and stretched her mouth into a drunken smile. If it was meant to be comforting, she'd supremely failed.

"No, thanks. I think I'll get out of here."

"And go where?"

"I don't know." Toby sniffed back tears that threatened to surface. "I just need to go…somewhere."

She called Daisy and asked if she wanted to go out. Her friend readily agreed and said she'd be there in an hour.

Toby went upstairs and showered, then dressed in a tight-fitting black cocktail dress. She smoothed stockings on and slipped her feet into high heels, fluffed her hair around her shoulders, applied eyeliner and dark red lipstick, and headed down.

Daisy showed up a few minutes later, and Toby climbed in beside her in the red Ford convertible.

"Where to?" Daisy asked. She wore a form fitting silver dress with matching pumps. Her hair was pulled back at the temples in glittering pins, with the ends hanging in fat curls.

"Let's go to Blue Moon."

Her pink-painted lips pulled down at the corners. "Blue Moon? But you don't drink."

"I do tonight."

"What's going on, hon?"

Toby told her what had happened, from her encounter with Wes, to the conversation with Mr. Rivers.

"Oh my God, you poor thing." Anger shook her voice. "That…jerk, that creep, that…*asshole*. I'm glad you hurt him."

"I almost killed him."

"Ha! That's what he deserved." She fell silent for a few moments as she navigated the streets. "No doubt you've had a rough couple of days, but do you think going out and getting smashed is the answer?"

Toby closed her eyes and rubbed her thumb on her forehead. "I'm not looking for answers. I just want to forget. Even for a little while."

"All right, then. I'm with you."

In moments, they were pulling into the parking lot of the club. Jazz music reached her ears before they made it to the door. Inside, loud laughter rose. The cigarette smoke was so thick, she could only see silhouettes of people. A moment's indecision made her pause. The place was dark, loud, crowded. She drew in a deep breath. Exactly what she needed to escape.

Daisy took her hand and led her between tables to a bar. Liquor bottles of all hues and designs lined the shelves. The bartender was a guy with reddish brown hair and black-framed glasses. He looked to be a few years older than she and Daisy. He leaned his hands on the bar. "Hey, Daisy, who's the knockout?"

Toby flushed with discomfort, yet, the compliment bolstered her ego. He hadn't said it in a smarmy way that made her want to take a shower, like Wes did. Somehow, it came out polite and kind of naughty in a good way.

"Cotton, this is my best friend, Toby. She's a novice, so set her up with something mild."

"Sure, darlin'. The usual for you?" At Daisy's nod, he grabbed a bottle of whiskey and poured it into a glass, added a shot of coke, and slid the drink to her. "Now for you, honey, something sweet, like you." He moved so quickly, Toby could barely keep track, but he poured rum, a few juices, and some pink liquid in a tall glass, added a slice of orange, and set the concoction in front of her. "Planter's Punch. It has a kick, but the juices hide the liquor taste."

She took a cautious sip. When the sweet, tangy liquid hit her tongue, she nearly moaned in delight. "Delicious! Thank you."

They hadn't been there five minutes when a man asked Daisy to dance. She followed him out to the floor. Toby watched them with a smile. Daisy was a great dancer. The two of them looked like Fred Astaire and Ginger Rogers. They started another dance just as Toby finished the punch, and Cotton made her another. Her limbs had started to relax, and her brain felt a little like the bartender's name, cotton. She liked it that way. She wasn't worrying about Noah or her future or how badly she'd let Miss Murdock down. She was in the now, and it was exactly where she needed to be—no past, no future.

A middle-aged man wearing a blue suit with a bow tie asked her to dance, and she slid from the barstool and took his hand. They swing danced to "In the Mood", and by the time the song ended, she was breathless—and elated. Excitement pumped through her blood. Look at what she'd been missing! Not any longer. She hadn't been this carefree in...well, never.

Half way through her third cocktail, she leaned over and yelled into Daisy's ear, "They got any rock and roll in this joint?"

She flinched and laughed. "Hey, you don't need to shout when you're right in my ear. I'll go play some. Hang on." She wove through the crowd and returned a few moments later. "Should be starting soon. Are you having fun?"

"A blast."

"I'm glad, but you might want to take it easy on the booze. You're not used to drinking. It can really put you under the first time."

"I'm jushh—" Toby halted, swallowed, enunciated carefully, "Just fine."

"All the same, maybe you shouldn't have any more."

She opened her mouth to respond when "That'll be the Day" by Buddy Holly played. "Oh my God, I love this song!" She jumped from the barstool. Dizziness swam through her head, and she nearly lost her balance. She grabbed the edge of the bar until she was steady. "Let's dance." She tugged Daisy out on the floor with her. They were soon joined by several others, and the floor became packed with bodies. After that song ended, "Shake, Rattle, and Roll" by Elvis started. Adrenaline shot through her, and she whooped loudly.

"This is a total blast!" she shouted to Daisy.

A man grabbed Toby around the waist and danced with his body pressed to hers. Even in her happy daze, it felt…nauseating, but she wasn't going to spoil this night by making a scene.

Daisy took hold of her arm. "Come on, I think it's time to go now."

Toby tugged out of her grip. "Go? No way. I'm having the time of my life."

"Yeah, but things are getting a little too wild for your first time out. We need to call it a night."

Toby poked a finger in her chest. "*You* call it a night, and I'll get a ride home."

"I'm not—"

Toby shut her out and continued dancing. She wasn't sure how many songs had played before she became aware of wooziness crowding her brain. She squinted and glanced around the bar. No sign of Daisy. Had she really left?

Oh well, Toby had told her to. To hell with her and everyone else. She didn't need anyone. She had Elvis and Planter's Punch and a ton of new friends.

"I Was the One" by Elvis started, and one of the men took her hand and pulled her into a slow dance. He bent his head, and his mouth landed on hers. She frowned, not liking the way his lips felt. He was a stranger, and he was…*gross*. She was about to pull back when a hand landed on her arm.

"Toby? What the hell are you doing?"

Noah? Oh God. She pushed her dance partner away, He frowned and seemed about to say something, then looked over his shoulder. Shaking his head, he disappeared into the crowd. She turned to find Noah, his eyes blazing with anger, staring down at her.

Although relieved he'd rescued her, she wasn't going to let him know that. "What am *I* doing? What are *you*?" The words seemed to be missing something. She frowned, searching her brain. *Oh yeah…* "doing here, I mean."

"Daisy called me, and it's a good thing she did. Come on, I'm getting you out of here." He took hold of her hand and tugged.

"She-she's s'pose to be my friend. She'sa traitor, a Judas, a Benedict. Wait 'til I see her…" Toby continued to mumble while Noah pulled her through the crowd.

Wait a minute. Who did he think he was? She dug her heels in and stopped. Noah halted too, turning back to her with a deeper scowl than the one he'd worn before. "Come on, we're getting out of here."

"Nope. I'm not done having fun. I want to dance." She stepped toward him and looped her arms around his neck. A slow song she didn't recognize was playing. "Dance with me, Noah."

A muscle ticked in his jaw. His body was warm against hers, and she thought she detected a slight hitch to his breath. "I need to get you home." His voice had lowered so much it was barely audible, but she heard him.

"Not quite yet." Being held in his arms felt

so…right…so perfect. Even though her senses were dulled by the alcohol, she could easily detect the difference in dancing with him and dancing with strangers. Her heart thudded hard, and she stared into his amber eyes. "Kiss me."

He squeezed his eyes shut for a moment, then opened them. His muscles tightened beneath her hands. He took hold of her arms and pried them from his neck. "I'm getting you home," he said in a voice that sounded unsteady.

She stood on her tiptoes and plastered her mouth and body to his. He tensed and tried to pull back, but she gripped the back of his head with her hands and pressed harder against his lips. A few catcalls and whistles barely penetrated her consciousness. This was *Noah*. This was right.

She sensed when his body relaxed, and he returned the kiss. His hands slipped down to her hips and pulled her tighter to him. He deepened the kiss, probing her lips with his tongue. She opened for him, and his tongue searched the recesses of her mouth. Heaven, pure Heaven…

An ugly thought intruded on her ecstasy…had it been like this with her mother? Resentment penetrated her fog of euphoria, and she tugged away long enough to murmur, "Who kisses better? Me or my mother?"

He blinked as if not sure what he'd heard. Then, a hard look came into his eyes, and he set her from him with a not-so-gentle shove. "What the…? I should just leave your ass right here. It would serve you right."

She ran her nail along his cheek. "Ah, come on, Noah. You wouldn't do that to me, would you? How about you and I go somewhere private and finish what we started at Make Out Point? We're grownups now. No reason to hold off."

He raked a hand through his hair and shook his head. "Good God, Toby, what's gotten into you?"

"What's the matter?" Unexpectedly, a sob rose to her chest. She suddenly wasn't happy anymore. She was deeply, thoroughly sad. "I thought men liked tramps."

His expression softened, and he gave her a tender smile. "You're not a tramp, Toby. For God's sake, your mother really did a number on you." A dark look crossed his face. "And that bastard, Wes... I wanted to kill him when I found out what he tried to do to you. Don't let a scumbag like that make you feel bad about yourself. Other people might hold your mother's reputation against you, but not me. I know the real you."

Easy for him to say, but he didn't walk in her shoes, didn't suffer the ridicule, the shame of being Constance Lawson's daughter.

She sighed and lifted a hand to brush the hair out of her face. His rejection might sting tomorrow, once she sobered up, but for now, she was spent. She just wanted to crawl into bed and pull the covers over her head. Sleep for a week.

"Please take me home," she whispered.

She barely remembered the drive. Noah took her key and opened her front door. Her mother was in the living room. She jumped to her feet and rushed over to them. "Where on Earth have you been? It's two in the morning. I was worried sick."

Maybe it was just because of Toby's own inebriated state, but she seemed...sober.

"I just went..." She had no energy to even finish the sentence. The room spun, and she was afraid she would be sick if she didn't lie down soon.

"Come on, honey. I'll get you to bed." Noah threw a glance over his shoulder at her mother. "I need to talk to you before I go."

A twinge of worry that they would do more than talk arose, then she had no thoughts at all. Only the feel of Noah's arms beneath her shoulders and knees when he lifted her and carried her up the stairs, tucked her into her big soft bed, laid a feather light kiss on her forehead, turned out the light…

****

"Sugah, are you awake?"

Someone had packed Toby's head with cement and was using a jack hammer to drill through it. Her mouth was filled with sand, and her stomach roiled. She blinked her eyes open. Her mother sat on the edge of the bed, wearing a tailored suit, matching beret, and gloves. Toby hadn't seen her this together in years. Her hazel eyes were clear. Sober again?

As shocking as the knowledge was, she felt too lousy to care. She groaned and closed her eyes, tugging the covers over her head.

"Come on, now. We need to get you up and about."

"I'm dying," she mumbled into the pillow.

Her mother's light laughter tinkled through the air. "Don't be silly. You just *feel* like you're dying. Wish you *could* die. Welcome to your first hangover." She patted Toby's arm. "Come on, sit up. Drink this."

"I'll never drink anything again."

"This will help, I promise."

Toby moved the pillow aside and sat up. The room spun, and she closed her eyes.

"Don't do that. Closing your eyes only makes it

171

worse." She thrust two aspirin and a glass toward her. "Here you go. I have some dry toast for you, too. You need something on your tummy."

Toby took the aspirin and red liquid and brought the glass to her nose. The smell of pepper sauce and tomato juice assaulted her nostrils. She frowned, but popped the aspirin in her mouth and turned the glass up, draining the contents. A slimy, odd taste mingled with the spicy liquid. She shuddered. "What's in that?"

"A few special ingredients, among them, a raw egg."

She coughed, almost retching, and shuddered. "Disgusting."

"It's good for you. Eat this and hop in the shower." She picked a saucer up from the nightstand that held two pieces of dry toast.

"Why can't I just stay in bed all day?"

"Because, we have something to take care of. If it works, it will be better than any hangover cure in the world."

Toby's head was still foggy, but even if it hadn't been, she was sure she wouldn't understand her meaning. She choked down as much of the toast as she could, then took a shower. The water revived her some, but she still wanted to die.

She sat in silence while her mother drove. How long had it been since her mom had been sober enough to get behind the wheel?

Toby studied her calm, confident demeanor. "Mom, what's going on? You're...different this morning."

She was silent for several moments, then said, "I suppose I am." A small secret smile touched her mouth. "We'll talk about that later. Right now, we have business to transact."

She slowed the car at the school and turned into the lot.

"What are we doing here? I can't go in there."

"You can, and you will. Trust me."

Toby let out a long, put-upon sigh and followed her into the school building. Her mother's heels clacked on the floor, echoing in the silence. Class was in session, and the halls were deserted. She stopped at Principal Rivers' office and went inside. Dread pooled in Toby's stomach, but she didn't speak. Constance was a woman on a mission and apparently wouldn't be swayed.

"We're here to see Daniel," she told the secretary.

Toby flinched at her use of his first name. Georgia frowned. "One moment please." She picked up the receiver. "Mr. Rivers, Toby Lawson and her mother are here to see you." She listened for a moment. "Yes, sir."

She hung up and plastered a professional smile on her face. "I'm afraid he can't see you right now, but if you would like to make an appointment, I can try to schedule you in."

Constance smiled. "Tell him to check his calendar one more time. If he can't see us now, we'll drop by his *home* this evening to speak with him."

Georgia tightened her lips, but made the call. In moments, Mr. Rivers' office door swung open. Scowling, he motioned them inside. He didn't offer them a seat, and he didn't take one himself. "What's the meaning of this?"

Constance crossed her arms and smiled. "I'll make this short, Daniel. You've been ramrodding and treating my daughter shabbily for too long. You treat her like some piece of…trash. Much like you did me, but she's not like me. And you of all people should know that."

His scowl deepened. "I'm sure I don't know what you mean."

"Oh, I'm sure you do. After all, you have...*intimate* knowledge of me. If you don't back off now, reinstate her to the committee, and approve her application, I'll tell everyone about our little rendezvous last year when your wife and daughter went to visit her sick mother. By everyone, I mean I'll start with Mrs. Rivers."

His face reddened. "You—that's a lie. No one would ever believe it."

"No? If I'm lying, how would I know exactly what the inside of your bedroom looks like? And how would I know about that birthmark on the inside of your upper thigh." She turned to Toby. "Does Noah have a birthmark like his father?"

Toby's face burned. "I—I don't know."

"Well, anyway." She turned back to Mr. Rivers. "I'm sure you understand the position you're in. I suggest you act quickly. You have until five o'clock to make all this go away and confirm the dance is still on." She sauntered to the door, and Toby followed. With a hand on the knob, Constance paused, turned back to Mr. Rivers, and winked. "Tick tock, darling."

They headed to the car, Toby's mind whirling with what she'd just witnessed—what she'd heard. Her mother had been...intimate with Noah's father? For cripe's sake, what wouldn't she do? Toby tried to be angry at her, but she was so pleased at what she'd done, she couldn't even work up irritation.

"Thank you," she said once they were in the car. "I—I can't believe you did that for me."

She gave a wry chuckle. "Oh trust me, sweetheart, I

owe you much more than that."

"What…what brought that on?"

"You can thank young Noah. After he put you to bed last night, he read me the riot act."

"Noah did that?"

"He did. He said, 'Between you and my father, you're wrecking her life. And the sad part is, you don't give a damn any more than he does.'"

Toby cringed. Noah had really let her have it. "I'm sorry." She really wasn't, but felt she should say it.

"Don't be. I deserved it. He was wrong about one thing. I do care, but he made me realize I haven't shown that I do. Not in years, and that's so unfair to you." She put a cool, soft hand on Toby's cheek. "You are the best daughter a mother could have, and I've been just horrible. I've made a mess of being a mother. I've left you to your own. You've had to take care of *me*."

"You haven't been that bad."

She smiled. "If I'd been the mother I should have, I'd have taught you not to lie, but you just told a whopper."

Toby laughed. "Well, maybe I did stretch the truth."

"You're so smart, so strong. But you're compassionate, too. I don't want you to end up like me." She gave a small, humorless chuckle, and her eyes took on a faraway expression. "I wasn't always like this, though. I was once a lot like you, except not nearly as brave. But I had a good heart. I was happy, and I tried to make others happy, too. After your father passed away, I was a wreck. Nothing else seemed to matter, and it should have, because I had a wonderful, beautiful daughter who needed me. But I was so focused on my own pain, that I failed to consider yours." She wiped tears from her eyes with a handkerchief. "I went to pieces when I lost the love of my life. Don't let that happen to you. Hold on to Noah with all your might."

She shook her head. "No, we can never—"

"Never say never, darling." She took Toby's hands and squeezed. "Listen to me carefully. I had no choice in losing the man I loved. You do. The only way you could possibly end up like me is if you're foolish enough to let love pass you by. And if I know my daughter, you're not that foolish."

Chapter Six

The week leading up to the dance was so busy, Toby barely had time to do anything except work and prepare for the event. But in the back of her mind, her mother's words kept pushing through. Would she really end up like Constance if she lost Noah? No, that was ridiculous. Like she said, Toby was stronger than she was. Although, she was starting to wonder why she was fighting her feelings so hard. Noah hadn't done anything with her mother. Constance had initiated it. But how could she really be sure it had all been one-sided? He was a man, after all, and apparently her mother could have just about any man she wanted.

Did that include Noah?

Toby shook her head. No time to dwell on that. The dance started in an hour, and she had to arrive early to make sure the DJ was there and everything was ready to go. The hall was ablaze with lights and inside, crepe paper in black, red, and white draped from the ceiling and adorned the columns. Balloons floated loose over the large dance floor. On the walls were posters of Elvis, Jerry Lee Lewis, Buddy Holly, Little Richard, and other rock and roll singers. Blue paper cut in the shape of guitars and drum sets were scattered between the posters. Blanche and Suzette had done a phenomenal job on the decorations.

A portrait of Miss Murdock rested on an easel next

to the DJ booth. Her kind eyes smiled from the canvas, and a lump rose to Toby's throat. Cal Megalorn was in place, wearing headphones. He was a local radio disc jockey who'd been Miss Murdock's student, and he'd volunteered to spin records for the dance.

At seven sharp, the doors opened and ticket holders poured into the concert hall. Music and laughter rose around Toby, and her heart swelled with pride. Miss Murdock would have been thrilled at the turnout.

Cal's voice came over the mic when "The Wanderer" ended. "Welcome, ladies and gents. Tonight is about having a ball, but it's also about honoring a special lady. Florence Murdock was an angel with a heart of gold and a fist of iron. I'm sure she touched most of the lives in here tonight. I'd like to thank the committee for the fine work they did in putting this shindig together. Here's a song I'm sending out to Miss Murdock. She will forever be missed."

He played "Special Angel." Although Toby tried not to cry, tears welled in her eyes. Her heart was heavy with sadness over losing Miss Murdock, but she took comfort in the thought that she was watching from Heaven, and found the homage fitting.

The crowd livened up when Cal played more upbeat music following his tribute song. Toby poured a cup of punch and tamped down the urge to join the people on the dance floor.

She was taking a sip of her drink when she spotted Noah. He headed toward her, wearing a black suit with satin lapels and a gray shirt with a narrow black tie. His dark hair had grown out some from his military cut, and he looked…dreamy.

She gulped the punch to wet her dry mouth.

"Hi, Toby." His low, husky tone caressed her. "You look beautiful."

She wore a silky beaded white dress with her hair piled atop her head and ringlets hanging down at her ears. When Noah looked at her that way, she *felt* beautiful.

"Thank you. You look nice, too." She was proud of the strength of her voice when her insides were quivering.

"I've requested a song from Cal. When it plays, you're dancing with me."

She opened her mouth to protest his presumptuous attitude, but there was nothing she wanted more at that moment than to be in his arms, regardless of how he'd asked her—or what song was playing.

A teasing light came into his eyes. "What? No indignation? No tongue-lashing?"

She shrugged, trying to play it casual. "It's a dance, after all. I suppose we're expected to dance."

"Playing for Keeps" started, and Elvis' rich, magical voice permeated her heart, her soul.

Noah held out his hand. "May I have this dance?"

She couldn't speak, could only move into the circle of his arms, melt against him as they glided across the dance floor. The crowd faded away. Noah's chest against her ear, his hand searing the skin on her lower back, were all that she was aware of.

She thought she felt his lips on her hairline, felt him place a gentle kiss there, but she couldn't be sure. Everything was surreal; she didn't know what was true and what was fantasy. She only knew that she never wanted the moment to end.

Noah's lips moved from her hairline to her cheek.

He whispered into her ear, "I'm playing for keeps, too, Toby. I'll never stop loving you. Not even when I take my last breath."

Her heart squeezed. Chills moved over her skin. This was heavenly, *he* was heavenly, and she'd been such a fool. Nothing could ever replace the way he made her feel. She was alive, fulfilled when she was with him. Although she wasn't necessarily happy around him all the time, even when she was angry or sad, she was *content*. Whole.

Did she want to risk losing that when she was certain she could never find it with another guy?

She pulled back and looked up at him. She opened her mouth, thinking she was going to confess her love. Instead, she heard herself say, "Your father hates me."

His jaw clenched, and he shook his head. "Another excuse? Are you for real? I don't care what my father thinks. And you can't hold what happened with your mother against me. You know it wasn't my fault. That's not even the real reason you're resisting your feelings. You're just scared."

The song ended, and Noah took hold of her hand, pulling her through the crowd and into the evening air.

"Noah, we can't. I have to stay for the—"

"This is it. I meant what I said, I will love you until my last breath, but I can't keep beating my head against a wall. Do you love me or am I just wasting my time?"

She did love him, so why did the words freeze up in her vocal cords? He was right. She was afraid. She'd been holding onto the excuse that she couldn't get past his kissing her mother, but the truth was, she was afraid she wasn't good enough for him. And if she gave their love a chance, he'd realize it, too.

She'd been quiet for several moments, and he finally shook his head and released her. "I guess that's all the answer I need." He took a step back, then waited. He was still giving her a chance, even after as stubborn as she'd been.

Tell him. Just tell him you don't want to lose him. You can figure the rest out later…

"Excuse me, Toby?" She turned toward the shaky, male voice and found Johnny standing behind her. "Uh, I'm sorry, but…there's been a fire. It's your house."

Panic nearly drove her to her knees. "Oh, God. My mother…she's at home…" She must be drinking again. She'd gone to sleep with a lit cigarette like before. Sirens wailed in the distance.

"Come on." Noah put his hand on her back and hurried her to his car. She shook so badly her teeth chattered. "Don't worry," he soothed. "She's okay, I'm sure of it." His words were meant to be reassuring, but she heard the underlying alarm.

Toby wanted to scream, "How can you be sure?" But her throat closed and no words would come, just a clog of tears trying to escape into sobs.

Noah sped to her house and screeched to a stop at the curb. Fire trucks were there, spraying water from hoses in large streams, but orange-yellow flames climbed from the roof into the night sky.

Toby fumbled for the door handle and nearly fell from the car before Noah could come around and help her out.

"Where's my mother?" she shouted, finally finding her voice.

No one paid attention to her. Noah rushed over to a fireman and grabbed his arm. "There was a lady in the house. Where is she?"

He frowned. "A lady? We didn't think anyone was home."

"Oh God." A tortured scream tore from Toby, and she ran toward the front door. Noah caught up to her and pushed her back.

"I'll go in. You stay here."

"No, don't you see, I have to—"

He gripped her shoulders and shook her, hard. "If she's in there, I can get her out much easier than you can. And I don't want to have to rescue you both. Got it?"

She hesitated for a split second, then nodded.

Noah started toward the door, and one of the firemen rushed up to him. "Sir, you can't go in there. We've sent one of our guys to look for the occupant." Noah turned to him. "Oh, it's you, Rivers. Still, you need to stay back."

"I know the layout of the house." Noah spoke briskly, still heading for the door. "I'm going in."

The fireman followed him and yanked off his jacket and helmet. "Then at least put these on."

Noah did, running as he donned them. Toby's heart filled with terror as he entered the inferno. The smell of smoke filtered through the air and ashy cinders flew from the house. Some landed on her face, but she was barely aware. She clasped her fingers together beneath her chin, praying with all her might that Noah and her mother would be all right.

All those times she'd had the horrible thought that her life would be easier if her mom died. And now, the thought of losing her was unbearable, devastating. She had to be okay. *Please, God, please let her be okay.*

It seemed like eons, but was probably less than a minute when a figure stumbled out of the front door. Noah...and he held her mother in his arms. A fireman followed behind.

Toby ran toward them, tears streaming down her face. Before she could reach them, a burly fireman grabbed her and held her back.

"Please." She tried to pull away from the steel grip. "That's my mother. Please, I have to see if she's okay."

A paramedic rushed over with a gurney. Noah settled Constance onto it, and the paramedic placed a mask over her face. Her eyes were closed. Black streaks marred her pale skin. She looked so...still.

"Mommy!" Toby screamed and fought harder to break loose. "Please, let me go to her." She kicked the fireman in the leg. He let out a surprised yelp, and she was free. She rushed to her mother. The paramedic was rolling her toward the ambulance. "Is she okay?" Fear nearly choked off the words. "Is she *alive*?"

The paramedic flicked a quick glance at Toby over his shoulder. "She's alive. She took in a lot of smoke and suffered some burns. Beyond that, we can't tell until we get her to the hospital. We'll do everything we can to help her."

Strong arms snaked around her. Without turning, she knew it was Noah. "She—she could die," Toby whimpered.

"She's not going to. Come on, I'll take you to the hospital."

Toby nodded, dazedly stumbling beside Noah—praying that her ghastly thoughts of the past wouldn't come true—that her mother wouldn't die.

****

The waiting room at the hospital was nearly empty. Other than she and Noah, only a handful of people occupied the plastic chairs.

They waited in silence for the doctor. It had been half an hour according to Toby's wrist watch, but each second dragged by in agonizing slowness. Noah's comforting hand on her back had kept her grounded. He'd murmured a few placating words, but nothing had really registered—nothing other than his warm, soothing touch.

When footsteps sounded on the linoleum floor, she snapped her head up to find the doctor entering the waiting room. She jumped to her feet and rushed over to him. Noah followed.

"How is she?"

The doctor's grim expression sent icy fear shooting through her veins.

"She inhaled a lot of smoke, but we've been giving her breathing treatments, and we're hoping there will not be any lasting lung damage." He put his hands in the pockets of his white coat. "She suffered second degree burns. If they hadn't found her when they did, she likely wouldn't be with us."

Toby glanced over her shoulder at Noah, her heart swelling with love. He'd saved her mother's life. She gave him a small smile of gratitude and turned back to the doctor.

"When can I see her?"

"She asked for a...Toby?" He glanced around the waiting room. "Do you know the young man?"

In spite of her worry, she had to smile. "I'm Toby."

He chuckled. "Oh, well, pardon me. Yes, you can see her. But please only stay a few moments. She's down the hall in room three-twenty-three." The doctor smiled, and she thanked him.

"Want me to go with you?" Noah offered, his voice low.

She shook her head. "No, thank you." He squeezed her hand and gave her a reassuring nod.

Toby walked down the hallway, her legs quivering. She paused outside her mother's room, took a deep breath, then pushed the door open.

Her heart sank to her stomach, and she couldn't control the cry that escaped when she saw her mother lying in the bed. Her skin was ashen, her eyes closed, and white bandages nearly covered her forehead and arms.

"Mom?" Toby ventured, not wanting to wake her if she was sleeping.

Constance turned her head, opened her eyes, and smiled. "Hi," she rasped out.

She moved quickly to the bed and laid a gentle hand on the blanket covering her mother. "Hi yourself. How are you feeling?"

"Nothing that a…stiff drink won't fix." She gave a hoarse chuckle.

Toby forced a smile. "That's probably the last thing you need."

"You're probably right. Maybe just water. Can you get it for me?"

She took the blue plastic pitcher from her bed table and poured water into the matching cup. "Here."

Constance drank, then let her head fall back on the pillow.

"Better." Her voice was clearer, but a slight roughness remained. "I'm so sorry, darling."

"Sorry?"

"The fire was my fault. I—I did a careless thing, and your young man risked his life to save me."

"Oh, Mom. I'm just glad you're okay. I thought—for a minute there, I thought—"

"That I'd died?" Tears filled her eyes. "Wouldn't you be better off if I had?"

Hearing her mother echo the same thought she'd had more than once sent remorse through her. God, what if she'd lost her? How would she have lived with herself?

"No, no I wouldn't have been better off." The words ended on a sob. "I love you. So much."

"Still? After all I've done?"

"Of course I do."

"I love you too, baby girl." She rested her hand on Toby's. "Is Noah here?"

"Yes, he's in the waiting room."

"Would you tell him thank you for me?"

"Sure I will."

"And one more thing…tell him you love him. That you don't want to lose him."

Toby grimaced. "I'm not sure if Noah will still want me."

"Honey, that man will never stop wanting you. Go to him. You two need to go on with your lives and stop worrying about me."

Toby raised her brows. "Stop worrying about you? After tonight?" She wasn't yet sure how much damage had been done to the house, but she knew it was unlivable at the moment. But the worst part was, people could have died…namely her mother and Noah.

Constance waved her free hand dismissively. "Oh, I

know I set fire to our house, but what I mean is, I won't be alone."

"You won't?"

She shook her head. "I've been seeing someone. He wants to marry me."

"Seeing? Who?"

"Butch Markham."

"What? Wes's father?" Wes had mentioned the two of them sleeping together, and Toby had only half believed him, but marriage? "You're marrying Wesley Markham's father?"

"I am. He's a good man. Good for me. And he loves me very much. Has for years."

"Oh no." She dropped her head into her hands. "Wes Markham is going to be my step-brother?" She wanted to say, *did you know he tried to rape me?* But her mother had been through enough tonight.

"Oh, don't you worry about Wes. His father is making him go into the military."

"Making him? Wes is a grown man."

"Yes, but Butch threatened to cut him off if he didn't join. He said Wes needed discipline that he could never give him. The man was widowed when Wes was a baby, and he indulged him his whole life."

"Well, I'm not sure if the military can make a changed man of him, but at least we'll be rid of him for a few years."

She laughed. "Indeed." Just as quickly, she sobered. "Do one thing for me. Promise me that you'll be happy. That you won't let my awful mistakes keep you from the joy you deserve."

"Sure, I promise." She placed a gentle kiss on her mother's forehead. "Get some rest. I'll be in to check on you later."

Toby let herself out and headed down the hall to the waiting room. Now that she had seen her mother, now that she knew she was going to be okay, she had something else to take care of—begging Noah to forgive her and telling him she loved him.

But what if, between her failure to confess her love for him, and her mother's last stunt, he'd decided to wash his hands of her drama-filled life?

She let out a sigh and pushed the thoughts from her mind. She wouldn't know until she spoke with Noah. No sense dwelling on the worst case scenario—a lonely life without the only man she could imagine ever loving.

****

When Toby entered the waiting room, she found Noah sitting in one of the small plastic chairs, his long legs stretched out before him, a copy of *Look* Magazine in his hands. He glanced up and tossed the magazine aside. "How's your mom?"

"She's good. She's going to be fine. She said to tell you thank you. And I want to thank you, too. What you did was really brave."

He shrugged. "No thanks necessary. I'm just glad she's okay." He stood and stretched. "Listen, I'm beat. Are you going to stick around for a while, or do you need me to run you to get your car?"

Dread settled in her chest. He seemed so...distant. "Actually, can you stay for...just a little while? I wanted to talk to you."

"Sure, what about?"

She glanced around at the curious gazes pointed in their direction. "Can we go outside?"

He nodded and led her out the emergency room

doors. The night air held a hint of rain, and she took a deep breath of the refreshing scent, trying to steel her resolve. Nerves settled in the pit of her stomach. She chewed on her thumbnail as she searched for words.

"Toby?" His voice was soft. "What is it?"

She raised her head. Her heart gave a little skip when she looked into his golden-brown eyes. "I know that you've given up on me. I don't blame you, but please hear me out."

He narrowed his eyes, but didn't speak.

"I realize I've been stubborn, and unfair, and—"

"Pig-headed?" he supplied.

She gave him an irritated frown. "That means the same as stubborn. Anyway, yes, I've been all those things. I shouldn't have rejected you…your love. I was just so confused, so hurt. But then…when I saw you run into that burning house…" Her breath caught on a sob. "You risked your life to save Mom. You could have died."

He shrugged. "But I didn't."

The remembered panic filled her again. "I couldn't stand the thought of losing you…forever. You were right, rather than being angry or mistrustful because I saw you with my mother, I was frightened. I was afraid I would be just like her, and you would figure that out, then you wouldn't want me anymore."

He crossed his arms and narrowed his eyes. "Why would you think you're like your mother?"

"Because, I…" She shrugged. "That night at Make Out Point, I wanted to…have…" She paused, her face heating. "Well, you know."

"You wanted to make love with me."

His quiet words sent a rush of warmth through her

veins. "Yes," she whispered. "You were the one who…who put a stop to it. I was loose and easy. I—"

"Loose and easy mean the same thing."

She shot him a glare. His lips twitched in amusement.

"You're not making this very easy for me," she snapped.

"Well, maybe you should get to the point."

"The point is, only a…bad girl…would do that. If I'm not like my mother, then why was I ready to give you my…"

"Virginity?"

She nodded and dropped her gaze.

He tucked a finger beneath her chin and lifted until she was looking at him. "Why did you want to make love with me?"

A quiver ran through her chest and settled in her lower belly. "Uh…why? Because, I'm a tramp."

"How many other guys have you made out with, wanted to sleep with?"

She frowned. "None. Just you.

"Why?"

"I-I don't know."

"Yes, you do. Is it really because you're a tramp? You have no feelings for me? You would have sex with just anyone?"

"No, no. of course I wouldn't."

"Then why?"

"Because…" She squeezed her eyes shut briefly, then opened them. Now was the time. She was tired of holding back. "Because I love you. I've always loved you."

A smile lit his face. "And you're not a tramp."

She smiled back. "And I'm not a tramp."

"That's more like it." He tugged her to him, and his firm lips found hers in a mind-drugging kiss. Desire stole through her limbs. Heat settled low in her belly. She looped her arms around his neck and returned the kiss, moaning a sigh of pleasure. He lifted his mouth only slightly. His gaze was hooded, the gold of his eyes turning to a rich amber. "You know, I took in some smoke myself. I'm feeling a little weak. You could easily take advantage of me."

She laughed, and just like that, the loneliness lifted from her soul. "You think I'm going to take advantage of a wounded hero? Is that what you want?"

He gave her a devilish wink. "I was hoping." His expression turned serious. "What I want, all I've ever wanted, is to marry you."

She closed her eyes momentarily, basking in the joy of hearing those words from Noah. He wanted to marry her...even after all they'd been through. "Oh, Noah, I want that too, but I need to finish college. I want to be a teacher. I can't let that go."

"Then you can finish school while we're married. I'll help you. Or we'll get married after you finish. I'll wait. I will do anything you want me to. Anything except walk away."

As wonderful as being Noah's wife sounded, was she really the kind of woman who could make him happy? "I want this, so much. But..." She shook her head. "What kind of wife would I make? Look at where I come from."

He cupped her face in his hands and planted a deep, warm kiss on her lips, then pulled away, still holding onto her. He took her hand and wrapped it in his, placed it on his chest. Through the material of his shirt, heat radiated to her skin. "It doesn't matter where you come from." He slid her hand until it was over his heart. "This is where you are now."

Truly Madly

by

Alicia Dean

Dedication

To Ruth and Sheri,
my wonderful sisters who have always stood by me.
And to J, for her tireless dedication to
making my stories better.

Chapter One

"I heard that after Daniel Connelly killed his wife, he wrote her name in blood on the wall. Then, he shot himself."

"The way I heard it, he wrote the name of her *lover* in her blood."

The voices came from the next aisle over, but they were increasing in volume, getting closer. I froze, my face burning with mortification and rage. They were talking about me, or rather, about my parents.

I recognized Deanna Summers' voice, but I couldn't identify her companion. I closed my eyes, willing their hateful voices away. When I opened them, the cashier at Truelove's Grocery, Brandon, was looking at me, his kind, brown eyes sympathetic.

Although it made me feel mean and small, I hated the pity almost as much as the gossip.

"You know," Deanna continued, "Carmen, Isabelle's sister, is locked up in some crazy hospital out in California."

The two women rounded the aisle then faltered when they saw me standing at the counter. I recognized the woman Deanna was with as Mindy Crawford, the librarian. Mindy had the decency to look ashamed; Deanna only gave me a self-satisfied smile.

"Brandon," Deanna said as she and her items

crowded in next to where I stood waiting for Brandon to finish bagging my purchases, "I'll take an apple pie, too."

"Ah, I'm sorry, Deanna. I just sold the last one to Isabelle." He turned to the bakery case behind him and retrieved a pie. He slipped it into a bag and added it to my purchases. I hadn't bought the pie. It was Brandon's sweet little dose of revenge. All the sweeter since Deanna was his sister.

Brandon was twenty-two, six years younger than my twenty eight, and he had a huge crush on me. I don't think it was so much my looks—which I thought were, at best, average—as it was the 'town bad girl' thing I had going.

Not that I'm *un*attractive. To use one of my father's expressions, I wasn't so ugly I had to sneak up on a water fountain to take a drink, but I'm far from beautiful.

People said I looked like my mother, but the features I shared with her were somehow muted on me, plainer. Where my mother's jet black hair had been long and glossy, I was a brunette with shoulder-length hair that sometimes seemed to have a mind of its own. My unruly mane almost always made me appear as if I'd just crawled out of bed, no matter how much I tried to tame it. Where my mother's eyes were a dynamic, electrifying, sapphire, mine were simply blue. Her skin had been flawless, her full lips always smiling, her makeup seemingly applied with an artist's brush. Although I made my living creating art, I was doing well if I managed to slap on eyeliner and lip gloss.

The appeal I held for Brandon might have more to do with the fact that I was something of a pariah in the small town of Jessup, Missouri, where I'd grown up, escaped from seven years ago, then returned to almost a year ago.

Just as Deanna and Mindy were doing now, people in town seemed to shrink from me, as if whatever had made my relatives lunatics might be contagious.

Although the two women thought they knew a great deal about my family, they had some of their facts wrong. My father did not write my mother's name, or her lover's, in blood. He simply shot her, wrote a note, and shot himself. My sister, Carmen, was not in a mental hospital. She was living in sunny California, and frequently visited a luxury spa in Palm Springs.

I had also been living in California until the murder/suicide, at which time I'd returned to Jessup. I intended to stay only long enough to settle my parents' estate and tie up loose ends, but here it was nearly a year later, and I was still here. I'd given up a successful design business to stay in Jessup and take abuse from the townspeople.

Maybe what they said about my family being insane was true, because only a crazy person would have stayed here this long.

Eyes down, anxious to flee from Deanna's not-so-subtle hostility, I grabbed the plastic bags from the counter and headed out of the store. I walked briskly toward my Jeep Cherokee, but before I made it, I collided with something large and solid, almost dropping the pie Brandon had given me.

"Oh, God, Isabelle, I'm sorry." Sheriff Rick 'Hutch' Hutchings grabbed my upper arms to steady me, and I looked up and found myself staring into his eyes. Concern had darkened their silver hue to gunmetal grey. "Are you okay?"

"I'm fine. It was my fault. I wasn't paying attention."

He studied me a moment then dropped his hands. He indicated his cruiser, which was parked near my jeep. "Damn thing won't start. You'd think a county vehicle could get better maintenance than this, but I've had it in the shop twice this month."

I nodded, not sure what kind of response that required. Hutch was wearing his uniform, including the hat that concealed most of his dark hair. He had a smudge of grease on one sleeve, and a bit on his cheek.

He took a rag from his back pocket and wiped at the grease on his hands, not very successfully. "Did I get any on you?" he asked, studying my torso for the effects of our collision.

"No, don't think so. No big deal."

"Good." He smiled. "I haven't seen you around much lately. How have you been?"

I shifted uneasily, adjusting the grocery bags in my arms. Every time I saw him, which fortunately wasn't often, I thought about our past, about how things had been between us when we were both much too young to know anything about life, or love.

I looked away, afraid he could read the emotion in my eyes. "I'm fine."

"Here, let me get those bags for you."

I stepped back and shook my head. "No, I've got them. Thanks, though. See you around."

I carried my bags to the jeep, threw them inside, and drove out of the parking lot, tempted to take the highway that led out of Jessup to freedom. Freedom from the gossip, freedom from the lingering attraction I felt for Hutch, and freedom from the strange hold this town had on me.

****

It was almost dusk by the time I finished my errands and headed home. As I drove, I squinted through my windshield at the overcast sky. Ominous black clouds seemed ready, at any moment, to spew a torrent of water on the land. I felt a kinship with them. My mood was also black, and I was ready to do some spewing of my own.

Even though I empathized with the clouds, I hoped they'd hold off until after I arrived home. The road that led uphill to my property could be tricky under normal conditions. It was positively treacherous in a heavy rain.

If my mood had been rotten before, when I pulled into my drive, it became as rancid as an open, festering wound.

An older model, baby-blue, Ford pickup sat in my driveway.

Patrick. Damn.

Patrick was my uncle, my father's brother, but he and I were not on the best of terms. I'd never been close to him. He and my father had been estranged because of an argument over their inheritance. My father had invested his share and done quite well. Patrick spent his on booze and women.

I climbed out of the jeep and waited. The truck's door gave a creaking protest as Patrick shoved it open. I could smell the rain in the air, and I took a deep, soothing lungful of it, bracing myself for the battle ahead.

Patrick staggered toward me and when he was

within six feet or so, the smell of sour booze eradicated the sweet smell of the rain.

Patrick had once been good-looking, a ladies' man, but years of hard living and heavy drinking had changed that. His longish, dark brown hair was scraggly, and although he was only thirty-eight, it was mostly gray. His blue eyes were rheumy and yellowed. Purplish veins spidered over his always red nose.

He pointed a finger at me, but missed his aim and directed it somewhere to the left of me. "You owe me some money, missy. You're nothin' but a damn thief." He ran the words together, canting slightly to the side as he spoke.

Since my parents died, Patrick had been regularly dunning me for 'his fair share' of the money my parents had left me and my sister. I refused to give him a dime. Partly because he wasn't entitled to it, partly because I didn't particularly like him, and partly because it would never be enough. Whatever I gave him, he'd drink up, and then he'd be back for more.

"I can't deal with this today, Patrick." I started around him, but he lurched into my path. I drew back, not wanting to get any closer to him than I was already.

"You're *gonna* deal with it. I want what's rightly mine."

I shook my head. "You need to get help."

"Get help?" He tried for a sneer, but all he managed was a drunken, clownish grimace. "Did you tell your loony-toons daddy to *get help* before he offed your mama?"

I gritted my teeth, determined not to engage in a war of words with him. "That's enough, Patrick."

He came closer, ducking his head, staring into my

face. "We all got it, ya know." His eyes became even more unfocused, the pupils almost disappearing in the yellowish-blue orbs. "Yer daddy killed his. I chose to anesthe...anesthe..." He frowned, brushing his hands along his shirt pocket as if he'd tucked the elusive word inside there. He blew out a breath and said, "...to numb mine. How do you make yours go away, Issy? How do *you* push back the crazy?"

I'd always regarded Patrick with a sort of pitying dislike. But at that moment, I hated him. Hated his weakness, his greed, his deluded sense of entitlement. But mostly, I hated his words, because I'd wondered that myself.

I had escaped, had been moderately successful and well adjusted, content. But the death of my parents had brought me back and now I didn't believe I'd ever really been free of it. It was as if I'd been on a boat, sailing over the waters of my family's madness. My father's desperate, tragic act had been my iceberg, and now I was punctured and being sucked into insane waters.

Patrick looked at me, his eyebrows raised as if for my answer, but I didn't respond. Instead, I took out my cell phone and dialed Rodney Sandford.

"Ah, shit, whatchyadoin?" Patrick whined. "Calling the sonofabitchin cab? Screw that, I'm leaving."

"You're not driving," I said.

"The hell I'm not. It's not like you give a damn what happens to me."

"It's not you I'm worried—" I stopped as Rodney answered the phone, saying to him, "It's Isabelle."

His heavy sigh came over the line. "Be there in a

few."

We'd been through this so many times, more words were not necessary.

Patrick whirled toward his truck, but forgot to move his feet and nearly toppled to the ground. He righted himself and mumbled, "I can drive my own damned self."

"You will not. I don't care what you do to yourself, but I won't be responsible for you killing someone else. You're not leaving."

Without turning around, he waved a hand back at me in a 'go away' gesture and lurched for the truck.

I followed.

"I said you're not leaving. You can either ride with the cab or the cops." I held up my cell phone to substantiate my threat.

By now, he had the driver's door open. He looked back at me, then away. He stared off for a moment then sighed, bowed his head, and dropped onto the seat, his feet still hanging out to the ground, waiting, defeated.

****

After Rodney and I loaded Patrick into the cab, and the two of them drove off, I spent the rest of the evening puttering around my house, a two-bedroom log cabin I'd purchased after selling the family home. I didn't want to live in the house where I'd grown up. It was too big and held too many memories.

My current abode suited me much better. It was rustic and cozy with its hardwood floors, hand-woven rugs, and comfy, overstuffed furniture. The house sat among towering pines and oak trees, and came with a detached shop I'd turned into a studio, which was where I should be right now. I should be completing the handbags for the fall festival coming up. I made purses for a living, and I intended to donate twenty of them to the festival, for which all proceeds would go to the children's hospital.

In California, I'd had a boutique where I sold the purses, but since moving to Jessup, I'd begun taking orders online. The purses I made were customized to buyers' specifications. If they chose to do so, they could send me items and I'd incorporate them into the design. People sent things like concert tickets, locks of hair, photos, baby shoes, etc, although once I'd received a used condom. I'd declined that particular sale.

I currently had an order for a special handbag that I'd almost completed. The customer, Tamra, had sent me a tie, along with a heart-wrenching letter. Her father had died tragically in a plane crash, and the tie had been his favorite. He'd worn it on his wedding day, and again on the day each of his six children had been born. She and her siblings wanted the purse to give to their mother for Christmas. I'd basically completed it and was in the process of embedding the gray and black tie into the soft leather, after which, I would seal it over with a plastic protector.

It wouldn't take me long to finish it if I'd just get started, and I could also work on the festival purses. But I couldn't stop thinking about Patrick. I was antsy and restless. I didn't do my best work under these conditions.

A little before ten, I slipped on my 'Kiss Me I'm Irish' nightshirt, knowing already I wouldn't be able to sleep. Not without some help.

I took one of the sleeping pills my doctor had prescribed almost a year ago. I didn't take them often—

which was why I still had some—but there were nights when I knew one would be my only chance at respite. Tonight would be one of those nights.

I slipped between the cool sheets, beneath the thick comforter, and lay on the feather pillow, pulling the covers up to my chin. I felt cocooned, shut off from the world. The narcotics and my comfortable bed worked together like synchronized swimmers. My limbs grew mercifully heavy, relaxed, and my mind drifted closed. My body shut down, and I slept.

Some time later, although I wasn't sure how much, something jerked me from my slumber.

I lay there, heart thudding, my stomach a flutter of unease, listening for the noise that had awoken me. I knew it had to be something out of the ordinary, or I wouldn't have been pulled from my state of nocturnal euphoria.

I heard it again and looked at the clock. Four a.m. Damn. What was it? It sounded like someone had dropped something very heavy, or hit something with a hammer...my brain wasn't functioning well enough to identify the noise.

Then I heard a car door slam and the rev of an engine.

I kicked off the blankets and struggled out of bed, fighting the cotton-headed, lethargic, zombie thing, which was the only drawback to the little white bits of heaven. If I could stay in bed for at least eight hours after taking them, I was fine. If not, I was as muddled and stumbly as Uncle Patrick.

I pulled my fluffy, mint green robe on and grabbed a flashlight. Walking out onto the porch, I swung the beam around my property, stopping when I saw the door to my studio.

It was open.

A tremor of fear buzzed through my veins, but I still stepped out into the night and made my way toward the studio. Halfway there, I realized I didn't have a weapon. I didn't own a gun, which suddenly seemed foolish since I lived out here alone, and half the town either feared me or hated me, or both.

I hefted the flashlight in my hand. It was one of those heavy-duty Coleman lanterns and might do in a pinch if the intruder wasn't much bigger than I—and didn't have a weapon of his or her own. I gripped the Coleman in both hands and held it in front of me in what I hoped was a threatening manner.

Almost to the studio, I stumbled over something on the ground and I gasped, afraid to look down, afraid it might be a body. But it had been hard. Too hard for a corpse. I shone the flashlight at my feet and gave a nervous, relieved laugh.

A chunk of concrete. The damn walk was cracking so badly, there were places where it was just chunks of loose stone. I'd have to get that replaced before long.

When I reached the studio, I eased the partially open door all the way back and swept the light over the room.

I did it once more because I couldn't quite believe what I was seeing. The adrenaline kick had erased most of the cobwebs, but my head still felt a little befuddled. Maybe that's why I had to look a third time before I really grasped the scene.

I didn't turn on a light, because I didn't want to view the carnage that closely. Walking slowly forward, I gazed in horror at the handbags I'd worked so hard to create. They were a jumble of slashed leather, almost indistinguishable from one another. Something red, paint, I hoped, was smeared all over them, all over the room. The words 'Crazy bitch, you'll get yours' were written in red on the floor next to the mess.

I'd had fifteen of the twenty purses for the festival complete, and they were in the mangled pile. But the object I focused on was not part of that batch. It was the gift for Tamra's mother. The whole thing was shredded, the tie in pieces and soaked in red. Ruined.

I dropped to my knees and picked it up, cradling it against my chest as the tears flowed.

I don't know how long I knelt there, holding the purse, but when I stood, my thighs had gone to sleep and they tingled painfully as feeling returned.

I made my way back to the house, barely noticing the morning dew that dampened the hem of my robe. The sun had just started to rise and the sky was tinged pink with its appearance and the passing of night. It was early. Very early. But when I went inside and found my cell phone, instead of dialing 911, I called Hutch.

Chapter Two

While I waited for Hutch, I took a quick shower, put on jeans and a pink sweater, and pulled my hair back into a ponytail. I brewed a pot of coffee and drank the first mug black, chasing away the last dregs of the sleeping pill.

I heard Hutch drive up when I was on my second cup, this one with cream.

I opened the front door, and my heart did a little stutter when I saw him walk toward me. He wasn't in uniform, probably because he'd been off duty—and asleep—when I'd called. He wore Wranglers and a camel-colored coat with a sheepskin collar. He was hatless and it occurred to me I hadn't seen him like that in years. His dark hair was damp, making it look ebony in the morning sun.

He stepped up on the porch and smiled, looking at me with his sleepy grey eyes. "Are you okay, Izzy-B? What happened?"

The old nickname slipped out effortlessly. He didn't seem to notice, but I did, and it brought back a flood of memories, a flood of feelings that left me temporarily breathless. For a moment, I couldn't speak, then I cleared my throat, and stepped back to let him inside.

"I'm fine," I said, my voice sounding like I'd

swallowed sandpaper, in spite of the throat clearing. I led him into the kitchen where his very presence, masculine and imposing, seemed to dominate the room.

I hadn't been alone with him since I was twenty-one. I thought about our first time, and how he'd kissed me and made love to me, if you could call our anxious, fumbling passion lovemaking. Although the rest had been a little frightening, I'd enjoyed the kissing immensely, and I wondered how much better he'd be at it now with a few years experience under his belt.

I flushed hotly as my mind moved to 'under his belt.' But when I once again thought of Tamra's desecrated purse, I wondered how I was going to tell her that her beloved daddy's tie had been demolished beyond repair. With that sobering notion, my silly, shallow thoughts fled.

Hutch took his coat off, slung it over the back of a kitchen chair and sat at the table. I poured him a cup of coffee and he took a sip. "What happened?"

On the phone, I'd only said there'd been a break-in. Now, sitting in the chair next to him, I explained exactly what had taken place, the knot lodged in my throat making the process slow and difficult. Once again, I saw the pitiful, revered, mangled tie and the tears burst forth, streaming down my cheeks as a deep, wracking sob tore from me.

"Izzy, honey? What is it? Are you sure you're okay?" He looked puzzled, as if mere vandals couldn't possibly cause such sorrow. I couldn't tell him why. It was too personal, too intimate.

His large, warm hand slipped over mine where it rested on the table. I felt a tingle work its way from his touch up through my arms and into my breasts. I tried to ignore it.

"I'm sorry," I said miserably. "I should have just called 911 instead of bothering you with this."

"Don't be ridiculous. I'm your friend. You can always call me."

I nodded, withdrawing my hand from his. "Thank you for coming."

"Tell me what you heard, exactly, that woke you up." He produced a notebook from his pocket and jotted as I spoke.

"I'm not sure. It was some banging noise I couldn't identify. Then, I heard a car leave just before I went outside."

"And this was around four?" I nodded. "And you called me at five-thirty. What were you doing between those times?"

"I went to check it out. I was so upset, I think I just sat there in disbelief."

His lips compressed, and a muscle ticked in his jaw. "You went to check it out on your own?" He shook his head. "You should have called me, or 911, the moment you saw that the door was open. Going out there on your own was—"

"Crazy?" I finished for him, giving a bitter laugh.

"Don't do that, Izzy," he said quietly. "I was going to say dangerous."

I wiped at my tears and sucked in a breath. "I wasn't thinking. I just wanted to find out what had happened."

"Do you have any idea who might have done this?"

"Maybe."

I told him about Patrick's visit, watching him closely as I spoke. Hutch was four years older than I and Patrick five years older than him, but they had been friends way back when. I wasn't sure if they still were, but if so, Hutch wouldn't like me accusing his buddy.

He nodded, but I couldn't tell if the information upset him. He put on his coat and slid the notebook in a pocket.

"I'll see what I can find out. I can't promise we'll catch whoever did this, but I swear I'll do my best."

"Thanks," I said.

"I need to go take a look. Want to come?"

I nodded, even though I really didn't. I led him out to the studio, wrapping my arms tightly around my middle as we surveyed the damage, somehow even more disturbing in the fresh light of morning.

He made some more notes. "I'll have someone come out and see if they can get fingerprints or evidence of any kind. Don't touch anything until they're finished, okay?"

"Okay," I promised, trying to keep the tears out of my voice.

I walked him to his car and watched him drive away, feeling an odd, unsettling loneliness after he was gone.

****

I stood at the back of the town hall, shifting nervously from one foot to the other. The only reason I'd come to the meeting was because everyone who had something to sell at the festival had to be here to present it to the city council. I didn't want to be here, didn't want to be anywhere near this many citizens of Jessup.

The smell of coffee wafted to me, and I looked at the table sitting a few feet away. A large Bunn coffee maker had been placed at one end and next to that was a tray of pastries. I eyed the cinnamon rolls, and my mouth watered, my stomach rumbled. Cinnamon rolls were one of my weaknesses, and these looked like the good kind with thin icing and lots of cinnamon. I was starving.

If I hadn't been late to the meeting and didn't feel so much like an ostracized interloper, I might have helped myself to a cup of coffee and one of those enticing cinnamon rolls.

But I *was* late. All because the 'forensic team' Hutch had sent, which consisted of Deputy Trevor Denkins and Hutch's secretary, Mable, took forever to check my studio for evidence. When they'd finally left, I'd had to quickly finish up the last of the purses and rush to the meeting. Late...conspicuous...and *so* hungry.

The meeting was in full swing and my nemesis, Deanna Summers, city councilwoman extraordinaire, had the podium.

"Is that everyone who has something to contribute to the Jessup Fallfest?"

My fingers suddenly went numb where they gripped the Dillard's shopping bag that held the purses. My stomach lurched and my knees trembled. Clearing my throat, I said quietly, maybe too quietly, "I have something."

"Okay, if that's all, we'll move to the next—"

"I have something," I said more loudly, and this time, it was a shout. Fifty or so heads turned in my direction, and I wanted to fall through the over-waxed wood floor.

Deanna's piercing gaze focused on me. She was a tall woman, attractive, in a female wrestler sort of way.

She had wide shoulders and streaked blonde hair. Her eyes were a deep brown that darkened to onyx when she was angry. They were onyx right now.

"The council recognizes Isabelle Connelly," she said grudgingly.

I walked on quivering legs to the front of the room and stepped up on the stage next to Deanna. "There are twenty purses in here I'd like to donate for sale at the festival," I said into the mic. "Handmade," I added quickly, although I wasn't sure why.

Deanna's thin lips turned up in a smug parody of a smile. "I don't believe folks around here can afford your fancy California purses, Isabelle."

"Oh, no, they're not. Not at all. They're cheap." A small titter went through the crowd and my face warmed. "I mean, I'm selling them for twenty dollars each. They're not fancy."

I dared to look out into the sea of faces. Relief coursed through me when my eyes met Liza Loomis's. Liza was gorgeous and leggy, with coppery red hair and dazzling pale green eyes. She had always been nice to me, one of the few in town who had, and she probably had more reason to dislike me than anyone.

Hutch and I had dated for two years, but when I moved to Houston to go to design school, due to the difficulty of keeping up a long-distance relationship, we'd broken up. Not long after, Liza started dating him and became pregnant. Even though he and I were no longer a couple, the news crushed me. I'd had this futile notion that one day, Hutch and I would get back together.

Liza and Hutch were going to marry, but before the wedding, she miscarried. Hutch stayed with her for a while, but the wedding never took place, and eventually, they broke up. Rumor around town was, he didn't want to be with her because he wasn't over me. I didn't believe it, but I would have thought there would be awkwardness, maybe resentment, between me and Liza. Surprisingly, there never had been.

She smiled at me and said, "I think the purses are a fantastic idea. Thanks so much, Isabelle."

Deanna tightened her lips. She and Liza were best friends. Not much Deanna could say now. "Great. Fine. Please have them at the fairgrounds half an hour before the festival."

"You don't need to look at them first?" I asked.

Deanna gave a quick shake of her head and curled her nose at the bag I held. "No, that won't be necessary. But please stay until the end of the meeting so you can fill out the proper forms for the donation."

Oh crap. I'd intended to leave the purses here and take off. I didn't want to stay for the meeting, and I didn't want to bring the handbags back for the festival. I should've gone with my first instinct and only made a cash donation. But, I felt I should contribute work of some kind, since I knew the festival coordinators wouldn't want me to help at the actual event.

If I were honest, part of me hoped the ladies in town would see the purses and like them. Hoped they might be a little impressed at my talent and maybe, just maybe, think there was *something* good about me. Pathetic, I know. I shouldn't care what these people thought of me. But apparently, I did.

I waited through the rest of the exceedingly dull meeting, pining after the cinnamon rolls the entire time. When the meeting was over, Liza came up to me and reached out for my hand, giving it a squeeze. "It's so good to see you, Isabelle. We don't see enough of you."

"Thank you. Good to see you, too."

"I heard about your break-in. I'm so sorry."

I nodded but before I could respond, Deanna walked up behind Liza, glaring at me. "Yes, we heard," she said, but she didn't say *she* was sorry.

"Was anything very important taken?" Liza asked.

"No. It was mostly just a big mess," I replied, thinking if they gave out awards for understatements, I should get one for that.

Deanna laughed harshly. "Sort of like you and your family, huh? Just one great big mess."

"Deanna!" Liza shrieked. "What an awful thing to say."

"Well, its true, isn't it? Her family was nothing but trouble, and now, it's the same with her."

I felt tears at the back of my throat, partly from embarrassment, partly from anger. I wanted to lash out at her, but the last thing I needed was a scene, especially one with the venerable Deanna Summers.

"Where do I go to fill out paperwork?" I asked Liza.

"Come on, I'll show you." She threw a look over her shoulder at Deanna, but the woman only gave a self-righteous smile.

When we were out of earshot, Liza said, "Please don't pay attention to her. She's just bitter and takes it out on everyone. Did you know about her husband leaving her for another woman?"

I nodded. I'd heard the gossip.

"Well," Liza continued, "She seems to hold it against every woman who's not in her inner circle.

And, she knows what happened, with us, and Rick."

I looked at her in surprise. Was she insinuating I'd come between her and Hutch? I hadn't even been in the state. "That was a long time ago. And Hutch and I were over before..."

"Oh, I know. She knows it, too. She just wants to blame you for our breakup because it's a way of re-directing her anger at the woman who ran off with her husband. Plus," she said, her green eyes twinkling, "she knows her brother has a mega-crush on you."

We'd reached the table where the festival paperwork sat, saving me from a response as I filled out a form. When I finished, I said my goodbyes and hurriedly left the building.

"That was pretty brutal."

I drew in a sharp breath and whirled, clasping a hand to my chest. "You scared me half to death!" I said to Hutch, who was leaning against the wall next to the door.

He straightened. "Sorry, didn't mean to startle you. I just wanted to tell you I'm sorry about what happened in there."

"How did you know? Were you there?" Surely I would have noticed him in the crowd.

He shrugged. "Sort of. I was in the office attached to the meeting hall going over some documents they wanted me to look at. I heard."

"Ah, well." I laughed self-consciously. "You can't be the town leper without expecting that sort of treatment."

His eyes narrowed, and I thought he was going to argue with me, but instead he said, "I heard my crack forensics team came out this morning. If they found anything, we should know in the next day or two."

"Good. Have you talked to Patrick?"

"No. I went by, but he's sleeping off a humdinger of a drunk. I couldn't get one coherent word out of him. I'll keep trying, though."

I bet you will, I thought, and immediately felt bad about it. Maybe he really was trying to find out who'd broken into my studio. Even if it was Patrick.

"Okay, well, just let me know."

He nodded, then said, "Hey, how about if I buy you dinner this evening? We haven't seen much of each other since you came home. I wanted to wait a while, you know, with what happened to your parents. But, I've missed you. I'd like to take you out."

"You mean, like a date?"

"If you want to call it that." He smiled.

I shook my head. "I'm sorry, Hutch. I can't. I mean...I don't think..." I couldn't tell him that the very thought of socializing with anyone, especially a man, especially a man from Jessup, terrified me. That this town, and everyone in it, represented the fear and tragedy that my life had become. I had no room, no enthusiasm, for a social life. And, even though it had been years ago, I hadn't forgotten what it felt like to be hurt by Rick Hutchings. "I'm not going to be here much longer, and—"

"No need to explain. It was just a thought." He gave me another smile, but his eyes looked wounded. "I'll let you know what I find out about your break-in. See you around."

He walked away, not looking back, and I sighed, somehow feeling even more dejected than I had earlier, when Deanna skewered me in front of the whole town.

****

On Sunday evening, three days after the meeting, I had just finished piecing together the remnants of the tie, trying to create something that would at least resemble the original, when I heard a car drive up. I walked out of my studio and saw Hutch climb out of his cruiser.

When I approached him, he didn't speak, just peered at me from beneath the brim of his hat.

"Do you have news?" I asked. "Did you speak to Patrick?"

"I'm afraid not," he admitted.

"You're not going to question him about the break in, are you?"

He looked up at the cabin. "Can we go inside?"

I stalked to the house, frustration mounting as I closed the door behind us. I crossed my arms and turned to face Hutch. "Why won't you talk to him?" I demanded, exasperated.

"Because..." He hesitated, then said bluntly, "He's dead."

I gasped and shook my head. "What? How?"

"We're waiting for the autopsy results, but it looks like poison."

"Alcohol poison?"

"No. *Poison*. Deadly poison."

"You mean, murdered?"

He nodded. "There are accidental poisonings, but the evidence suggests it was intentional. So, yeah, murdered."

"Oh, my God." I walked on wobbly legs to the kitchen and dropped into a chair. He followed, removing his hat and rain slicker, but remained standing.

I knew I should feel sad. Patrick was my uncle. But I didn't. Just a numb sense of disbelief. Maybe the grief would come when the shock wore off. I hoped when that happened, I wouldn't feel what had briefly flashed through my mind...relief.

"Who would want to murder Patrick?" I asked.

"I don't know. There are a lot of people who didn't care if he lived or died, but probably very few who actually *wanted* him dead."

"Do you have any suspects?"

"Not yet." He shrugged and said casually, almost too casually, "Did you know poison is most often the chosen method for women who kill?"

"No."

He nodded, his expression grave, considering. Rain started falling, hitting the roof with a noisy dissonance. Hutch looked skyward, then back at me. "Gets pretty muddy out here when it rains, huh?"

"Yes." I fiddled with an oven mitt I'd left lying on the table as I answered.

"That distinctive, hard to remove red mud."

"Yes," I responded slowly, cautiously. This wasn't just idle chatter.

"Has Patrick been back out here lately? Since Tuesday, when you two argued?"

"No. Why?"

Again, the casual shrug. "Red mud was found in his home, near where his body was discovered."

My fingers stilled, and my gaze flew to his. "Do you think I did this? Am I a suspect?"

"I didn't say that. We're just beginning the investigation. I can honestly say I can't see you as a killer."

"But?"

"There are a lot of people who don't like you, and maybe a few who like you a little too much."

"I'm not following."

"Whoever did this may have done it because they dislike you, or they may have done it because they like you a great deal. Patrick hurt you by vandalizing your studio. Assuming, of course, Patrick is the one who did it. And, whether he did it or not, that's the general opinion around town, so his killer may have been getting revenge for you."

I shook my head. "That's crazy. And I can assure you *no one* in this town likes me enough to do anything like that."

"Not even Brandon?"

There was something in his voice. Jealousy? I looked at him, but couldn't read his expression. He couldn't be jealous, could he?

"Funny how there are no secrets around here," I muttered, wondering how on earth Hutch knew about Brandon's crush.

"Small town like this, there aren't many. Is there anyone who's made threats to you lately? Seemed particularly angry? Any altercations you've been involved in?"

I thought for a moment. "Deanna Summers. You heard her at the town meeting. And afterward, she was...she seemed highly upset with me. Very confrontational." I sighed and ran a hand through my hair. "But, I'm not saying she'd do something like this. No way."

"You never know. I'll talk to her."

The rain intensified, sounding like a million tiny rocks falling on the roof. I looked up toward the ceiling, then at Hutch. "You'd better go if you want to make it out of here before the water gets too high on the road. Makes it kind of tough to navigate in the dark."

He nodded and put on his hat and raincoat. "I'll be in touch," he said, and I wondered why it sounded a teeny bit like a threat.

I walked him to the porch, watching him duck as he went out into the rain and got into his cruiser. I heard the engine turn over and sputter. He tried again, and again, but no luck. Apparently, he still hadn't gotten it fixed.

In a few seconds, the car door opened, and Hutch ran through the rain back to the house.

"Won't start, dammit. I'll have to call for a ride."

I shook my head. "No one should try to come out here with the rain like it is." I pointed out the door at the drive, which had started to swell with water. "The road leading here is bad, too. They might not even make it up here."

"Ah, hell."

"You can stay," I said, then wondered why I'd said it. "Maybe tomorrow it will clear up and you can get your car started. It's not so bad in the daylight."

He studied me silently for a moment, and suddenly the air between us was palpable with implication. "Sometimes it starts randomly," he finally said. "I'll keep trying. And I'm not afraid of the road."

Maybe not, but I could tell, he was afraid to stay here with me.

Chapter Three

Hutch hung his hat and rain slicker on hooks out on the porch and followed me inside.

He sat at one end of the couch, while I sat at the other, my feet drawn up under me, clutching a throw pillow to my chest. The curtains were pulled back, and I watched as the rain beat against the windows. A huge burst of thunder rattled the cabin.

"It doesn't bother you?" Hutch asked. "The storm doesn't scare you?"

I pulled my attention back to him and shook my head. "I like storms. They make me feel alive." I smiled. "When I was small, my father would take me driving in them, I'd stare, fascinated, out the window as jagged lighting ripped through the sky and the car vibrated with the force of the thunder."

He laughed. "Sounds a little odd."

"It was one of those memories of my father that I cherish. Before I knew he was..." I stopped, feeling a lump form in my throat. I swallowed and said, "Tell me about my father. About those last months before he died." I'd heard rumors about the peculiar things he'd done, but I didn't know details, facts.

Hutch looked away, then back at me. "I don't think you really want to hear about that."

"I do. People around town act like, at any moment, I'm going to pounce on them and infect them with my lunacy. I need to understand what he did, what made people so afraid of my family."

My father's mother had also been mentally unbalanced. When I was a toddler, she was committed to an asylum and was there until she died fifteen years ago. But, as far as I knew, she was never dangerous. Not like my dad had been at the end.

Hutch blew a burst of air out through pursed lips. He sighed, then said, "Did you know about the time Daniel pulled a gun on the Smith's dog because he thought the dog was mocking him?"

I almost laughed, but it really wasn't funny. "No. God, I had no idea. What happened?"

"A neighbor called me and no one, including the dog, was injured. I put your father in jail for a few hours. His doctor checked him out. He seemed to be okay and I let him go."

"He should have been in some kind of facility. I had no idea. The times I was here to visit..." I stopped, feeling guilty. I had only visited every year or two. "I never saw any of that."

"Your mother didn't want him hospitalized, and the doctor said he'd be fine as long as he took his medication. I don't know if he stopped taking it, but the episodes continued."

"What else?"

"There was the time when the Franklins woke to find him going through their medicine cabinet in the middle of the night. When they confronted him, he said he was counting their ibuprofen, because he was sure they'd stolen some of his."

"Good grief. No wonder people are afraid of me." I shook my head. "You know something? I'm afraid, too."

"Why? You're not..."

"No. But he wasn't either, at first." I shuddered. "I mean, how would I know? He probably thought he was fine, too."

"You're fine, Izzy. Don't worry about that, okay?"

I studied his concerned face, his warm eyes, and I nodded. "It's all so hard to make sense of. Hard to sort out. I loved my parents dearly, both of them. When it first happened, I hated my father. Or at least, felt like I should hate him. But I also missed him and I loved him and I couldn't really hate him. Then I felt like I was being disloyal to my mother because I *didn't* hate him. I wasn't sure how to feel, what was right, you know?"

"I can't say I know how you feel, but I understand what you're saying."

"If it happened to you, do you think you could hate your father?"

"I'm don't know. I don't think anyone can say for sure unless they've been through the same thing."

"No, I guess they can't." I smiled grimly. "But it doesn't seem to stop the people in town from talking, from judging."

"Don't pay any attention to them. You know how people like to gossip."

"Yes, but have you seen the way they look at me? They're actually *afraid*. I just can't figure out why I haven't left. Why I'm still here."

"I don't know either, but I'm glad you are."

I didn't respond, was afraid to respond. I didn't want those old feelings brewing again between us. Or did I? Maybe I wanted them to, but I was afraid to let them.

"You know, I think maybe the reason I've stayed is because I feel guilty for leaving in the first place. If I'd been here, it wouldn't have happened. I know staying here now doesn't help. It *did* happen. Maybe I think of it as some kind of penance."

"You have no reason to feel guilty. You couldn't have stopped it. And, if you'd been here..." He sucked in a deep breath and said, "He might have killed you, too."

"I've thought about that. I want to believe he wouldn't have hurt me. He was my daddy. But, who knows? I know he was mentally ill. But supposedly, he killed my mother because she cheated on him. I don't even know if that's true. Do you know? Was my mother having an affair?"

"I don't know for sure. It was just gossip and I seldom believe gossip. It's possible, but it's also possible it was just part of your dad's increasing delusion and paranoia."

"Yeah, seems like there was a lot of that."

He leveled me with a steady gaze. "You've been through a lot lately. I can't believe how you've dealt with it all. I'm sure sometimes you feel like you've reached your breaking point."

I shrugged. "I manage." I gave him a chagrined look. "I bet you thought I *had* reached it the morning you came out after the break-in. I was a mess."

"You certainly seemed distraught. I mean, it would be upsetting to anyone, but you seemed so...sad," he finished quietly.

I took a deep breath. "Yes, I was crushed." I explained about Tamra's purse. "It's my fault. She lost her dad, and now, thanks to me, she lost something precious of his that she can never get back."

"It's not your fault." He reached out and placed a hand over mine where it rested on the pillow.

I looked at his hand, but didn't pull away. "That's what she said, but I feel responsible. She entrusted it to me, and I should've protected it. Sometimes, I just feel like everything I touch turns into..." I thought of Deanna's words, "...into a mess. Like I'm just a great big mess."

"Hey," he said softly. When I didn't look up, he hooked a finger under my chin and lifted my head until I met his gaze. "You're not a mess." His eyes dropped to my mouth, and he brushed the pad of his thumb over my lower lip. Little tremors of desire shook through me. He raised his eyes back to mine, imprisoning me with their intensity. His voice gruff, he said, "You're perfectly... incredibly..." He shook his head and ended on a husky sigh, "...perfect."

His eyes, a warm, molten shimmer of silver lava, never left my face. He slid his fingers gently along my jawbone and brushed my hair back from my cheek, letting his touch trail down the side of my neck. My breath caught and I couldn't move. The only thing in motion was the steady thump of my heart.

Kiss me, please, I silently begged, and for a moment, I thought he would. He leaned closer, his gaze still trapping mine. My throat went dry, and I was mesmerized by his mouth, so close to mine, his touch...so warm...so...

A flash of lightening lit the room, immediately followed by a deafening crash of thunder that rattled the windows. I jumped, giving a startled shriek and his touch fell away. I laughed, a breathless, nervous sound.

"Wow! That was close."

He looked at me a moment longer, then his gaze slid away, and he gave a curt nod. "Yeah, too close." He stood abruptly and headed for the door. "I'm going to try the car again."

"I meant what I said earlier," I told him as he took hold of the doorknob. "If it doesn't start, you could just stay here for the night."

He went still for a few seconds before slowly turning to face me. He narrowed his eyes, looking at me as he'd probably looked at my father while he held the pistol to the poor dog's head. "It'll start," he said, and it sounded more like a prayer than a statement.

It didn't start. Not with the first attempt. But this time, he stayed out in the car between tries. The engine caught on the third effort, some thirty minutes later.

I went to the window, lifting my hand in a wave as he drove off. I thought maybe he didn't see me, because he didn't wave back.

****

The next morning, I loaded the purses to be sold at the festival into my jeep and drove into town. When I pulled into the parking lot of the fairgrounds, Liza was getting out of her black Audi. She waved exuberantly and rushed over to me, almost before I was completely in the space.

She gave me a warm smile. "Hi, Isabelle. I'm so glad you're here." She wore a stylish, mocha-colored pantsuit with a silky white blouse. She looked beautiful, as always.

"I just came to drop the purses off," I said, climbing out of the jeep with the Dillard's bag in my hand.

"I heard about your uncle. I'm so sorry. Is there anything I can do?"

I shook my head. "No. Thank you, though."

The funeral would be held in Texas, where Patrick lived during his marriage. His ex-wife was taking his body back once the medical examiner released it. I wouldn't even have to make an appearance and suffer the awkward condolences. "Could you take the purses in for me?"

"I can, but why don't you stay for the festival? You could help me in the funnel cake booth."

Oh, sounds like ever so much fun, I thought peevishly, but said, "That's nice, but I really shouldn't."

The loud roar of a motor drowned out her response, and I turned to the source. Brandon had rolled into the parking lot, driving a souped-up red Camaro. He had his window down, and he pulled up beside us, grinning. "Hey, Isabelle. You're looking good."

Deanna sat in the passenger seat, glaring at me. I ignored her and smiled at Brandon. "How are you?"

"Fine, but not as fine as you are." His boyish attempt at flirtation made me feel a little uneasy...and flattered.

"We need to go, Brandon," Deanna's churlish voice cut in.

"See you inside?" he asked me.

"I'm afraid I'm just dropping something off. You have fun, though."

As they drove away, Deanna shot me one last glower, her eyes holding a wealth of hatred.

I tried to shrug it off and turned to Liza. "Listen, I need to go. Can you take these in for me?" I held up the shopping bag.

She nodded. "Sure, if I can't talk you into staying."

"Thanks." I handed her the purses and climbed back into the jeep.

Driving away, I couldn't get the image of Deanna's expression out of my mind. The other people in town generally regarded me with scorn and wariness. Deanna's feelings seemed to go deeper, were more intense, more personal, somehow. There was something there, something dark and angry.

But was it enough to make her kill?

****

A few days after the festival, I flipped on the small television in my kitchen while I drank my coffee and made cinnamon toast.

I liked listening to the local news, even though it's not normally very exciting. It also isn't very upsetting. Although there was an occasional serious crime, most of the news involved drunk and disorderlies, social events, city council reports, things of that nature. Of course, a year ago there had been the murder/suicide. *That* had been big news. It had stayed on the front page and led the evening newscast for several days.

But, other than that, not a lot of newsworthy incidents in Jessup. That's why, when I heard 'house fire' and 'Liza Loomis', it caught my attention.

Since cinnamon toast burns after about eight seconds under the broiler, I had to take it out before I could turn up the television and concentrate on the report. By then, it was pretty much over. All I'd caught was that Liza had escaped with minor injures, and that Sheriff Rick Hutchings said his department was investigating it as a possible arson.

Arson? What was happening around here? In a town that probably had no more than one malicious crime a year, we'd had a vandalism, a murder, and now a suspicious house fire where a woman had been injured, could have been killed, all within the span of a week. For that reason alone, they almost had to be related, but otherwise, it seemed highly unlikely.

I believed Patrick had broken into my studio, but to think someone killed him because of it was preposterous. And Liza's home burning? As far as I knew, she shared no link with Patrick other than living in a place where he was the resident town drunk. The entire population of Jessup shared that link. So, what? Why all these bizarre occurrences lately?

I felt I should call and check on Liza. After all, she'd been so nice after Patrick's death. Yesterday, she'd stopped by with a plant. But, I didn't know where to call. I didn't have her cell phone number. If she were in the hospital, they wouldn't give me any information, although they would most likely ring her room. But after what she'd been through, if she were still in the hospital, I didn't want to disturb her. Brandon might know the status of her condition since his sister and Liza were best friends, but I didn't want to risk encouraging his crush, provided he was even working at the store right now, which was the only way I knew to reach him.

I was debating calling Hutch to ask about Liza when the phone rang and, as if my thoughts had conjured him, I heard Hutch's voice on the other end.

"I'd like to drop by if I could," he said abruptly.

"Why?"

"I need to ask you a few questions."

"About?"

"I'm gathering information about the fire. I'm sure you heard about it, right?"

"Yes. I saw it on the news."

He was silent for a moment. "I really need to come out. Will you be home?"

Reluctantly, with dread and curiosity surfacing in me, I replied, "Sure, come on out."

Hutch arrived fifteen minutes later. I let him in, glancing at the darkening sky. Were we due to get more rain? I'd have to make this quick. Otherwise, Hutch might be stranded here again.

"Liza told me she was out here yesterday," he stated as soon as we were inside.

"Yes, she wanted to offer her condolences about Patrick."

He nodded. "Kind of funny how things are happening to people who come to visit you lately, huh?"

I went cold, then something seized around my heart. "You think I had something to do with this?"

He peered at me, his eyes cold and assessing. "I think there are some pretty odd things happening, and you're at least mildly connected to all of them."

"Other than her visit, how am I connected to Liza's house fire?"

He reached into his shirt pocket and pulled something out, opening his hand so I could take a look. "Recognize this?"

A small, silver thimble rested in the center of his hand. I shrugged. "I'm not a crack investigator like you, but I'd say it's a thimble."

He ignored my sarcasm and said, "Yes, I'd say it

is. Where were you last night just before midnight?"

"Sleeping."

"Alone?"

I wanted to say 'None of your business' or 'What the hell do you think?', but I didn't want to agitate the situation, and it *was* his business. I was a suspect.

"Yes, alone," I replied tightly.

He closed his hand around the thimble and dropped it back into his pocket. "Liza doesn't sew. This was found in the general vicinity of where the fire started."

It took a moment for his meaning to sink in. "You think it was me? That I carry a pocket full of thimbles and I inadvertently dropped one while skulking about, doing my dirty deed?"

"I'm not saying that. I'm just saying, you sew, Liza doesn't. I'm sure, at one time or another, various objects wind up in a jacket pocket and a person may not remember them being there. I'm also sure that they can occasionally fall out unnoticed."

I sucked in a breath, hardly believing what I was hearing. "Are you here to arrest me?"

He shook his head. "Right now, everything we have is circumstantial. Not enough to press charges."

"I see. You want to be sure you can get a conviction before you take me in."

"That's pretty much how it works, but we need all the information before we take *anyone* in. Right now, we're just asking questions."

"Very accusatory questions."

"Fact-gathering questions. A thimble is just a thimble. Lots of people own them, I would imagine."

"Yes, I would imagine."

"But not everyone who owns a thimble recently

had their property vandalized. Or had a hated uncle conveniently die, or had a woman with whom they share a—*tense*—past almost perish in a mysterious house fire."

"Oh my God, you can't be serious. You really think I did those things? That I'm capable of doing something like that?"

"I'm a cop and I have to think like a cop. Be objective. Everyone is a suspect or no one is a suspect."

I stepped closer, tears brimming, my voice a whisper. "What about as a man?"

The air grew heavy with tension. Outside, I heard the low rumble of thunder, just like the anticipation rumbling through my body. I could barely breathe as I waited for his response.

His gaze bore into mine, glimmering with intensity. "As a man, I have to remember that things are not always what they seem. My heart wants you to be innocent, but I can't let my love for you blind me to the truth."

Stunned, I nearly took a step back. I was speechless for a moment before repeating incredulously, "Love? You love me?"

"Yeah," he said miserably. "I love you. I never *stopped* loving you."

I wasn't sure how I felt about him. I knew I felt something. I just didn't know if it was love. I knew I got this little thrill every time he was near. I knew the other night our almost passion had left me yearning and feeling desperately hollow inside.

But, was that love?

"That was a very long time ago," I said, bewildered. "And since then..."

"Since then, nothing's changed. I've loved you all these years, every second, every minute, of every day," he said, although he didn't really sound like a man declaring his undying love. He sounded like a man who'd just been informed football had been outlawed, and Budweiser made you impotent.

"Then why? If you love me, how could you think...?" I couldn't finish. It was mind-boggling, both that he thought me a killer, and that he loved me. I wasn't sure which one shocked me more.

He raked a hand through his hair, his expression tormented. "I don't know what to think. But I have to consider the evidence. And, there's your family history—"

I gasped, stepping back, a jagged pain ripping through me. The air left my body as if he'd punched me in the stomach. I thought maybe I did love him; otherwise, he wouldn't have the power to hurt me this much.

"Get out," I said hoarsely.

"Isabelle, I'm..." He reached out to me then let his arm drop.

"Get out," I repeated. "And don't come back until you're ready to arrest me."

He stared at me a moment longer then walked out the door. I watched him leave, my soul as dark and cold as the night into which he vanished.

I shut the door and went into the living room where my mind did a macabre version of *he-loves-me, he-loves-me-not*, that went, *he-loves-me, he-thinks-I'm-a-killer, he-loves-me, he-thinks-I'm-a-killer*...

What if I really was charged? I'd never even entertained the thought of going to prison. I mean, if you didn't do anything wrong, you couldn't wind up in jail, right?

Wrong.

Innocent people were sometimes convicted. I wasn't sure about the statistics, but I knew it happened. And the thought scared the hell out of me. Almost as much as the whispers, the speculation, the very real threat that I, like my father and grandmother, could possibly someday go insane. Maybe if I went to prison, I'd *want* to be insane. Maybe it would be easier to cope that way.

No, I didn't want to be crazy, didn't want to go to prison, and I didn't want to love a man who thought I might be a killer.

But I was afraid all of those were very real possibilities, and an abject sadness filled the spot in my heart where the fear had been.

I don't know how long I sat there, or how long I cried, but just before bedtime, the sky opened up and cried with me.

Chapter Four

I spent the next two days waiting for the authorities, hopefully not Hutch, but most likely him, to show up at my door, slap on the cuffs, and haul me to jail.

Instead, one evening just after I'd eaten dinner and settled in front of the television to watch a mindless sitcom, Liza stopped by.

I opened the door, shocked to see her looking a little less striking than usual. She wore gray sweatpants and an oversized Old Navy T-shirt. Her mass of red-gold hair was in wild disarray, making it look as though shimmering flames surrounded her face.

"Liza, come in." She did, without speaking, stalking past me into the living room. Her tennis shoes creaked as she paced the hardwood floor.

"I'm so sorry about what happened," I said. "I wanted to check on you, but I wasn't sure how to reach you, where you were staying..." I trailed off, out of excuses, especially when none of them were valid.

She raked her hands through her hair over and over, pacing and breathing fast, almost panting. "I tried so hard. Nothing has worked. Nothing has worked and now I have to take care of it myself." She muttered the words, some of them almost indecipherable, under her breath.

A sliver of anxiety trickled through me. She didn't

look...*right*, didn't *sound* right. Was she on drugs?

"Liza? What's wrong?"

She whirled on me, her expression twisted in a mask of such fury I took a step back. "You!" she screamed. "*You're* what's wrong. Always have been."

"What do you mean?" I asked in barely a whisper, shock rendering me almost mute.

"I thought you were leaving, thought you wouldn't be here long. But you just...stayed." Her eyes were wild, glinting with something angry...something evil. "You stayed around until Rick started paying attention to you again. Started wanting you."

"He doesn't want me. We're just friends. Barely even that."

"Ha! You think I haven't seen? Think I don't know? Just like years ago. It's always been you."

"Liza, you're not making any sense," I said, starting to back away. And then it dawned on me. She must be behind what had been happening. She... "Are you the one who destroyed my studio?"

She smiled triumphantly. "You thought it was Patrick, didn't you?"

Patrick...surely she hadn't...I was trying to assimilate all of this when she reached into her jacket pocket. Her hand came out, holding a small black pistol.

Oh, shit.

I stopped, my heart speeding up, knocking against the wall of my chest like a bass drum. "Liza, what are you doing?"

"Oh, don't worry," she said, waving the gun around, which had the exact opposite effect. It actually made me worry very much. "I'm not going to kill you with this. I'm going to use poison. After all, that's your *modus operandi,* and this whole thing has to be perfect, convincing, down to the last detail."

"What thing?" My brain worked frantically, trying to remember what I'd done with my cell phone and how I could get to it once I figured it out. Escaping through the front door was no longer an option. She'd shoot me in the back, in spite of her fondness for poison.

She reached into her pocket again and retrieved a tiny vial of liquid. Poison, I assumed, and my heart beat even faster. Without commenting, she slipped it back in the pocket. Maybe she just wanted me to see it. Wanted me to think about what she was going to do to me.

"I only wanted to scare you away," she said. "But you wouldn't go. I've worked so hard." She shook her head. "You know why Deanna hates you so much?" She didn't wait for my response. "I told her that when you would come back to visit, even when I was engaged to Rick, you slept with him. That you did it while I was pregnant."

"That's a lie!"

"*That's a lie*," she mimicked in a nasal, little girl voice. "I also told her that her husband was sleeping with your mother."

"*What?*"

She shrugged. "It wasn't true, but Dave was a cheating piece of shit and most of the men in town wanted Audra. Even when your mother got older, she never lost her looks. It was easy to convince Deanna there was something going on between Dave and Audra. She couldn't keep hating Audra after she was murdered, so she turned that hate on you. With Deanna's position in Jessup, your crazy family, and

Patrick's antics, it didn't take long for the whole town to feel the same way. Everyone in town hated you. Except me, of course. I was the long-suffering, kind-hearted, generous soul who loves everyone, no matter what."

Stay calm, I told myself. Stay calm and maybe *she'll* stay calm. "Liza, we can work this out. Whatever you've done. Let's just talk about this and work it out."

"First, I need you to tell me what he said in the note," she said.

"Who? What note?"

She sighed impatiently. "Don't act stupid. I don't have time for this. You know what I mean. Daniel's suicide note. The one you're going to write, in addition to confessing to the recent crime spree, needs to say something similar to his note so they'll think it's authentic. So they'll believe you really wrote it, which you will, but they need to think you wrote it of your own accord, which I'm fairly certain you won't. What Daniel wrote is not widely known, so when they see the same thing in yours, they'll be convinced."

"Since it's not widely known, they won't realize my note said the same thing."

She clenched her jaw, speaking through gritted teeth. "You're really trying my patience. We both know they'll learn what the note said in the course of the investigation. If nothing else, Carmen knows. She'll see the similarities."

"Look, if this is because of Rick, you don't have to do this. We're not together, we never will be."

Her face scrunched into something ugly and not quite sane. "Maybe not, but you took him from me. I was pregnant with his child, and you took him. We were going to be married, but his stupid bitch of a mother wanted to plan a 'real' wedding, wanted to take our time with it. Then I miscarried and Rick no longer wanted to marry me. He was only going to in the first place because it was the *honorable* thing." She spat the word as if honor were something vile.

My cell phone rang. The sound came from the kitchen. *That's* where I'd left it. On the counter.

"Don't move," she commanded, although I wasn't aware that I had.

"If I don't answer, whoever is calling might decide to come out here."

She mentally debated that for only a moment before nodding. "Go get it. I'll be right behind you, so don't try anything stupid."

She followed me into the kitchen, and I picked up my phone. The missed call showed to be from Hutch. Funny how earlier I'd feared being arrested for a crime I didn't commit, and now it was the preferred choice in two very disastrous predicaments.

"It was Hutch," I told her. "If I don't call him back, he'll be suspicious."

"Call him back, but leave it on speaker so I can hear what both of you say. I swear to God, if you say one thing that sounds out of line, I'll shoot you before Rick can possibly ride to your rescue."

I called and when he answered, he said, "Is Liza with you?"

I looked at Liza and her eyes rounded, reflecting my own surprise at the question.

"No, why would she be?" I asked, trying to keep my voice steady while at the same time, searching my mind for some kind of code word that would tip him off, but wouldn't rouse Liza's suspicions. Maybe that only worked in the movies.

"I'm not sure," Hutch replied. "But Deanna is here with me. She and I have been comparing notes. Maybe we should come out and talk to you in pers—"

"No! I'm not even at home. Tell me over the phone."

"When will you be there? I really need to see you."

"It's going to be a while. Please, just tell me what's going on."

He sighed heavily. "Well, nothing's for sure, I'm trying to piece it all together. But, you could possibly be in danger. What Deanna's told me and what I've discovered in the investigation could mean Liza is behind everything that's happened, including burning her own house down," he ended incredulously.

Briefly, Liza closed her eyes, her mouth tightening as she gave a frustrated shake of her head.

"Why, that's absurd," I said, smiling sardonically at Liza. She gave a grim, cold smile in return.

"It sounds that way, but looking at the facts, it seems less and less absurd. Deanna was concerned about something she found, so she came to see me tonight. That, coupled with Liza's strange behavior lately, made Deanna realize Liza may be the perpetrator. Liza could be coming after you, Isabelle."

Still looking at Liza, I saw her eyes narrow and her lips mouth, "That bitch."

"Thanks for the warning," I said into the speaker. "I'll let you know if I hear from her."

"Okay. And call me when you get home. I really want to come out and talk to you."

"I will." I pushed one of the numbers instead of the

end button, hoping I could keep the line open long enough for Liza to say something Hutch could hear, but not long enough for him to say something she could hear.

Liza must have been wise to my plan, because she raised the gun and pressed a finger to her lips in a shushing gesture. Then, she reached her hand out for the phone. I slapped it into her palm, and she punched the 'end' button herself, shaking her head.

"I should punish you for that, but we're running out of time and need to get straight to the killing-you-but-making-it-look-like-suicide part." She pulled back the hammer and pointed the gun at my face. "Now, tell me what the note said, or I'll blow your head off."

The expression behind the deadly pistol was menacing, the green eyes snapping with fury and determination.

But, suddenly, I'd either become resigned, or overly confident. I laughed and lifted my hands, palms up. "You know what? I'm tired of the threats. You're going to kill me no matter what. Why should I make it easy for you? Go along with a plan that assures you'll get away with my murder, in addition to the others? What have I got to lose?"

She smiled, coldly, like a serpent might if it could smile. "In a word, Rick."

"Rick?" I parroted, some of my bravado fading.

"Yes. No matter what, I kill you. But if I'm going down for the crime, if I can't make it look like suicide, I'll kill him, too. And don't think I can't take him out before he gets to me. He'll be here eventually to check on you, and I'll be waiting. Even tough-guy Rick can't survive a surprise ambush."

I shook my head. "You love him."

"Yes, I do." She sighed regretfully.

"You love him, yet you'd murder him?"

"I know!" she exclaimed in a *can-you-believe-it* tone of voice. "It's, well, *crazy*, isn't it? Funny how, out of the three of us, *I'm* the one who got it."

I furrowed my brow, hopelessness giving way to confusion. "Three of us? Got what?"

"The insanity gene. From your father. *Our* father."

I went cold, not believing, yet somehow...believing. "He was your father, too?"

She nodded. "He had an affair with my mother. My dad, who raised me, thought *he* was my father. Then, after he died, my mother told me the truth. But she made me swear not to go to Daniel. Not to confront him. She was worried because of his reputation. Worried he might do something to harm me. Ironic, huh?" She barked out a maniacal laugh. "The man who raised me was poor. We never had any money growing up. But your family was rich, and you got Dad's inheritance. It wasn't fair. Was never fair. All I got from him was the lunacy. Do you know how hard that's been to hide all these years? How liberating it is to finally express it?" I didn't respond. "It's positively euphoric. Now, once you're dead, my parentage will mysteriously be revealed and I'll be entitled to your half of the inheritance. And, when I have money, maybe Rick will want me. Once you're dead, he'll have to stop wanting you."

I stared at her, trying to see if I could detect a family resemblance. Not really, although she did have the red hair of my father's Irish ancestry, where Carmen and I had our mother's Italian features.

"Did he know?" I asked, thinking how ironic it was that my father had killed my mother because he believed *she* was cheating. And he'd conceived a child with another woman.

She shook her head and her voice turned hard, angry. "I've spent way too much time explaining all this to you. It's time, now, to tell me what the hell was in the note."

Thinking quickly, hoping at least to stall a little, that maybe a miracle would happen, I said musingly, "So, that's what he meant."

"What who meant?"

"Dad. In the note. It must have been about you."

A glimmer of something, hope maybe, flickered in her unbalanced gaze. "What are you talking about? What did it say?"

"He said he'd tried to be a good father. He said he only wished he could have also been a father to *her*. He didn't give a name, just said 'her.' That puzzled us, but we figured it was just part of his unstable rantings. But now it makes perfect sense."

Every word of that, of course, was a lie. Dad's note had simply said, *I'm sorry. I can't live with the pain and I couldn't let your mother live after what she's done. I love you. Dad.* It was written in bold, firm, neat strokes, as if he were making a grocery list.

We couldn't know for sure, but we speculated he'd written it after he'd killed mom. Otherwise, he'd probably have said "I *can't* let your mother live," not *couldn't*. I would be forever haunted by the image of my father steadily penning the note while my beautiful, dead mother lay only a few feet away.

I looked at Liza. Tears pooled in her eyes. She

appeared hopeful, yet at the same time haunted. I felt a tug of remorse and, for just a few seconds, the slightest bond with this woman. She was my sister. Then I looked at the gun and my *Gilmore Girls* moment vanished. She also wanted to kill me.

"Do you have the note?" she asked softly, her expression one of wondrous awe.

"Yes." I was lying again. Carmen had the note. I'd wanted to destroy it, but Carmen had insisted on keeping it. She said that someday our children may want to see it. *Yeah, right.*

"Where is it?"

"It's out in my studio."

I was getting so good at lying, if I survived this, I might consider a career in politics. The hope was that during the trek to my studio, in the dark, the terrain would be unfamiliar and treacherous enough for her that I might find an opportunity to overpower her. If that didn't happen, and we made it all the way to my studio, well, I was basically screwed. I didn't have a plan B, unless, once we got inside, I could convince her to hold her hand underneath the needle of my sewing machine while I stepped on the presser foot. It wouldn't kill her, but it would hurt like a sonofabitch.

"Let's go," she said, motioning toward the door with her gun hand.

I took the flashlight from the table in the foyer and led my captor outside. I held the Coleman tightly, remembering my earlier consideration of it as a weapon. Somehow, a flashlight vs. a gun didn't seem like a very even match-up.

When we were halfway to the studio, I pretended to stumble over a section of the cracked sidewalk.

"Watch your step," I said over my shoulder. "This sidewalk is uneven in some places."

"Right, like you care."

I stopped and turned to look at her, hoping my expression was one of sincerity. "I do care. I just wish I'd known before that you were my sister. I've always liked you." I gave a wistful smile. "And if I'd known..."

"What do you mean?" Her voice held suspicion, yet there was something else there, a longing to believe?

"I wish we could have known each other as sisters, could have grown up together."

The gun wavered and I dared to hope.

She shook her head in disgust, and said, almost apologetically, "*Men*. If it weren't for our father and Rick, I wouldn't have to kill you."

A chill coursed through me at the matter-of-fact way she spoke of my impending murder. When I looked into her face, the features were a bit distorted in the shadows, making her look truly insane, just as she'd claimed.

She once more raised the gun and motioned me forward. "Now, let's go."

I tried to remember the exact spot where the sidewalk was coming apart, where the chunks of cement were completely loose. I kept the flashlight beam aimed at the ground in front of me, but I had to know just a few seconds *before* we reached the spot, so I would know exactly when to fall.

About six feet in front of the door to the studio, I saw it. I stumbled again, this time going down on my hands and knees, the flashlight bobbing, falling away from me. Liza reached out, probably instinctively, to try to catch me. I gripped the loose chunk of cement. I sensed her leaning over me and felt the roughness of the stone against my fingers.

The reality of it sunk in at that moment. Could I actually *hit* her with it? Maybe kill her?

If you don't, she's going to kill you.

With that sobering thought, I clutched the weapon in my hands and twisted sideways, bringing it up and slamming it into her forehead.

Her eyes rounded, and her pupils rolled back to where only the whites were showing. Her hand reflexively squeezed the trigger.

I'd never heard gunfire, other than on television, but I would've expected it to make a huge noise like a cannon going off. Instead, there was a snapping sound, sort of like the noise those little popper things made, the ones kids played with that exploded when thrown on the ground.

I thought I'd been hit, but felt nothing. Didn't they say when you were shot, at first you felt numb? Then the pain started? But there was no pain. No blood. No bullet holes.

Once the shots stopped, the hiss of rain was the only sound. Otherwise, the world had gone eerily silent. Faintly, I heard the hum of an engine and the slamming of car doors.

I trembled from a combination of fear and relief, still clutching the concrete. Rain sluiced over me, through me, running in my eyes and under the collar of my shirt.

Then Hutch was there, pointing his gun at Liza where she lay in a heap on the sidewalk. But, she wasn't moving. Deanna followed behind him and rushed over to Liza, dropping to the ground beside her.

I let go of the stone. Strong arms lifted me, and I was wrapped in Hutch's warmth as he enfolded me in his embrace. Burying my face into his chest, I let the tears fall, mixing with the rain and the smell of him, the feel of him.

"Are you okay?"

I felt the words rumble from his chest, reassuring and real. I nodded, wanting to say so much. Wanting to tell him that, yes, I was okay, and I would always be okay, as long as I could stay right here, forever. And that I loved him.

But all I said, so quietly I was unsure he heard me, was, "She's my sister."

****

Shortly after Hutch and Deanna's arrival, two ambulances came. Liza was alive and Deanna went with her to the hospital after apologizing to me half a dozen times for the way she'd treated me, for what Liza had put me through. She hadn't known Liza was my sister, but she'd seen signs of instability and felt she should have said something sooner. I assured her I didn't hold it against her.

The paramedics checked me over, but I convinced them I was fine, and they didn't insist I go to the hospital.

After they and the police, other than Hutch, had gone, I took a warm, soothing shower and put on black, cotton athletic pants and a white sweatshirt.

Hutch was in my kitchen waiting for me. He'd made a pot of coffee and rummaged around until he found a bottle of rum I didn't remember having. He poured a healthy shot into my steaming mug before handing it to me.

I took a sip and grimaced. It tasted awful, but it *felt* wonderful. It traveled through me, where I still felt cold on the inside, and left a trail of heat and tranquility.

"Are you okay?" he asked gently, tentatively.

I nodded. "Can you believe it was Liza? I can't imagine how it must have been for her to hold in those feelings all these years." The knowledge that she had felt her mental illness coming on for a long time made me think maybe I was okay. Maybe I would know if I had inherited the psychosis.

"She was obviously disturbed," Hutch said. "I wonder if she was telling the truth. About your father."

I'd given Hutch my statement earlier and told him Liza was my sister. I had nothing to back it up, but I knew it was true. "Yes, I'm sure of it. Carmen will be blown away." I hadn't called her yet. I needed some time to process it all. Time to wind down. "So, what, exactly, made you figure out Liza was the one behind all this?"

"There were several little clues, and when they all added up, and when Deanna came to see me, it was suddenly crystal clear. The night of the fire, one of Liza's neighbors called 911 a couple of minutes before Liza's call came in. The woman said she looked outside and saw Liza standing in the yard, watching the house burn. She thought it strange that Liza was standing so close, and she figured Liza had already called herself, but just to be sure, she also called. Listening to Liza's 911 call, you can easily tell she's outside. But, she claimed to be just waking up in the smoke-filled house when she phoned it in. Deanna told me she found a package of thimbles, with one missing, in Liza's house.

She didn't think much of it, even though Liza didn't sew, but later she heard about the thimble being found near where the fire started and it made her suspicious."

"Good God, to think she went so far as to burn down her own house." I couldn't wrap my mind around the depths of Liza's—my sister's—insanity.

Hutch reached out and took my free hand in both of his. "I'm sorry," he said softly, looking not at me but at our linked hands. He raised his head and I nearly gasped at the tortured look in his eyes. "I'm sorry you almost died, sorry I wasn't here for you, and so very sorry I doubted you, even for a second."

"Is that all?" I asked, my throat clogged with emotion, with loving him.

"Should there be more?" he asked warily.

"What about for waiting so long to tell me you love me? For waiting until I'm a *murder* suspect before telling me?"

"I told you years ago."

"We were kids. I didn't know..."

He leaned forward and kissed me, quickly, sweetly, tenderly. "You know it now. I love you."

I smiled, tears burning my eyes, but this time, they were tears of happiness. "I love you, too."

He let out a breath, as if he'd been waiting to hear those words. Waiting a lifetime.

He stared at me for a moment, then took the coffee cup out of my hand and placed it on the counter. Pulling me against him, he bent his head and claimed my lips in a fierce, consuming kiss. My head spun as I clung to him, returning the kiss, yearning, wanting him. Now.

"Wow," I said breathlessly when he lifted his mouth away from mine. My heart pounded and heat tingled through me.

"We've wasted too many years," he growled, still holding me against his hard body. "Marry me."

A passion-filled daze had me in its grip, but his words penetrated the fog and I stepped back, shaking my head. "You can't. You're the sheriff. You can't marry a woman the whole town hates."

"When all of this comes out, when Deanna sets them straight, they won't hate you. If they do, we'll move away. We'll start a new life somewhere else."

"You would do that for me? Move away from here?"

"There's nothing—short of murder," he amended with a grin, "that I wouldn't do for you."

His words, his eyes, seared into me, into my heart and soul.

"But, the..." I almost couldn't get the words out, but they had to be said. "My family. The insanity. What if that happens to me?"

"It won't," he said firmly. "You know it won't. You would have seen signs of it by now. And if it does, we'll deal with it. We'll get you help, whatever it takes." His gaze was tormented, longing. "I can't lose you again. If I do, *I'll* go crazy."

I saw the depth of Hutch's feelings, the love shining in his beautiful, silver-grey eyes and I stepped back into his arms, placing my hands around his neck and pulling him into a kiss to seal the deal.

Now I knew why I'd stayed.

The Twelfth Day

by

Alicia Dean

Acknowledgments

I'd like to thank my son, Presley, and my ex-husband, Terry, for their assistance in answering my research questions. The murder and mayhem couldn't have been accomplished without you. And, as always, thank you to my critique partners, friends, fellow writers, and family. You make my world a better place.

Chapter One

Sabrina Spencer relaxed her stranglehold on the steering wheel as she rolled her Ford Infiniti to a stop in the cabin's driveway. Between the snow-packed roads and holiday traffic, the eighty-mile trip from Sturgeon Bay to Lily Lake had taken two hours.

She shut the engine off and reached for the door handle. Her cell pinged with an alert. The song "Twelve Days of Christmas" played and the words, *On the first day of Christmas...* popped onto the display. A grainy image of a strip of duct tape waved across the screen. She frowned. *What the hell?*

She hated Christmas music, that song in particular. Her hands shook as memories surfaced, and she drew in a deep breath to calm herself. She didn't know what the image meant, or how it had come up on her phone, but it had nothing to do with her past. It was just some crazy fluke.

Determinedly, she pushed it out of her mind. She was here at the lake, where it was peaceful, with no holiday reminders. She wouldn't let some annoying technological glitch ruin that.

The lake house was a two-story wooden structure with a second floor balcony that stretched around the entire house. The first level's façade was stone, the second story logs, giving it a mismatched look that was oddly appealing. Behind it, the blue lake shimmered in the late afternoon sun that glinted off the small islands of ice floating on the water.

She climbed from the car. Her UGG boots crunched over icy snow as she hauled in her suitcase and laptop and closed the door, shivering at the bite of the cold wind.

She was stomping snow off her boots on the entryway rug when her phone rang. She looked at the display. *Great. Mitch.* She cringed, debating whether to ignore his call. Guilt prodded her to answer.

His chipper voice came over the line. "Hey, did you make it okay?"

"Yeah, finally. Just got here, getting my stuff out of the car."

"I really wish you would reconsider and let me come down and stay with you. I don't like the idea of going through the holidays without you."

Sabrina nearly groaned out loud. *Here we go again.* She and Mitch were co-workers, fellow high school teachers. They'd gone out once, but he had been pressing her for more ever since. He was nice enough, but she wasn't interested in him as more than a friend. Perhaps she'd been too kind and hadn't made her feelings clear enough. Or maybe he was just irritatingly persistent.

Silence and aloneness pressed in around her. Keeping the phone to her ear, she walked around opening shades to bring some light into the room. The spaciousness kept her from feeling like the walls were closing in.

For a moment, she was tempted to take Mitch up on his offer. Anything would be better than being alone.

She opened her mouth to agree, but Mitch spoke

before she could. "You can't keep putting me off like this. You need to decide, are we going to be together or not?"

Annoyance tensed her jaw. "I've tried to tell you that we're not. I like you as a friend, but nothing more." Ugh…maybe some things *were* worse than being alone.

"You went out with me. I thought we were getting along great."

"I can't have this conversation over and over. We are either friends, or we are nothing, but I am not in a place to get involved with anyone, definitely not someone I work with." The truth was there was zero attraction, zilch. He was a good-looking guy, but there was no chemistry. Not that she had chemistry with anyone, but until she did, she was not going to bother with the hassles of a relationship. "I need to finish unloading the car."

Mitch let out a long, heavy sigh. For a guy, he was such a drama queen. "Okay, call me if you need anything at all. Maybe I could come down and visit for at least a day or so?"

Because he was a nice guy, she didn't want to hurt him. But she didn't want to lead him on either. Despite her better judgment, she found herself saying, "We'll talk about it in a few days. For now, I need to get settled in so I can start on my black-capped chickadee project."

"I can't believe you're spending your time off working on a project for your students."

She hated to admit it, but, other than her friend and roommate, Lindsey, her students were pretty much all she had. Besides, there was nothing she loved more than teaching science. "Yeah, well, since I won't be celebrating the holidays, I don't have a whole lot else to do."

Even speaking the word *holiday* caused a pang in her chest. She used to love Christmas, but now the very mention sent chills through her body. Losing your entire family on Christmas pretty much sucked the joy out of the holiday. She pushed those thoughts away. In a remote cabin, while she was alone, was not the time to dwell on the horror from ten years ago.

They ended the call with vague plans about his visit, and she started a fire. "Bless you, Jess," she murmured aloud. The man she rented the cabin from every year always left her firewood and basic staples. He and his wife had been friends of her parents, and they had looked after her when her family died.

She went out to the car to retrieve her last few items. Snow pelted her, but she didn't mind. The cold was invigorating, just what she needed to rejuvenate her after the drive.

Once the car was unloaded and the food put away, she bundled up in her jacket and scarf, slung the bag containing the feeder, tools, and seeds over her shoulder, then slid open the patio door and tromped outside.

The icy snow raining down spurred her to make quick work of the feeder. She'd chosen the tube feeder because it seemed to be the most comfortable for the tiny birds. She installed it near a tree so the birds would be more likely to come around. They preferred having a nearby shelter in case they were threatened. It would also give them a place to roost at night, so hopefully, they would hang around the area. She finished by filling the tube with sunflower seeds, then hurried back inside.

After putting away her clothes and toiletries, she made a cup of hot cocoa and settled in front of her computer. She really just wanted to plop on the sofa and unwind after her hectic day, but she had promised Halley, one of her students, that she would check in when she arrived and stay in touch with her during the break. Halley was a little too dependent on Sabrina, a little too attached, but Sabrina didn't have the heart to put distance between them. She was rather attached to Halley, too, and the girl needed someone to care about her. She certainly didn't get that at home.

Sabrina opened up Skype and, in moments, Halley's face appeared on the screen. Sabrina smiled at her favorite student. "How is your vacation so far?"

A shadow passed over Halley's face, and Sabrina immediately regretted the question. Halley had an alcoholic mother, absent father, and no siblings, no friends. What the hell kind of vacation *could* she be having? Guilt pricked Sabrina for abandoning her.

Halley shrugged. "It's okay. How is yours?"

"So far, so good. I've got the feeder set up for the chickadees. I'll be bringing you guys all kinds of stuff for the new semester. You'd better be ready."

Her eyes behind the glasses lit up. "I can't wait until school starts again."

How many kids actually looked forward to the end of vacation? The poor girl was overweight and had severe acne; the other kids picked on her unmercifully. It was pretty bad that, even though she was bullied at school, it was preferable to her home life.

"Well, just try to enjoy your time off, and we'll keep in touch."

"Thanks." She smiled. "I think my aunt is coming

for Christmas. That will make things a lot better. Usually, it's just me and Mom."

"That's great."

"Yeah." Her lip trembled, and she glanced down.

"What is it?"

"Nothing."

"I know there's something. Spill."

"It's just these kids. They made some threats."

Rage boiled Sabrina's blood. "Who?"

After a slight hesitation, she said, "Chet and Marcie. They said I was going to get it for sucking up to you and getting them suspended."

That figured. Freaking bullies. Just before the break, they'd shoved Halley partially into her locker, laughed, and took pictures, then posted them on the internet with captions about how she was so fat they couldn't fit her all the way in.

Sabrina had reported it and demanded they be punished. They would be suspended after the break, and Chet would have to sit out the first two football games next season. But that was a slap on the wrist. Those two and their friends had tormented Halley all year.

She blinked back tears of sympathy. She was already too emotionally involved with her students, Halley in particular. She shouldn't reveal how much this affected her. But she was determined to do something about it when she returned to school.

"Promise me something. If they bother you again during break, let me know, okay?"

"Okay."

In the background, a woman's strident voice came from the hallway. Halley's mother screamed something unintelligible, and Halley's face tensed. "I guess I need to go."

Sabrina offered a smile. "Take care of yourself and try to have fun okay? We'll talk again in a few days."

"Sure, yeah. Talk to you soon."

As soon as the connection was broken, the room thrummed with loneliness. She should go down to the lodge. The owner, Theresa, didn't believe in Christmas, so Sabrina never had to worry about trees, decorations, Christmas music, or other reminders.

The wind howled against the windows, and she shivered. Maybe she wasn't ready to go back out just yet.

She started an oldies playlist on her MP3 player. With the songs of Otis Redding and Elvis Presley filling the room, she felt less lonely.

A pot of spaghetti was simmering on the stove when a noise came from the front door. Someone trying the knob. The living room and kitchen were one big open space, separated only by a long bar. Her gaze flew to the door.

Who can that be? Surely, Mitch hadn't driven up. If he had, he would have knocked. Someone was actually trying to get in.

She grabbed a knife from the counter. Her heart fluttered into her throat as she crept to the front door. Before she could reach it, the door flew open. Two men stood on the threshold.

Jerking her arm high over her head, holding the knife in what she hoped was a threatening gesture, she yelled, "Stop right there. I have a weapon."

The younger, smaller man jumped back with a squeak.

The taller guy held his hands up. "Whoa, whoa,

careful now. You want to put that thing away?"

She clutched the knife more tightly. "You want to tell me who the hell you are and how the hell you got in here?"

"My name is Josh Cravens, this is Dustin Reynolds. We got in because I have a key. We're here to make some repairs to the bathroom. Who are you?"

"Why didn't Jess tell me you were coming?"

He kept his hands raised and shrugged. The guy next to him remained silent, his eyes rounded, his trembling hands above his head. She almost felt sorry for him. But he could be a thief, a rapist, a murderer. She'd reserve her sympathy until she knew.

"I don't know why he didn't tell you, but I promise...we're contractors. We were hired by Jess Cofield, who owns the cabin. I've done work for him before." His eyes narrowed. "Come to think of it, how do I know *you're* supposed to be here?"

She barked out a shaky laugh. "You're questioning me?" She backed up a few steps, heading to the bar where her cell phone lay. "You stay right there. I'm calling Jess."

The Josh guy gestured with his hand. "By all means. Please do. My arms are getting tired, and Dustin here is about to have a coronary."

Sabrina punched in the speed dial for Jess, keeping a wary eye on the intruders. Admittedly, they looked like contractors. Looked harmless, but why wouldn't Jess have told her, and why were they coming in the *evening* to begin work on a job?

Jess answered. "Hey, Sabrina. Did you get settled in?"

"Yes, thanks. Uhm, but there's a little bit of a

problem."

"What's that, hon?"

"These guys, Josh and..." She'd forgotten his name. She lifted her brows toward the trembling one. He opened his mouth, but rather than words, chattering came out.

"Dustin," Josh supplied.

"Dustin," she said to Jess. "They say you hired them to do some work on the cabin?"

"Oh, shoot. Yeah, I forgot to tell you. Sorry. With the kids and grandkids coming for the holidays, Marge and I have been running around like chickens with our heads cut off. I hired Josh and his friend to make some repairs. Sorry it coincides with your time there. Josh has a few weeks off his regular job, and it's the only time he could do it. He's the one who built that new utility room off the kitchen. I put in a washer and dryer last week. Now you don't have to lug your laundry up to the lodge."

Relief and embarrassment flooded her. "No problem. I just wanted to make sure. Thanks again for letting me use the cabin."

"You're welcome, dear. Marge says hi and Merry..." He stopped. "Uh, enjoy the cabin."

She cringed. She hated the fact she couldn't look at Christmas normally, like everyone else did. "Thanks, Jess. Give her my love, and you guys enjoy your kids and grandbabies."

She punched the end button and tossed her phone on the bar. Feeling foolish, she lowered the knife. "I'm sorry. I just...Jess didn't tell me."

Josh dropped his hands. "No problem. I'd have reacted the same way. Except, I might have used a bigger knife." He grinned.

She looked at the four-inch paring knife she still held. Josh could have easily disarmed her. She flushed. "It was the closest one."

Josh elbowed Dustin. "You can drop your hands now, she's not going to filet us to death."

Dustin's cheeks reddened. "Oh, yeah."

"Let's start over. I'm Sabrina Spencer. Nice to meet you. Come on in."

"Thanks." They moved inside, and Josh pushed the door shut.

"Can I ask why you're starting so late? Wouldn't it be better to wait until the morning?"

"We just wanted to come by and assess the work so we'd know how much time to plan and what tools to bring. Jess didn't tell us about you either. We were as surprised as you were." His lips curved in a grin. For the first time, she noticed his dimpled jaw and ice-blue eyes. Her heart performed an annoying little flutter. She attributed it to the remnants of her fright, rather than the unexpected male attractiveness that suddenly landed in her living room.

"Feel free. Do whatever you need to." She pointed down the hallway. "Bathroom's that way."

"Got it, thanks." They shed their coats and hung them on the rack by the door, then headed to the back of the house.

Half an hour later, the two men reemerged.

"That's all we need," Josh said. "Sorry for the scare."

Sabrina lifted a shoulder. "Sorry for brandishing a knife." The thought of them leaving produced a trickle of unease. She'd be alone...and it was so much worse after having human contact. "Listen, I made spaghetti. Would you guys like to stay for dinner?"

Dustin rubbed his hands together. "Spaghetti's my favorite. Can we, Josh?"

Josh ruffled his hair. "Sure. Let's go wash up."

During dinner, Sabrina thought she'd be uncomfortable, trying to make conversation with two strangers, but Dustin eliminated that problem by chattering non-stop, between stuffing his mouth full of spaghetti and garlic bread.

She learned that he and Josh lived in Green Bay, they were neighbors, and Josh worked for the City of Green Bay as an engineer. He hired Dustin to help on side jobs he did for friends and family. They'd done some work on Lambeau field. The mention of which incited Dustin into an enthusiastic monologue filled with praise for the Packers. He talked non-stop for several minutes about how he missed Brett Favre, but what an awesome quarterback Aaron Rodgers was, so on and so forth. Although Sabrina had lived in Wisconsin her entire life, she didn't follow football. In this part of the country, that made her an oddity, but her youth had been spent partying and her young adult years studying and teaching. Football never appealed to her.

Josh held up a hand. "Let's let the lady talk for a bit, 'kay, bud?"

Dustin nodded. "Sorry. I'm a chatterbox."

Josh favored him with an affectionate grin, and Sabrina warmed toward him. He was obviously good to the kid—well, maybe 'kid' wasn't accurate. Dustin was probably in his early twenties, but he was obviously slightly mentally challenged.

"So," Josh took a drink of tea. "Tell us about you."

"I'm a high school science teacher," she said. "I'm renting the cabin for the holidays."

Dustin swallowed a mouthful. "You're going to be all by yourself during Christmas?"

"It's all right. I don't like Christmas anyway."

Dustin's eyes rounded. "How can anyone not like Christmas?"

Sabrina grimaced. "It's just...too much of a hassle." No way was she going to tell her life story to these strangers. But then again, anyone from the area likely knew what had happened. When a serial killer wipes out an entire family, except one member he kept locked up and tormented, it was big news.

If they recognized her, they didn't let on. It had been ten years, but everyone in Wisconsin knew about the Rosewood murders—dubbed so because the house they lived in, that her family died in, was on Rosewood Lane.

In an attempt to shift the focus off her distaste for the holiday, she said, "Even worse than that, I don't like football."

Dustin jumped to his feet. "You what? No Packers?"

She shook her head. "If I were going to like football, it would definitely be the Packers. Does that help?"

He scrunched his nose. "Not much."

She laughed. "Sorry."

Josh stood. "Thanks for dinner. We'll help you with the dishes, then get out of your way."

"No need to help, I can handle them."

"I insist. We're not leaving you with a mess after

your hospitality."

Dustin frowned. "Don't you need to get to Shady's? I thought Chastity was meeting you there at eight."

Sabrina lifted her brows. "I'm keeping you from a date?"

Josh shrugged. "Not a date. I just—"

"Chastity is a girl," Dustin cut in. "Her hair's red, not dark like yours, and she's got bigger..." He stopped, his cheeks reddening. "Bigger eyes. But her eyes are green instead of brown like yours. But she's not his girlfriend. Josh don't date. He just hooks up. I drive him."

Josh clamped a hand over Dustin's mouth. "Hey, buddy, we don't need to spill all our info, right?"

Sabrina's estimation of him dropped by about a hundred points. "You have this young man drive you around to your hook ups? What, does he wait in the car while you...?" She cut a look at Dustin. His expression showed misery. She didn't want to make him feel worse. "Sorry, none of my business."

"It's not like that," Josh said. "Sometimes when Dustin and I go out, I have him drive if I've had too much to drink. That's all he meant."

"Yeah, me and Josh hang out together, but I drive home 'cause sometimes Josh is too wasted. When he hooks up, he takes a cab so I don't have to wait all night." Dustin beamed up at Josh like he'd rescued a kitten from a tree.

"*Well*." She turned a sarcastic expression on Josh. "It's quite admirable he doesn't make you wait outside all night."

Josh flinched. "I guess we will let you take care of

the dishes. We'd better head out. See you in the morning. Is six too early?"

"I'll be up. I'm an early riser."

"Thanks for dinner." They grabbed coats from the rack by the front door. "Hope we're not wrecking your vacation by working these next few days."

"Not at all." In spite of her less than stellar opinion of Josh, she liked Dustin, and it would be nice to have company.

Chapter Two

Early the next morning, Sabrina went out back to set up a recorder, nestling it inside a box and placing it in a nearby tree. She hoped to catch the adorable little birds in person, but in case that didn't happen, she wanted to get them on tape.

Her students would love this. Well, most of them. Brutes like Chet thrived on tormenting rather than learning and discovery. Why couldn't she get through to him? She'd tried on more than one occasion, but he'd been more focused on her breasts than her words.

Cold wind seared her unprotected face between her scarf and hat. She might have to start wearing a ski mask as much time as she'd be spending outside.

Once everything was set up, she hurried into the cabin. She peeled off her coat, gloves, and scarf and poured a large mug of coffee.

A knock came, and she went to the front door to let in Josh and Dustin.

Josh wore a white Henley shirt, faded jeans, and a tool belt around his hips. His dark hair was sprinkled with crystals of snow. Her heart gave a little skip, much to her dismay. He was even better looking than she remembered.

She stepped back and swept her arm out. "Come in. Coffee?"

Josh rubbed his hands together as he stepped

inside. "Sounds great."

She poured them both a cup. Josh leaned his hip against the bar and sipped his.

She sat at the table and wrapped her hands around her mug. "So, did you have fun last night?"

Dustin grinned. "He must have 'cause I ended up picking him up this morning."

Josh shoved his shoulder. "What did we talk about?"

Dustin pursed his lips. "About me being a blabbermouth."

"Right. Keep it on the down low."

"On the down low." Dustin stuck his clenched hand out, and they fist-bumped.

Of course, the guy was a whore-dog party-hound. *Figures.* But, that was actually a good thing. It might keep her from noticing how his blue eyes sparkled when he smiled, and his deep dimples creased on either side of his full mouth.

She clenched her jaw. At least, she hoped it would.

The guys headed to work in the guest bathroom while she pulled out her laptop and made notes about the chickadees, along with grading papers the students had turned in before the break. The sounds of hammering and the murmur of male voices filtered to her, soothing, comforting. Once in a while, a loud burst of laughter came from Dustin.

Three hours passed, and Sabrina's attention was caught by a loud howling wind that creaked the house. Tiny shards of ice pelted the windows.

She rose and looked outside. If Josh and Dustin didn't leave soon, they'd have trouble traversing the icy roads. She was about to go suggest they knock off for the day, when a ping sounded from her laptop.

A strain of "Twelve Days of Christmas" started. *What the hell?*

She rushed over to the computer. Another image wavered on the screen—a length of rope, this one with the text, *On the second day of Christmas…*

Chills washed over her. Probably just some kind of odd pop up glitch. Nevertheless, a shudder ripped through her body.

She went into Chrome settings to turn off pop ups. That should stop it.

But the first one was on your phone…

Well, she wasn't a computer expert, but her phone had internet as well. It was all connected, and the changed setting would likely resolve the issue in both places.

She headed down the hall and stopped in the doorway to the bathroom. Josh was setting cream-colored tiles into the shower wall. Dustin was meticulously spreading grout between new tiles on the floor.

"Hey guys, the roads are getting bad. Thought you might want to go home before it gets too treacherous."

Josh looked at her over his shoulder. "We're not at a good stopping place. The snowplows will take care of the roads. We'll be fine."

She shrugged. "Suit yourself."

She left them to their work, put on her coat and gloves, poured another mug of coffee, and went outside on the deck to watch the feeder. It was empty at the moment, but might not be for long. The little birds were hardy. The weather wouldn't keep them away, and if she hoped to catch a glimpse, it needed to be in the daytime. At night, they were still. They possessed the amazing ability of going into hypothermia to survive the bitter cold.

She'd been out for fifteen minutes, without a single sighting, when the sound of the glass door sliding made her turn.

Josh came out on the deck. "Are you insane?"

"Why?"

"Oh, I don't know. It's ten degrees, and you're sitting outside in an ice storm."

"I'm hoping to catch sight of a chickadee."

"You can't watch from the window?"

"I like being outside." In spite of the roominess of the cabin, if she didn't get out a few times throughout the day, she started to feel short of breath, felt the walls closing in on her. This was more or less preventative maintenance.

"Dustin and I are heading out. See you in the morning. Are you sure you don't want to come inside?"

"I'll go in soon. Don't worry about me. I'll see you guys in the morning. Be careful out there."

"Us be careful? You're the crazy one."

She made a face at him, and he grinned, sliding the door open and disappearing inside.

The cold seemed somehow more severe once he was gone.

****

The next day, Dustin and Josh had been hard at work for several hours when they came down the hallway.

"We're going up to the lodge for lunch," Josh said. "Want to come?"

"Sure." She had been meaning to go up and say hi

to Theresa anyway. And she was starving.

"Come on, we're driving."

They bundled up and stepped outside. A single-cab Chevy pickup sat next to her Infinity.

She halted. Riding in that tiny cab, squished between two bodies? *No way in hell*.

"I'll drive," she said.

Josh shook his head. "Too dangerous on these slick lake roads."

Her ire rose. "You mean because I'm a woman driver?"

His mouth twisted. "Don't get all women's libby and defensive. I meant because my truck has snow tires, front wheel drive, and it's heavier."

"My car has front-wheel drive and snow tires. It might not be as heavy as your truck, but it does fine on the roads, and I'm more accustomed to the route."

Josh lifted his arms to his sides and let them drop. "Suit yourself."

They piled into her car and drove the half mile to the lodge. Inside, the room was warmed with a roaring fire in the stone fireplace.

Theresa met her at the door and hugged her tightly. She was in her early sixties, with silver hair and a red-trimmed white apron tied around her plump waist. "I was wondering when you were going to come up and see me." Theresa released her and gave Josh and Dustin a questioning look. "Who are your friends?"

Sabrina introduced them, and Josh turned his charming smile on the older woman, causing a pink blush to rise in her cheeks.

"Nice to have you. Come on, we're having pot roast, potatoes, asparagus, and chocolate cake."

Sabrina's mouth watered. Theresa was a phenomenal cook.

In the dining area, an elderly couple and a middle-aged couple sat at a long table in the center of the room. Theresa made introductions. The elderly couple were Henry and Doris Buckingham, the others were Ben and Tracy Stewart.

While Theresa owned the lodge itself, the cabins were owned by individuals and rented out, when the owners themselves weren't occupying them. Theresa's staff took care of the upkeep on the properties while the owners were away.

Sabrina slipped her coat off and she, Dustin, and Josh sat on the bench across from the Stewarts. Still feeling the cold, Sabrina shivered. She smiled at Tracy. "I suppose this isn't the ideal time to visit the lake."

The woman was blonde, dainty, with a makeup-less fresh-scrubbed look. Ben was handsome, with short dark hair shot with gray at the temples. He took his wife's hand. "We love it here. Nice and peaceful. Gets us away from the holiday rat race."

"But no tree?" Dustin asked.

"Theresa doesn't believe in Christmas," Sabrina told him.

Dustin wrinkled his forehead. "What kind of crazy nonsense is that? Christmas is real, how can you not believe in it?"

Josh bent to his ear. "Down low, buddy, remember?"

Dustin's face scrunched. "Sorry."

Lunch was delicious. Ben and Tracy were friendly, and Ben kept them laughing with anecdotes about his job as a used car salesman.

The older couple was subdued. They confessed they had recently lost their only child and escaped to the lake to avoid holiday memories. Sabrina could empathize.

"Oh yeah, I almost forgot." Theresa stood and went to a sideboard, picked up a small, wrapped box, and handed it to Sabrina. "This was left on the porch for you."

"Thanks." Heat warmed Sabrina's cheeks. It was probably from Mitch. She didn't want to open it in front of everyone. She set the box on the bench beside her.

"Come on, open it." Dustin's eyes were bright with excitement.

"I think I'll wait."

"Oh, come on," Ben chimed in. "The kid wants to see what you got. We all do."

Tracy punched his shoulder and rolled her eyes. "You're worse than a child at Christmas."

With the expectant stares glued to her, Sabrina felt put on the spot. Reluctantly, she peeled off the wrapping. Hopefully, it wasn't something sappy and romantic. Mitch had a tendency toward that sort of thing.

She opened the box lid. "The Twelve Days of Christmas" played from one of those little discs like they put into greeting cards. A silver bracelet lay amidst crumpled red tissue paper. And a note. *On the third day of Christmas…*

She gasped. The box fell from her trembling hands and landed on the table.

"Hey," Josh's low voice spoke beside her. He put his hand over hers, and a slight sense of calm stole through her. "You all right?"

All eyes were on her. "I-I thought I saw a spider in the box. I'm fine."

"You sure?" His gaze captured hers. Doubt lingered in their blue depths.

Sabrina nodded. Everyone went back to eating, but she could barely focus on the remainder of the meal. This wasn't just a computer glitch. The bracelet was just like the one she wore often, had been wearing when she was rescued. Someone was purposely referencing her past. *But why*? Was it a sick joke?

Everyone knew Samuel Goodman had hummed "Twelve Days of Christmas" over and over while he held her captive. They would know he used duct tape and rope and would know about the bracelet. She'd been wearing it in the photographs shown on the news. All the information she'd given to the police had made it into the media. So it could be anyone, someone just screwing with her. It couldn't be Goodman. He was serving a life sentence in a maximum-security prison. Or was he…

If he'd escaped, she'd have heard, right? She needed to call Detective Keller who'd headed up the case. But, he would have let her know if Samuel Goodman escaped. Hell, it would be all over the news.

No, this is just some sick prank. Maybe Chet or one of the other troublemakers at school. They were fascinated with her past. She probably should have moved away from Sturgeon Bay after the tragedy, but she couldn't stand the thought of leaving her family, even though they would forever reside in the cemetery.

She couldn't stay in the home, though. She'd sold the house, although doing so hadn't been easy. She'd taken a loss. No one wanted to live in a house where a couple and their young son were murdered. A knot clogged her throat, and she swallowed back tears.

"Are you ready to go back?" Josh's voice brought her out of her musings.

She nodded. The conversation had steered away from her, and for that, she was grateful.

"I'll drive, if that's okay," he offered.

"Yes, fine." She wouldn't let him know how relieved she was. Her shakiness and preoccupation with the strange messages might cause her to drive them off the road.

****

Each of the following two days, another odd message appeared—one on her phone, one on her laptop. Both had played the song. One had been a rose, the other a block of wood. She easily solved the puzzle—Rosewood Lane. Yes, there was no doubt. These incidents were related to the murders.

She'd called Detective Keller, who assured her Goodman was locked up nice and tight. Although it wasn't his jurisdiction, he offered to come check things out, and she said she'd call on him if she didn't figure it out soon, or if they became more threatening.

She wouldn't let this cripple her. Some asshole was playing a sick game, and whoever it was, she'd be damned if she'd let them win.

It was Monday morning, and she was finishing up her second cup of coffee when Josh and Dustin arrived. Josh's eyes were red, and his hair looked like he'd gotten caught in a windstorm.

Sabrina narrowed her eyes and spoke to Dustin. "What's wrong with him?"

"Too much celebrating. Packers won, and he met a

hot blonde."

Josh groaned. "Jesus Christ, Dustin. Down low."

Sabrina's mouth tightened. "Maybe you shouldn't expose him to all your shenanigans, and he wouldn't have to be deceptive."

Josh's lips quirked. "*Shenanigans*? What are you, eighty? And it's not being deceptive, since it's none of your damn business what I do."

Dustin hung his head. "Sorry, Sabrina. Josh is grouchy when he's hungover. Even if he gets laid."

Josh growled and clenched his fists. "Son of a bitch, Dustin. Don't apologize for me, and don't tell her," he pointed a finger at Sabrina, "another damn thing about my business or you're off the job, got it?"

Sabrina's blood heated with anger. "Don't take it out on him."

"I don't need this bullshit from two nags. Jesus, it's like I'm fucking married." His mouth twisted. "And if I ever was stupid enough to get married, it wouldn't be to some buttoned-up, judgmental shrew."

Unwarranted, a shaft of pain shot through her. Why should she give a damn what he thought? She lifted her chin and glared at him. "Shrew? Now look who's eighty!"

He tossed her a scowl and stomped down the hallway.

Dustin's lip trembled. "He's a really good man, promise. He just doesn't feel like himself today."

Sabrina hated that her hands shook and her heart ached. "Oh, I think he's shown *exactly* who he is today."

"It's all my fault. My big blabbermouth."

She put a gentle hand on his shoulder. He reminded

her of Halley, beaten down and unwanted. "It's not your fault at all. Don't let Josh bully you and treat you like crap. He just uses you."

Dustin jerked away. He lifted a finger and shook it in her face. "Don't ever say Josh is a bully. He's my best friend. No one else wants to hang out with me. Josh could hang out with *any* of his other buddies, but he hangs out with me all the time. Plus, he…" He sniffled. "He saved me."

Sabrina flinched. "I'm sorry, I didn't mean—"

"Momma said if I couldn't find a job, they'd have to put me in a special home. Josh was the only one who gave me a job, so don't never, *ever* say that about him again."

Misery swamped her. "Okay, okay. You're right. I'm sorry. Josh is a good man."

"A *very* good man."

"A *very* good man," she repeated.

"He just has his moods."

"Right." Fine, so he wasn't all bad. He'd rescued the kid. That was great, but he was a promiscuous drunk, and she'd had her fill of those. She'd actually *been* one of those. An out of control teen with no thought for anything other than fun. And look what had come of that.

She offered Dustin an apologetic smile. "I am sorry about what I said. I'll let you get to work."

Dustin patted her shoulder. "Okay, Sabrina. Sorry I had to yell at you. Sorry Josh treated you like shit, too."

"It's all right. Friends?" She stuck out her hand.

He took it. "Yeah, but Josh is still my *best* friend."

She smiled. "I can live with that."

Chapter Three

Sabrina bundled up and went out to check the feeder. Winter sunlight glinted off the smooth surface of the lake. Not a bird in sight, but some of the seeds were missing. She retrieved the recorder and checked the video.

Excitement bubbled when a tiny chickadee hopped onto the feeder and was soon joined by two others. They flitted around in their signature flying/hopping movements. The recorder had caught their faint whistles and chirps, and even the call they made that sounded like an alarm. She smiled. This was gold. She sent the recording to her email and erased it, then set it to record again.

Inside, she fixed lunch, but Josh and Dustin stayed in the bathroom, working. Their usual chatter was absent. She tried to tell herself she was okay with that, but she was lying. The house seemed too silent and cold without their voices and laughter. What would she do when they left? In spite of Josh being a dick sometimes, it was nice to have company.

A knock sounded at the door.

She looked through the peephole to find Ben and Tracy standing outside. She opened the door. "Hello, what a surprise." She moved back and gestured for them to come in, and they stepped inside.

Tracy said, "Sorry to bother you. Our electricity is

out, and that maintenance guy is fixing it. He kind of gives us the creeps. Mind if we hang out here for a little bit?"

Richard *was* a little creepy. Sabrina avoided him as much as she could. "Not at all. I was about to make stroganoff. Would you like to stay for dinner?"

"We'd love it." Ben hoisted a bottle of wine she hadn't noticed him holding. "We brought this, just in case you invited us in." He grinned.

She smiled back. "That's great. I'll open it with dinner."

Just as they settled in the living room, Josh and Dustin entered from the hallway.

Sabrina gestured to the couple. "Remember Ben and Tracy?"

Josh narrowed his eyes. "Yeah, hi." *Not the friendliest greeting.*

"Maintenance is working on their electricity so they're hanging out here. We were about to have dinner. Would you care to join us?" She was only being polite. She had barely enough for the three of them. If Dustin and Josh accepted her offer, she'd have to throw some things together to go with it.

At the same time, Dustin said yes, and Josh said no.

Josh frowned. "Sorry, bud. It's been a long day. I need a shower and to take care of some things at home."

Dustin looked crestfallen.

Sabrina said, "He could stay, and I can drive him home later."

"No, I don't want you out on the roads." As if realizing he sounded too caring, Josh clamped his mouth shut, and his frown deepened. "Dustin needs to get home to his mother anyway. Thanks for the offer. You folks have a good evening."

When the door closed behind them, Tracy said, "Damn, he's hot."

Ben narrowed his eyes and gripped his wife's arm. "Now, honey, you know how jealous I get when you look at other men."

Tracy laughed uncomfortably. "I was just teasing. You know you're the only man for me." She kissed him on the cheek, her expression almost pleading. Something felt off about the exchange. Did Ben abuse her?

The conversation turned to the weather, wine, and Richard's creepiness; tensions eased. Ben was loving and attentive toward Tracy. As usual, Sabrina had overreacted. Why did she have to always look beneath the surface of every word or action and try to find the hidden motive? People were people, humans. Imperfect humans, and sometimes jealousy was just jealousy.

After dinner, they drank wine and talked until close to midnight. Sabrina's promise to Skype with Halley pricked her conscience, but time got away. Once her company left, she just wanted to go to bed. She shot Halley a quick text and told her they'd Skype tomorrow.

Sabrina showered and brushed her teeth, then slipped into her warm, flannel gown. Loneliness seeped through her more so than usual. Maybe it was because the house had been full this evening, or maybe it was because she was growing accustomed to having Josh and Dustin around, but whatever the reason, the quiet screamed at her like a banshee.

She flipped the hall light on, pushed the bedroom door open wide, then climbed under the covers. But sleep eluded her.

After an hour of tossing and turning, she got up and warmed a cup of milk. Sipping from the mug, she wandered around the house, stopping at the window to peer outside at the feeder. But the birds hibernated at night, there was nothing to see.

She picked up her cell from the bar. Maybe she should tell Mitch to come out after all. It was late, but she could shoot him a text, and he'd see it tomorrow.

But, was she really prepared for what that would entail?

No, she wasn't. She laid the phone back down.

She finished her milk and headed back to bed. Snuggled beneath the covers, she went through her relaxation rituals, *clear your mind, deep breaths, relax your entire body, starting with the toes, moving slowly up through the legs, through your stomach, your arms...*

Sometime later, she was pulled out of sleep by the inability to breathe. She struggled to draw in air and fought against the pressure on her chest. Her eyes flew open, and she sat up abruptly, heart pounding. What had woken her?

She tried to look around the room, but it was pitch black. What the hell? The door was shut. She knew she had left it open before going to bed.

Gasping, she flung the covers off and raced to the door. She grabbed the knob and whipped the door open. The lights were off. Maybe a power outage? But how had the door closed?

She stumbled into the hall and scrambled her hand

along the wall until she found the switch. She hit it, and light bathed the area. Letting out a cry of relief, she took in deep pulls of oxygen.

She pressed against the wall and wrapped her arms around her body. Images of the room in the back of the carriage house flooded in. The thick darkness, the musty, moldy stench, no windows, no air…

But worse, so much worse, the monster in the darkness, his cold hands touching her flesh. "No, no, no," she muttered. She squeezed her eyes shut, trying to banish the memories.

A violent shudder racked her body. The counselor she'd seen the year following the ordeal had advised that, when the memories overcame her, she take her mind somewhere pleasant, somewhere light and safe, where nothing could harm her. But it never worked. The reality, the horror, was much, much stronger than any fantasy she tried to conjure.

She turned to head back to her room. A figure loomed in front of her. Hands gripped her shoulders.

She let out a scream and wrenched away, stumbling against the wall. God, he was here, her nightmare was here, and she was going to die…

"Sabrina? For God's sake, what's wrong?"

The familiar voice registered at the same time her eyes brought him into focus. "Josh? Is it really you?" Her control dissolved, and sobs wracked her body. Her entire frame trembled so violently, her teeth clacked together.

"Hey, hey, what's the matter?" Josh brushed the hair back from her face and took her shoulders gently in his hands. "Tell me."

She concentrated on the concern in his eyes, the

soft tone of his voice. No terror had ascended, no monster. Just Josh. Then why couldn't she stop shaking?

His arms went around her, and he pulled her close to his body. She buried her face in his chest and snuggled into his warmth. He held her until the trembles subsided.

Slowly, he eased her away and tilted her chin up with his finger. "Tell me what happened."

She swiped at tears and stepped away from him. Embarrassment heated her skin. "Did you close the door and turn off the light?"

His brow creased. "Yeah, I did. I didn't want to disturb you."

She didn't want to tell him that she had to sleep with a door open and the light on, but since she'd made such a fool of herself perhaps she should come clean.

But the real question was… She frowned up at him. "What are you doing here?"

He scrubbed his hands over his face. "Dustin picked me up at the bar and brought me here. I told him to take me home, but he drove here." He grimaced. "I sort of…well, I dozed off in the truck after I said to take me home and when I woke, we were in your drive."

"Why did he bring you here?"

"I don't know. Sometimes the kid baffles me. He pretty much kicked me out of my own truck and left. He said I needed to learn to get along."

"With me?"

He cocked a crooked grin, and her heart pounded, but this time not from fear. *Dammit.*

"I don't know if he's trying to play matchmaker, or if he just doesn't want two people he likes so much to be at odds."

"Well, just because I think you're a woman-chasing drunk, it doesn't mean we're at odds."

He laughed. "And just because I think you're a stuffy, frigid science nerd, it doesn't mean that I don't like you."

She smiled. "Touché." She peered at him. "You don't seem all that drunk."

"I slept for a few hours. I think I slept it off."

"Do you literally drink every day?"

"Not every day, but probably more than I should."

Conflicted emotions battled inside her. Did Josh only hang out with Dustin so he'd have a driver for his escapades? No, he could take Uber if that was all he wanted. So, why? "I told Dustin a few days ago that you were just using him for a designated driver, and he nearly tore my head off." She grinned at the memory of Dustin's defense of his hero. "I probably shouldn't have said that, but I have to wonder…are you using him?"

He frowned. "Of course not. I would never do anything to take advantage of that kid. He loves going out with me and really loves driving my truck." He chuckled. "I guess you could say it's a win-win for us both. And, just for the record, I don't 'hook up' as much as Dustin insinuated. I think he has me built up in his mind as some kind of macho, ladies' man who beds a different woman every night. Trust me, that's not me."

Inexplicably, his explanation reassured her, though why it should matter so much, she had no idea. She just knew that she was extremely glad he was here, and suddenly, the darkness, the loneliness, didn't seem so pronounced. "I'm going to make some hot chocolate. I can't go back to sleep right now anyway. Would you like some?"

"Oh yeah, hot chocolate. That's exactly what I want."

She lifted her brows. "I'm not feeding you alcohol."

"Exactly what I would expect from a Polly Poindexter."

She rolled her eyes. "Last chance, hot chocolate or not?"

"Sure, I'll take some hot chocolate, thanks."

He followed her into the kitchen. She warmed milk in a saucepan on the stovetop and added cocoa, sugar, and vanilla.

"Wow." Josh whistled. "You go all out on hot chocolate preparation."

She handed him a mug. "It's much better than the powder kind."

He took a sip. "Damn straight it is." He raised his gaze. "Oh, wait. I didn't offend you with my cursing, did I?"

She twisted her mouth. "Ha, ha."

They went into the living room and sat side by side on the sofa.

A contented quiet settled over them. She no longer felt lonely. She was oddly peaceful, happy, in spite of the horrific images that had plagued her moments before.

"So," Josh's warm, husky voice caressed her. "You want to tell me what that was all about earlier?"

She lifted her hot chocolate to her lips, blew on it, and took a sip. "I'm not sure if I do." The only people she'd discussed the tragedy with were the police, her counselor, and her best friend, Lindsey. And, she hadn't told them everything.

"Sometimes talking makes the nightmares go away."

She let out a humorless laugh. "These nightmares will be with me for the rest of my life."

Josh took her hand and rubbed his thumb along the back. "You don't have to talk about it if it's too painful."

Warmth filtered from his touch and blossomed in her stomach.

She remained silent for a few moments, sipping her hot chocolate. The need to talk outweighed her need for privacy. Although she didn't know Josh well, and she wasn't sure what she truly thought of him, his presence inspired security, comfort. Drawing in a deep breath, she said, "How long have you lived in Green Bay?"

"Five years, why?"

"Maybe you didn't hear about the murders that took place in 2005. The Rosewood murders."

"I did hear something about that. I don't know all the details, though."

Her lips pinched together. "I do. I know more than I want to."

He frowned, but didn't speak.

She took another deep breath. "My family were the ones who were murdered that night."

"Oh, my God, Sabrina." He took her hands and squeezed. "I'm so, so sorry. I don't know what to say."

She gave a jerky nod. The events of that evening two weeks before Christmas unfolded in her mind. The party at the bar she'd been too young to get into. Dancing, drinking. Unaware she'd been targeted. That

Samuel Goodman had chosen her as his next victim and followed her home.

Her voice was steady as she relayed the details. "I got home, somehow. I could have killed someone on the way as much as I'd been drinking." She grunted a half sob, half cry. "Instead, I led a killer home to my family."

Josh's grip tightened on her hands, but he didn't speak.

"I let myself into the quiet house, glad my parents weren't awake to chew me out. I'd just fallen asleep when I heard the screams." Her tone remained calm, but trembles moved over her body. "I jumped out of bed and raced down the hallway to my parents' bedroom. My father and mother lay in their bed, bleeding. A man stood over them, holding something in his hand. I didn't realize until later, it was a knife.

"I screamed and tore down the hallway to my brother's room. I burst through his door, planning to grab him and escape." An image of Adam's lifeless body rose, and a sob jerked in her chest. "He-he was only thirteen years old. He wanted to play football for the Packers." She wiped tears off her cheeks. "The killer had gotten to him first. He'd been stabbed in his bed too. I whirled, screaming hysterically. I ran out of the room, looking for a phone, suddenly stone cold sober. Maybe they weren't dead. Maybe I could call an ambulance, and they would be fine.

"When I reached the hallway, he was standing there, breathing heavily. I remember that loud breath, going in and out from behind that black mask covering his face." She shuddered. "A knife in his right hand dripped blood onto my mom's carpet. I knew I would be next and, in that moment, I honestly didn't care. But, somehow, my survival instincts must have kicked in. I ran to my brother's window and smashed through it with his baseball trophy. I climbed out onto the roof. Glass shredded my bare feet, but I scarcely felt the pain. I slid to the edge of the roof, looking down below into the bushes, knowing that the fall might kill me. Behind me, the man was getting close. He climbed out the window, and I decided I would take my chances with the two stories and hard ground over a maniac with a knife. I jumped and landed in the bushes."

She closed her eyes briefly. "I scrambled to disentangle myself from the shrubs and lunged to my feet. I'd only taken a few steps when a figure came hurtling out the front door. He grabbed me and yanked me back inside." His hands…still wet with her family's blood…the feel of him grabbing her in the dark, the helplessness, hopelessness… A cry escaped her throat.

"Sabrina, you don't have to tell me this."

Her mind was back, in that place. She couldn't stop now if she wanted to. "He dragged me into the carriage house. Tied me to a chair with ropes and duct taped my mouth. I just knew he was going to kill me. After a few days, I wished he had."

"How long did he keep you there?"

Her mouth twisted with bitterness. "Ten days." Ten long, pain-filled, terrifying days.

"The police didn't find you when they found the bodies?"

"They weren't found for almost two weeks. It was the Christmas holidays. School was out, my dad was off work. No one expected to hear from us." The grief, the fear, the smell of that stuffy room in the carriage house washed over her so strongly, she could taste it on her tongue.

"What did he do to you during that time?" The words were low, hesitant.

"You're wondering if he raped me. No, thank God, he never did. He got his sadistic kicks from frightening me, tormenting me day after day. He dragged our Christmas tree from the house and stuck it into that tiny room with me. The smell of pine was nauseating. And all the while, he hummed Christmas tunes. His favorite seemed to be "The Twelve Days of Christmas." He told me he was counting the days down, and on Christmas day, I would die, just like my family."

"My God."

The most vile, most heinous occurrence of her captivity pushed at her consciousness. She'd never spoken of it, but she wanted to now. *Needed* to. "There's something that I've never told anyone, not even the police." The memories shuddered through her, and bile rose to her throat. "He made me wear my mother's nightgown, the one she died in. Her dried blood was all over it."

Josh closed his eyes and dropped his head back. "Oh, baby. I'm so sorry."

A small part of her mind registered he'd called her baby, acknowledged she liked hearing that word come from his mouth. How she could even think about something like that while reliving horrific events was baffling. But it was also a glimmer of pleasantness in the world of horror she'd plunged into. She'd hold onto that and not question.

She told him of how one day when Goodman left for work, one of the PTA members had stopped by to see if her mother would help with a fundraiser. The woman—Charlotte, her angel of rescue—smelled the odor and called the police. They found Sabrina in the carriage house, and a few days later, arrested Goodman.

When she finished her story, she was emotionally drained. The fire had died down to ashes, and the room was freezing. She shivered.

Josh took the mug from her hand and set it on the coffee table. He folded an Afghan around her and pulled her against his chest, leaning back into the arm of the sofa and pulling her with him. They didn't speak. He held her, and they sat there and, after a while, the cold and the memories seeped away.

Chapter Four

Sabrina opened her eyes and frowned. Her bed was warmer than normal. And harder. What the…?

She lifted her head, leaned an elbow on…Josh's chest.

The events of last night rushed in. Oh my God. She had slept on him all night. Had he gotten any sleep at all? She peered into his face. He seemed to be sleeping pretty deeply at the moment.

She tried to ease gently away from him, and he shifted. His blue eyes opened and looked directly into her face.

"Mornin'," he mumbled.

"Morning." She moved off of him and ran a hand through her tangled hair.

He sat up and yawned, rubbing his hands over his face. "How are you feeling?"

Embarrassed, ashamed, happy… "I'm fine. Thank you for…well, for last night."

He cocked a grin. "Usually when a woman says that, we've—"

She held up her hand. "I know, I know. Spare me the details." Disappointment deflated her happiness bubble. Here they were, back to the same old Josh.

She rose and headed to the restroom to use the facilities and brush her teeth. When she came out, Josh had folded the Afghan over the back of the couch and was in the kitchen.

"Coffee?" He was filling a pot with water. At least he wasn't fleeing out the door after her lengthy and emotional confession of the night before.

"Yeah, sure. Coffee would be great."

When the pot sputtered to a stop, he filled a cup with coffee. The warm, comforting aroma filled the air. She took the mug from him and sipped, then let out a satisfied sigh. Nothing better than strong, hot coffee first thing in the morning. "You made it strong just the way I like it. How did you know?"

"Because you've been serving me coffee I could pave a road with every morning."

"Oh." *Duh.* She chuckled self-consciously, not even minding his little dig. She was just glad to have him here.

"Listen, I hope you're not embarrassed about last night. I'm sure it felt good to unburden yourself. I only offered you comfort, and we fell asleep. Nothing more."

Of course it was nothing more. She wasn't his type. "No, I'm not embarrassed. I'm sure that's the tamest night you've spent with a woman. I just hope whoever you were due to service wasn't terribly disappointed." Her face heated, and she nearly groaned. What the hell was wrong with her? Maybe she should have had more coffee before speaking.

His mouth compressed. "You always have to make those little jabs at me, don't you?"

"Sorry," she muttered, not sounding as sincere as she meant. She really was sorry. Her remark was totally out of line.

"Have you always been this judgmental and sharp-tongued, or have you gone so long without getting laid, you just take it out on the nearest target? Maybe loosening up and having a drink or two would erase some of the condemnation in your eyes."

Anger and hurt pierced her heart. "No, I haven't always been this way. Remember? I used to be wild, all about fun, only concerned about the next party, just like you." She pushed to her feet and slammed her cup onto the bar. Hot coffee sloshed over the sides. "Don't you remember? That's how my entire family ended up slaughtered." As soon as the words were out of her mouth, she regretted them.

Josh's face paled. He set his coffee down, his jaw rigid, and stormed out the front door. Into the cold. Without a coat.

She rushed to the door and flung it open. Josh was stomping through the snow, shivering, his arms folded around his body.

"Josh," she called. "Come back."

He ignored her and kept walking.

"Come on. I'm sorry. You'll catch your death."

He shot a glance over his shoulder. "Trust me, sweetheart," he spoke through chattering teeth, "it's much colder in there with you than it is out here."

Her shoulders slumped. He'd been so kind to her last night, and she repaid him by being bitchy this morning.

The closest cabin was thirty feet down the road, but he'd rather walk that far in the freezing cold than spend another second with her. Who could blame him?

It was rather counter-productive, though. He'd have to see her when he came back to finish the bathroom. Unless he quit in the middle of the job. If that happened, Jess wouldn't be very happy with her. But then, she wouldn't be very happy with herself.

Never seeing Josh again? That would suck. Badly. She'd only known him a few days, but she was really, *really* starting to like him.

Yeah, you sure act like it...

Shit. She was an idiot.

She took a quick shower and ate breakfast, watching the clock, hoping Josh would show up with Dustin and act as though nothing had happened.

At nine, they still hadn't arrived. It was late enough to call Halley without fear of waking her. She booted up her laptop and opened Skype.

While they were chatting, Josh and Dustin arrived. Relief, sharp and deep, shot through her. Josh didn't speak to her, although Dustin said hello as they headed down the hallway. Well, maybe he was still pissed, but at least he was here.

She ended the call with Halley and was about to shut down the laptop when the song started. Holding her breath, she warily eyed the screen. A note appeared.

On the sixth day of Christmas...

You cheated death a decade ago, but time is running out.

She let out a scream and jumped from the chair.

Footsteps pounded. She glanced back to see Josh and Dustin standing behind her.

Josh frowned at the screen. "What's that all about?"

She slammed the laptop shut. "Nothing."

"You're trembling. It's not *nothing*. Tell me."

She wrapped her arms around her body. "I-I really don't know what it is. I've been getting these crazy

294

messages."

Josh's frown deepened. "That's not the first one?"

She shook her head.

"Have you called the police?"

"And tell them what? That somebody, I have no idea who, is sending me creepy messages?"

"After what happened to you, don't you think this might be a little more than that?"

Her cheeks were numb, and she had trouble forming words. "The killer is behind bars."

Dustin's eyes rounded. "The killer? Is there a killer?"

Sabrina forced a reassuring smile. "No, there's no killer. Everything is fine."

His confused expression turned petulant. "Don't lie to me. Are you in trouble, Sabrina?"

"I'm not lying. There's something a little…freaky going on, but I'm sure it's nothing to worry about."

Josh pulled out a chair and sat at the table. "Maybe you should tell us everything."

Sabrina sat as well and explained what had been going on since the day she arrived at the cabin.

By the time she finished, Josh's scowl had become ferocious. "I don't like this. Not at all."

"I'm a high school teacher. I'm sure it's just one of the kids playing a prank."

"It's not a very damn funny prank."

She grinned without humor. "I never said it was funny."

"Maybe you should leave here, go back home."

"What good would that do? If they're going to screw with me, they can do it as well at home as they can here." And at home, she would be endangering

Lindsey. Plus, reminders of Christmas would be all over the place. No thank you. She'd rather deal with a demented prankster.

Josh rubbed his hand over his chin. "Maybe Dustin and I should stay here until the job is finished."

"Isn't it supposed to be finished tomorrow?" Dustin said.

Josh shushed him.

Dustin rolled his eyes. "I know, I know. On the down low."

Disappointment bit at her. They'd be leaving soon. She'd be alone again. "You'll be finished tomorrow?"

"We thought we might, but we've run into snags. I think it's going to take a little longer than that."

Thank God for snags. *If* there were snags. "You don't have to pamper me and stay here to protect me. I'll be fine." She infused her voice with resolve, but inside she was screaming, *don't leave. don't leave. don't leave.*

"I'm not pampering you, swear to God. It will take at least a few more days to complete the job."

"That's very nice of you." She bit her lip. "I'm sorry, about what I said this morning. It was rude, and you didn't deserve it."

He smiled. "Forget about it. We're good, okay?"

She nodded. "Okay, thanks."

"How about we finish up working for the day and go down to the lodge for dinner."

"Sounds great to me."

Dustin held up both hands. "Double high five."

Sabrina laughed and slapped his hands.

At the lodge, Tracy and Ben were there, but the elderly couple was absent. It was a good evening with good food, good company, and lots of laughter.

On the drive home, Sabrina was content…more than content, *happy*. Odd. It seemed she was happy whenever Josh was around, even when they were arguing. Oh no…

She couldn't be falling for him. Not so quickly and not with someone so different from her.

When they pulled into the drive, her phone rang. Josh's frown mirrored her concern. She breathed a sigh when the display showed Mitch's number.

"No worries," she said before answering. "Just a friend."

She went inside with the phone to her ear. "Hi, Mitch. What's up?"

"Just checking on you. How are you doing?" Mitch asked.

"I'm fine."

"I miss you. I want to see you."

She wandered down the hallway so she could talk privately. "I don't know if now's a good time."

"Look, I agreed I wouldn't be staying with you, but you said I could come and visit."

She rolled her eyes. Did he not know how needy and pathetic he sounded?

If he did come see her, how would she explain her sexy handyman? Well, not *her* handyman. A guy like Josh wouldn't give her a second glance. The night she poured her heart out, he hadn't given her a second glance, only an ear to bend and a shoulder to cry on. And a chest to sleep on.

A very strong chest… Tingles washed over her flesh.

"Sabrina? Are you listening?"

Mitch's sharp words brought her out of her musings. "I'm sorry. Lost signal for a second. What did you say?"

"I'm coming out to see you. I don't like the way you're sounding. Something's wrong."

He was more intuitive than she thought. Something was definitely wrong, but her hesitation had nothing to do with the creepy messages. She just really didn't want to deal with him.

"It's been a long day. We'll talk tomorrow and plan a day for you to come out, okay?"

He huffed out a loud sigh. "Don't try to placate me. I'm not one of your errant students."

No, but you're acting like a child. The words almost tumbled out, but she stopped them. She didn't want to hurt his feelings any further.

"I need to go. I promise, we'll talk tomorrow."

"Fine, okay. Tomorrow it is. Have a good night."

"Thanks, you too."

"And, Sabrina…" She didn't respond in the silence that followed. "I love you. Goodnight."

I love you? Oh no… "Mitch, please don't say that—" Damn. He'd already hung up.

Dear God. He'd just said he loved her. Now there was no way she could let him come to the cabin. As a matter of fact, she'd have to quit her job and move to Alaska

"Boyfriend troubles?"

She jumped at the sound of Josh's voice and whirled. She gave a self-conscious laugh. "No, not a boyfriend. Just a friend who thinks he's my boyfriend."

Josh crossed his arms and leaned against the doorjamb. "Soooo, nerdy little teacher's got a wild side."

She grinned. "Maybe, but I wouldn't say Mitch exactly brings out the wild side in me."

He sauntered closer, ran his gaze over her body, then back up to her face. "Oh? What does bring out the wild side in you?"

A band tightened around her chest. Her mouth went dry, and she licked her lips. His gaze dropped to her mouth. He narrowed his eyes and huffed out a resigned sigh. His head dipped, and his mouth touched hers. Her lips parted, and he slid his tongue inside. Rockets went off in her brain…her stomach tightened…her knees buckled. Warmth seeped through her while chills washed over her skin. She lifted her arms to wrap them around his neck.

"You guys okay?"

They jumped apart. Dustin stared at them with a question in his eyes.

Sabrina brought a shaking hand to her mouth. "Yeah, we're fine. We were just…"

Josh chuckled. "He knows what kissing is." He punched Dustin gently on the shoulder. "We were kissing, bud."

He nodded and brushed his blond hair from his eyes. "Yeah, that's what I thought."

They were kissing…Josh had kissed her. She gave herself a mental shake. In what possible world would a guy like Josh be attracted to someone like her?

She cast a look at him from beneath her lashes. His expression was unreadable, but it didn't seem to hold revulsion *or* regret.

"Dustin and I are going to go grab a few things then we're going to stay here for a while until the job's done."

"Look, I appreciate the offer, but it's really not necessary."

"It will be better for us, too. The drive back and forth is kind of a bitch on these icy roads."

Relief seeped through her. "Okay then, that would actually be great."

The men were gone for a few hours. When they returned, the three of them spent the evening playing board games. Sabrina tried to focus on Scrabble, to rein in the ecstasy of Josh's kiss, but it was no use. Her gaze kept straying to Josh, and each time she caught him looking back, a thrill raced through her heart. Her inattention came at a price. Dustin kicked her ass at every game they played.

Chapter Five

The next morning, Sabrina woke feeling better than she had in ages. Last night, she hadn't been plagued with her usual nightmares, and she had slept peacefully. She told herself it was because she had someone with her in the house. But at home, Lindsey was around. No…the fact that the *someone* was Josh was most likely responsible. So, how would she feel when he was no longer around? She didn't want to think about it, but the reality was inevitable.

She had been up for an hour when Josh made an appearance. His hair was mussed, and his eyes were droopy with sleep. Dark whiskers shadowed his jaw. Something pleasant kicked in her stomach. She swallowed hard. She handed him a cup of coffee, and he winked at her.

"Thank you. Just what I needed."

"You want breakfast?"

"You're going to cook for me?"

"Sure, for you and Dustin. Want to wake him?"

He closed the space between them and lifted her chin to look into her eyes. "What's the matter? You afraid to be alone with me?"

She gave a nervous laugh and pulled away from his touch. "Of course not. I just thought he might be hungry."

His mouth quirked. "He's sleeping, so he's

probably not all that hungry." The teasing light made his blue eyes even sexier.

"I just meant...you two will probably start work soon, and..."

Josh chuckled and moved away. "Just messing with you. Sorry. I'm kind of an ass like that. But then, you already know what an ass I am."

She smiled. "Actually, I'm beginning to think you're a pretty decent guy."

His brows lifted. "Wow, high praise from a Polly Poindexter."

She threw a dishtowel at him. "Go wake Dustin before I change my mind about breakfast."

He caught the dishtowel and left the kitchen wearing a cocky grin.

After breakfast, Josh headed back to the bathroom to get to work, while Dustin lingered at the table, sopping up the last bit of gravy with a biscuit.

Sabrina bundled up to go outside to check the feeder.

Dustin finished off the biscuit and stood. "Where you going, Sabrina?"

"Out to check my bird feeder."

"You have a bird feeder? Don't birds fly south for the winter?"

"Well, many birds do, but these are black-capped chickadees. They hang around during winter. They're pretty resilient, smart little birds."

"Really? How so?"

"Oh, there are all kinds of amazing things about them. Chickadees are social birds and live in flocks. To keep up with changes within the flock—and to remember where food stores are located—they're able to replace old neurons with new ones. Basically, it wipes out their old memories and gives them more space to store new ones." She was jealous of that particular ability. How great would it be to replace the memories of her family's deaths? But then, she'd lose the first seventeen years of her life, the happy times, and she wouldn't trade those for anything.

Dustin's eyes grew large. "Wow. Can I go see them?"

"I'm not sure if there are any out there, but you can go with me to check if your boss doesn't mind."

"I'll be back."

He disappeared into the hallway and came back in moments, grinning. "Josh said it was fine if I wanted to freeze my balls off."

Sabrina grinned back. "Then let's go."

Dustin put on his cap, coat, and gloves and followed her outside.

Excitement raced through her. Four chickadees perched on the feeder, pecking the seeds.

Dustin's smile split his face. "What are they eating?" he whispered.

"Sunflower seeds. Chickadees love them, and their high fat content helps with the birds' winter survival."

"Awwweeessoommmee."

His voice rose, and Sabrina put a finger to her lips. "Shh. We don't want to scare them away. They aren't all that skittish around humans, but loud noises might startle them."

Dustin pressed his lips together and clapped his gloved hands over his face. His brown eyes lit with pleasure. She knew how he felt. Chickadees were not only adorable, they were pretty amazing to observe.

Dustin threw his arm over her shoulder, his gaze fixed on the feeder.

Her heart squeezed. Not good. She was getting attached to them both. She planted a kiss on his cap-covered head, and they stood there for another few minutes watching the birds.

This was incredible. Not only did she have them on tape, but she was able to see them with her own eyes. And to share them with someone who was as excited as she.

After a while, the birds flew away. Sabrina went to the box that held the recorder.

"What you doing?" Dustin came up beside her.

"I set up a recorder to tape them so I could see what was going on when I'm not out here. I wasn't certain I'd get to see them in person, but I sure did. And you did too."

"Yep. Maybe I'm your good luck charm."

She laughed. "Maybe you are at that."

"Can we watch the tape?"

"Of course."

"It's almost lunchtime. Maybe Josh can take a break and watch with us."

"Maybe, but I doubt he's all that interested in birds."

Dustin grinned. "Well, I know he likes chicks!"

He guffawed at his own joke, and she laughed along with him despite the sting of its truth.

Inside, they shed their coats. Josh came down the hallway, and Dustin let out a string of chatter about the birds, impressively repeating every fact Sabrina had shared. He finished with, "Want to come watch the tape with us?"

"When do you plan on actually getting some work done?" Josh's teasing tone took the bite out of the words.

"After lunch, promise. You gotta see this."

Josh slipped the tool belt off his hips and laid it on the bar. His worn jeans gently hugged his muscular thighs. Her heart crept to her throat. He was just too damn sexy.

Dustin nestled on the sofa between Sabrina and Josh, his eyes glued to the television.

Sabrina fast-forwarded through hours of nothing, then pressed play when, just after sunrise, a group of birds flew in and landed on the feeder.

Dustin clapped his hands and bounced on the sofa. "Did you see? Did you see 'em? I saw 'em. Aren't they cute?"

Josh laughed. "They're cute all right. That's pretty cool."

"Fast forward to the end, Sabrina, and show Josh how me and you were watching them with our own two eyes."

She hit fast forward, stopping the tape when a black shape appeared. A bear. He lumbered around the yard, sniffed at the feeder, then disappeared into the trees.

Dustin pointed at the screen like they wouldn't see the bear otherwise. "Oh wow, oh man, this is the best thing ever!"

Sabrina was excited too. She'd have plenty to show and teach her students. She wished Halley was here to share this with them.

She fast-forwarded to where she and Dustin went outside.

"See!" Dustin shouted when the birds appeared. He shoved off the sofa, pacing and chattering.

When Sabrina kissed Dustin's head onscreen, Josh smiled at her. He stretched a hand across the back of the couch and ran a thumb down her cheek. Shivers skipped over her flesh.

"Thank you for being so kind to him." His voice was low, gentle.

"He's a great guy."

"He's got the biggest heart of anyone I've ever known."

"He thinks the world of you."

"The feeling is mutual."

She smiled. "I can tell."

Josh squinted at her. "Are we actually getting along, Polly Poindexter?"

"I believe we might be. I'd better go fix lunch before you screw it up."

"Before *I* screw it up?"

She jumped off the sofa, and he popped her on the bottom with the cushion as she went by.

****

They had just finished lunch when Sabrina's phone dinged, and the music started. She didn't want to see, but still, she grabbed her phone.

On the seventh day of Christmas...

An image appeared—a long-bladed knife, blood dripping from the tip.

She slapped her hand to her mouth and let out a cry.

"Sabrina? What's wrong?" Josh's concerned voice barely registered.

She couldn't take her eyes of the screen. Couldn't

speak.

He looked over her shoulder at the phone. His mouth set in a grim line. "We're calling the police." He snatched up his phone and punched in numbers, then spoke to someone on the other line.

Half an hour later, two officers arrived. One was a middle-aged man, the other younger, a woman.

They took a report, but since nothing had actually happened, there wasn't much they could do.

"There are a lot of sickos in this world. I know what happened to your family brings out the weirdness in people," the man, Officer Harvey, said. "I'm sorry. It's a shame when a tragedy is used as a source of someone's enjoyment."

They agreed to speak with Chet and keep an eye out. Officer Harvey asked Sabrina to call if anything more happened; he put a slight emphasis on the more, sending a clear message. A handful of images wasn't enough. But there were five days left before Christmas. Sabrina hoped that *more* didn't result in someone getting hurt, or killed.

****

That night, it took Sabrina several rounds of her relaxation routine before she finally dozed off. She shifted and tossed, unable to fall into a deep sleep.

A sound at the door woke her. Her heart pounded and she sat up.

Josh stood in the doorway.

She pushed hair out of her face. "Is everything okay?"

"Not really."

"What's the matter?"

"You."

"Me? What about me?"

He looked at the floor, then back up at her. "You're just too…close."

She frowned. "I'm sorry?"

"I thought I could do this, but I can't."

"Do what?"

"Sleep with you in the next room. I can't stop thinking about what it felt like to kiss you."

A thrill tingled over her skin. But logic overruled her libido. "I-I don't know what you expect to happen. I'm not a one-night stand kind of girl. I'm not one of your party girls."

He chuckled. "I don't think you have to tell me you're not a one-night stand kind of girl."

"Right, *Polly Poindexter*."

He grinned. "But, incredibly sexy Polly Poindexter."

"Me, sexy?"

His gaze raked over her body, and he strolled to her bedside.

Electricity zipped through the air. She held her breath.

He bent, cupped her face in his hands and pressed his lips to hers. "I'm thirty years old, and I've spent a majority of my adult life seeking a good time. I always thought a good time was a string of women and endless booze, but hanging out here with you, having dinner together, conversing, and just sitting quietly, have been some of the best times of my life."

Her pulse jumped. "You…mean it?"

He swept his thumb down her cheek and along the side of her neck. Goosebumps raced over her flesh, stirring heat in her core.

"I've never meant anything more." He kissed her again, this time tasting her with his tongue. She kissed him back, letting a small moan escape.

He lifted his head. His eyes were dark sapphire, his voice hoarse. "I don't want to take advantage of you. Say the word, and I'll leave. I just…I want you."

An achy yearning blossomed between her thighs. It had been so long, so very long. Josh may be a man whore, but he was kind-hearted, too. She didn't need promises. She just wanted him. Without thoughts of what it meant, she would be with him.

She gripped his shoulders, and her eyes drifted shut. She fastened her mouth to his, and he groaned, scooping her up and holding her body tightly against his.

His erection pressed against her stomach through her nightshirt. A smile curved her lips, along with a heady feeling of power at the effect she had on him.

She ran her hands over his shoulders, his chest. He shoved her nightshirt up and thumbed her nipple, sending zings of lightning through her body.

She pressed into his touch, and he eased her back onto the bed and swept her sleepshirt off her. His hands grazed her hip, up her side to cup her breast. "So lovely." His husky murmur sent a thrill through her body.

She moaned and grasped the waistband of his sweat pants, shoved them down his hips. He gritted out a sigh and kicked them away.

"Make love to me, Josh," she choked out.

"Hold on, baby. I'll be right back."

He released her and disappeared down the hallway, his absence leaving a chill on her skin. Where was he going? God, what if Dustin saw him coming to her room, naked?

She had no more time to worry about it, to think about it before Josh appeared in her bedroom again.

He shut the door behind him and held up a small square package. "Condom."

Her relief spilled out in a chuckle. "You came in with the intention of ravishing me, but didn't bring a condom?"

He grinned. "I didn't plan to ravish you. I didn't even plan to wake you. I just looked in on you, and I couldn't leave. I guess that's what you get for sleeping with your door open."

He joined her in bed. She smiled and plucked the condom out of his hand, ripped open the package, and rolled the condom over his erection. "No," she whispered. "This is what I get."

He pushed her back on the mattress and slid on top of her. His fingers caressed her nipples as his erection pushed into the insides of her thighs. With a gasp, she took hold of him and guided him to her.

He let out a long, tortured moan and plunged inside her. Her hips arched as she met his thrusts with an urgency she'd never felt before.

Pleasure rocketed through her. Warmth built with the friction of his movements. Her breath caught, and she tensed as a long, throbbing orgasm sent waves of delight from her center throughout the rest of her body. Josh gave one final thrust, his orgasm warming, pulsing inside her. She let out a deep, contented sigh.

He pushed her damp hair off her forehead and kissed her gently on the mouth. "That was incredible."

"Yeah. Amazing."

He rose and went into the bathroom—to dispose of the condom, she assumed. When he returned, he slid back into bed and tucked her into his side. "Goodnight."

"You can't stay here."

He lifted his head. "What?"

"Dustin might see you."

He laughed. "So what? Dustin's not a child."

"No, but I like him. I don't want him to think of me as another one of your fly by night women."

He peered at her in the darkness. "No one could ever think of you like that. You're something special."

His words warmed her insides, but she made her voice stern. "Go."

He planted another quick kiss on her lips and climbed from bed. "Sleep tight, Polly Poindexter."

Her smile remained long after he left the room.

Chapter Six

The next morning, Sabrina was as nervous as she was excited about seeing Josh again. How would he act? Like nothing had happened? She wasn't sure how she even wanted him to act, but she would be heartbroken if he blew it off like it was just another one-night stand.

When he and Dustin came into the kitchen, Josh bent and kissed her cheek. "Mornin'."

She smiled, feeling almost giddy. "Morning."

Dustin narrowed his eyes and wrinkled his forehead. "What's happening here? Are you two dating now?"

Josh raised his brows at Sabrina. "I don't know, are we?"

Sabrina couldn't wipe the smile from her face. "I don't know. Maybe."

"Whoop, whoop!" Dustin gave a fist pump. "Best couple ever."

Josh chuckled and held up a hand. "Slow down, there. We're not exactly ready to walk down the aisle."

"Aisle? Are you going to the grocery store? Can you get some Skittles?"

Sabrina ruffled his hair. "Yeah, sure. I'll get some Skittles, whenever I go."

"Awesome." Dustin nodded and took a drink of coffee.

The rest of the day was spent with Sabrina wandering out to check the feeder, and the guys working in the bathroom. The routine felt so comfortable, so right that it was…unsettling. What would happen when the break was over? Would she see Josh again? They lived forty-five miles apart, but that wasn't much.

She wouldn't think past the now. Today had been a good day—no crazy messages—and her heart felt at peace. For the time being, that was enough.

****

That evening, when her Skype notification dinged, Sabrina accepted, and Halley's tear-ravaged face appeared on the screen.

"Halley, sweetie, what happened?"

"It's Chet. You didn't hear?"

Sabrina took in a deep breath and clenched her fists. "No, what did he do?"

"Nothing, he…" She sucked in a deep breath. "He died."

Shock rendered Sabrina silent for several moments. "What, how?"

"Someone—someone murdered him. Last night. Shot him."

Sabrina's mind spun. Grief kicked her in the stomach. She didn't like the kid, but he was just a kid. For God's sake…

A ping sent icy chills over her skin. The familiar, terrifying music played and the words, *On the eighth day of Christmas* appeared. Along with an image of a figure—a young man, blank eyes staring at the ceiling—lying in a dim room. *Chet.*

Sabrina screamed.

"What?" Halley's voice rose to a screech. "What happened?"

"N-nothing. I need to go. We'll talk later, okay?"

She barely gave Halley time to respond before she ended Skype and pushed to her feet, knocking the chair over.

Josh rushed into the room. "What? What's going on?"

Tears streaked her cheeks. She couldn't get the words out, all she could do was gasp and draw in deep, sobbing breaths.

Josh pulled her into his chest and stroked her hair, brushing his hand down her back, murmuring soothing words over and over.

Finally, her breathing leveled out and she whispered, "Call the police."

****

This time, a detective came. He was more interested in the goings on than the officers had been, especially since she'd received the photo of Chet. He questioned her in detail, but she had little to offer.

After he left, Sabrina fixed dinner, but none of them had much of an appetite. They sat in silence, picking at their food.

Since Sabrina had been unable to save the message and photo, there wasn't that much to help the detective. He told her to keep him posted if anything else happened, and he'd let her know when they caught the guy.

She tried but failed to take comfort in his use of *when* rather than *if*.

After dinner, Josh and Dustin watched television, and Sabrina worked on grading papers. Her cell pinged with a text message notification from Mitch.

Have to see you. Let me know what day is best.

She typed back, *I think it's best if you don't come. I have a lot going on. I'll see you when I return.*

She did not want to deal with him, did not want him to ask questions about Josh and Dustin. Too much stress already. She was not going to add fielding his advances to it.

Please don't shut me out.

I'm going to start ignoring your texts. I really can't deal with this right now. Bye, Mitch.

She backed out of her text messages, refusing to feel guilty. She didn't owe him anything. She hadn't led him on, and he was being too damn pushy. Maybe she'd let him down too easily. She'd remedy that when she returned. If she started dating Josh, he'd surely get the hint...

Ridiculous. She didn't need another man to help her get rid of one, and it was pretty pathetic that she was wondering if she'd date a guy she'd already slept with. Talk about putting the cart before the horse.

A frantic pounding on the door made her jump. For one crazy second, she thought Mitch had arrived. But there was no way he could have made the eighty mile drive so quickly. Unless he was already on his way when he texted her.

Anger brought her to her feet. If it was him, she'd...well, she didn't know what she'd do, but it wouldn't be pretty.

Josh stood. "Let me get that."

"No, I'll see who it is." If it was Mitch, she didn't want him to meet Josh. She would send him on his way.

She looked through the peephole to find Ben

standing in the cold without a coat. His expression was ravaged.

She threw the door open. He stepped inside, and she shut the door. "Ben, are you okay? What happened?"

A sob burst from him. "It's Tracy, she's…"

"What, Ben?" Dread climbed up her throat and clamped onto her heart. *Don't say dead, please don't say dead.*

He pinched the bridge of his nose and let out another sob. "She's dead. Tracy… My wife is dead."

The strength left Sabrina's legs. "How?" Her voice was barely a whisper.

Josh and Dustin joined them in the foyer. Their expressions were grim.

"Someone broke into our cabin this afternoon. I was only gone for a little while. I ran to the liquor store. They, they stabbed her. The police just left."

Terror gripped her throat. What was happening?

She forced her mind onto Ben and put a hand on his shoulder. "My God, Ben. I don't know what to say. I'm so sorry."

He wept loudly and wrapped his arms around her. She patted his shoulder, making soothing sounds. She felt awful for him, but also a little awkward. She barely knew him. But perhaps she knew something about his wife's death. Definitely more than she wanted to. It had to be the same guy.

Would the police be back to speak with her? They had to suspect all the craziness was related. But then, how much more could she tell them? She had no idea what the hell was going on.

But maybe it was time to get out. Head home.

Really? Right in the thick of Christmas joy? When whoever was doing this was obviously reaching out to those in town, and he might hurt someone else, like Halley?

No, going back wouldn't solve anything. She had to think, had to figure out if she was missing something that might help the police.

Ben pulled away from her. He retrieved a note from his jeans pocket and stared down at it. "I wanted to ask you if you knew anything about this."

He held the paper out, and she took it. Her hands shook as she read. *On the ninth day of Christmas… Bye, bye, Tracy.*

Josh looked at the note over her shoulder. "Son of a bitch," he muttered.

She gaped at Ben. "Was this at the scene? Why don't the police have it?"

"They have the one the killer left. It was—" Another sob hiccupped out of him. "It was splashed with Tracy's blood. I wrote down exactly what it said so I wouldn't forget." His eyes narrowed on her. "I know you got some kind of strange gift that day we met. It seemed to freak you out. Was it anything like this? Do you know something about what happened to Tracy?"

Sabrina shook her head. "No, God, no." The man had lost his wife. The least she could do was give him honesty. "I mean, I don't know anything about who is behind this, but yes, strange things are happening. Including that gift I received at the lodge."

She told him everything, leaving out the part about her family's murders and her kidnapping. Whether or not they had to do with what was going on now, he didn't need to know. He wasn't from here and likely hadn't heard. She didn't want to keep reliving it over and over.

"My God. Do the police know?"

"Yes. One of my students"—her voice broke, and she drew in a shaky breath—"was killed as well."

"Jesus Christ." He wiped his nose on his sleeve. "I don't know what to do. I can't leave, not until they catch this bastard. I can at least do that for Tracy. I just feel, helpless."

She rested a hand on his arm. "I know, Ben. I'm so sorry. If there's anything I can do. If you just need company, be sure to call on me."

He nodded. "Thanks, I will. You're a good person, Sabrina."

"So are you." The response was automatic. She had no idea if he was a good guy or not. But he obviously loved his wife very much. And now she was dead. As terrifying as the thought was, the woman had likely been killed because of Sabrina. "If you want to hang out here, you're welcome. I'm sure you don't want to be alone."

Ben shook his head. "No, thank you. Teresa put me up in a rental cabin until the police are finished with ours. I appreciate the offer, but I need to be by myself."

He left and Sabrina turned to Josh. Her entire body shook, and she wrapped her arms around herself. Once again, Josh pulled her into his chest and offered comfort. This time, it didn't help. Someone with a horribly twisted plan was out there. If he wasn't stopped soon, more people would die.

****

That night, Josh came to her room. Without

speaking, he slid into bed beside her.

Their lovemaking was slow, precious. He made love to her as though he *loved* her. And she returned his passion. Without words, she told him, the one bright spot in this nightmare was, she had fallen in love with him.

Afterward, he tucked her into his chest and placed a gentle kiss on her forehead. "It's going to be okay, baby. We'll find this asshole and stop him. I won't let anything happen to you. I promise."

She tightened her hands on his arm that lay over her breasts. She knew he meant it, and she wanted to believe him. But whoever they were dealing with was clever, vicious. And it would take more than Josh's determination to defeat him.

Chapter Seven

The next morning, Sabrina went out to get the
recorder. Maybe watching the adorable little chickadees
would bring her some pleasure, some peace. It was a
few days before Christmas, and Josh had taken Dustin
back to his family so he could spend the holidays with
them. He'd be back soon, but not soon enough.

She put the tape in and lowered to the sofa. Her
phone showed a voicemail received at nine last night.
She picked it up and pulled up the message. Half her
attention was on the television as she fast-forwarded on
the slowest setting so she wouldn't miss anything. A
dark shape appeared on the tape. The bear again?

Mitch's voice spoke from her phone. "I know
there's something wrong. This isn't like you. I'm not
waiting until you get back. I need to talk to you, now."

She narrowed her eyes on the screen and pressed
play. Not a bear. A man wearing a black ski mask. He
held another man in a chokehold.

Mitch's message continued, "I'm coming out now.
I'll call you when I'm close. If you get this message,
call me."

Dread uncoiled in the pit of her stomach. Last
night... He'd never made it. Oh God. Her gaze flew to
the television. Or had he?

The man in front came into focus. Mitch...

His captor lifted a knife.

"No!" Sabrina shot to her feet, her body vibrating with fear. "God, please, no…" As if she could stop it. As if the horror playing out on the screen hadn't already happened.

"Say it," the man growled into Mitch's ear.

Mitch shook his head and cried out, "Please, just let me go."

The assailant pressed the knife to his throat. "Say it!"

Mitch drew in a sobbing breath. "O-on the tenth day of Christmas—"

The knife sliced along his neck.

"Noooo!" Her scream reverberated through her body, her soul. She trembled violently.

Mitch's lifeless body dropped to the snow.

Josh came through the front door. "Sabrina? What is it? What happened?"

She pointed a shaking finger at the television. The man with the bloody knife stood there smiling. Just like he had ten years ago. Hysteria rose in her throat, choked the breath from her. She was barely aware of Josh wrapping an arm around her and lowering her next to him on the sofa…dialing his phone.

The detective arrived. The EMTs. Why were they here? It was too late for Mitch.

She couldn't stop crying, couldn't stop shaking. "He's back." The words rose to a fevered pitch. "Goodman. He's out. He's back. Oh my God. He's back."

Josh's arm tightened around her.

Detective Bateman shook his head. "No, Ms. Spencer. He's still in prison. Some other sicko is out there. We'll find him, though, I promise."

You said that before, you said you'd find him, and now Mitch is dead...

"Here, Miss, this will calm you."

An EMT slid a needle into her arm. A sedative. Yes, she needed that. She felt like her entire body would disintegrate.

The murmur of voices rose around her. Detective Bateman was saying they found Mitch's body. The killer had dragged him into the trees. Heavy overnight snowfall had covered the blood. He ended with, "We'll be taking the video in for evidence."

She nodded. She didn't want it anyway.

A strange calmness flowed through her. Her hysteria disappeared, and she just felt...numb.

She turned her head to the detective. "It's him. Goodman. It has to be him."

"Ms. Spencer, I assure you, he is still locked up. I don't know who is doing this, but it's not Samuel Goodman."

"But he knows so much."

"It was all over the news. Everyone knows. Trust me, he's locked up tight."

She nodded. But the detective didn't know what she knew. You could never lock the devil up tightly enough.

****

The next morning—Christmas Eve, her mind acknowledged with dread—Sabrina made bacon and eggs for breakfast. They sat at the table. She drank coffee, but couldn't eat with the stone lodged in her stomach.

She wrapped her hands around the mug and looked at Josh. "You should be with your family today.

Tomorrow's Christmas."

He placed his hand over hers. Warmth tingled from his touch up through her shoulder and into her heart. "I wouldn't want to be anywhere else but with you. I'm not leaving your side until this bastard is caught."

She offered him a grateful smile. The last thing she wanted right now was to be alone. She'd called Lindsey and Halley to make sure they were okay. They both assured her they were fine. Lindsey tried to talk her into coming home, but she declined. She didn't want to bring danger to her friend, and she had no desire to part from Josh.

Someone knocked on the door. Josh answered it and opened it back to let Ben inside.

"How are you doing?" Sabrina asked.

He drew in a stuttered breath. "One moment I seem to be getting better, the next, I…" He rubbed his hands over his face. "I feel like I'm dying. And I wish I had. Right along with Tracy."

Sabrina took his arm and led him over to the sofa. "Don't say that, Ben. She wouldn't want that for you. She loved you very much." Sabrina had no idea if that was true; she barely knew the couple. But it was the right thing to say. "Can I take your coat?"

He shook his head. "I'll keep it on. Since Tracy died, I can't seem to get warm." He lowered to the sofa. "Do you have coffee?"

"Sure, I'll make a fresh pot."

Josh joined her in the kitchen. "So, I guess he's going to hang out here all day?"

"Maybe. Is that a problem?"

"It might be. What do you really know about this guy?"

323

She gave him an irritated scowl. "I know he just lost his wife, tragically, and he needs a friend right now. Surely, you can't think we should turn him away."

"Something about him just doesn't sit right with me."

"With all that's been happening, I'm sure we're all just overly suspicious. Please be nice to him, okay?"

He took a cup from the cabinet and poured in coffee. "Fine. I'll be nice to him." He winked. "But later, you have to be nice to me."

Her pulse fluttered, and she smiled. "Deal."

They took coffee into the living room and Josh handed Ben his mug.

An awkward silence settled over them. What did one say to a man whose wife had just been murdered? Especially when her death might have something to do with you?

Sabrina's cell pinged, and she picked it up. Her stomach heaved when the tune played, and a message appeared on the screen.

On the eleventh day of Christmas…

How did it feel to wear your dead mother's clothes?

She yelped and tossed the phone to the table.

"Sabrina?" Josh put his hand on her arm. "What's the matter?"

Josh. He was the only one she'd told. Even the police didn't know…

She jerked her arm away and leapt to her feet. "You!" She didn't know how he'd sent the message when he was right here in front of her, but he probably had it set on some kind of delayed timer.

"Me, what?" Confusion creased his features.

Panic and anguish welled in her chest. She had made love with him. Had *fallen* in love with him. Although, really, she barely knew him. And all the trouble started at almost the exact moment he arrived in her life... Tears filled her eyes. "Stay back."

Ben stood. "What's going on?"

Sabrina pointed a shaking finger at Josh. "It was him. He was behind it all. He killed your wife."

Josh let out a strangled grunt. "Sabrina, have you lost your mind?"

She snatched up her phone and held it in front of his face. "You were the only one who knew about my m-mother's gown." A sob wrenched her throat. "The *only* one."

His gaze fell to the screen, and his face paled. "I don't know what's going on, but for God's sake, you can't really think that I'm a killer? That I would hurt you in any way."

She backed away from him and punched 911 into her phone. When the operator answered, she gasped out, "Send the police. A killer is in my house."

She answered the woman's questions and was assured officers would be there soon. She hung up and glared at Josh. "The cops are on their way."

He barked a humorless laugh. "Good. Maybe they can talk some sense into you."

Detective Bateman arrived fifteen minutes later. During the wait, Josh pleaded his case, but didn't try to escape, didn't harm her or Ben. Did he think he was that clever? That he could convince the authorities he was innocent?

Sabrina explained about the gown to Detective Bateman. "You need to arrest him."

The detective narrowed his eyes on Josh. "I'm afraid that's not enough for an arrest, but I can assure you, we'll investigate him."

"You can't arrest him? Are you kidding me?" Anger, grief, and fear battled in her soul.

"I promise, Ms. Spencer, we'll keep close tabs on him. If even the slightest blip comes on our radar, we'll haul his ass in."

Josh shook his head. "This is insane." He turned to Sabrina. "Please, Sabrina. You have to believe me."

"Get out." She whirled on the detective. "You can make him leave, at least."

"Mr. Cravens, you need to go."

"I can't leave her. Don't you understand? This is some kind of crazy scheme. I can't leave her unprotected."

"Ha!" The word caught in Sabrina's clogged throat. "Unprotected? You're the monster behind all of this. Behind everything."

"I'll stay with her," Ben said. "I couldn't help Tracy, but I'll be damned if I'll let anything happen to Sabrina."

Josh favored him with a ferocious scowl. "She's not in any danger from me."

"That remains to be seen." Detective Bateman held out a hand. "Come on, Cravens. Time to go."

Josh let out a growl and stalked to the door. He cast a look over his shoulder at Sabrina. The expression in his eyes was tortured, and she could almost believe it was sincere. But the image on the phone proved otherwise.

Chapter Eight

Sabrina couldn't think, couldn't move. Her heart was shattered, her body numb. How could she not have known? His entire good guy act had been a ruse. Was Dustin part of all of this? No, she refused to believe that. He was a sweet, innocent pawn in a madman's sick game.

Her phone pinged. God…was Josh so sure he wouldn't be caught that he was actually pulling this bullshit again so soon?

Fine, I'll bite, you asshole. The police would catch him, and he'd pay. Angrily, she snatched up her phone and checked the display.

On the twelfth day of Christmas… You die.

A shudder trembled through her. "We'll see about that."

She was only half aware of Ben's presence in the room. He'd been quiet since Josh and the others left. But now, he was humming…

Her gaze shot to him. A malicious, satisfied smile spread across his face. She recognized the tune…

She gasped and shot to her feet. The pieces fell into place like a gigantic, macabre puzzle. "You!"

"Finally! I thought you'd never figure it out." He laughed and stalked toward her.

She whirled and ran toward the front door. Only a few feet away…

Ben caught her just before she reached for the knob. He grabbed a handful of hair and dragged her backward. Piercing shards of pain shot through her scalp, and moisture sprang to her eyes.

"Oh, no you don't," Ben rasped into her ear. "We're going to have some fun before your much delayed demise. Samuel told me all about your time together."

She frowned in confusion. "Samuel?"

"That's right." He flung her down onto the sofa and towered above her. "He was my cell mate for four years. We became closely acquainted. He loved reliving his glory days, culminating with the incident with your family. I don't have the luxury of enjoying you as long as he did. I can't take the chance someone will come along and ruin our evening. But I plan to make the most of the little time we have."

She hadn't noticed before, but now, a gleam of insanity drifted in his hazel eyes.

Dear God. She was going to die. And, Josh. She'd accused him of murder. She'd driven him away. She'd never have the chance to tell him she was sorry. That she loved him.

"You won't get away with this. The police will figure it out. They'll find out about you, about your past."

"You might be right. But you won't be around to see it."

Terror exploded in her heart, but she forced calmness in her voice. She had to keep him talking, stall until she figured a way out of this. "How were you released from prison if you're a murderer?"

"I wasn't in for murder. Until recently, I'd only

328

killed one person. That was a girlfriend when I was eighteen. No one ever knew. They thought she committed suicide." He spoke matter-of-factly. "I was in for computer hacking. My skills have come in particularly handy during all of this. I programmed the software to send you messages at precise times, even when I was with you. Clever, right?"

"You're twisted."

"Twisted?" He shrugged. "Maybe. Samuel was definitely twisted. A twisted genius. I listened to his stories over and over. I couldn't stop thinking about what it would be like to take up where he left off, but ten years later, with the woman the girl had become." His lips widened in a smile that sent chills coursing through her. "And you do *not* disappoint."

"You-you killed your own wife."

"Tracy? She was starting to wear on me. Questioning me and whining. She'd outworn her usefulness. But she wasn't my wife."

"Won't the authorities figure it out? Whoever she really is, that she didn't have a husband named Ben?"

"Oh, but she did have a husband named Ben. She and I killed him. We took off together. My real name is Tobias Elliott. Nice to make your acquaintance."

He jerked her up by the arm and dragged her into the utility room. She fought him, kicked his shin, punched his arms, his chest, but couldn't get loose. He grabbed a chair from the kitchen and set it down in front of the side-by-side washer and dryer. "We don't have a carriage house, but this room is small enough to be a good substitute."

"You're a sick, warped son of a bitch."

He grinned. "Now, now, no call for insults. I like

you, Sabrina. I thought you liked me." He slammed her into the chair and pulled a length of rope from his coat pocket. He bound her feet and hands to the legs and chair back. The knots were so tight, the rope bit into her skin. She jerked on her bindings, but it only made them tighter. She cried in frustration.

"I'll be back shortly." His lips stretched into a demented grin. "I have some things I want you to wear."

Nausea curdled her stomach, and tears coursed down her cheeks. This couldn't be happening...

She took in a deep breath. *Think*... She had to keep a sharp mind, come up with a plan.

He closed the door behind him, and the walls shrunk around her, sucking the air out of the tiny room. It was so dark... She gasped for air, squeezed her eyes shut, and pictured sunlight and wide, open spaces.

Breathe, just breathe...

The door opened, and she was almost relieved when Ben—Tobias returned. She sucked in long, deep breaths of air from the kitchen, but then he shut the door, and her lungs closed up again.

He flipped on a light and untied her from the chair. She rubbed at the soreness in her wrists.

He held something out to her. "Here, put this on."

A gown. Goodman had made her wear a different nightgown each day he held her captive. Oh God, she couldn't...

"Put it on!" The command was sharp, fierce. He whipped a knife out of his back pocket and held it to her throat. "You'll put it on, or I'll put it on your dead, mutilated body."

She trembled so badly she almost couldn't

function. She slipped the gown over her head, still dressed.

"Clothes, off."

Anger and humiliation burned through her. At least the gown would cover her while she shed her clothes. She slipped her jeans and shirt off from beneath the gown and dropped them to the floor.

Tobias's smile was eerily reminiscent of Goodman's.

She shivered in the thin gown, trying to draw air into her lungs.

Tobias hummed "The Twelve Days of Christmas" and ran the knife over the skin next to her eye and down to her jaw. "I bet it was so much more exciting when the bodies of your family were lying only twenty feet away."

Her teeth clenched, and anguish shot through her heart. Sick motherfucker…

"I'm almost jealous of Goodman, but I've had a pretty good run myself. And, he's locked up. Yet here I am, free as a bird." He pushed the knife point into her cheek. She flinched at the sting. Blood trickled down her face.

A knock sounded on the front door. His eyes widened momentarily, then he frowned. "Son of a bitch. Who is that?"

"How the hell should I know, genius?"

Anger flickered in his eyes, and his mouth tightened. "You better shut that pretty, spiteful mouth of yours, or I'll cut your tongue out." He pressed the knife to her lips. "I'm going to see who that is, so we don't rouse suspicion. If you make a sound, I'll kill whoever it is, got it?"

He tied her up and covered her mouth with duct tape, then left, plunging her into darkness.

She listened closely. Maybe the police were at the door, and they'd search the house. They'd find her, and this nightmare would be over.

Voices filtered to her. "Let me talk to Sabrina."

Oh my God, Josh…

"She doesn't want to see you."

"Where is she? She can tell me that for herself."

"I think she already told you, pal."

"I asked you where she is." Josh's voice was louder. Had he come into the house?

With her mouth taped, she couldn't make noise, even if she wanted to, and if she did, the asshole would kill Josh.

"She's in her room, working on some kind of project for school. I told her I'd give her some time to herself. She doesn't want to be disturbed."

Silence fell.

Was Josh leaving? At least she'd heard his voice in the last moments of her life. She couldn't tell him she was sorry she'd thought such horrible things about him, but surely he would know. She had been such an idiot. How could she not have seen? Josh hadn't trusted Tobias, and rightly so. But she'd driven Josh away. And now, she was going to die. Tears welled and spilled down her cheeks. She wanted to be brave, but she was so afraid, she could barely think.

The front door closed, and footsteps neared the utility room. For one, brief moment, she thought that maybe, maybe Josh would be the one to open the door. She let out a muffled scream of disappointment when Tobias appeared.

He grinned and ripped the duct tape off her mouth. "Whew! That was close. Your boyfriend is pretty persistent. Wonder how he shook the cops? Inept bastards probably didn't even tail him." He laughed. "Boy, it was priceless when you accused him. That was an added bonus I hadn't counted on. I thought I'd have to get rid of him, too, and that's not something I looked forward to. He's a pretty big guy. I'd have had to get the jump on him for sure."

She curled her lips. "Yeah, I'm sure. You're just like that wimp, Goodman. Your victims are usually teenagers and helpless women."

His expression darkened, and he slapped her hard across the face. The sting brought tears to her eyes.

He shook his finger in her face. "You need to watch that smart mouth of yours. This isn't part of the plan. I'm recreating the events of ten years ago, and you're throwing me off. So just shut up and play along, you hear me?"

Her mind clicked, searching for something, anything to give her a moment's advantage where she could escape. But how? She was bound to a chair, in a closed up room that stole her ability to breathe, to think, with a psychotic maniac.

"Let's see…he made you wear the gown. And he played Christmas music. Back then, you had a tree. He brought the one from your home out into the carriage house. We need a tree." He frowned. "I'll go get the one from my cabin. It's small. I won't be long."

After he left, she tried to clear her mind and focus on breathing. He'd be gone for several minutes. If she was going to do something, it had to be now. She tugged at the ropes around her wrists. This time, they weren't tied as tightly. He didn't see the need. He thought he had her at his mercy. He was getting complacent.

She worked her wrists back and forth, loosening the ropes. She squeezed and tugged, the rough fibers scraping the flesh on her wrists, but she was finally able to slip one hand out.

Hope soared in her heart. She was out, free…thank God.

She quickly loosened the bindings around her feet and rushed to the door. She turned the knob and pushed. It didn't open. Didn't budge. *Son of a bitch.* He'd blocked it somehow.

She rested her back against the door and slumped to the floor, sobbing in frustration. Had the bastard purposely left the ropes loose so she would think she had a chance at freedom? Goodman used to play those same games. Relishing in her defeat, laughing at her pathetic attempts to flee.

Well, in the end, she *had* gotten free. And look where Goodman was today. She could do the same now. She wouldn't have the benefit of someone coming to her rescue, but she was a grown woman, tougher, more resourceful. Determined as hell to survive.

She jumped to her feet and flung open cabinet doors, searching for something to use to bust out of the room. Nothing. Detergent, dryer sheets, that was it.

Wait…pliers, a screwdriver. Jess must have left them behind when he installed the washer and dryer. She grabbed the tools and rushed to the door. Fingers damp with sweat, she worked the screwdriver into the doorjamb and shoved. Nothing, not even a smidgen of movement. What now? It was hopeless.

Think, dammit, think…

She climbed onto the washer and searched the cabinets above. A hammer, maybe? Would one need a hammer to install a washer and dryer? Probably not. She found no hammer, nothing else in the cabinets.

She hefted the pliers in her hand. Not much of a weapon. No way could she hurt Tobias badly enough with them to escape.

Her shoulders slumped with defeat. He'd be back soon. And she would die. Tears filled her eyes.

Dammit, why had she trusted him? After what she'd been through, how could she not recognize evil?

Deflated, she sank to her knees on top of the washer and leaned her back against the wall. The plug in the outlet dug into her back, but she welcomed the discomfort. It was mild compared to—

An idea slammed into her brain.

The plug.

A smile curved her mouth. If her idea was successful, she wouldn't just overpower Tobias. She would kill him. And he would never hurt another soul.

Chapter Nine

Holding onto the tools, Sabrina jumped off the washer, unplugged the dryer, then tugged it away from the wall. The machine was on rollers, so it slid easily.

She removed the back panel and unscrewed the wires connecting the cord.

Quickly, she climbed onto the washer, still holding the cord. She loosened the hoses with the pliers and dripped a large puddle onto the floor. She lifted the lid and dropped the hose into the washer drum to let the water continue to drain.

Heart pounding loudly in her ears, she plugged the cord into the outlet and settled onto the dryer to wait.

Minutes ticked by. "Come on, you bastard. I have two-hundred forty volts with your name on it."

Would it work? What if she failed? If so, she'd die. It was that simple. She couldn't fail.

Humming filtered to her. Tobias was returning. The cocky asshole. *Let's see how much you like that song a few seconds from now…*

The door pushed open. A small tree laden with decorations appeared. "It's not much, but it's—"

He stepped inside. Frowned down at the water, the empty chair. Then his gaze found hers. He looked at the cord, and his eyes widened.

She gritted her teeth and dropped the cord into the water.

Sparks flickered, and his body flew back. The tree fell from his hand. He screamed, slammed against the wall, and jerked sporadically.

His eyes bugged out. He staggered forward…reached out for her…his grappling fingers came within inches…

Then, he halted, and his body vibrated. His hair and the skin on his face sizzled. His bulging eyes latched onto hers, and his mouth opened in a silent scream. He toppled onto the wet floor, spasmed once more, then lay still.

Relief and horror flooded her. She slumped to her bottom on the dryer top. Her teeth chattered, and her body shook so violently she thought she'd tumble to the floor. And if she did, she'd die. Like Tobias.

The stench of burning flesh rose. Nausea gripped her stomach, and she gagged.

The door rattled. "Sabrina? Are you in there?"

She jerked her head toward the door. "Josh?" she sobbed.

"Hang tight. I'm coming in."

"No!" Her chest was so constricted, the word was barely audible. She drew in a deep, quick breath. "No, don't come in! You'll die."

The body lay in front of the door. It pushed open slightly, moving Tobias back a few inches. Josh was about to come in. He'd be electrocuted.

"Josh! There's water on the floor, and electricity. Tobi—Ben—is dead. If you come in, you'll die, too."

The door pushed the rest of the way open, but Josh remained in the doorway. His gaze found hers. He closed his eyes and breathed out a long sigh. "Thank God."

"Don't move. You'll be electrocuted."

"It's okay. I'll be careful. I'm going to get you out of here."

She shook her head rapidly back and forth. "No, just call someone. You can't. It's too dangerous."

"I called the police, but I'm not leaving you stuck there until they get here. I can help you."

She scrubbed at the tears on her face. "You can?"

"Yeah." He smiled. "I love you too much to let anything happen to you."

A choked laugh shuddered out of her. "You love me?"

"Like crazy."

She drew in a shaky breath. "I love you, too."

"Then let's do this. Together." His gaze captured hers. The ice-blue eyes warmed, lit by his smile. "Come on. Stand up and step over to the washer toward me, nice and easy, hold onto the walls."

"I-I can't. My legs are too shaky."

"You'll be fine. Just stay calm and listen to my voice."

"O-okay."

"Get as far on the edge of the washer as you can."

She focused on Josh's soothing voice and followed his orders.

He reached out. "Now, take my hands."

Her arms shook as she gripped his hands.

"On the count of three, I want you to leap, as hard and as far as you can."

She nodded.

"One, two, three…"

She leapt and slammed into him. The momentum knocked him back to the floor, and she landed on top of him. She looked behind her. She was free of the water, free of the room.

Josh's arms shot around her, and he held her to him, raining kisses over her face. "You're okay. I've got you, you're okay."

She didn't know how long they lay there, but sirens caught her attention. Josh slipped her off him and got to his feet, then pulled her up and once more enclosed her in his embrace.

"How did you know?" she whispered into his chest. "Why did you come back?"

"After I left, it occurred to me. He told me you were in your bedroom. You wouldn't have been in your bedroom with the door closed."

"That's right. I wouldn't have."

"I was afraid if I came back to the door, he'd kill you right then. If you weren't already dead." A shudder moved through his body. "I circled the house, trying to figure out where you were. When I heard him scream, I busted down the door and found you."

"I'm so glad you did."

"You seemed to have it under control yourself." His voice held admiration. "How did you figure out how to do that? How to electrocute him?"

She shrugged. "It's basic science. I guess being a nerdy science teacher has its advantages."

He chuckled. "I suppose it does."

The reality of her actions sank in. Her body trembled. "Oh my God...I killed a man."

"Shhh...you had no choice. He would have killed you. He's killed others."

He was right, but she'd taken a life. She squeezed her eyes shut and tightened her arms around him. Now wasn't the time to worry about that. She'd deal with it later. For the moment, she was glad to be alive. Glad Josh was with her. "I'm sorry, so sorry I doubted you."

He pressed a kiss to her head. "It's okay, baby. It's all over now."

She leaned back and looked into his face. "Did you mean it when you said you loved me?"

He tenderly kissed her lips. "Absolutely."

She smiled. "Then I think it's just beginning."

Caster's Unfriendly Ghost

by

Alicia Dean

Dedication

To Reba Dearion,
a beautiful person and wonderful friend.
The world's loss is Heaven's gain.

Chapter One

Percy, Oklahoma, October 1ˢᵗ

Reese Caster blinked twice at the keyhole—make that *two* keyholes, and they were blurring together—of his high rise apartment door.

Maybe that fifth scotch and soda was a bad idea.

"Shit," he mumbled and made another stab at it. This time, the key slid into the lock. "Ha, ha! Got ya!" He pushed the door open and stumbled through the entrance.

Chilled air blasted him in the face. "What the…?" He kept the temp down in the apartment—he liked it cool—but this was mother freakin' freezing.

He rubbed his hands briskly on his arms and headed down the hallway. Once he was under the blankets, he'd pass out, and it wouldn't matter. He'd mess with the thermostat tomorrow.

He pushed his bedroom door open and fell back onto the bed. Now, if he could just manage to actually get under the blankets…

A replay of Jessica's tirade surfaced in his mind. He chuckled. Man, was she pissed. He'd been too smashed to close the deal. Oh well, he'd bang her twice next time. If there was a next time. One thing he couldn't stand was a shrewish, demanding woman. Maybe it was time to move on. After all, they'd had two great weeks together—fun times, good sex. No point in dragging things out.

The room stopped spinning, and he was just thinking of trying to wrestle under the blankets when a voice penetrated his consciousness. "Caster, hey, Caster."

He frowned and squeezed his eyes shut tighter. That sounded like Joey, his old pal. But it was impossible…

"Caster! Are you awake?"

Caster forced his eyes open. Joey stood over him, snapping his fingers in his face. "Hey, rise and shine, I need to talk to you."

"Son of a bitch!" Caster sprang from the bed, and fell to the floor, then jumped to his feet, suddenly and completely sober. "What the hell?"

"That's better." Joey chuckled. "What'sa matter? You act like you've seen a ghost." The chuckle became a rocking belly laugh. He finally regained control of himself and gasped out, "A little cliché, maybe, but still funny as hell."

Caster's gut clenched, and chills raced through his blood. "It can't be." He shook his head, trying to clear the alcohol from his brain. "You're…dead."

"Yes, it *can* be." Joey crossed his arms and plopped down into the easy chair next to the bed. "See, you're talking to my ghost. Unfinished business and all that."

Caster shook his head and backed out of the room. He was never, ever drinking again. Never.

Wait…he was dreaming, that was it. He'd come home, gone to bed, and fallen asleep. Why he was dreaming about Joey Tillman, he had no idea. But that's what was happening. All the same, he'd sleep on the sofa. He scrubbed his hands over his face, then pulled back to study them.

Hmmm…that sure felt real…

Nope, he was dreaming. Had to be. He went into the living room and dropped onto the sofa, put his forearm over his eyes, and tried to make himself fall asleep again. But his heart was pounding out of his chest, making it hard to relax. That had been one hell of a real dream.

"Damn, Caster, you're making this harder than it has to be."

Caster jerked his arm off his face and shot to his feet. Joey stood in the room—looking the same as he had the last time he'd seen him five years ago, dark, wavy hair, even darker eyes, his usual attire of jeans and a T-shirt—this time a Thunder basketball shirt—that big, shit-eating grin he always wore.

"You're not real." Caster shook his head. "This cannot be happening. I'm wasted. I'm imagining things." Caster kept a litany of denial going until Joey/not Joey held up a hand.

"Let me save us some time. I died in a plane crash a year ago; you came to my funeral. You haven't seen or spoken to my wife since. I, however, have been keeping an eye on her. She's about to make a huge mistake, and I need your help to keep that from happening. I'm sure you'll help me because, in spite of the fact that you pushed the two of us together, you care about Emily, and you don't want to see her hurt." Joey moved toward him, and Caster stepped back. "Before we proceed, though, I apparently have to make you see that this is real, that I'm here. Pinch yourself."

Caster shook his head. "I'm not going to do that. You're not real."

"I would pinch you if I could, but I can't touch people. Only inanimate objects. Guess I'll have to prove it another way."

Joey held his arms out to his sides and lifted off the ground. Just hovered there, like a…*ghost*. No way in hell…it couldn't be.

"See, I'm really, truly a ghost. Now, are you ready to hear me out?"

Caster nodded, although he was anything but. He was ready to call the police—or a psych ward.

"I have been unable to move on since my death. My otherworldly mentor—for lack of a better title—told me it was because I can't rest until Emily is happy. She took my death hard, and now she's starting to see some dickwad. He's planning to ask her to marry him, but he only wants her money."

In spite of the impossibility of the situation, Caster could no longer deny it. Joey Tillman's ghost was here, in his apartment, asking for a favor. He shook his head. *Son of a bitch.* "How do you know he only wants her money?"

"I've been keeping an eye on him—and her. He's a greedy bastard. He found out Emily received a large insurance settlement from the insurance company—dying in a plane crash is quite a profitable way to go, FYI—and now he wants to get his hands on that money. He's had a vasectomy, but he told Emily that he hopes to have children one day. The thing Emily wants most is children. I wasn't able to give them to her." He fell silent, cleared his throat, but his voice was still hoarse when he spoke again. "Like I said, he's tricking her, using her, and I can't allow that to happen." He blinked rapidly and pressed his thumb and forefingers into his eyes. "Emily doesn't deserve that. She's the best."

Emily *was* the best, Caster couldn't argue with that. "So, where do I come in?" Okay, it was official. He was actually convinced Joey's ghost was here, and that he needed a favor. Wow.

"I want you to go after her."

"Go after her? You want me to kill your wife?" Maybe he wanted Emily to join him on the other side?

"No, of course not. I meant, go after her romantically. Sweep her off her feet."

Caster snorted a laugh. "I thought you didn't want her with the wrong guy. I'd be worse than the bozo gold digger."

Joey was nodding before Caster finished speaking. Hell, he didn't have to agree so vehemently.

"Oh yeah, you definitely would. But you see, he'll marry her and ruin her life. You'll break her heart, but you won't marry her. She'll stay away from men for a period of time, while she's getting over you, and by then, maybe I will have found someone right for her."

"You're out of your mind." Caster headed to the kitchen and popped a Keurig pod into the maker. No way in hell he was getting back to sleep tonight.

Joey followed. "I know it sounds crazy, but I'm desperate. I'd have to be to ask you, of all people, to romance my wife."

Caster shot him a look over his shoulder. "Flattery will get you everywhere." The coffee finished, and Caster gulped the scalding liquid, burning his tongue. Nope, he was definitely not dreaming. "Why don't you just appear to her and tell her the jerk is all wrong for her? Keep me out of this."

"I've thought of that. But I don't want to traumatize

her. And, even once she accepts that my ghost has appeared to her, she won't necessarily believe the guy is wrong for her. She might think I'm just jealous."

Caster took another drink. "Are you?"

Joey's mouth tightened. "Of course it's hard to see her with another man. But I've accepted she has to move on." His voice dropped. "She deserves someone great in her life. And, yeah, I'm jealous, but that's not the reason I want to break them up. He's bad for her."

Caster let out a long breath through clenched teeth. What would it be like to rekindle the old flame with Emily? Exciting? Yes. Fulfilling? Yes. Wise? Hell, no. He'd barely gotten away unscathed the first time. "Forget it. Not going to happen. Now get out and let me *try* to get to sleep. Maybe when I wake up tomorrow, this will all have been a dream." Caster stumbled back to the bedroom and threw himself on the bed.

Joey followed him. "If you don't, you'll regret it."

Caster grunted a laugh. "Oh, what are you going to do, haunt me?"

Joey grinned. "You'll wish that was all I'm going to do."

Caster growled and closed his eyes. Maybe if he ignored Joey, he'd go away. A few moments ticked by with nothing happening, and Caster relaxed. He was just about to doze off when the sound of shattering glass jerked him awake. "What the hell?"

Joey stood next to the nightstand, holding a baseball bat over his shoulder. Caster's expensive, Gherkin etched glass lamp lay in fragments on the carpet.

"Are you out of your mind? You dug in my closet and found my bat, then destroyed my thousand dollar lamp?"

Joey shrugged. "Guess that's what you get for paying a grand for a lamp." He moved to the dresser and swung the bat into the mirror. Caster ducked when pieces of glass flew around the room. Joey grinned. "I can do this all night."

Caster let out a heavy breath. Talk about your proverbial rock and a hard place.

Chapter Two

Covington, Oklahoma, October 3rd

Emily Tillman carried a caramel macchiato and cinnamon scone over to where her best friend, Rachel Ramos, sat in the booth at Java Hut. She slid into the seat across from her and tucked a strand of short, dark hair behind her ear. "Okay, so, I think we just about have everything covered for the haunted forest. The guys are coming over tomorrow to build the plywood walls." Emily was in charge of the fundraiser for elder care at the hospital where she was an assistant administrator. She'd decided to host a haunted forest on her land. She lived out in the country, and there were plenty of woods surrounding her house.

Rachel pinched off a piece of scone and popped it into her mouth. "You have all the spooks lined up?"

Emily grimaced. "Well, I did, but Michael Myers is having a root canal, so I'll have to find a replacement."

"Better make it quick. It opens in a few weeks, and we have to rehearse."

Rachel was playing Lizzie Borden, and she was just a little too excited about portraying the murderess.

"I know. We'll find someone."

"Emily?" A deep voice spoke from behind her. "Emily Tillman?"

Before Emily could turn, she caught a glimpse of

Rachel's horrified expression. Her hazel eyes shot sparks, and her lips compressed into a thin line.

Emily looked over her shoulder and suddenly found it difficult to breathe. "Reese Caster?" Her words came out in a faint whisper.

He looked good. Damn good. He wore a dark gray suit, sans tie, with the first few buttons of his white shirt undone. A hint of a five o'clock shadow darkened his jaw line.

He approached their booth and reached out a hand. In a daze, she placed her trembling fingers in his. His white teeth flashed in a smile. "How have you been?" Solemnity overtook his expression. "I haven't seen you since Joey's funeral."

"And that's not *nearly* long enough." Rachel's words scorched the air.

Rachel hated Reese because he'd broken Emily's heart. Emily wanted to hate him too, but couldn't bring herself to. She'd known he was a playboy when she'd dated him. At the time, he was a surgeon at the same hospital where she worked in admissions, and his prowess was legendary. Although she'd always thought herself strong-willed, she found she was totally helpless when he turned those crystal green eyes on her. It hadn't seemed to matter he had bedded half the women who worked at the hospital. When he looked at her, she felt like she was the only one in his world.

Caster shot Rachel a smile. "I see you haven't softened toward me, even after five years."

"You dumped my best friend. On her birthday."

Emily's face heated. "Rachel, that was a long time ago. And things turned out fine. After all, Caster was the reason I met Joey." Her husband had been a friend of

Caster's. She'd met him just before Reese broke up with her. One thing led to another, and she and Joey started dating, then married within a year. Joey had definitely helped her get over Caster. Sometimes, she wondered if that had been part of the reason she married him.

No…she loved Joey. That's why she'd married him. And they'd had a good marriage, until Joey's death. Anxious to change the subject, Emily said, "What have you been up to? Are you still at Saint Francis?" She knew he was, but didn't want him to know she knew. He'd left Jarman Memorial and transferred to the hospital in the neighboring town of Percy shortly after their break up. She'd kept tabs on him—through the grapevine—since that time. She hadn't wanted to, but was unable to resist. She refused to dissect the reason behind *that* insanity.

"Yes, still there. What's going on with you?"

"Still at Jarman. We're actually discussing a charity haunted forest the hospital is putting on."

"Nice. Need any help?"

Emily swallowed a knot in her throat. Working with Reese again? Based on her reaction to him now, that wouldn't be wise. In spite of the logic of her thinking, she heard herself say, "As a matter of fact, we just learned our Michael Myers actor backed out."

His grin did funny things to her insides. "Hey, that's perfect. I know how to walk slowly, and I'm good with knives."

Emily laughed.

In a so-sweet-it-was-sarcastic tone, Rachel said, "Plus, you're tall and evil."

Caster threw his head back and laughed. "Ah, Rachel, I've missed the barbs."

She flipped a handful of platinum blond hair over her shoulder. "There's plenty more where that came from."

Emily blew a breath out. "Come on, now. We're adults here. Can't we have a fresh start?" Although he'd broken her heart, she was ultimately relieved, because he would never give her what she wanted—marriage and children—so marrying Joey had been the smart move, despite its tragic ending.

"I'm game." Caster lifted his brows to her friend. "Rachel?"

Her lips tightened, then she gave a quick nod. "Fine. I guess if we'll be working together, I can be civil."

"Working together?"

"Yeah, I'm helping with the haunted forest, too." A wicked gleam came into her eyes. "Better watch your step. I have an ax." At his confused expression, she said, "Lizzie Borden."

"Touché." He grinned and turned to Emily. "So, maybe we can get together this evening, and you can show me the ropes?"

"I'm sorry, I have a da—dinner. I have a dinner this evening." Why was she reluctant to tell him about her date?

"How about tomorrow?" He looked at his watch. "I've got rounds at Covington Special Care until five, but I can come by after that."

"Covington Special Care?"

"Yeah. I volunteer at the nursing home here once a week, provide health care to the elderly."

She couldn't control a surprised lift of her brows. She hadn't known of him doing anything so selfless when they were together. Was it possible he'd changed?

"What a coincidence. Our charity is for elder care."

"Well, then, I guess this was meant to be. So, I'll see you tomorrow evening?"

She nodded. "It's being held on my property south of town. A crew will be there tomorrow to start building walls." *So we won't be alone.* "Tomorrow is perfect."

****

The next evening after work, Emily pulled into her drive, tires crunching over scattered orange and yellow autumn leaves. Her mood was a mixture of excitement and trepidation. She would be seeing Reese this evening, and if he actually went through with his offer, she'd be working with him for the next three weeks—one week of rehearsals and two weeks while the haunted forest was in operation.

She took a deep breath and closed her eyes. *You can do this. The thing with Reese ended a long time ago.* And she'd been married to Joey for three years in the interim. So why couldn't she put aside the memories of another man?

With a long sigh, she climbed from the car. The sound of a vehicle behind her sent her pulse racing. He was early. She wasn't ready to face him yet. Her body tensing, she turned. A flash of relief when she saw it was Ken Anderson, not Reese, quickly morphed into irritation.

What was he doing here, uninvited?

The man was nice enough—and easy on the eyes, with his ripped physique and piercing blue eyes—but he was coming on awfully strong. They'd known one another for a month, and he'd been after her to go out with him. She'd finally agreed. They'd been on three dates, and now he was showing up at her house uninvited?

Ken climbed from his car and approached, greeting her with a big smile and a kiss on the cheek. "Hi, hon. I missed you."

Hon? Missed her? She'd seen him last night.

"What are you doing here?"

He pulled his arm from behind his back and produced a bouquet of multicolored carnations. "I wanted to bring you these. And to see if you're free for dinner."

She took the flowers. "They're lovely, Ken. But as I told you earlier today, I have plans this evening."

"Right. I was hoping something changed."

She gritted her teeth. The sound of an engine drew her attention. Her heartbeat sped up when she recognized Caster, arriving in a black Lexus.

"So, *that's* your plan?" Ken's voice sounded peevish. "What's this all about?"

Before she had a chance to tell him she didn't owe him an explanation, Caster was striding toward them. The evening sun reflected like sparks of fire in his jade eyes. She struggled to swallow a lump in her throat.

"Hope I'm not late." He looked at Ken and stuck out his hand. "Reese Caster."

Ken introduced himself and shook Caster's hand, but his mouth was set in mutinous lines.

Emily said to Ken, "I'm going to show Reese around. He'll be playing Michael Myers. So, if you'll excuse us?"

Ken frowned, but gave a quick nod and headed to his car.

Caster turned a dimpled smile on her. "The guy seemed a little ticked. Did I interrupt something?"

"No, he just wasn't happy that I had plans."

"So…are you two…"

Emily shook her head. Was that accusation she saw in his eyes? He and Joey had been good friends. Maybe he thought she was betraying Joey's memory? "We've gone on a few dates." She drew in a deep breath. "You know, Joey's been gone a year. I—I miss him, and I always will, but I have to move on." Tears rose in her eyes, and she quickly thumbed them away.

"Hey, hey." His voice was low, soothing. He hooked his finger beneath her chin and tilted her face up. "You don't have to explain anything to me. I understand." He brushed his thumb across her cheek, sending goose bumps over her flesh. "You okay?"

She nodded and stepped back from his touch. She couldn't breathe when he was that close. "Yes, I'm fine. Sorry. I guess I sound a little defensive. Probably just guilt about dating again. I'm not exactly—comfortable with the idea."

"You need to do things in your own time. No one except you knows what that timetable is. And, if this Ken is a good guy, and you enjoy being with him, then give him a chance, see where it goes."

That was just it. She really didn't enjoy being with him, not all that much. And now that she'd seen Reese again, all her memories of him came rushing back. They'd dated a few months, and she'd fallen fast and hard. He was charming, sexy, kind, and his lovemaking, his kisses…tingles traveled over her skin. Involuntarily, her eyes went to his lips. Her mouth dried, and she pulled her gaze away. "Yeah, we'll see where it goes. Now, let's find that costume, and I'll show you around."

She led him up the porch steps. He glanced around

at the white swing and pots of colorful fall plants.

"Beautiful place you have out here."

"Thank you. Joey and I dreamed of having it built together. I finally did." Sadness clogged her throat. "But not until after I lost Joey."

Caster put his hand on her arm, a small touch, but it sent quivers to her toes. "I'm really sorry. It was difficult for me, too."

She sniffed back tears. "He was a good man. We had a wonderful marriage." She smiled. "And without you dumping me, I'd never have met him."

He winced. "Uh…you're welcome?"

She smiled. "Let me put these in water, and I'll grab your costume. Would you like anything to drink?"

"No, thanks. I'm good."

She added water to a crystal vase, then put the carnations in. They were pretty, but the rainbow colors clashed with her dark red cabinetry and red and brown checkered handmade throw rugs. She placed them on the breakfast nook anyway, and returned to the living room.

Caster was roaming around, among the antiques and plaid furniture. He looked up at her. "You know, this has a real homey feel, but it's not too feminine. A man could be completely comfortable here. I bet Joey would have loved it."

"I like to think he would have." They'd planned it out together. Now, he'd never see it, never share it with her. Sadness weighted her chest, but she forced a smile. "The costumes are this way."

He followed her into the den. She lifted a box onto the sofa and opened the lid, retrieving a jumpsuit, mask, and a large, plastic—but very authentic-looking—knife.

Caster took them from her and chuckled. "You

always did like those Halloween horror flicks."

"Yeah, and I think they scared you a little."

"Who me?" He winked. "Nah, they scared me a lot. Maybe playing the psychotic slasher will be therapeutic."

"Glad to be of service."

"I'm sure you are." He chuckled. "You hungry? I'd like to buy you dinner."

"Sure, that would be great." Her pulse skipped, and she had to remind herself, *it's only dinner…*

Chapter Three

The next few weeks went by in a whirlwind of work, rehearsals, and dates with Ken. Emily had gone out with Caster a few times, but she'd made sure it wasn't any more than that. Made sure she spent more time with Ken than with Caster. Not because she had feelings for Ken—she didn't. And she might be leading him on a little—using him as a buffer to keep her from falling for Caster all over again.

Because falling for Caster would be a very, very bad idea. Ken was more settled, more open to marriage. Not that she knew him even remotely well enough to consider the prospect, but at least with him, marriage was on the table. Ken had actually hinted at the idea a few times. She'd quickly steered the conversation to other topics, but she had a gut feeling he was racing toward a proposal, even though she'd known him less than two months.

With Caster, there was no way in hell he'd ever commit to a woman. That's why, as difficult as he was to resist, she'd made certain to keep their outings casual. Just a few dinners. She'd made a point to make comments like, "It's great to spend time with an old friend of Joey's" and "Being around you somehow makes me feel closer to Joey"—keeping the specter of her deceased husband between them. She had to put up some kind of barrier between her and his irresistibility.

Being swept up into Caster's sexual charms made a woman forget every other man she'd ever known.

She shook off thoughts of her love life and focused on the event at hand—opening night of the haunted forest. Tickets for the first few nights of the event had sold extremely well. Word of mouth would likely determine how the remaining nights went.

"Emily!" Pennywise the psycho clown—aka Bob Ferrell—rushed up to her. "Have you seen Megan? She's not here and now, Destiny is saying she'll be Michael's victim instead of mine. I need a victim, asap."

Emily rolled her eyes. No doubt the curvy, young blonde would love to trade out horror monsters— Michael aka Caster had it all over Pennywise aka Bob. "Destiny will be your victim, just like we rehearsed, if she wants to be a part of this at all." Destiny was a switchboard operator at the hospital who was bucking for a promotion, so she'd likely do whatever the administrative assistant asked of her. "I'll call Megan, and if she doesn't show then—"

"Then maybe you can be my victim?"

Emily turned at the sound of Caster's voice. He wore the Michael Myers jumpsuit, but was holding the creepy mask beneath his arm, making it look even creepier.

"Uh, yeah…well, I'm sure Megan will be here." Granted, it was do-able. She wasn't needed to actually run the haunted forest. A few of the nurses from the hospital were manning the ticket desk. Everything was in place, and everyone had their roles. She was just there for problems that might arise. But being held in the dark so close to Caster…she shuddered. More dangerous than encountering *the* Michael Myers.

She stepped away and dialed Megan. The girl answered, sounding like she'd swallowed sandpaper. "What's wrong?" Emily asked. "Are you sick?"

"Yes," she croaked. "I thought I'd texted you. I've been so out of it."

Emily could tell speaking was agony. She bit back a groan and took mercy on her. "That's okay. I'm so sorry. Get better soon."

Very soon. Otherwise, Emily would be stuck with the delightful torture of being way too near Caster for too many nights.

She walked back over to the group. "Well, looks like I'll be Michael's victim. Megan is ill."

A smile curved Caster's mouth. He leaned in and whispered, "Don't worry. I'll be gentle."

His warm breath vibrated against her ear, sending the blood rushing hotly inside her veins. Gentle? Right, when the slightest look, the slightest touch set off tiny explosions through her entire body.

****

Slivers of moonlight filtered through the leaves of the oak trees above Emily's head. Thick fog floated on the ground, leaving only the tops of the phony headstones they'd set up showing. The fog was phony too, but it looked so real, the effect was downright spooky—as was standing in the woods with Michael Myers. Even though she knew Caster was beneath the mask, a little quiver of fear raced over her skin. She gave a breathless laugh. "Okay, let's do this."

"I'm ready," he said, his voice muffled beneath the mask.

She turned her back to him, and he slipped an arm around her waist. The large plastic knife in his left hand was pointed toward her chest. Cold wind blew through the trees in the dense woods, but her shiver had more to do with being pressed to Caster's hard, warm body. She ground her teeth together, fighting the urge to sink into him. To tilt her head back and feel his hot mouth on hers…

Just when she thought she couldn't stand it any longer, the sound of laughter and squeals rose in the night air. The first group was close.

"Showtime," Caster whispered in her ear.

Emily's heartbeat escalated. She had no time to think about the heated blood pumping through her veins. She had a performance to put on.

As the group rounded the curve in the path, Caster lifted the knife and plunged it downward. Emily let out an ear-piercing, terrified shriek. Girls in the group screamed, and a couple of the guys with them laughed.

Caster pushed Emily aside and held the knife above his head, moved slowly toward the group. The teens backed away, stumbling into one another, then took off in a dead run toward the exit through the gate.

Caster chased them, wielding the knife. Once they were out of sight, he returned to Emily and pulled the mask from his head. In the light of the moon, his green eyes glittered with mirth. "That was the most fun I've had in ages."

Emily rested her hands on her hips and shook her head. "I think you have a sadistic streak, Reese Caster."

He sauntered up to her and stopped with only a few inches separating them. "Yeah, but it's one of the things you love about me."

A heavy silence settled between them. Love? The comment was meant to be offhand, but Emily couldn't take it that way. At one time, she did love him. She wasn't falling again, was she?

She cleared her throat and stepped away. "The next group will be coming by soon."

Caster replaced his mask and they once more took their places. He bent his head close to hers. "By the way, I liked making you scream. Reminds me of old times."

She gave a shaky laugh. "Cut out the suave playboy routine. Remember, I've been there, done that."

She felt him shake his head. "It's not a routine. I haven't forgotten how good we were together. And you haven't either." His fingers moved slowly over her stomach, slightly lifting her shirt until a cool breeze blew over her flesh. His fingers skimmed the strip of skin just above the waistband of her jeans. Her mouth went dry, and heat pooled between her thighs.

"Come on, Caster. Knock it off."

"Tell me something." His voice as a low growl in her ear. "Does the Ken doll make you feel like this?"

In an instant, anger replaced desire. She jerked from his hold and whirled to face him. "It's always been about sex with you, hasn't it? Good God, Caster, there's more to a relationship than the physical."

He shook his head. "It isn't just about sex. Not with you. It never was. You know how much I cared about you."

She barked out a bitter laugh. "Yeah, so much that you dumped me without an explanation, then disappeared from my life."

He shrugged. "You were with Joey. Which, by the way, certainly didn't take long after we split up."

She shook her head. "Are you kidding me right now?" A low growl of frustration rumbled from her throat. "I'm not sure what you expect from me, but the next group will be here soon. Let's just drop it."

Reese seemed about to say more, then he gave a quick nod, replaced his mask, and resumed his position.

Emily managed to get through the rest of the night without exploding, but each minute in Caster's arms made it more difficult to remember the bad that had happened between them. Everything about him just felt so…right. And so damn scary.

No way could she do this over and over again until the haunted forest was over. She'd have to find someone else to cover for her. Maybe Rachel would trade roles? Nah, she took too much glee in playing the ax-wielding murderess, and if she had to spend too much time around Caster, she'd likely become a real-life murderess. But there had to be something she could do. Whether or not Pennywise liked it, maybe it would be a good idea to switch out the victims.

After everyone else had left, Rachel hung behind. She crossed her arms and scowled at Emily.

"You're doing it again."

Emily raised her brows. "Doing what?"

"Falling."

"I don't know what you're talking about." Emily focused on gathering the tickets and other items, refusing to meet Rachel's gaze.

"For Caster. You're falling in love with him all over again."

Emily was silent for several moments, and her friend let out an exasperated breath. "Come on, we've been friends since we were kids. You've never lied to me before. Admit it."

Emily cleared her throat and let out a long sigh. "I

don't ever think I unfell."

Rachel raised her brows as if she hadn't expected her to admit it so quickly. "Oh Lordy, girlfriend, are you in trouble."

"Most definitely a possibility."

"What are you going to do?"

"I don't know exactly."

"Maybe you should take things to the next level with Ken. It will keep you from making a mistake with Caster."

"I don't need one man to keep me from making a fool of myself over another." *I hope...* "But I do need your help. Trade me roles. I can't keep doing this with Caster night after night."

"You want my Lizzie Borden ax? You want me to cozy up to that...monster?"

Emily winced. "Yeah, please? For me?"

Rachel let out a heavy sigh and tugged the wildly frazzled wig from her head. "Fine, then. Anything to keep you out of Satan's clutches."

Emily chuckled. "So don't hold back. How do you really feel about him?"

Chapter Four

Caster pulled off his surgical cap and sank into the comfort of the sofa in the doctor's lounge. He rubbed his hands roughly over his face. God, he hated days like this. He leaned back and closed his eyes, grateful he was alone. He needed to de-stress, work on letting it go. But, that wasn't easy to do after watching a kid die.

What he really wanted was to be with Emily right now. Her presence settled him, somehow helped him feel at peace. And being in her house had felt like…well, coming home. He'd always been proud of his stylish bachelor pad. The decorator he'd hired said the abstract artwork, the modular design, the black, gray, and white leather furniture was the in thing. But now, it all felt a little cold, pretentious.

A chill in the room made him snap his eyes open.

Joey hovered in front of him. Caster rose and glanced quickly around. "Jesus, Joey, what are you doing here?"

"We need to talk. Don't worry, no one can see me, unless I choose for them to. So, if anyone happens in, it will just look like you're talking to yourself."

"Great." Caster grunted. "What do you want?"

"It appears you need a pep talk. You're playing like the third string."

"I've been my usual charming self. I even did as you suggested and started volunteering at the nursing home."

"I know. Nice touch. But I've been watching you and trust me, we need more. You need to step up your game."

"Watching me? With Emily?" Caster grimaced. "How come I haven't felt that icy coldness that accompanies your appearances?"

"That only happens when I'm manifesting. When I hover, no cold air."

Unbelievable. This whole damn thing was just...unbelievable. "You need to stop the hovering bullshit when Emily and I are together. I don't like that. It creeps me out."

"I have to. I gotta know if you're keeping up with your end of the deal."

Caster shook his head. "No, not if you want me to go along with this ridiculous charade. I'll be tense, unnatural. And I definitely won't be bringing my *game*, if I know you're watching."

"Okay, okay. Fine."

"How do I know you'll keep your word?"

Joey shrugged. "I have to. Ghosts can't lie. It's a weird little side effect."

Caster wasn't sure he was telling the truth now, but he was too weary to concern himself with it.

When he didn't speak, Joey continued. "Whatever you're doing isn't working. That asshole is still around."

"Emily is the kind of woman you have to take things slowly with."

"Sure, if this was real. But you have to step it up, turn on the charm. You need to show you care, that you know her, buy her things that she loves. Her favorite flowers are white roses, she loves dark chocolate, and her favorite wine is Merlot. You need to move in on her, hard."

Caster gave a humorless laugh and shook his head. "Do you hear yourself? You were her husband, for God's sake. Have some respect."

Joey's face flushed. "I do respect her. That's why I don't want this asshole putting one over on her. She deserves to find someone who will truly love her and give her the things I couldn't."

A note of pain in his voice almost made Caster feel sorry for him. But not as sorry as he felt for the family who lost a loved one less than half an hour ago. "Listen, I've performed back-to-back surgeries today, and had my night capped off by an emergency surgery that ended with a young girl's death. So, you'll understand why I'm not in the mood for this right now."

"I'm sorry, but there's nothing I can do about that. My concern is with Emily. And I need you to follow through with your end of the deal."

"Deal, my ass. You blackmailed me into going along with this bullshit. Well, I'm out. I'll finish the haunted forest thing, but no more of this romancing Emily crap. I can't use her like that. I can't break her heart again."

"Break her heart? You sound pretty sure she'll fall for you. My, my. Someone's full of himself."

Caster stood and stalked to the door. "Look, I don't know if she will or not, I just know I can't do this any longer. You can destroy everything I own, keep me up every night for the rest of my life, but I'm done."

He put his hand on the door, but Joey's voice stopped him. "I'll tell her."

Caster paused and turned to face him. "You'll

what?"

"Not only will I continue to screw with you, even on the job, but I'll appear to Emily, tell her about our little scheme. What do you think she'll think of you then?"

"You're bluffing. You wouldn't hurt her like that."

Joey shook his head and closed his eyes. When he opened them, they were suspiciously damp. "I don't want to. But I'll do anything to keep her from making the biggest mistake of her life."

Caster let out a resigned sigh and shook his head. "Nah, getting mixed up with the two of us was the biggest mistake of her life."

****

The trees closed in around them, and she and Caster were in their own secluded world, where no one could intrude. Caster was looking at her with love in his eyes, and she knew…he was about to ask her to marry him. She held her breath, waiting. Finally, all her dreams were coming true…

He opened his mouth to speak, but a large tree toppled into another with a loud snap. That one also toppled. Then another, and another. No!!! Their sanctuary was disappearing with a loud succession of booming cracks…

Emily's eyes flew open, and she sat up in bed, pulse pounding in her ears. It was a dream…just a dream.

Was the sound she heard the beating of her heart?

No, she could still hear it. Someone was banging on the door.

She climbed from bed and threw on a robe. The clock on the nightstand showed three a.m. Who would be here at this time of night?

Crossing the living room, she grabbed a fireplace poker. Her neck muscles tightened with wariness as she hurried to the door.

Cautiously, she peered through the peephole. Her tension eased when she found Caster standing on her porch.

She threw the door open. "Caster?" He wore olive green scrubs, and his face looked haggard, his mouth drawn into a frown. The porch light reflected in his eyes, making them look like chipped emeralds. "Is everything okay?"

He stepped inside and snaked his arms around her waist, pulling her against him in a tight hug. She wrapped her arms around his shoulders and held on fiercely. His muscles tensed, then relaxed beneath her hands.

"I'm sorry, I just..." He pulled away and looked into her eyes. One of his hands left her waist and cupped the back of her head. "I just...need you." He bent his head and clamped his mouth onto hers. He coaxed her lips apart, slipping his tongue inside, searching, seeking, ravaging her with his kiss.

The scrape of his whiskers on her flesh was slightly painful, yet at the same time sensuous. Her knees weakened, and she stood on tiptoes, pressed her body into his, and returned the kiss. His hands slipped inside her robe, his fingers finding the flesh between her pajama top and bottoms. Heat scorched her skin, and she moaned deep in her throat.

With a strangled groan, he lifted his head, breaking the kiss. He squeezed his eyes shut and let out an unsteady breath. "I'm sorry. I didn't plan to..." He released her and stepped back.

She brought a trembling hand to her lips. Tingles washed over her skin, and she wrapped her robe more tightly around her body. "It—it's okay." She moved back and swept her arm out. "Do you want to come in?"

"I shouldn't have come here at this time of night. You were sleeping."

"I can see you're upset. Want to tell me what happened? I can make coffee."

"You sure?" His expression was a mixture of uncertainty and gratitude. She'd never seen Caster looking so...vulnerable, and it chipped away a little more at her heart. *Danger...danger...*

Ignoring the warning, she said, "Of course. Come in. Have a seat."

She expected him to sit on the sofa, but he followed her into the kitchen and settled at the breakfast nook. There was something intimate and comforting about having him in her dimly lit kitchen in the wee hours before dawn. She brewed two cups of coffee in her Keurig and slid one to Caster. "You take anything in it?"

He shook his head. "Black is fine."

She settled onto the stool across from him. "Want to tell me about it."

Releasing a heavy sigh, he took a sip from his mug, then set it down with a plunk. "I performed an emergency surgery tonight. A rough one. Eighteen-year-old twin sisters went out shopping for their birthday. A carload of boys who were drag racing hit them head on." He shuddered and took another gulp of coffee. "The boys were fine. One of the girls died at the scene. The other was in...bad shape. We went in knowing her chances were slim." He shook his head, cleared his throat, but his voice was still hoarse when he spoke.

"She didn't make it. I had to go out and face her parents. Tell them I lost their only surviving child on the table."

Tears sprang to her eyes, and she reached out and rested her hand on his. "Oh, Caster. I'm so sorry."

He turned his hand over and caressed her fingers. Chills raced over her skin. "It was selfish of me to come over here and put this on you. To wake you in the middle of the night." He raised his head and captured her eyes. His were filled with torment. "But you were the only one I wanted to see. To talk to." He laughed without humor. "It's crazy, but I—needed you."

Her chest tightened, and she swallowed hard. "I'm glad you came to me. Glad we have that kind of friendship."

His lips tightened. "Friendship? Is that what this is, Emily? Is that what the kiss was? Friendship?"

She pulled her hand from his and summoned all her willpower. "That kiss was a mistake. You needed human contact. That's all."

He studied her for a moment, his gaze moving over her hair, down to her lips, to her breasts. Fire burned everywhere the emerald orbs grazed. "You know, I hated myself for letting you go."

Oh God, what was he doing to her? "It was best. We wanted different things."

"But now, we can have a new start."

"We still want different things."

"Maybe not. Maybe I want it all."

She peered closely at him. "I find that hard to believe."

"Give me a chance to prove I've changed."

"I—I'm seeing someone." She couldn't believe she played the Ken card. She couldn't care less about Ken.

"Do you love him?"

She shrugged. "I don't know how I feel right now, but I know it's very late, and you've been through a horrible ordeal. You're not thinking clearly."

He gave a curt nod, pushed off the stool, and stood. "Again, I'm sorry for disturbing you. Thanks for the coffee." He swallowed the last of it and set his cup down, then moved into the living room. She followed.

At the front door, he said, "I'll see you tomorrow."

"Okay, sure. See you tomorrow."

He hesitated, as if struggling for words, then turned his intense gaze back on her. "No matter what happens, know that I care about you a great deal."

"What do you mean, no matter what happens?"

A shadow of pain crossed his features. "Nothing. I guess I'm just feeling maudlin. A day like this will do it to you."

"I know." She placed a gentle kiss on his cheek. "Goodnight, Caster."

After he left, she leaned against the door and closed her eyes. Resisting him tonight had been one of the hardest things she'd ever done. Could she continue to do so? He was...Caster. He always had and still did just...melt her.

Chapter Five

Two nights later, Caster showed up at the hospital, holding a bouquet of white roses, a box of dark chocolates, and a bottle of Merlot.

She widened her eyes. "These are all my favorites."

"I wasn't sure if I remembered right."

"You did." She inhaled the heady, sweet fragrance of the flowers and smiled. "These are perfect. That's very thoughtful. Thank you."

"You're welcome. Are you free for dinner?"

"I'm not. I have plans."

His jaw tightened. "Ken?"

"Yes, Ken." Was he jealous? While it might not be the most mature attitude, she couldn't help but experience a little thrill at the thought.

He gave a curt nod, then leaned forward and placed a whisper of a kiss on her cheek. "Have fun. But not too much fun."

She nodded, biting the inside of her mouth as he left her office to keep from calling him back, telling him she'd changed her mind, that she'd cancel plans with Ken and spend the evening with him…that she only wanted to be with him.

Her enthusiasm level for the date with Ken plummeted to zero.

Half an hour later, she met Ken at the Café Monique, one of her favorite restaurants, but she was barely able to focus on dinner. How could she guard her heart against Caster? Even though she would no longer be forced in close proximity with him, just being near him was…delightful torture.

Ken reached across the table and took her hand. "Emily, I have something very important to ask you."

A knot of dread settled in her stomach. *Please don't propose, please don't propose…*

Sure, that's what she wanted, marriage and children, before it was too late. But mainly, she wanted love. And, she most definitely didn't love Ken. Caster coming back into her life had proven that beyond all doubt.

"Maybe we should order first—"

"No, I have to say it now." His eyes gazed into hers. "Emily, I love you. I know we haven't been dating long, but you're a very special woman, and there's nothing I want more than to be with you." He reached his free hand into his inside suit pocket and pulled out a small box. With his thumb, he flipped open the lid. A solitaire diamond blinked at her from the black velvet. "Emily, will you marry me?"

No, no way…

She looked into his eyes and opened her mouth…and couldn't do it. He looked so eager, so sincere. She just couldn't disappoint him. Yet. She needed time to let him down gently. "Ken, this is so unexpected. The ring is beautiful, and I like you a lot. But you're right. We haven't known one another that long. Let's give it a little more time and see how it goes."

He scowled like a child denied a toy. "But a lot of women would kill to be in your shoes."

She almost laughed. Seriously? Did he just say that?

"Maybe so. But I'm not one of them. For now, the answer is no. If you don't want to see me anymore, I'll understand. But I can't marry you. Not right now."

He seemed to weigh her words, then gave a quick nod. "I'll give you time. I don't want to lose you." He slipped the ring back in his pocket and scowled at the menu.

Throughout dinner, he remained sullen and moody, and she couldn't wait for the evening to end. Although, tomorrow wouldn't be much better. Now, she had to get through the remaining nights of the haunted forest feeling awkward around *two* men.

Chapter Six

Caster wasn't pleased to learn Rachel would be his victim instead of Emily.

He scowled and crossed his arms over his chest. "It's because of the flirting, isn't it? I was just playing around. I'll stop, I promise."

"No, that's not it. Rachel twisted her wrist and can't hold the ax right," she lied. "That's the only reason."

He narrowed his eyes. "You wouldn't be lying to me, would you?"

"Of course not." She smiled brightly and checked the time on her cell. "We'd better get started." She turned her back on him and walked over to the group of monsters who were preparing to take their places.

Ken pulled his Freddy Krueger knife-glove from his pocket, and a sheaf of papers fell out and blew across the ground. Emily and the others quickly helped gather them before the wind took them away.

Without conscious thought, Emily glanced at the papers in her hand. The blood in her veins chilled when she recognized pages from her bank statement. Her gaze flew to Ken's face. "What the hell?"

He frowned. "What? I don't know what that is or where it came from. I didn't have papers in my pocket."

Rachel scoffed. "The hell you didn't. We all saw them fall out. And now we see what they are."

Emily gestured toward him with the wadded papers.

"Why do you have these?"

He didn't answer, but Rachel spoke for him. "It's obvious. He's been scoping you out. He wants your money."

His panicked gaze swung from Emily to Rachel, then back to Emily. "No...I swear. Why would I carry something like that with me?

"I don't know, but my eyes aren't lying."

He stalked over to Emily and gripped her shoulders, shaking her roughly. "You have to listen to me, dammit. I proposed to you tonight. You really think I would do this?"

Caster stepped forward and shoved Ken from Emily. "Hey, ease off."

Ken whirled on him. "You go to hell. Everything was fine until you showed up. Things were going just as—"

Caster's mouth quirked in a humorless grin. "Just as planned?" He grabbed Ken's upper arm. Ken tried to jerk away, but Caster held on. "I think it's time you cleared out of here."

Ken turned a pleading gaze to Emily. "Come on, Emily. Tell him to butt out."

Emily let out a disbelieving laugh. "You're kidding, right? I want you out of my sight, forever. If you show your face again, I'll press charges against you for illegally accessing my bank records."

Caster hauled Ken to his car, and Rachel placed a gentle hand on Emily's arm. "And I thought Reese was the devil. Ken could give him a run for his money." Her mouth tightened in a sympathetic grimace. "I'm sorry. Are you okay? Want me to stay?

Emily shook her head. "You go on. I'll be fine. I

didn't know him all that well, you know."

"Yeah, but it still sucks to be taken advantage of. And you, of all people, do not deserve that." Rachel hugged her tightly, then headed to her car.

****

Caster knew he should leave now that he'd seen Ken off the property, but he couldn't resist going back. Just to make sure Emily was okay.

She was sitting in the porch swing with her sweater wrapped tightly around her. Waiting, as if she knew he'd come back. She offered a small smile when he approached.

He settled on the swing next to her. "I'm sorry about all that. What an ass."

She nodded. "Yeah, but it's okay, really. It's not like I was in love with him or anything. I just..." She tucked a strand of hair behind her ear. "I just hate that I suck so badly at relationships."

He slipped an arm around her shoulder and tried to ignore how much he enjoyed touching her, even slightly. She smelled faintly sweet with a hint of spice—like there was a bad girl beneath all that innocence. "Ah, come on now. You and Joey had a successful marriage."

"Yes, it was a good marriage, but..." She paused, then said softly, "But I often felt like I was the only one really *in* the marriage, you know? Joey was good to me, but he was sort of...absent. I didn't feel like he really listened to me. And he knew how much I wanted children, yet we were married for three years, and he still wasn't ready to start trying. I sometimes wonder if he ever would have been." She laughed self-consciously. "I'm sorry. I don't know why I told you that."

He smiled and brushed his knuckles along her

cheek. "Because we're friends, remember?"

"Yes, we are. Thank you for everything." She looked up at him, her dark blue eyes shimmering in the glow from the porch light, and he had to use all of his fortitude not to kiss her full, tempting lips. There was something in her gaze, in the expression on her face that told him maybe…maybe she wanted him to?

She looked away, and the moment passed. "I'm just tired of making bad choices. But if I don't put myself out there, I'll never have the family I want. I'm almost thirty, I want children."

"You'll find the right man, make the right choice."

She gave him a wistful smile. "Promise?"

He smiled back. "Promise." He placed a brotherly kiss on her forehead and stood. "I'm going to head out. Do you have anyone to play Freddy?"

"Dang! I hadn't even thought that far."

"I'll get one of my buddies to do it. No sweat. I mean, if Ken doll can play the part, pretty much anyone can, right?"

She laughed, a free, delighted sound that reached deep down inside his gut.

Damn. This whole charade couldn't be over quickly enough. Suddenly, babies and picket fences didn't sound all that terrifying. At least not with her. He inwardly groaned. *Shit*. He needed to put as much space as possible between him and Emily Tillman. And he needed to do it soon.

****

Instead of heeding his own, very wise advice, Caster found himself at the grocery store the next morning, shopping for ingredients to make breakfast for Emily. He had the pancake mix, peach preserves, and cinnamon and sugar. He was reaching for canned icing, when a chill made him shiver. *Ah, hell...*

Joey stood behind him, wearing a scowl. Caster quickly glanced around, but he was the only shopper on the aisle.

"What are you doing here?" Caster kept his voice low.

"What are *you* doing is the question. That's not for Emily, is it?"

"Actually, it is."

His dead friend shook his head. "What's with the lame pancakes?"

Caster tossed a can of cream cheese icing in the basket. "I'm making her favorite breakfast. Peach pancakes."

"I don't remember her saying anything about liking peach pancakes." Joey scoffed. "And if she likes them so much, she can just make them herself, right?"

"I don't know man, it's just a gesture, okay?"

Joey shrugged. "Suit yourself. Although, I'm not sure how necessary this is. The asshole's gone. Pretty clever move, huh? Planting those papers on him."

"Yeah, clever." Caster thought Joey must have had something to do with it. Surely, the goober wouldn't be dumb enough to carry around evidence of his duplicity. "I figured another day or two of charming her won't hurt. Just to make sure." *Right*, because that's the only reason he was doing this...

"Sure. A little insurance is always good."

****

Emily woke feeling lighter than she had in days. In spite of being duped, she was immeasurably relieved that Ken was out of her life. And that Caster was back in it. Maybe she was wrong to hold him at arm's length. Maybe he had changed—or at the very least, maybe they could have some good times together while she was looking for Mr. Right...

No, if she got involved with Caster, there would be no room in her heart for another man. He literally consumed her every thought and emotion. Danger...that's what Reese Caster was. Pure danger.

She was sipping her first cup of coffee when a knock sounded at her front door. Frowning, she went into the living room. Her heart squeezed when she saw Caster through the peephole. She should be annoyed at his unannounced visits, but she was just too damn happy to work up any other emotion.

Smiling, she opened the door. He held a paper grocery sack in his arms. "Good morning." He gave her a lopsided grin. "Hungry?"

She stepped back and allowed him inside. "What have you got? Breakfast?"

"Ah, not just any breakfast." He went into her kitchen, and she followed. "I seem to remember someone saying their favorite breakfast as a child was peach pancakes." He unpacked the groceries as he spoke. "With cinnamon and icing instead of maple syrup?"

Her heart dropped into her stomach. For a moment, she couldn't speak. "How did you...did I tell you about that?" She hadn't told anyone, other than Rachel. Not even Joey.

"You told me that you loved them, and you hadn't had them since you were a little girl." He shot her a dazzling smile. "The look on your face made me realize they were pretty special to you. I thought maybe something comforting and familiar was just what you needed."

Tears welled, and she brushed them away. "Thank you."

Caster frowned. "Hey, hey, what is it? I thought you'd be happy."

She nodded. "I am. I just…I didn't tell you why I loved peach pancakes so much?"

He shook his head and took her hands in his, leading her to the breakfast nook. "Here, sit. Tell me."

Could she really bare her soul to Caster like that? She shook her head. "No, it's not anything you'd be interested in. Just know, it means a lot to me that you remembered."

"You're not getting out of it that easily. I'm not cooking until you tell me." He grinned at her raised brows. "That's right, I'm heartless enough to let you starve to death."

She smiled through her tears. Maybe she could open up to him. He really seemed interested, seemed to care. She drew in a deep breath, then let it out slowly. "I think you know I was raised in foster homes?" At his nod, she continued. "I was treated well for the most part, but never really felt like I belonged. Like I really had a home, you know?" She sniffed back tears. "But one of my foster moms, Della, was different. She was good to me. She loved me. Really loved me. She was an excellent cook, and my favorite thing she made was peach pancakes. We'd sit together in the kitchen in the early morning hours before anyone else was awake, and we'd talk about…everything. She was the first person in my life who made me feel important. Who really seemed to care about me." She paused. Bittersweet memories assailed her. Della's comforting hugs. Her special smile. Listening to Elvis Presley music with her and watching her sweet face as she seemed transported to another time. Then, the night her husband came home from the hospital, looking ten years older…

Caster took her hand and closed it between both of his strong, warm ones. "You don't have to tell me the rest if you don't want to."

"No, I do." She drew in a deep breath. "Della decided to adopt me. I was so excited. We were both so excited. I'd finally found a home. A family that wanted me." She bit back a sob. "There was a car accident. Della didn't survive. I never even had a chance to tell her goodbye. Her husband fell apart, and I was sent back to the orphanage." She released a long, shuddering breath. "So, you see. They're more than just peach pancakes. And…I'm touched that you remembered."

Caster stood and tugged on her hand. "Come here." She went into his arms. He wrapped her in a tight hug, and she clung to him. She couldn't fight it any longer, she *was* in love with this man. Maybe she always had been.

She pulled back and looked into his face. "Caster, I…" Could she say the words, knowing they'd only bring heartbreak?

He slipped his hand in her hair and cupped the back of her head. "Yes?" he whispered.

She couldn't do it, couldn't open herself up to that kind of heartbreak. "Thank you."

He stared at her for a few, silent heartbeats, then dipped his head and slanted his mouth over hers. Her lips softened beneath his, opened to him, allowed him access. Currents of desire, stronger than any electrical charge, rocketed through her. If anything, his kisses were even more explosive than they had been. Or, maybe it was her feelings for him that had exploded. She only knew, she had to get closer…she wanted more. She moved her tongue against his, tasting, reveling in the feel of him, and pressed her body tightly to his.

Lost…I'm completely lost…

Chapter Seven

Caster drove away from Emily's house, feeling like the tires weren't touching the pavement. His heart was light, and he'd never been happier. They hadn't gone any further than the soul-rocking kiss—leaving him a confusing mix of elated and frustrated. But it didn't matter, because he was alive. And he'd just kissed Emily for the second time in less than a week.

Was this what love felt like? Maybe, maybe not, but the fact that he could see himself spending the rest of his life with her—and only her—had to mean something. Funny how it didn't scare him like he thought it would. No…it actually sounded like paradise.

"Okay, I'll admit, the pancakes were a nice touch."

"Shit!" Caster swerved and nearly ran off the road when Joey materialized in the passenger seat. "Dude! While I'm driving? What the hell's wrong with you?" The last thing he wanted to deal with right now was Joey, but obviously, he didn't have a choice.

"Sorry, man. I just couldn't wait to talk to you. You did it, you really did it. Operation 'run off the dickwad' is a success."

Caster scowled, his euphoria shattered. "How did you know the pancakes were a hit? You weren't supposed to come around when we're together."

"I didn't. She called Rachel after you left, gushing about what a sweet thing you did, about what a great morning you two had."

Caster couldn't prevent a smile from emerging. She called her girlfriend to talk about him. That had to be a good sign.

"Okay, now it's time to break things off. Let her down easy, maybe do the whole, heartbroken, 'I'm not good enough for you' thing. Tell her she deserves a man who can give her the commitment she wants."

Caster tapped his fingers on the steering wheel and chose his words carefully. "I think I need a little more time, just to be sure the guy is gone. Besides, I promised her I'd find someone to play Freddy Krueger. She'd have to find two replacements the last week of the haunted forest. That wouldn't be fair."

Joey snorted a laugh. "Since when do you care what you promise women?"

Since I fell in love... Caster shrugged. "I just can't let her down like that. She's been through enough."

Joey remained silent, and Caster shot him a glance. He was studying Caster with narrowed eyes. Joey shook his head. "Oh no, oh no you don't."

Caster raised his brows and turned his gaze back to the road. "What?"

"You're falling for her."

"Don't be ridiculous."

"No, no, you are. I've never seen that goofy-ass smile on your face before when you talked about a woman. Well, except when you were dating Emily years ago. You insisted you didn't care about her, but there was this look in your eyes...And you've got that same look now."

Caster needed to examine his feelings for Emily more closely before he confessed them to anyone—

especially her dead husband's ghost. "You're nuts."

"Okay, prove it. Stand her up."

"I can't do that."

"You know it's going to end, anyway. Might as well walk away now."

Maybe Joey was right. Not only was he hurting her again, this time, his own heart was in jeopardy. Perhaps a clean break would be best. "Fine. I'll stand her up."

Joey nodded in satisfaction. "Great, then it's settled."

****

Emily looked at her watch. The haunted forest was supposed to start in five minutes. Not only had Caster not brought a replacement Freddy Krueger, he wasn't even here himself. And he wasn't answering his cell. Damn him. She should have known she couldn't trust him. Peach pancakes or not, he was a jerk who didn't care about anyone but himself. Maybe now she'd finally learned her lesson.

"Emily?"

She whirled at the sound of his voice. Happiness swelled in her heart and, if she hadn't been holding the Freddy Krueger costume against her to block it, it might have burst from her chest. He hadn't let her down after all. Well, not completely. "Caster, you're late."

He smiled, a sheepish little boy grin that turned her into a puddle of goo. "Sorry, but I had to pick up John." He looked behind him where a man was approaching. "He'll be your Freddy Krueger."

John was stocky, medium height, with a goatee and an open, pleasant smile. He was shorter and heftier than Ken, but the costume should still fit.

"Wonderful!" Her relief was more that Caster

hadn't disappointed her than that he'd found a replacement for Freddy. But, she'd take both. "Let's get you in the costume, quickly, so we can start. The natives are getting restless."

"I'll take him to the dressing rooms," Caster offered. "I need to change, too."

She smiled and handed John the costume, then looked at Caster. "Thank you. For everything."

"You bet." He winked, then led his friend away.

Emily shook her head and closed her eyes. God, he was close to perfect. Why couldn't he fall in love with her, want the same thing she did? Was she destined to love a man who wouldn't give her what she needed? Or, maybe she didn't really need marriage and children. Maybe being with Caster was enough. *Yeah, right.* For how long before he got bored and moved on to the next woman?

She was heading toward the entrance to the haunted forest when a freezing gust of wind—even colder than the forty-eight degree temperature—raced over her. Goosebumps broke out on her skin, and she whipped around to look behind her.

A man stood a few feet away. She squinted in the semi darkness. Oh my God, not just any man…

Her knees buckled, and a yelp of fear left her throat. It was…impossible, but…it was him. She lifted a trembling hand to her mouth. Barely able to make a sound, she managed to whisper, "Joey?"

"Emily, I'm sorry."

She gasped out a strangled cry. "You—you can't be real."

Strands of his dark hair lifted in the breeze. His chocolate brown eyes gazed at her with that same look of adoration that had made her fall for him. "I know. It's a shock."

She shook her head and backed away. "No, you can't be real. I'm imagining things. You're—"

"I'm real. Yes, I'm dead, but it's really me. My spirit, at least."

"No, no, no. Those things can't happen. Ghosts aren't real." Hysteria bubbled up in her throat, threatening to choke her. What was happening? Was she going insane?

"Listen, I'm sorry. I know this is a shock, but we don't have much time. There's something I need you to know. I need to warn you."

In spite of the impossibility of the situation, she found herself asking, "About what?"

"Caster. He's using you, just like Ken did."

She frowned. "You know about that?"

"Yes, I know all about what's been going on."

This was real. Her husband's ghost was here. Oh my God…"Joey, I can't believe it's really you. I've missed you so much." She stepped forward. "Can I…touch you?"

Moisture filled his eyes, and he shook his head. "No, I can't feel another human. I can feel solid objects, but not people." His charming smile appeared briefly, then faded. "I'd love to stay forever and talk to you, but you need to hear me out. This is important."

Emily nodded. "Sure, yeah, okay."

"You need to stay away from Caster. He's a dog, a womanizer. You know he can't be faithful. And he'll definitely never marry you."

Her heart hurt for him, and she offered a sympathetic smile. "I know it's hard for you, seeing me with another man, but Caster makes me happy."

"He's all wrong for you. You want different things."

She shrugged. "I'm not so sure anymore. Maybe we've both changed. Maybe we can want the same thing. He's different. I feel I can trust him now."

Joey let out a harsh laugh. "Oh, really? Maybe you won't be quite so trusting when I tell you what he's doing."

A tremor of dread skittered through her. "What do you mean?"

"Caster has been playing you all along. He came back into your life, because I insisted. I wouldn't leave him alone until he agreed to romance you."

She shook her head. "No, Caster wouldn't…and why would you do that? Why would you want me with him, then warn me away from him? None of this makes sense."

"I wanted him to come between you and Ken. I knew the jerk was out for your money, and I needed someone to put an end to his scheme. I was afraid you'd marry him."

A chasm opened in her stomach, filling with an ache so strong, she couldn't draw a full breath. "So, you convinced Caster to pursue me." Her voice sounded as hollow as her heart felt.

"Right. I even coached him on your favorite things. The roses, the chocolate, the wine. That was all me."

She sniffed. "And the peach pancakes."

Joey let out a sigh. "If you need any more convincing, check out the date he started volunteering at the nursing home. That was another ploy to win you over. He started the day he *accidentally* ran into you at the coffee shop."

Needles of agony pierced her heart. Maybe it was true. Was Joey telling the truth?

"And his deception started a long time ago. The only reason you and I met is because Caster wanted to push you off on another man, so you wouldn't try to hang onto your relationship with him. He timed the break up perfectly, just after he introduced you to me."

She shook her head from side to side. "No, that's not...he wouldn't do that."

"I'm afraid he would. I'd like to say I'm sorry. I knew what he was doing at the time, but I'm not sorry. Because it gave me you. And you're the best thing that ever happened to me. That's why I want to protect you. Even after my death."

Tears she'd been fighting flowed freely down her cheeks. This was too much. Joey here, but not here. Now, she'd have to grieve him all over again. And the pain of Caster's betrayal. Shouldn't she have known better? How could she have thought, for one second, she could trust him?

Joey glanced over his shoulder. "He's coming. I'm going to...well, I'll leave you two alone. I'm sure you have a lot to say to him."

Emily nodded, unable to speak around the knot in her throat. When Caster and John approached, she brushed tears from her cheeks and said to John, "Can you give us a moment? If you'll go see the young lady at the desk over there, she'll show you around."

"Sure." He frowned, looking between the two of them, then headed toward the desk.

"What is it, Emily? What's wrong?"

She brought her gaze up to his face—his gorgeous,

lying face. "When did you start volunteering at the nursing home?

He frowned, then chuckled. "What? Where did that come from?"

"Just answer me, please."

He didn't speak. Was he debating whether to tell her the truth? Or searching his mind for a plausible lie?

The cold blast of air came again. She shivered, and Joey materialized, standing next to Caster.

Caster shot him a look, then plastered an innocent expression on his face. "I don't remember, exactly, but I can check it out and let you know."

He was pretending Joey wasn't there, thinking she couldn't see him. Boy, was he a piece of work. She shook her head. "It won't be necessary. I know exactly when. It was the day I saw you at the coffee shop."

"What? How do you know that?"

She pointed at Joey. "He told me."

Caster closed his eyes. "Ah, hell."

"So it's true. All of this with…us…was a lie. You only spent time with me because my dead husband forced you to."

Caster scowled at Joey. "How could you do this, man? How could you hurt her like this?"

Joey shook his head. "No way. You're not putting this on me. You're the one who hurt her. I just made her see it before it was too late." He turned to Emily. "I'm heading out now."

"Will I see you again?"

He shrugged. "I'll be around. I'm stuck here until you find the happiness you're looking for. I'm sorry about my part in this."

She nodded. "I know you were trying to protect

me."

He reached out a hand toward her, then blinked out in the darkness.

She turned back to Caster. "You can go now. We'll handle these last few nights without a Michael Myers. And, if you want to take Freddy with you, that's fine, too. We'll manage."

"Please don't do this, Emily. Give me a chance to explain."

"Unless your explanation involves proof that what Joey said was a lie, I'm not interested."

He lifted his hands, then let them drop to his sides. "He wasn't lying. But you're wrong about my spending time with you because Joey forced me to. That's the way it started, but I care for you. Really care. I don't want this to end."

She curved her mouth into a sarcastic smile. "Well, since a good time isn't what I'm looking for, and since the jig is up, it's no longer necessary for you to hang around. Please leave."

"I can't. I don't want to lose you."

"No, really, it's fine. I'm sure Joey will leave you alone now. He's probably off tormenting some other guy into dating me." She lifted her chin and took a deep breath. "Goodbye, Caster." She turned and walked away, forcing herself to not look back. To keep her head high, though the leaves crunching beneath her feet mirrored the cracking of her heart.

Chapter Eight

One week later

Man, am I the biggest dick on Earth, or what? Joey leaned against the counter and watched Emily move around the kitchen like a zombie—a heartbroken zombie. He'd been watching her for days, hoping she'd snap out of it, realize learning the truth about Caster was the best thing for her. And now she could move on. But she didn't look like a woman who would ever be ready to move on.

He was forced to admit a truth he'd denied since he'd met her. Even during their marriage, Caster had occupied a piece of her heart. She might not have been fully in love with him—Joey was pretty sure these past few weeks and the peach pancakes had pushed her into the love zone—but Caster had always been there between them. Like the ghost of a past love. He chuckled at the irony.

And now, the only woman he'd ever loved, the woman he'd do anything to protect, was miserable. Caster wasn't faring any better. He looked like a man who'd been beaten down by life, and then life had dealt him a nice, hard kick to the balls, just for good measure. They both had Joey to thank for this. *Nice job, dick head.*

"I'm so sorry, Emily." He resisted the urge to kiss

her cheek—neither of them would feel it anyway—and headed to Caster's.

****

Caster rolled out of bed and glanced bleary-eyed at the clock on his nightstand. Seven a.m. on a Saturday, and he was up. Could be because he hadn't been able to sleep well in the past week. Nothing unusual for him, but this time, he couldn't blame it on his party life style. He hadn't touched a drop of alcohol—or a woman—since Joey had made an appearance and his life a living hell.

He pushed to his feet and went into the kitchen, stuck a pod in the Keurig, and closed the lever. The machine was making its last few spitting gurgles when icy air filled the room. *Damn.*

Caster swigged down half the coffee and turned to scowl at Joey. "If you're here to gloat, be done with it and get the hell out."

"I'm not here to gloat."

"Then what do you want?"

"You're one miserable son of a bitch, aren't you?" Joey didn't wait for an answer. He chuckled. "You really love her."

Caster shook his head, knowing it was a lie as the words left his lips. "I do not. I just didn't like hurting her like that."

"Huh. Looks like you hurt yourself, too."

"Whatever. Is there a point to all of this?"

Joey shrugged, then said softly, "Go after her. Tell her how you feel."

Caster shot him an incredulous look. "Are you out of your mind? You drop a bombshell that breaks us apart, now you're telling me to go after her? What kind of sick game are you playing?"

Joey shook his head. "Not a game. My job is to make sure Emily's happy. From the looks of her, that's going to be impossible. Without your help."

In spite of himself, Caster's interest was piqued. "What do you mean, from the looks of her?"

"She's as miserable as you are. I've never seen two more miserable human beings, and I've seen a butt load of dead people."

Caster grudgingly smiled. "So what do you want me to do? It's too late."

"Ha! Too late is when you're in my shoes. As long as you're breathing, there's hope. Now, get your ass over there. Unless you want me and the Louisville Slugger to give you another show."

Caster considered for just a moment, then drained his mug and headed for the shower.

****

Emily stalked toward her house, pausing to divide the trash from the haunted forest into the recycling bins. God, was she relieved it was over. They'd raised a good deal of money, but the last few weeks had taken a toll on her heart, and her spirit. To think that her husband's ghost was out there…watching. She shuddered. Then, of course, there was the fiasco with Caster. How could she have been so gullible? So blind?

"Emily."

She spun around. Caster stood on her porch, looking devilishly sexy in jeans, a black oxford shirt, and brown leather jacket.

"What are you doing here? I think we said all we had to say to one another."

He shook his head. "Huh uh, not me."

She brushed her hands on the seat of her jeans and crossed her arms. "Say it and leave."

He stepped off the porch and sauntered toward her. She held her breath, fighting the urge to step back. She would not retreat. Would not show him the effect he had on her.

"I never said I love you."

The words lanced her heart. Words she'd wanted to hear—for years, if she were honest. But now, they rang hollow. She knew they were false.

"Look, I don't know what you're up to now, but I really am over this. Please just go."

"I have a note."

She raised her brows. He wore a charming, sheepish smile that wreaked havoc with her insides. "A note?"

"From Joey."

"You're kidding, right? My husband's ghost wrote a *note*?"

"He wanted to tell you some things, but didn't think it was a good idea to appear to you again. He didn't want to upset you. He really just wants to be able to move on. He wants you to move on, too." He held a folded sheet of paper toward her.

She hesitated, then snatched it from his hand. The quicker she read it, the quicker she could get this over with.

She unfolded the note, tears rising in her throat at the familiar scrawl.

Dear Emily,

I've wronged you, deeply, and I can never say how sorry I am. I claimed I wanted your happiness, but I came between you and the only person who can give it to you. Yes, I mean

Caster. He really does love you. I know I didn't listen to you like I should when we were married. I know I didn't make you feel special, but you are. Very special. You deserve a man who knows that and who values you, who listens to you. I didn't tell Caster about the peach pancakes. I didn't even remember that you loved them. He did. I know it's not exactly moving mountains, but it's something...right? Please don't let me stand between you and the happiness you deserve. I can't rest until you're happy. And, I've grown weary of straddling two worlds. I'm ready to move on. So should you be.

All my love for eternity,
Joey

Emily lifted her face to Caster, not even caring about the tears that flowed down her cheeks. "Is it true, did you remember the pancakes yourself?"

Caster nodded and shoved his hands in his jacket pockets. "Yeah. I knew they were special to you. I thought you could use some cheering up."

She was touched, but that didn't mean she could trust him. She waved the paper in the air. "I'm not sure what to do about this. I mean, I want Joey to move on, but I'm not sure being with you is what will make me happy. You've caused me too much heartache over the years."

"Things are different now. I promise. I can't lose you again. I meant what I said. I've fallen in love with you."

She shrugged. "Even if that's true, it doesn't really matter, does it? Since we want different things."

"All I know is I want you. More than I've ever wanted anything. I'll even do the whole marriage thing if that's what it takes to keep you."

She let out a disbelieving laugh. "Oh, would you really? Oh wow, I must be the luckiest woman in the world that you would suffer through the whole, dreaded *marriage* thing for me."

He huffed out a breath. "That didn't come out right. Marriage has never held appeal, but when I'm with you, somehow it does. You are the only woman I can see spending the rest of my life with."

God. He was wearing her down. But could she trust him? Her heart couldn't take another hit.

He stepped closer, and this time, she did back up. "Don't run from me, Emily. It's truth time."

"Truth time?"

He narrowed his eyes on her, and she was powerless to look away. "Do you love me?"

"That—it doesn't matter. We'll never work. I can't—"

He slipped an arm around her waist and pulled her to him. His head tilted forward, and he captured her lips with his. She clung to him, returning the kiss, drowning in sensations only Caster could evoke.

"Do you love me," he murmured against her lips.

She tugged away, and he released her. Shoving a strand of hair behind her ear, she let out a sigh. "Yes, dammit, yes, I love you. So now what?"

A grin split his face, lighting his ice green eyes. "Now, we get married and make babies."

She laughed. "Really?"

"Oh, yes, most definitely."

She saw the sincerity, the love in his eyes, and knew

she could trust him with her heart. Stepping into the circle of his arms, she turned her face up for his kiss.

A blast of icy wind surrounded them, and she looked over her shoulder. Joey appeared behind her, wearing a sad, loving smile. He lifted his hand in a wave, then faded away.

A word about the author...

Alicia Dean lives in Edmond, Oklahoma, and is the mother of three grown children. Alicia loves creating spine-chilling stories that keep readers on the edge of their seats. She's a huge Elvis Presley fan, and loves MLB and the NFL. If you look closely, you'll see a reference to one or all three in pretty much everything she writes. If she could, she would divide all her time between writing, watching her favorite television shows—such as *Dexter* (before it was canceled; she's still hoping he comes back), *Vampire Diaries*, *Justified*, and *True Blood*—and reading her favorite authors...Stephen King, Dennis Lehane, Michael Connelly, Lee Child, and Lisa Gardner, to name a few.

Find her here:

Email: AliciaMDean@aol.com

Website: http://aliciadean.com/

Facebook: https://www.facebook.com/pages/Alicia-Dean/131939826889437?ref=br_tf

Twitter: https://twitter.com/Alicia_Dean_

~*~

Other Alicia Dean titles
available from The Wild Rose Press, Inc.

END OF LONELY STREET (January, 2015)

KILLER LOVE (boxed set with 4 suspense stories)

NOTHING TO FEAR

TEARS OF THE WOUNDED

POETIC INJUSTICE

TRULY MADLY

THICKER THAN WATER

A KNIGHT BEFORE CHRISTMAS